D0182929

The Chocolate War
and
Beyond the Chocolate War

Robert Cormier was born in Massachusetts, USA. He began writing at school, where he was praised for his poetry. At the age of nineteen he had his first short story published in a national magazine. His first novel for teenagers, *The Chocolate War*, was published in the UK in 1975, and was followed by others, including *I Am the Cheese*, *After the First Death* and *Beyond the Chocolate War*. He quickly established a reputation as a brilliant and uncompromising writer for young people. Robert Cormier died in November 2000.

CORMIER

The Chocolate War

and

Beyond the Chocolate War

PUFFIN

This one's for my son, Peter.
With love

PUFFIN BOOKS

Published by the Penguin Group: London, New York, Australia, Canada,
India, Ireland, New Zealand and South Africa
Penguin Books Ltd, Registered Offices: 80 Strand, London WC2R 0RL, England

puffinbooks.com

First published in one volume 2008
1

The Chocolate War copyright © Robert Cormier, 1974
First published in the USA by Pantheon Books, a division of Random House Inc. 1974
First published in Great Britain by Victor Gollancz 1975
Published by Hamish Hamilton 1977
Published in Puffin Books 2001

Beyond the Chocolate War copyright © Robert Cormier, 1985
First published in the USA by Alfred A. Knopf, Inc. 1985
First published in Great Britain by Victor Gollancz Ltd 1985
Published in Puffin Books 2001
All rights reserved

The moral right of the author has been asserted

Page 160 of *Beyond the Chocolate War*, two lines from 'The Laws of God, the Laws of Man' from
The Collected Poems of A. E. Housman, reprinted by permission of The Society of Authors, as the
literary representative of the Estate of A. E. Housman and Jonathan Cape Ltd Publishers.

Set in New Caledonia
Typeset by Rowland Phototypesetting Ltd, Bury St Edmunds, Suffolk
Made and printed in England by Clays Ltd, St Ives plc

Except in the United States of America, this book is sold subject to the condition
that it shall not, by way of trade or otherwise, be lent, re-sold, hired out, or otherwise
circulated without the publisher's prior consent in any form of binding or cover other than
that in which it is published and without a similar condition including this condition
being imposed on the subsequent purchaser

British Library Cataloguing in Publication Data
A CIP catalogue record for this book is available from the British Library

ISBN: 978-0-141-32483-8

www.greenpenguin.co.uk

Mixed Sources
Product group from well-managed
forests and other controlled sources
www.fsc.org Cert no. SA-COC-1592
© 1996 Forest Stewardship Council

Penguin Books is committed to a sustainable future
for our business, our readers and our planet.
The book in your hands is made from paper
certified by the Forest Stewardship Council.

Introduction

The Chocolate War was written during weekday evening hours and Saturday mornings in parts of 1969, 1970, and 1971, while I was working full-time as a newspaper editor and columnist.

Writing the novel was a labour of love. Although the setting was a Catholic boys' high school, I regarded the school as a metaphor for the world. On the other hand, I knew that, on its primary level, this was a story about a school chocolate sale. Who would be interested in reading such a story? I sometimes wondered. Yet I was having such a good time as the words leaped and danced on the page and the characters of Jerry Renault, Archie Costello, and Brother Leon came alive that I didn't worry about it.

It seems incredible to me that, more than two decades later, *The Chocolate War* continues to be read and taught and to cause problems in classrooms here in the United States and in such places as England, Australia, Sweden, France and Japan, among others.

Yet the novel was almost stillborn and existed for more than a year in a kind of literary no-man's-land. Seven major publishers rejected it over the course of thirteen months in 1972 and 1973. The reasons? Too complicated. Too many characters. A downbeat ending, which teenagers of the 1970s would find difficult to accept. Too violent. Not quite an adult novel, too sophisticated to be a juvenile novel. Too unbelievable. That frustrating "not for us", without further comment. One publisher, however, seriously considered accepting it if some changes were made, particularly to the ending.

I decided not to change or revise the novel. This was not a heroic gesture but an act of innocence. I knew nothing of the young adult market, was unaware of its then traditions and taboos, the domination of safe stories with role-model heroes walking off into the sunset of happy endings.

Although *The Chocolate War* does not have that hoped-for happy ending, its history has had happy moments and its share of heroes.

My son, Peter, inspired the novel when he refused, as a matter of principle, to sell the chocolates at his school's annual sale.

Marilyn E. Marlow, my literary agent at Curtis Brown Ltd., supported my decision against revisions and insisted that the novel, as written, would find its place in the world of young adult literature, convinced that the young adult market was entering a period of change, heralded by the earlier appearances of S. E. Hinton's *The Outsiders*, and Paul Zindel's *The Pigman*.

Finally, Fabio Coen, Publisher of Books for Young Readers at Pantheon Books and Knopf, the eighth publisher to whom the book was submitted, accepted it for publication in April of 1973.

I worried about revisions. Needlessly, as it turned out. At a brief editing session at Fabio Coen's office, his suggestions were few and minor, scrawled on a single sheet of paper. But he was doubtful about a short chapter toward the end of the novel. Astonished, I realized it was a chapter I had agonized about earlier, actually removing it at one time, then reinstating it. I had found an editor who shared my instincts and my intentions. The chapter was removed. Otherwise, the novel was published essentially as I had written it, in April of 1974. Fabio Coen became my mentor and remained so until his retirement several books later.

The success of *The Chocolate War* is testimony to all the other heroes involved in its history: teachers who have taught the book in the face of censorship attempts that sometimes threatened their jobs; librarians who had had to fight to keep the novel available to readers; critics, writers, and educators who supported the novel in countless reviews and essays; all the young people who continue to write me letters, who call me up, who organize protests when the book faces yet another banning threat; Pantheon Books, followed by Knopf and Delacorte Press/Dell Laurel Leaf, who have kept the book in continuous print in the USA in hardback and softcovers.

Talk about happy endings!

Robert Cormier
Leominster, MS,
1997

1

THEY murdered him.

As he turned to take the ball, a dam burst against the side of his head and a hand grenade shattered his stomach. Engulfed by nausea, he pitched toward the grass. His mouth encountered gravel, and he spat frantically, afraid that some of his teeth had been knocked out. Rising to his feet, he saw the field through drifting gauze but held on until everything settled into place, like a lens focusing, making the world sharp again, with edges.

The second play called for a pass. Fading back, he picked up a decent block and cocked his arm, searching for a receiver—maybe the tall kid they called The Goober. Suddenly, he was caught from behind and whirled violently, a toy boat caught in a whirlpool. Landing on his knees, hugging the ball, he urged himself to ignore the pain that gripped his groin, knowing that it was important to betray no sign of distress, remembering The Goober's advice, "Coach is testing you, testing, and he's looking for guts."

I've got guts, Jerry murmured, getting up by degrees, careful not to displace any of his bones or sinews. A telephone rang in his ears. Hello, hello, I'm still here. When he moved his lips, he tasted the acid of dirt and grass and gravel. He was aware of the other players around him, helmeted and grotesque, creatures from an unknown world. He had never felt so lonely in his life, abandoned, defenseless.

On the third play, he was hit simultaneously by three of them: one, his knees; another, his stomach; a third, his head—the helmet no protection at all. His body seemed to telescope into itself but all the parts didn't fit, and he was stunned by the knowledge that pain isn't just one thing— it is cunning and various, sharp here and sickening there, burning here and clawing there. He clutched himself as he hit the ground. The ball squirted away. His breath went away, like the ball—a terrible stillness pervaded him—and then, at the onset of panic, his breath came back again. His lips sprayed wetness and he was grateful for the sweet cool air that filled his lungs. But when he tried to get up, his body mutinied against movement. He decided the hell with it. He'd go to sleep right here, right out on the fifty yard line, the hell with trying out for the team, screw everything, he was going to sleep, he didn't care anymore . . .

"Renault!"

Ridiculous, someone calling his name.

"Renault!"

The coach's voice scraped like sandpaper against his ears. He opened his eyes flutteringly. "I'm all right," he said to nobody in particular, or to his father maybe. Or the coach. He was unwilling to abandon this lovely lassitude but he had to, of course. He was sorry to leave the earth, and he was vaguely curious about how he was going to get up, with both legs smashed and his skull battered in. He was astonished to find himself on his feet, intact, bobbing like one of those toy novelties dangling from car windows, but erect.

"For Christ's sake," the coach bellowed, his voice juicy with contempt. A spurt of saliva hit Jerry's cheek.

Hey, coach, you spit on me, Jerry protested. Stop the spitting, coach. What he said aloud was, "I'm all right, coach," because he was a coward about stuff like that, thinking one thing and saying another, planning one thing and doing another—he had been Peter a thousand times and a thousand cocks had crowed in his lifetime.

"How tall are you, Renault?"

"Five nine," he gasped, still fighting for breath.

"Weight?"

"One forty-five," he said, looking the coach straight in the eye.

"Soaking wet, I'll bet," the coach said sourly. "What the hell you want to play football for? You need more meat on those bones. What the hell you trying to play quarterback for? You'd make a better end. Maybe."

The coach looked like an old gangster: broken nose, a scar on his cheek like a stitched shoestring. He needed a shave, his stubble like slivers of ice. He growled and swore and was merciless. But a helluva coach, they said. The coach stared at him now, the dark eyes probing, pondering. Jerry hung in there, trying not to sway, trying not to faint.

"All right," the coach said in disgust. "Show up tomorrow. Three o'clock sharp or you're through before you start."

Inhaling the sweet sharp apple air through his nostrils— he was afraid to open his mouth wide, wary of any movement that was not absolutely essential—he walked tentatively toward the sidelines, listening to the coach barking at the other guys. Suddenly, he loved that voice, "Show up tomorrow."

He trudged away from the field, blinking against the afternoon sun, toward the locker room at the gym. His knees were liquid and his body light as air, suddenly.

Know what? he asked himself, a game he played sometimes.

What?

I'm going to make the team.

Dreamer, dreamer.

Not a dream: it's the truth.

As Jerry took another deep breath, a pain appeared, distant, small—a radar signal of distress. Bleep, I'm here. Pain. His feet scuffled through crazy cornflake leaves. A strange happiness invaded him. He knew he'd been massacred by the oncoming players, capsized and dumped humiliatingly on the ground. But he'd survived—he'd gotten to his feet. "You'd make a better end." Was the Coach thinking he might try him at end? Any position, as long as he made the team. The bleep grew larger, localized now, between his ribs on the right side. He thought of his mother and how drugged she was at the end, not recognizing anyone, neither Jerry nor his father. The exhilaration of the moment vanished and he sought it in vain, like seeking ecstasy's memory an instant after jacking off and encountering only shame and guilt.

Nausea began to spread through his stomach, warm and oozy and evil.

"Hey," he called weakly. To nobody. Nobody there to listen.

He managed to make it back to the school. By the time he had sprawled himself on the floor of the lavatory, his head hanging over the lip of the toilet bowl and the smell of disinfectant stinging his eyeballs, the nausea had passed and the bleep of pain had faded. Sweat moved like small moist bugs on his forehead.

And then, without warning, he vomited.

2

OBIE was bored. Worse than bored. He was disgusted. He was also tired. It seemed he was always tired these days. He went to bed tired and he woke up tired. He found himself yawning constantly. Most of all, he was tired of Archie. Archie the bastard. The bastard that Obie alternately hated and admired. For instance, at this minute he hated Archie with a special burning hate that was part of the boredom and the weariness. Notebook in hand, pencil poised, Obie looked at Archie now with fierce anger, furious at the way Archie sat there in the bleachers, his blond hair tossing lightly in the breeze, enjoying himself, for crying out loud, even though he knew that Obie would be late for work and yet keeping him here, stalling, killing time.

"You're a real bastard," Obie said finally, his frustration erupting, like a coke exploding from a bottle after you shake it. "You know that?"

Archie turned and smiled at him benevolently, like a goddam king passing out favors.

"Jesus," Obie said, exasperated.

"Don't swear, Obie," Archie chided. "You'll have to tell it in confession."

"Look who's talking. I don't know how you had the nerve to receive communion at chapel this morning."

"It doesn't take nerve, Obie. When you march down to the rail, you're receiving The Body, man. Me, I'm just chewing a wafer they buy by the pound in Worcester."

Obie looked away in disgust.

"And when you say 'Jesus,' you're talking about your leader. But when I say 'Jesus,' I'm talking about a guy who walked the earth for thirty-three years like any other guy but caught the imagination of some *PR* cats. *PR* for Public Relations, in case you don't know, Obie."

Obie didn't bother to answer. You couldn't ever win an argument with Archie. He was too quick with the words. Especially when he fell into one of his phony hip moods. Saying *man* and *cat*, like he was a swinger, cool, instead of a senior in a lousy little high school like Trinity.

"Come on, Archie, it's getting late," Obie said, trying to appeal to Archie's better nature. "I'm going to get fired one of these days."

"Don't whine, Obie. Besides, you hate the job. You have a subconscious wish to be fired. Then you wouldn't have to stock the shelves any more or take crap from customers or work late Saturday night instead of going to the—what is it you go to?—the Teen-Age Canteen to drool over all those broads."

Archie was uncanny. How did he know Obie hated the stupid job? How did he know that Obie hated especially those Saturday nights stalking the supermarket canyons while everybody else was at the canteen?

"See? I'm doing you a favor. Enough of these late afternoons and the boss'll say, 'You're all done, Obie baby. Set free.' And you'll have one, right in front of him."

"And where'll my money come from?" Obie asked.

Archie waved his hand, signaling that he was tired of the conversation. You could see him physically withdraw although he was only a foot or two away from Obie on the

6

bleacher bench. The shouts of the fellows from the football field below echoed feebly in the air. Archie's lower lip dropped. That meant he was concentrating. Thinking. Obie waited in anticipation, hating the thing in him that made him look at Archie in admiration. The way Archie could turn people on. Or off. The way he could dazzle you with his brilliance—those Vigil assignments that had made him practically a legend at Trinity—and the way he could disgust you with his cruelties, those strange offbeat cruelties of his, that had nothing to do with pain or violence but were somehow even worse. It made Obie uncomfortable to think of that stuff and he shrugged the thoughts away, waiting for Archie to talk, to say the name.

"Stanton," Archie said finally, whispering the name, caressing the syllables. "I think his first name is Norman."

"Right," Obie said, scrawling the name. Only two more to go. Archie had to come up with ten names by four o'clock and eight were now listed on Obie's pad.

"The assignment?" Obie prodded.

"Sidewalk."

Obie grinned as he wrote the word. Sidewalk: such an innocent word. But what Archie could do with simple things like a sidewalk and a kid like Norman Stanton whom Obie recalled as a blustering bragging character with wild red hair and eyelids matted with yellow crap.

"Hey, Obie," Archie said.

"Yeah?" Obie asked, on guard.

"You really going to be late for work? I mean—would you really lose your job?" Archie's voice was soft with concern, his eyes gentle with compassion. That's what baffled everyone about Archie—his changes of mood, the way he could be a wise bastard one minute and a great guy the next.

"I don't think they'd actually fire me. The guy who owns

7

the place, he's a friend of the family. But I mean getting there late doesn't, like, help the cause. I'm overdue for a raise but he's holding it back until I get on the ball."

Archie nodded, all businesslike. "All right, we'll wrap it up. We'll get you on the ball. Maybe I ought to assign someone to the store, and make life interesting for your boss."

"Jeez, no," Obie said quickly. He shivered with dread, realizing how awesome Archie's power really was. Which is why you had to stay on the good side of the bastard. Buy him Hersheys all the time to satisfy his craving for chocolate. Thank God Archie didn't go in for pot or that stuff—Obie would have had to become a pusher, for crying out loud, to supply him. Obie was officially the secretary of The Vigils but he knew what the job really demanded. Carter, the president who was almost as big a bastard as Archie, said, "Keep him happy, when Archie's happy, we're all happy."

"Two more names," Archie mused now. He rose and stretched. He was tall and not too heavy. He moved with a subtle rhythm, languidly, the walk of an athlete although he hated all sports and had nothing but contempt for athletes. Particularly football players and boxers, which happened to be Trinity's two major sports. Usually, Archie didn't pick athletes for assignments—he claimed they were too stupid to absorb the delicate shadings, the subtle intricacies involved. Archie disliked violence—most of his assignments were exercises in the psychological rather than the physical. That's why he got away with so much. The Trinity brothers wanted peace at any price, quiet on the campus, no broken bones. Otherwise, the sky was the limit. Which was right up Archie's alley.

"The kid they call The Goober," Archie said now.

Obie wrote down "Roland Goubert."

"Brother Eugene's room."

Obie smiled in delicious malice. He liked it when Archie involved the brothers in the assignments. Those were the most daring, of course. And someday Archie would go too far and trip himself up. In the meantime, Brother Eugene would do. He was a peaceful sort, made to order for Archie, naturally.

The sun vanished behind floating clouds. Archie brooded, isolating himself again. The wind rose, kicking puffs of dust from the football field. The field needed seeding. The bleachers also needed attention—they sagged, peeling paint like leprosy on the benches. The shadows of the goal posts sprawled on the field like grotesque crosses. Obie shivered.

"What the hell do they think I am?" Archie asked.

Obie remained silent. The question didn't seem to require an answer. It was as if Archie was talking to himself.

"These goddam assignments," Archie said. "Do they think it's easy?" His voice dripped sadness. "And the black box . . ."

Obie yawned. He was tired. And uncomfortable. He always yawned and got tired and uncomfortable when he found himself in situations like this, not knowing how to proceed, surprised at the anguish in Archie's voice. Or was Archie putting him on? You never knew about Archie. Obie was grateful when Archie finally shook his head as if warding off an evil spell.

"You're not much help, Obie."

"I never thought you needed much help, Archie."

"Don't you think I'm human, too?"

I'm not sure. That's what Obie almost said.

"All right, all right. Let's finish the damn assignments. One more name."

Obie's pencil was poised.

"Who was that kid who left the field a few minutes ago? The one they wiped out?"

9

"Kid named Jerry Renault. Freshman," Obie said, flipping through his notebook. He searched the *R*'s for Renault. His notebook was more complete than the school's files. It contained information, carefully coded, about everyone at Trinity, the kind of stuff that couldn't be found in official records. "Here it is. Renault, Jerome E. Son of James R. Pharmacist at Blake's. The kid's a freshman, birthday—let's see, he just turned fourteen. Oh—his mother died last spring. Cancer." There was more information about courses and records in grammar school and extracurricular activities but Obie closed the notebook as if he were lowering a coffin lid.

"Poor kid," Archie said. "Mother's dead."

Again that concern, that compassion in his voice.

Obie nodded. One more name. Who else?

"Must be hard on the poor kid."

"Right," Obie agreed, impatient.

"Know what he needs, Obie?" His voice was soft, dreamy, caressing.

"What?"

"Therapy."

The terrible word shattered the tenderness in Archie's voice.

"Therapy?"

"Right. Put him down."

"For crying out loud, Archie. You saw him out there. He's just a skinny kid trying to make the Freshman team. Coach'll grind him up like hamburger. And his mother's barely cold in the grave. What the hell you putting him on the list for?"

"Don't let him fool you, Obie. He's a tough one. Didn't you see him get wiped out down there and still get to his feet? Tough. And stubborn. He should have stayed down on that turf, Obie. That would have been the smart thing to do. Besides, he probably needs something to keep his mind off his poor dead mother."

"You're a bastard, Archie. I said it before and I'll say it again."

"Put him down." Ice in the voice, cold as polar regions.

Obie wrote down the name. Hell, it wasn't his funeral. "Assignment?"

"I'll think of something."

"You've only got till four," Obie reminded.

"The assignment must fit the kid. That's the beauty of it, Obie."

Obie waited a minute or two and couldn't resist asking, "You running out of ideas, Archie?" The great Archie Costello running dry? The possibility was staggering to contemplate.

"Just being artistic, Obie. It's an art, you know. Take a kid like this Renault. Special circumstances." He fell silent. "Put him down for the chocolates."

Obie wrote down: *Renault—Chocolates.* Archie would never run dry. The chocolates, for instance, were good for a dozen assignments.

Obie looked down at the field where the guys were skirmishing in the shadow of the goal posts. Sadness seized him. I should have gone out for football, he thought. He had wanted to—he'd been hot stuff with Pop Warner at St. Joe's. Instead, he had ended up as Secretary of The Vigils. Cool. But, hell, he couldn't even tell his parents about it.

"Know what, Archie?"

"What?"

"Life is sad, sometimes."

That was one of the great things about Archie, you could say things like that.

"Life is shit," Archie said.

11

The shadows of the goal posts definitely resembled a network of crosses, empty crucifixes. That's enough symbolism for one day, Obie told himself. If he hurried he could make the four o'clock bus to work.

3

THE girl was heart-wrenchingly, impossibly beautiful. Desire weakened his stomach. A waterfall of blond hair splashed on her bare shoulders. He studied the photograph surreptitiously and then closed the magazine and put it back where it belonged, on the top shelf. He glanced around to see if he'd been observed. The store owner positively prohibited the reading of magazines and a sign said NO BUY NO READ. But the owner was busy at the far end of the place.

Why did he always feel so guilty whenever he looked at *Playboy* and the other magazines? A lot of guys bought them, passed them around at school, hid them in the covers of notebooks, even resold them. He sometimes saw copies scattered casually on coffee tables in the homes of his friends. He had once bought a girlie magazine, paying for it with trembling fingers—a dollar and a quarter, his finances shot down in flames until his next allowance. And he didn't know what to do with the damn thing once it was in his possession. Sneaking it home on the bus, hiding it in the bottom drawer of his room, he was terrified of discovery. Finally, tired of smuggling it into the bathroom for swift perusals, and weary of his deceit, and haunted by the fear that his mother would find the magazine, Jerry had sneaked it out of the house and dropped it into a catchbasin. He listened to it splash dismally below, bidding a wistful farewell to the squandered buck and a quarter. A longing filled him. Would a girl ever love him? The one devastating sorrow he carried within him was the fear that he would die before holding a girl's breast in his hand.

Out at the bus stop, Jerry leaned against a telephone pole, body weary, echoing the assault of the football practices. For three days his body had absorbed punishment. But he was still on the roster, luckily. Idly, he watched the people on the Common across the street. He saw them every day. They were now part of the scenery like the Civil War Cannon and the World War Monuments, the flagpole. Hippies. Flower Children. Street People. Drifters. Drop-Outs. Everybody had a different name for them. They came out in the spring and stayed until October, hanging around, calling taunts to passersby occasionally but most of the time quiet, languid and peaceful. He was fascinated by them and sometimes envied their old clothes, their sloppiness, the way they didn't seem to give a damn about anything. Trinity was one of the last schools to retain a dress code—shirt and tie. He watched a cloud of smoke swirl around a girl in a floppy hat. Grass? He didn't know. A lot of things he didn't know.

Absorbed in his thoughts, he didn't notice that one of the street people had detached himself from the others and was crossing the street, dodging cars deftly.

"Hey, man."

Startled, Jerry realized the guy was addressing him. "Me?"

The fellow stood in the street, on the other side of a green Volkswagen, his chest resting on the car's roof. "Yes, you." He was about nineteen, long black hair brushing his shoulders, a curling mustache, like a limp black snake draped on his upper lip, the ends dangling near his chin. "You been staring at us, man, like every day. Standing here and staring."

They really say *man*, Jerry thought. He didn't think anybody said *man* any more except as a joke. But this guy wasn't joking.

"Hey, man, you think we're in a zoo? That why you stare?"

"No. Look, I don't stare." But he did stare, every day.

"Yes, you do, man. You stand here and look at us. With your homework books and your nice shirt and your blue-and-white tie."

Jerry looked around uneasily. He confronted only strangers, nobody from school.

"We're not sub-humans, man."

"I didn't say you were."

"But you look it."

"Look," Jerry said, "I've got to get my bus." Which was ridiculous, of course, because the bus wasn't in sight.

"You know who's sub-human, man? You. You are. Going to school every day. And back home on the bus. And do your homework." The guy's voice was contemptuous. "Square boy. Middle-aged at fourteen, fifteen. Already caught in a routine. Wow."

A hiss and the stench of exhaust announced the arrival of the bus. Jerry swung away from the guy.

"Go get your bus, square boy," he called. "Don't miss the bus, boy. You're missing a lot of things in the world, better not miss that bus."

Jerry walked to the bus like a sleepwalker. He hated confrontations. His heart hammered. He climbed aboard, dropped his token in the coin box and lurched to his seat as the bus moved away from the curb.

He sat down, breathed deeply, closed his eyes.

Go get your bus, square boy.

He opened his eyes and slitted them against the invasion of the sun through the window.

You're missing a lot of things in the world, better not miss that bus.

A big put-on, of course. That was their specialty, people like that. Putting people on. Nothing else to do with their lives, piddling away their lives.

And yet . . .

Yet, what?

He didn't know. He thought of his life—going to school and coming home. Even though his tie was loose, dangling on his shirt, he yanked it off. He looked up at the advertising placards above the windows, wanting to turn his thoughts away from the confrontation.

Why? someone had scrawled in a blank space no advertiser had rented.

Why not? someone else had slashed in answer.

Jerry closed his eyes, exhausted suddenly, and it seemed like too much of an effort even to think.

4

"**H**ow many boxes?"

"Twenty thousand."

Archie whistled in astonishment. He usually didn't blow his cool that easily, particularly with someone like Brother Leon. But the image of twenty thousand boxes of chocolates being delivered here to Trinity was ridiculous. Then he saw the mustache of moistness on Brother Leon's upper lip, the watery eyes and the dampness on his forehead. Something clicked. This wasn't the calm and deadly Leon who could hold a class in the palm of his hand. This was someone riddled with cracks and crevices. Archie became absolutely still, afraid that the rapid beating of his heart might betray his sudden knowledge, the proof of what he'd always suspected, not only of Brother Leon but most grownups, most adults: they were vulnerable, running scared, open to invasion.

"I know that's a lot of chocolates," Brother Leon admitted, managing to keep his voice casual, for which Archie admired him. A smart one, Leon, hard to pin down. Even though he was sweating like a madman, his voice remained calm, reasoned. "But we have tradition working in our favor. The chocolate sale is an annual event. The boys have come to expect it. If they can sell ten thousand boxes of chocolates in other years, why not twenty thousand this year? And these are special chocolates, Archie. High profit. A special deal."

"How is it special?" Archie asked, pressing his advantage, none of that student-talking-to-teacher crap in his voice. He was here in Leon's office by special invitation. Let Leon talk to the real Archie, not the kid who sat in his algebra class.

"Actually, these are Mother's Day chocolates. We were—that is, *I* was—able to pick them up at a bargain price. Beautiful boxes, gift boxes, and in perfect condition. They've been stored under the best of conditions since last spring. All we have to do is remove the purple ribbons that say *Mother* and we're in business. We can sell them for two dollars a box and make a profit of almost a dollar on each one."

"But twenty thousand boxes." Archie performed some quick calculations although he wasn't a whiz at math. "We're about four hundred guys in the school. That means everybody's got to sell fifty boxes. Usually, the guys have a quota of twenty-five boxes each to sell and the price is a dollar." He sighed. "Now, everything is doubled. That's a lot of selling for this school, Brother Leon. For any school."

"I know that, Archie. But Trinity is special, isn't it? If I didn't think the boys of Trinity could do it, do you think I would take a risk? Aren't we capable of what others aren't?"

Bullshit, was what Archie thought.

"I know what you're wondering, Archie—why am I burdening you with this problem?"

Archie, in fact, *was* wondering why Brother Leon had laid his plans before him. He had never been particularly friendly with Leon or any other Trinity teacher. And Leon was a special breed. On the surface, he was one of those pale, ingratiating kind of men who tiptoed through life on

18

small, quick feet. He looked like a henpecked husband, a pushover, a sucker. He was the Assistant Headmaster of the school but actually served as a flunky for the Head. Like an errand boy. But all this was deceptive. In the classroom, Leon was another person altogether. Smirking, sarcastic. His thin, high voice venomous. He could hold your attention like a cobra. Instead of fangs, he used his teacher's pointer, flicking out here, there, everywhere. He watched the class like a hawk, suspicious, searching out cheaters or daydreamers, probing for weaknesses in the students and then exploiting those weaknesses. He had never taken on Archie. Not yet.

"Let me paint you the picture," Leon said, leaning forward in his chair. "All private schools, Catholic or otherwise, are struggling these days. Many are closing down. Prices are going up and we have only so many sources of income. As you know, Archie, we're not one of those exclusive boarding schools. And we don't have any wealthy alumni to draw on. We're a day school, dedicated to preparing young men from middle-class homes for college. There are no rich men's sons here. Take yourself, for instance. Your father operates an insurance agency. He makes a good salary but he's hardly wealthy, is he? Take Tommy Desjardins. His father's a dentist—very well off, they have two cars, a summer home—and that's about tops for the parents of Trinity boys." He held up his hand. "I'm not trying to put down the parents." Archie winced. It irritated him when grownups resorted to student language like *put down*. "What I'm saying, Archie, is that the parents are mostly in modest circumstances and can't absorb any more tuition increases. We have to find revenue wherever possible. Football barely pays for itself—we haven't had a winning season for three years. The interest in boxing has fallen off now that television doesn't feature boxing anymore . . ."

Archie stifled a yawn—so what else was new?

"I'm putting my cards on the table, Archie, to show you, to impress upon you, how we have to tap every source of income, how even a chocolate sale can be vital and important to us . . ."

Silence fell. The school was hushed around them, so hushed that Archie wondered whether the office was sound-proof. Classes were over for the day, of course, but that was the time when a lot of other action got started. Particularly Vigil action.

"Another thing," Leon went on. "We've kept this quiet but the Head is ill, perhaps seriously so. He's scheduled to enter the hospital tomorrow. Tests and things. The outlook isn't good . . ."

Archie waited for Leon to get to the point. Was he going to make a ridiculous pitch for the chocolate sale to be a success in honor of the sick Headmaster? "Win one for The Gipper" like some pukey late-night movie?

"He may be incapacitated for weeks."

"That's rough." So what?

"Which means—the school will be in my charge. The school will be my responsibility."

The silence again. But this time Archie felt a waiting in the silence. He had a feeling that Leon was about to make his point.

"I need your help, Archie."

"My help?" Archie asked, feigning surprise, trying to keep any trace of mockery out of his voice. He knew now why he was here. Leon didn't mean Archie's help—he meant the help of The Vigils. And didn't dare put it into words. No one was allowed to breathe a word about The Vigils. Officially, The Vigils did not exist. How could a school condone an organization like The Vigils? The school allowed it to function by ignoring it completely, pretending it wasn't there. But it was there, all right, Archie thought bitterly. It was there because it served a purpose. The Vigils kept things under control. Without The Vigils, Trinity might have been torn apart like other schools had been, by demonstrations, protests, all that crap. Archie was surprised by Leon's audacity, knowing his connection with The Vigils and bringing him in here this way.

"But how can *I* help?" Archie asked, turning the screw, emphasizing the singular of himself and not the plural of The Vigils.

"By getting behind the sale. As you said, Archie—twenty thousand boxes, that's a lot of chocolates."

"The price is doubled, too," Archie reminded him, enjoying himself now. "Two dollars a box, instead of one."

"But we need that money desperately."

"How about the bonus? The school always gives the boys a bonus."

"As usual, Archie. A day off from school when every chocolate has been sold."

"No free trip this year? Last year we were taken to Boston to a stage show." Archie didn't care about the trip but he enjoyed this reverse position—himself asking the questions and Leon squirming, so different from the classroom.

"I'll think of something as a substitute," Leon said.

Archie let the silence stretch.

"Can I count on you, Archie?" Leon's forehead was damp again.

Archie decided to plunge. To see how far he could go. "But what can I do? I'm just one guy."

"You have influence, Archie."

"Influence?" Archie's voice was coming out loud and clear. He was cool. In command. Let Leon sweat. Archie was sweet and cool. "I'm not a class officer. I'm not a member of the Student Council." Christ, if only the guys were here to see him. "I don't even make the Honor Roll . . ."

Suddenly, Leon wasn't sweating anymore. The beads of perspiration still danced on his forehead but he had become stiff and cold. Archie could feel the coldness—more than cold, an icy hate coming across the desk like a deadly ray from some bleak and lethal planet. Have I gone too far, he wondered. I've got this guy for algebra, my weakest subject.

"You know what I mean," Leon said, his voice like a door slamming.

Their eyes met, held. A showdown now? At this moment? Would that be the smart thing to do? Archie believed in always doing the smart thing. Not the thing you ached to do, not the impulsive act, but the thing that would pay off later. That's why he was The Assigner. That's why The Vigils depended on him. Hell, The Vigils *were* the school. And he, Archie Costello, was The Vigils. That's why Leon had called him here, that's why Leon was practically begging for his help. Archie suddenly had a terrific craving for a Hershey.

"I know what you mean," Archie said, postponing the showdown. Leon could be like money in the bank, for future use.

"You'll help, then?"

"I'll check with them," Archie said, letting *them* hang in the air.

And it hung.

Leon didn't pick it up.

Neither did Archie.

They looked at each other for a long moment.

"The Vigils will help," Archie said, unable to contain himself any longer. He had never been able to use those words—The Vigils—aloud to a teacher, had had to deny the existence of the organization for so long that it was

22

beautiful to use them, to see the surprise on Leon's pale perspiring face.

Then he pushed back his chair and left the office without waiting for the teacher's dismissal.

5

"**Y**OUR name is Goubert?"

"Yes."

"They call you The Goober?"

"Yes."

"Yes, what?"

Archie was disgusted with himself even as he said it. *Yes, what?* like a scene from out of an old World War Two movie. But the kid Goubert stammered and then said, "Yes, *sir*." Like a raw recruit.

"Know why you're here, Goober?"

The Goober hesitated. Despite his height, he was easily six-one, he reminded Archie of a child, someone who didn't belong here, as if he'd been caught sneaking into an Adults Only movie. He was too skinny, of course. And he had the look of a loser. Vigil bait.

"Yes, sir," The Goober finally said.

Archie was always puzzled about whatever there was inside of him that enjoyed these performances—toying with kids, leading them on, humiliating them, finally. He'd earned the job of Assigner because of his quick mind, his swift intelligence, his fertile imagination, his ability to see two moves ahead as if life were a giant checker or chess game. But something more than that, something nobody could find words to describe. Archie knew what it was and recognized it, although it eluded a definition. One night while watching an old Marx Brothers movie on the Late Show, he was held entranced by a scene where the brothers were searching for a missing painting. Groucho said, "We'll search every room in the house." Chico asked, "But what if it ain't in the house?" Groucho replied, "Then we'll search the house next door." "What if there ain't no house next door?" And Groucho, "Then we'll build one." And they immediately started to draw up plans for building the house. That's what Archie did—built the house nobody could anticipate a need for, except himself, a house that was invisible to everyone else.

"If you know, then tell me why you're here, Goober," Archie said now, his voice gentle. He always treated them with tenderness, as if a bond existed between them.

Someone snickered. Archie stiffened, shot a look at Carter, a withering look that said, tell them to cut the crap. Carter snapped his fingers, which sounded in the quiet storage room like the banging of a gavel. The Vigils were grouped as usual in a circle around Archie and the kid receiving the assignment. The small room behind the gym was windowless with only one door leading to the gymnasium itself: a perfect spot for Vigil meetings—private, the solitary entrance easily guarded, and dim, lit by a single bulb dangling from the ceiling, a 40-watt bulb that bestowed only a feeble light on the proceedings. The silence was deafening after the snap of Carter's fingers. Nobody fooled around with Carter. Carter was the president of The Vigils because the president was always a football player—the muscle someone like Archie needed. But everyone knew that the head of The Vigils was The Assigner, Archie Costello, who was always one step ahead of them all.

The Goober looked frightened. He was one of those kids

who always wanted to please everybody. The guy who never got the girl but worshiped her in secret while the big shot hero rode off in the sunset with her in the end.

"Tell me," Archie said, "why you're here." He allowed a bit of impatience to appear in his voice.

"For . . . an assignment."

"Do you realize that there's nothing personal in the assignment?"

The Goober nodded.

"That this is tradition here at Trinity?"

"Yes."

"And that you must pledge silence?"

"Yes," The Goober said, swallowing, his Adam's apple doing a dance in that long thin neck.

Silence.

Archie let it gather. He could feel a heightening of interest in the room. It always happened this way when an assignment was about to be given. He knew what they were thinking—what's Archie come up with this time? Sometimes Archie resented them. The members of The Vigils did nothing but enforce the rules. Carter was muscle and Obie an errand boy. Archie alone was always under pressure, devising the assignments, working them out. As if he was some kind of machine. Press a button: out comes an assignment. What did they know about the agonies of it all? The nights he tossed and turned? The times he felt used up, empty? And yet he couldn't deny that he exulted in moments like this, the guys leaning forward in anticipation, the mystery that surrounded them all, the kid Goober white-faced and frightened, the place so quiet you could almost hear your own heartbeat. And all eyes on him: Archie.

"Goober."

"Yes, yes sir." Swallow.

"Know what a screwdriver is?"

26

"Yes."

"Can you put your hands on one?"

"Yes, yes sir. My father. He has a tool chest."

"Fine. Know what they use screwdrivers for, Goober?"

"Yes."

"What for?"

"To screw things . . . I mean, to put screws into things."

Someone laughed. And Archie let it pass. A relief to the tension.

"And also, Goober," Archie said, "a screwdriver takes screws out of things. Right?"

"Yes, sir."

"A screwdriver, then, can loosen as well as tighten, right?"

"Right," The Goober said, nodding his head, eager, his attention fastened on the thought of the screwdriver, almost as if he were hypnotized, and Archie was carried on marvelous waves of power and glory, leading The Goober toward the ultimate destination, feeding him the information little by little, the best part of the lousy job. Not really lousy, though. Great, in fact. Beautiful, in fact. Worth all the sweat.

"Now, do you know where Brother Eugene's homeroom is located?"

The anticipation in the air was almost visible at this moment, blazing, electric.

"Yes. Room nineteen. Second floor."

"Right!" Archie said, as if giving The Goober an A for recitation. "Next Thursday afternoon, you'll make arrangements to be free. Afternoon, evening, all night, if necessary."

The Goober stood there, spellbound.

"The school will be deserted. The brothers, most of them, the ones who count, will be off to a conference at Provincial headquarters in Maine. The janitor is taking a day off.

27

There'll be no one in the building after three in the afternoon. No one but you, Goober. You and your screwdriver."

Now, the final moment, the climax, almost like coming—

"And here's what you do, Goober." Pause. "You loosen."

"Loosen?" The Adam's apple dancing.

"Loosen."

Archie waited a beat—in strict command of the room, the silence almost unbearable—and said, "Everything in Brother Eugene's room is held together by screws. The chairs, the desks, the blackboards. Now, with your little screwdriver—maybe you'd better bring along various and assorted sizes, just in case—you start to loosen. Don't take out the screws. Just loosen them until they reach that point where they're almost ready to fall out, everything hanging there by a thread . . ."

A howl of delight came from the guys—probably Obie, who had gotten the picture, who could see the house that Archie was building, the house that didn't exist until he built it in their minds. Then, others joined in the laughter as they envisioned the result of the assignment. Archie let himself be caressed by the laughter of admiration, knowing that he'd scored again. They were always waiting for him to fail, to fall flat on his face, but he'd scored once more.

"Jeez," The Goober said. "That's going to take a lot of work. There's a lot of desks and chairs in there."

"You'll have all night. We guarantee you won't be disturbed."

"Jeez." The Adam's apple was positively convulsive now.

"Thursday," Archie said, a command in his voice, no nonsense, final, irrevocable.

The Goober nodded, accepting the assignment like a sentence of doom, the way all the others did, knowing there was no way out, no reprieve, no appeal. The law of The Vigils was final, everyone at Trinity knew that.

Somebody whispered, "Wow."

Carter snapped his fingers again and tension quickly built up in the room once more. But a different kind of tension. Tension with teeth in it. For Archie. He braced himself.

Reaching under the abandoned teacher's desk he sat behind as presiding officer, Carter pulled out a small black box. He shook it and the sound of marbles could be heard clicking together inside. Obie came forward, holding a key in his hand. Was that a smile on Obie's face? Archie couldn't be sure. He wondered, does Obie really hate me? Do they all hate me? Not that it mattered. Not while Archie held the power. He would conquer all, even the black box.

Carter took the key from Obie and held it up.

"Ready?" he asked Archie.

"Ready," Archie said, keeping his face expressionless, inscrutable as usual, even though he felt a bead of perspiration trace a cold path from his armpit to his rib. The black box was his nemesis. It contained six marbles: five of them white and one of them black. It was an ingenious idea thought up by someone long before Archie's time, someone who was wise enough—or a bastard enough—to realize that an assigner could go off the deep end if there wasn't some kind of control. The box provided the control. After every assignment, it was presented to Archie. If Archie drew a white marble, the assignment stood as ordered. If Archie drew the black marble, it would be necessary for Archie himself to carry out the assignment, to perform the duty he had assigned for others.

He had beaten the black box for three years—could he do it again? Or was his luck running out? Would the law of averages catch up to him? A tremor ran along his arm as he extended his hand toward the box. He hoped no one had noticed. Reaching inside, he grabbed a marble, concealed it in the palm of his hand. He withdrew his hand, held the arm straight out, calmly now, without shiver or tremor. He opened his hand. The marble was white.

The corner of Archie's mouth twitched as the tension of his body relaxed. He had beaten them again. He had won again. I am Archie. I cannot lose.

Carter snapped his fingers and the meeting began to break up. Suddenly, Archie felt empty, used up, discarded. He looked at the kid Goober who stood there in bewilderment, looking as if he were going to cry. Archie almost felt sorry for the kid. Almost. But not quite.

6

BROTHER Leon was getting ready to put on his show. Jerry knew the symptoms—all the guys knew them. Most of them were freshmen and had been in Leon's class only a month or so but the teacher's pattern had already emerged. First, Leon gave them a reading assignment. Then he'd pace up and down, up and down, restless, sighing, wandering through the aisles, the blackboard pointer poised in his hand, the pointer he used either like a conductor's baton or a musketeer's sword. He'd use the tip to push around a book on a desk or to flick a kid's necktie, scratching gently down some guy's back, poking the pointer as if he were a rubbish collector picking his way through the debris of the classroom. One day, the pointer had rested on Jerry's head for a moment, and then passed on. Unaccountably, Jerry had shivered, as if he had just escaped some terrible fate.

Now, aware of Leon prowling ceaselessly around the classroom, Jerry kept his eyes on paper although he didn't feel like reading. Two more periods. He looked forward to football practice. After days of calisthenics, the coach had said that probably he'd let them use the ball this afternoon.

"Enough of this crap."

That was Brother Leon—always trying to shock. Using

31

words like crap and bull and slipping in a few damns and hells once in a while. Actually, he did shock. Maybe because the words were so startling as they issued from this pale and inoffensive-looking little man. Later on, you found out that he wasn't inoffensive, of course. Now, everyone looked up at Leon as that word crap echoed in the room. Ten minutes left—time enough for Leon to perform, to play one of his games. The class looked at him in a kind of horrible fascination.

The brother's glance went slowly around the room, like the ray of a lighthouse sweeping a familiar coast, searching for hidden defects. Jerry felt a sense of dread and anticipation, both at the same time.

"Bailey," Leon said.

"Yes, Brother Leon." Leon *would* pick Bailey: one of the weak kids, high honor student, but shy, introverted, always reading, his eyes red-rimmed behind the glasses.

"Up here," Leon said, finger beckoning.

Bailey went quietly to the front of the room. Jerry could see a vein throbbing in the boy's temple.

"As you know, gentlemen," Brother Leon began, addressing the class directly and ignoring Bailey completely although the boy was standing beside him, "as you know, a certain discipline must be maintained in a school. A line must be drawn between teachers and students. We teachers would love to be one of the boys, of course. But that line of separation must remain. An invisible line, perhaps, but still there." His moist eyes gleamed. "After all, you can't see the wind but it's there. You see its handiwork, bending the trees, stirring the leaves . . ."

As he spoke, he gestured, his arm becoming the wind, the pointer in his hand following the direction of the wind and suddenly, without warning, striking Bailey on the cheek. The boy leaped backward in pain and surprise.

32

"Bailey, I'm sorry," Leon said, but his voice lacked apology. Had it been an accident? Or another of Leon's little cruelties?

Now all eyes were on the stricken Bailey. Brother Leon studied him, looking at him as if he were a specimen under a microscope, as if the specimen contained the germ of some deadly disease. You had to hand it to Leon—he was a superb actor. He loved to read short stories aloud, taking all the parts, providing all the sound effects. Nobody yawned or fell asleep in Leon's class. You had to be alert every minute, just as everyone was alert now, looking at Bailey, wondering what Leon's next move would be. Under Leon's steady gaze, Bailey had stopped stroking his cheek, even though a pink welt had appeared, like an evil stain spreading on his flesh. Somehow, the tables were turned. Now it seemed as if Bailey had been at fault all along, that Bailey had committed an error, had stood in the wrong place at the wrong time and had caused his own misfortune. Jerry squirmed in his chair. Leon gave him the creeps, the way he could change the atmosphere in a room without even speaking a word.

"Bailey," Leon said. But not looking at Bailey, looking at the class as if they were all in on a joke that Bailey knew nothing about. As if the class and Leon were banded together in a secret conspiracy.

"Yes, Brother Leon?" Bailey asked, his eyes magnified behind the glasses.

A pause.

"Bailey," Brother Leon said. "Why do you find it necessary to cheat?"

They say the hydrogen bomb makes no noise: there's only a blinding white flash that strikes cities dead. The noise comes after the flash, after the silence. That's the kind of silence that blazed in the classroom now.

33

Bailey stood speechless, his mouth an open wound.

"Is silence an admission of guilt, Bailey?" Brother Leon asked, turning to the boy at last.

Bailey shook his head frantically. Jerry felt his own head shaking, joining Bailey in silent denial.

"Ah, Bailey," Leon sighed, his voice fluttering with sadness. "What are we going to do about you?" Turning toward the class again, buddies with them—him and the class against the cheat.

"I don't cheat, Brother Leon," Bailey said, his voice a kind of squeak.

"But look at the evidence, Bailey. Your marks—all A's, no less. Every test, every paper, every homework assignment. Only a genius is capable of that sort of performance. Do you claim to be a genius, Bailey?" Toying with him. "I'll admit you look like one—those glasses, that pointed chin, that wild hair . . ."

Leon leaned toward the class, tossing his own chin, awaiting the approval of laughter, everything in his manner suggesting the response of laughter from the class. And it came. They laughed. Hey, what's going on here, Jerry wondered even as he laughed with them. Because Bailey did somehow look like a genius or at least a caricature of the mad scientists in old movies.

"Bailey," Brother Leon said, turning his full attention to the boy again as the laughter subsided.

"Yes," Bailey replied miserably.

"You haven't answered my question." He walked deliberately to the window and was suddenly absorbed in the street outside, the September leaves turning brown and crisp.

Bailey stood alone at the front of the class, as if he was facing a firing squad. Jerry felt his cheeks getting warm, throbbing with the warmth.

34

"Well, Bailey?" From Leon at the window, still intent on the world outside.

"I don't cheat, Brother Leon," Bailey said, a surge of strength in his voice, like he was taking a last stand.

"Then how do you account for all those A's?"

"I don't know."

Brother Leon whirled around. "Are you perfect, Bailey? All those A's—that implies perfection. Is that the answer, Bailey?"

For the first time, Bailey looked at the class itself, in mute appeal, like something wounded, lost, abandoned.

"Only God is perfect, Bailey."

Jerry's neck began to hurt. And his lungs burned. He realized he'd been holding his breath. He gulped air, carefully, not wanting to move a muscle. He wished he was invisible. He wished he wasn't here in the classroom. He wanted to be out on the football field, fading back, looking for a receiver.

"Do you compare yourself with God, Bailey?"

Cut it out, Brother, cut it out, Jerry cried silently.

"If God is perfect and you are perfect, Bailey, does that suggest something to you?"

Bailey didn't answer, eyes wide in disbelief. The class was utterly silent. Jerry could hear the hum of the electric clock—he'd never realized before that electric clocks hummed.

"The other alternative, Bailey, is that you are not perfect. And, of course, you're not." Leon's voice softened. "I know you wouldn't consider anything so sacrilegious."

"That's right, Brother Leon," Bailey said, relieved.

"Which leaves us with only one conclusion," Leon said, his voice bright and triumphant, as if he had made an important discovery. "You cheat!"

In that moment, Jerry hated Brother Leon. He could

taste the hate in his stomach—it was acid, foul, burning.

"You're a cheat, Bailey. And a liar." The words like whips.

You rat, Jerry thought. You bastard.

A voice boomed from the rear of the classroom. "Aw, let the kid alone."

Leon whipped around. "Who said that?" His moist eyes glistened.

The bell rang, ending the period. Feet scuffled as the boys pushed back their chairs, preparing to leave, to get out of that terrible place.

"Wait a minute," Brother Leon said. Softly—but heard by everyone. "Nobody moves."

The students settled in their chairs again.

Brother Leon regarded them pityingly, shaking his head, a sad and dismal smile on his lips. "You poor fools," he said. "You idiots. Do you know who's the best one here? The bravest of all?" He placed his hand on Bailey's shoulder. "Gregory Bailey, that's who. He denied cheating. He stood up to my accusations. He stood his ground! But you, gentlemen, you sat there and enjoyed yourselves. And those of you who didn't enjoy yourselves allowed it to happen, allowed me to proceed. You turned this classroom into Nazi Germany for a few moments. Yes, yes, someone finally protested. *Aw, let the kid alone.*" Mimicking the deep voice perfectly. "A feeble protest, too little and too late." There was scuffling in the corridors, students waiting to enter. Leon ignored the noise. He turned to Bailey, touched the top of his head with the pointer as if he were bestowing knighthood. "You did well, Bailey. I'm proud of you. You passed the biggest test of all—you were true to yourself." Bailey's chin was wobbling all over the place. "Of course you don't cheat, Bailey," his voice tender and paternal. He gestured toward the class—he was a great one for gestures. "Your classmates out there. They're the cheaters. They

36

cheated you today. They're the ones who doubted you—I never did."

Leon went to his desk. "Dismissed," he said, his voice filled with contempt for all of them.

7

"WHAT'RE you doing, Emile?" Archie asked, amusement in his voice. The amusement was there because it was obvious what Emile Janza was doing—he was siphoning gas from a car, watching it flow into a glass jug.

Emile giggled. He, too, was amused that Archie should have discovered him performing such an act.

"I'm getting my gas for the week," Emile said.

The car, parked at the far end of the school's parking lot, belonged to a senior by the name of Carlson.

"What would you do, Emile, if Carlson came along and saw you stealing his gas?" Archie asked, although he knew the answer.

Emile didn't bother to reply. He grinned knowingly at Archie. Carlson wouldn't do anything about it at all. He was a thin, mild kid who hated getting involved in messes. Not too many people defied Emile Janza, anyway, whether they were fat or skinny, mild or not. Emile was a brute, which was kind of funny because he didn't look like a brute. He wasn't big or overly strong. In fact, he was small for a tackle on the football team. But he was an animal and he didn't play by the rules. Not if he could help it. His small eyes were imbedded in pale flesh, eyes that seldom smiled despite the giggle and the grin that sometimes flashed across his face, especially when he knew he was reaching people. That's what Emile Janza called it—reaching people. Like whistling softly in class so that it got on the teacher's nerves, a barely perceptible whistle that could drive a teacher up the wall. That's why Emile Janza reversed the usual process. Wise guys usually sat in back. Emile didn't. He chose seats near the front where he'd be in better position to harass the teacher. Whistling, grunting, belching, tapping his foot, stirring restlessly, sniffling. Hell, if you did that kind of stuff from the back of the room the teacher wouldn't notice.

But Emile didn't harass only teachers. He found that the world was full of willing victims, especially kids his own age. He had discovered a truth early in life—in the fourth grade, in fact. Nobody wanted trouble, nobody wanted to make trouble, nobody wanted a showdown. The knowledge was a revelation. It opened doors. You could take a kid's lunch or even his lunch money and nothing usually happened because most kids wanted peace at any price. Of course, you have to choose your victims carefully because there were exceptions. Those who protested found that it was easier to let Emile have his way. Who wanted to get hurt? Later, Emile stumbled upon another truth, although it was hard to put into words. He found that people had a fear of being embarrassed or humiliated, of being singled out for special attention. Like in a bus. You could call out to a kid, especially one who blushes easily, and say, "Jeez, you got bad breath, know that? Don't you ever brush your teeth?" Even if the kid had the sweetest breath in the world. Or, "Did you lay a fart, kid? What a dirty thing to do." Softly, but loud enough for everybody to hear. Stuff like that—in the cafeteria, during lunch, in study class. But it was better in public places, with strangers nearby, especially girls. That's when the kids squirmed. As a result, people went around being extra nice to Emile Janza. And Emile basked in that treatment. Emile was not stupid but he was not exactly bright in class. However, he managed to squeak by—no *F*'s, only a couple of *D*'s, all of which satisfied his father, whom Emile regarded as stupid and whose major dream was to have his son graduate from a fancy private school like Trinity. His father didn't know how cruddy the place was.

"Emile, you're a beautiful person," Archie said as Emile, satisfied with the overflowing glass jug, carefully screwed the cap of the gas tank on.

Emile looked up suspiciously, on guard. He was never sure whether Archie Costello was serious or not. Emile never fooled around with Archie. In fact, Archie was one of the few people in the world Emile respected. Maybe even feared. Archie and The Vigils.

"Did you say beautiful?"

Archie laughed. "I mean, Emile, you're something special. Who else would siphon gas in the middle of the day? Out in the open like this? Beautiful."

Emile smiled at Archie, suddenly wistful. He wished he could share with Archie some of the other stuff. But he couldn't. Somehow, it was too private but often he wanted to tell people about it. How he got a kick out of things. For instance, when he went to the john at school, he seldom flushed the toilet—and got a kick out of picturing the next kid who'd go in and find the mess in the bowl. Crazy. And if you told anybody, it would be hard to explain. Like how he sometimes felt actually horny when he roughhoused a kid or tackled a guy viciously in football and gave him an extra jab when he had him on the ground. How could you tell anybody about that? And yet he felt that Archie would understand. Birds of a feather, that was it. Despite that picture. The picture that haunted his life.

Archie began to walk away.

"Hey, Archie, where're you going?"

"I don't want to be an accessory, Emile."

Emile laughed. "Carlson's not gonna press charges."

Archie shook his head in admiration. "Beautiful," he said.

"Hey, Archie. How about the picture?"

"Yes, Emile. How *about* the picture?"

"You know what I mean."

"Beautiful," Archie said, walking away quickly now, wanting to keep Emile Janza sweating about the picture. Actually, Archie hated people like Janza even though he could admire their handiwork. People like Janza were animals. But they came in handy. Janza and the picture—like money in the bank.

Emile Janza watched the departing figure of Archie Costello. Someday, he'd be like Archie—cool, a member of The Vigils. Emile kicked at the rear tire of Carlson's car. Somehow he was disappointed that Carlson hadn't caught him siphoning the gas.

8

THE Goober was beautiful when he ran. His long arms and legs moved flowingly and flawlessly, his body floating as if his feet weren't touching the ground. When he ran, he forgot about his acne and his awkwardness and the shyness that paralyzed him when a girl looked his way. Even his thoughts became sharper, and things were simple and uncomplicated—he could solve math problems when he ran or memorize football play patterns. Often he rose early in the morning, before anyone else, and poured himself, liquid, through the sunrise streets, and everything seemed beautiful, everything in its proper orbit, nothing impossible, the entire world attainable.

When he ran, he even loved the pain, the hurt of the running, the burning in his lungs and the spasms that sometimes gripped his calves. He loved it because he knew he could endure the pain, and even go beyond it. He had never pushed himself to the limit but he felt all this reserve strength inside of him: more than strength actually—determination. And it sang in him as he ran, his heart pumping blood joyfully through his body. He'd gone out for football and there was a good feeling when he caught one of Jerry Renault's passes and outran everybody for a score. But it was the running he loved. The neighbors would see him waterfalling down High Street, carried by the momentum of his speed, and they'd cry out, "Going for the Olympics, Goob?" Or, "Got your eye on the world record, Goob?" And on he'd run, floating, flowing.

But he wasn't running now. He was in Brother Eugene's homeroom and he was terrified. He was fifteen years old and six-one-and-a-half and too old to cry but tears blurred his vision, as if the room was under water. He was ashamed and disgusted with himself but he couldn't help it. The tears were from frustration as well as terror. And the terror was different from any other kind he'd ever known: the terror of a waking nightmare. Like waking up from a bad dream in which a monster was gaining on you and breathing a sigh of relief as you realized you were safe in your bed and then looking toward the moonlit doorway and seeing the monster stalking toward your bed. And knowing you'd stumbled from one nightmare into another—and how do you find your way back to the real world?

He knew that he was in the real world at this moment, of course. Everything was real enough. The screwdrivers and the pliers were real. So were the desks and chairs and the blackboards. So was the world outside, a world he had been shut away from since three o'clock this afternoon when he had sneaked into the school. Now the world had changed, had grown blurred with day's leaving and then purple at dusk and then dark. It was now nine o'clock and The Goober sat on the floor, his head against a desk, angry at his damp cheeks. His eyes stung from strain. The Vigils said he was allowed to put on the small emergency night light each classroom was furnished. A flashlight was forbidden because it might look suspicious to outsiders. The Goober had found the job almost impossible. He had been in the classroom six hours and had only finished two rows of desks and chairs.

The screws were stubborn, most of them factory-tight, resisting the twists of the screwdriver.

I'll never get done, he thought. I'll be here all night and my folks will go crazy and it still won't be done. He envisioned himself being discovered here tomorrow morning, collapsed in exhaustion, a disgrace to himself and The Vigils and the school. He was hungry and had a headache and felt that everything would be all right if he could only get out of here and run, hurtle himself through the streets, free from the terrible assignment.

A noise from the corridor. That was another thing—it was spooky. All kinds of noises. The walls spoke their own creaky language, the floors crackled, motors hummed somewhere, the humming almost human. Enough to scare a guy to death. He hadn't been this scared since he was just a kid and woke up in the middle of the night calling for his mother.

Thump. There—another noise. He looked with dread toward the doorway, not wanting to look but unable to resist the temptation, remembering his old nightmare.

"Hey, Goober," the whisper came.

"Who's there?" he whispered back. Relief swept him. He wasn't alone anymore, someone else was here.

"How're you doing?"

A figure was advancing toward him on all fours, like an animal. The aspect of the beast—nightmare, after all. He shrank back, his skin hot and prickly, like the onset of hives. He was aware of other figures crawling into the room, knees scraping across the floor. The first figure was now in front of him.

"Need some help?"

The Goober squinted. The kid was masked.

"It's going slow," Goober said.

The masked figure grabbed the front of Goober's shirt

44

and twisted hard, pulling him forward. He could smell pizza on the kid's breath. The mask was black, the kind Zorro wore in the movies.

"Listen, Goubert. The assignment is more important than anything else, understand? More important than you, me or the school. That's why we're going to give you some help. To get the thing done right." The kid's knuckles dug hard into Goober's chest. "You tell anybody about this and you're through at Trinity. Got that?"

Goober gulped and nodded. His throat was dry. He was happy beyond belief. Help had arrived. The impossible had become possible.

The masked figure raised his head. "Okay, fellows, let's get going."

One of the other fellows raised his face, also masked, and said, "This is a gas."

"Shut up and get to work," the guy who was obviously the leader said.

He also let go of Goober's shirt and pulled out his own screwdriver.

It took them three hours.

9

JERRY'S mother had died in the spring. They had been staying up with her nights—his father and some of his uncles and aunts and Jerry himself—since her return from the hospital. They came and went in shifts that final week, everyone exhausted and mute with sadness. Nothing more could be done for her at the hospital and she was taken home to die. She'd loved her home so much, always had some project underway—wallpapering, painting, refinishing furniture. "Give me twenty workers like her and I'd open a small factory and make a million," his father used to joke. And then she got sick. And died. Watching her ebb away, seeing her beauty diminish, witnessing the awful alteration of her face and body was too much for Jerry to bear and he sometimes fled her bedroom, ashamed of his weakness, avoiding his father. Jerry wished he could be as strong as his father, always in control, masking his sorrow and grief. When his mother finally died, suddenly, at three-thirty in the afternoon, slipping off quietly without a murmur, Jerry was overcome with rage, a fiery anger that found him standing at her coffin in silent fury. He was angry at the way the disease had ravaged her. He was angry at his inability to do anything about saving her. His anger was so deep and sharp in him that it drove out sorrow. He wanted to bellow at the world, cry out against her death, topple buildings, split the earth open, tear down trees. And he did nothing except lie awake in the dark, thinking of her body there in the funeral home, not her anymore, but a *thing* suddenly, cold and pale. His father was a stranger during those terrible days, like a sleepwalker going through the motions, like a puppet being maneuvered by invisible strings. Jerry felt hopeless and abandoned, all tight inside. Even at the cemetery, they stood apart from each other, a huge distance between them even though they were side by side. But not touching. And then, at the end of the service, as they turned to leave, Jerry found himself in his father's arms, his face pressed close to his father's body, smelling the cigarette tobacco, the faint odor of peppermint mouthwash, that familiar smell that was his father. There in the cemetery, clinging to each other in mutual sorrow and loss, the tears came for both of them. Jerry didn't know where his own tears began and his father's left off. They wept without shame, out of a nameless need, and walked together afterward, arm in arm, toward the waiting car. The fiery knot of anger had come undone, unraveled, and Jerry realized as they drove back from the cemetery that something worse had taken its place—emptiness, a yawning cavity like a hole in his chest.

That was the last moment of intimacy he and his father had shared. The routine of school for himself, and work for his father, had been taken up and they both threw themselves into it. His father sold the house and they moved to a garden apartment where no memories lurked around corners. Jerry spent most of the summer in Canada, on the farm of a distant cousin. He had fallen into the routine of the farm willingly, hoping to build up his body for Trinity and football in the fall. His mother had been born in that small Canadian town. There was a kind of comfort walking the narrow streets where she herself had walked as a girl.

When he returned to New England in late August, he and his father fell into a simple routine. Work and school. And football. On the field, bruised and battered or grimy and dirty, Jerry felt as if he was part of something. And he sometimes wondered, what was his father part of?

He thought of that now as he looked at his father. He'd come from school to find his father napping on a sofa in the den, arms folded across his chest. Jerry moved soundlessly through the apartment, not wanting to awaken the sleeping figure. His father was a pharmacist and worked all kinds of staggered hours for a chain of drugstores in the area. His work often included night shifts, which meant broken sleep. As a result, he'd developed the habit of falling off into naps whenever he found a moment to relax. Jerry's stomach was weak from hunger but he sat quietly down across from his father now, waiting for him to waken. He was weary from practice, the constant punishment his body took, the frustration of never getting a play off, never completing a pass, the coach's sarcasm, the lingering September heat.

Watching his father sleep, the face relaxed in slumber, all the harsh lines of age less defined, he remembered hearing that people who had been married a long time began to resemble each other. He squinted his eyes, the way one inspects a fine painting, searching for his mother there in the face of his father. And, without warning, the anguish of her loss returned, like a blow to his stomach, and he was afraid that he would faint. Through some nightmarish miracle, he was able to superimpose the image of his mother's face on his father's—and for a moment the echo of all her sweetness was there and he had to go through all the horror of visualizing her in the coffin again.

His father awakened, as if slapped from sleep by an

invisible hand. The vision vanished and Jerry leaped to his feet.

"Hi, Jerry," his father said, rubbing his eyes, sitting up. His hair wasn't even mussed. But then how could a stiff crew cut get mussed up? "Have a good day, Jerry?"

His father's voice restored normalcy. "Okay, I guess. Another practice. One of these days, I'll get a pass off."

"Fine."

"How was your day, Dad?"

"Fine."

"That's good."

"Mrs. Hunter left us a casserole. Tuna fish. She said you liked it fine last time."

Mrs. Hunter was the housekeeper. She spent every afternoon cleaning up the place and preparing some kind of evening meal for them. She was a gray-haired woman who constantly embarrassed Jerry because she insisted on tousling his hair and murmuring, "Child, child . . ." like he was a third grader or something.

"Hungry, Jerry? I can get it ready in five or ten minutes. Heat the oven and there it is . . ."

"Fine."

He was throwing one of his father's *fines* back at him although his father didn't notice. That was his father's favorite word—fine.

"Hey, Dad."

"Yes, Jerry?"

"Were things really fine at the store today?"

His father paused near the kitchen doorway, puzzled. "What do you mean, Jerry?"

"I mean, every day I ask you how things are going and every day you say fine. Don't you have some *great* days? Or *rotten* days?

"A drugstore's pretty much the same all the time, Jerry.

49

The prescriptions come in and we fill them—and that's about it. You fill them carefully, taking all precautions, double-checking. It's true what they say about doctors' handwriting, but I've told you that before." He was frowning now, as if searching his memory, trying to find something that would please the boy. "There was that attempted holdup three years ago—the time that drug addict came in like a wild man."

Jerry made an effort to hide his shock and disappointment. Was that the most exciting thing that had ever happened to his father? That pathetic holdup try by a scared young kid brandishing a toy pistol? Was life that dull, that boring and humdrum for people? He hated to think of his own life stretching ahead of him that way, a long succession of days and nights that were fine, *fine*—not good, not bad, not great, not lousy, not exciting, not anything.

He followed his father into the kitchen. The casserole slid into the oven like a letter into a mailbox. Jerry wasn't hungry suddenly, all appetite gone. "How about a salad?" his father asked. "I think there's lettuce and stuff around."

Jerry nodded automatically. Was this all there was to life, after all? You finished school, found an occupation, got married, became a father, watched your wife die, and then lived through days and nights that seemed to have no sunrises, no dawns and no dusks, nothing but a gray drabness. Or was he being fair to his father? To himself? Wasn't each man different? Didn't a man have a choice? How much did he know about his father, really?

"Hey, Dad."

"Yes, Jerry?"

"Nothing."

What could he ask him without sounding crazy? And he doubted whether his father would level with him, anyway.

Jerry recalled an incident that had taken place years ago when his father worked in a neighborhood pharmacy, the kind of place where customers came to consult the druggist as if he possessed a doctor's certificate. Jerry had been hanging around the store one afternoon when an old man entered, bent and gnarled with age. He had a pain in his right side. What should I do, Mister Druggist? What do you think it is? Look, press here, Mister Druggist, do you feel the swelling there? Is there a medicine to cure me? His father had been patient with the old man, listening sympathetically, nodding, stroking his cheek as if he were preparing a diagnosis. He finally convinced the old man to go see a doctor. But for a moment there, Jerry had seen his father acting the part of a physician—wise and professional and compassionate. A regular bedside manner, even there in a drugstore. After the old man's departure, Jerry had asked, "Hey, Dad, did you ever want to be a doctor?" His father glanced up quickly and hesitated, taken by surprise. "No, of course not," he said. But Jerry had caught something in his manner, in his tone of voice, that ran counter to his answer. When Jerry tried to pursue the subject, his father suddenly became very busy with prescriptions and stuff. And he never brought up the subject again.

Now, seeing his father presiding in the kitchen, getting supper, for crying out loud—such a far cry from being a doctor—and his wife dead and his only son full of doubts about him, his life so pale and gray, Jerry was plunged into sadness. The stove signaled—casserole ready.

Later, preparing for bed and sleep, Jerry looked at himself in the mirror, saw himself as that guy on the Common must have seen him the other day: Square Boy. Just as he had superimposed his mother's image on his father's face, now he could see his father's face reflected in his own features. He turned away. He didn't want to be a mirror of his father. The thought made him cringe. *I want to do something, be somebody. But what? But what?*

Football. He'd make the team. That was something. Or was it, really?

For no reason at all, he thought of Gregory Bailey.

10

*L*ATER, Archie had to concede that Brother Leon had dramatized the sale too vividly and therefore put himself and The Vigils and the entire school on the spot.

To begin with, he called a special assembly at chapel. Following prayers and a lot of other religious hoopla, he started talking about all that school spirit crap. But with a difference this time. Standing at the pulpit, he gave the signal to a few of his stooges to bring in ten big cardboard posters which listed in alphabetical order every student in school. A series of blank rectangles had been drawn beside each name which, Leon explained, would be filled in as each student sold his quota of chocolates.

The student body watched with glee as Leon's stooges tried to scotch-tape the posters to the wall at the rear of the stage. The posters kept slipping to the floor, resisting the tape. The walls were made of concrete blocks, and tacks couldn't be used, of course. Hoots filled the air. Brother Leon looked annoyed, which increased the hoots and catcalls. There was nothing more beautiful in the world than the sight of a teacher getting upset. Finally, the posters were secured and Brother Leon took charge.

Archie had to admit that the Brother turned in one of his great performances. Academy Award caliber. He poured it on like Niagara—school spirit, the traditional sale that had never failed, the Headmaster lying sick in the hospital, the brotherhood of Trinity, the need for funds to keep this magnificent edifice of education operating on all gears. He recalled past triumphs, the trophies in the display case in the main corridor, the do-or-die determination that made Trinity a place of triumph through the years. Etc. Crap, of course, but effective when a master like Leon was at work, casting a spell with words and gestures.

"Yes," Brother Leon intoned, "the quota is doubled this year because we have more at stake than ever before." His voice an organ, filling the air. "Each boy must sell fifty boxes, but I know that each boy is willing to do his share. More than his share." He gestured toward the posters. "I promise you, gentlemen, that before this sale is ended each one of you will have the number 'fifty' inscribed in that final box, signifying that you have done your part for Trinity . . ."

There was a lot more but Archie tuned him out. Talk, talk, talk—that's all anybody ever heard in school. Archie squirmed uncomfortably in his seat, thinking of the Vigil meeting at which he had announced that Brother Leon had asked support for the sale and how he'd pledged the backing of The Vigils. Archie had been surprised at the ripple of doubt and skepticism from the members of The Vigils. "Christ, Archie," Carter had said, "we never get mixed up in this stuff." But Archie had overcome them as usual, pointing out that Leon's need for an endorsement from The Vigils was a symbol of how powerful the organization had become. And it was only a crappy chocolate sale. But now, listening to Leon sounding as if the school was embarking on the Crusades, for crying out loud, Archie was doubtful.

Looking at the posters and seeing his own name there, Archie plotted how his own fifty boxes would be sold. He wouldn't dream of selling the chocolates himself. He hadn't

54

touched a box since his freshman days. Usually he found some willing kid who'd gladly sell Archie's quota along with his own, figuring it was something special to be singled out by the assigner of The Vigils. This year, he'd probably spread the burden around, picking out five guys, say, and have them sell only ten boxes each. It was better than sticking one kid with the entire quota, wasn't it?

Sitting back in comfort, Archie sighed now, contented, gratified by the heights his sense of fairness and compassion could reach.

11

IT was as if somebody had dropped The Bomb.

Brian Kelly started it all when he touched his chair. It collapsed.

Then, everything happened at once.

Albert LeBlanc brushed against a desk as he made his way down the aisle and it fell apart after trembling crazily for a moment. The impact sent out vibrations which shot down two other chairs and a desk.

John Lowe was about to sit down when he heard the noise of collapsing furniture. He turned and in doing so touched his own desk. The desk disintegrated before his astonished eyes. Leaping backward, he hit his chair. Nothing happened to his chair. But Henry Couture's desk behind it shivered violently and tumbled to the floor.

The racket was deafening.

"My God," Brother Eugene cried as he entered the classroom and beheld the bedlam. Desks and chairs were falling apart as if being demolished by mysterious unheard dynamite explosions.

Brother Eugene rushed to his desk, that haven of security behind which a teacher always found protection. At his touch, the desk swayed drunkenly, shifted gears into a lopsided position and—miracle of miracles—remained

56

upright at that strange tipsy angle. But his chair collapsed.

Boys scrambled madly and merrily around the room. Once they realized what was happening they dashed around Room Nineteen testing all the desks and chairs, watching with glee as they fell apart, and toppling the stubborn pieces of furniture that refused to go down without help.

"Wow," somebody yelled.

"The Vigils," somebody else called out—giving credit where credit was due.

The destruction of Room Nineteen took exactly thirty-seven seconds. Archie timed it from the doorway. A sweetness gathered in his breast as he saw the room being turned into a shambles, a sweet moment of triumph that compensated for all the other lousy things, his terrible marks, the black box. Witnessing the pandemonium, he knew that this was one of his major triumphs, one of those long-shot assignments that paid off beautifully, certain to become legend. He could picture Trinity students of the future discussing in wonder the day Room Nineteen exploded. He found it hard to suppress a howl of delight as he surveyed the havoc—*I made this happen*—and saw Brother Eugene's trembling chin and horror-stricken expression.

Behind the brother, the huge blackboard suddenly tore loose from its moorings and slid majestically to the floor, like a final curtain dropping on the chaos.

"You!"

Archie heard the voice in all its fury at the same instant that he felt the hands spinning him around. He swiveled to encounter Brother Leon. Leon wasn't pale at this moment. Scarlet splotches glistened on his cheeks as if he had been made up for some grotesque stage show. A horror show maybe, because there was nothing funny about him at this moment.

"You!" Leon said again, a wicked whisper that spilled

into Archie's face the foul aftertaste of Leon's breakfast—the smell of stale bacon and eggs. "You did this," Leon said, digging the fingernails of one hand into Archie's shoulder while pointing to the chaos of Room Nineteen with the other.

Curious students from other classes had now gathered around the two entrances to the room, drawn by the crash and clatter. Some of them regarded the rubble with awe. Others glanced curiously at Brother Leon and Archie. No matter where they looked, it was great—an interruption of school routine, a diversion in the deadly order of the day.

"Didn't I tell you I wanted everything to go smoothly? No incidents? No funny business?"

The worst part of Leon's fury was the way he whispered, this terrible tortured hissing from his mouth, giving his words a tone more deadly than a shout or a yell. At the same time his grip on Archie's shoulder got tighter and Archie winced with pain.

"I didn't do anything. I didn't promise anything," Archie said automatically. Always deny everything, never apologize, never admit anything.

Leon pushed Archie up against a wall as the boys began to fill the corridor, pouring into Room Nineteen to view the destruction, and milling around outside, talking and gesturing, shaking their heads in wonder—the legend had already begun.

"I'm in charge, don't you see? This entire school is now my responsibility. The chocolate sale is ready to start and you pull something like this." Leon released him without warning, and Archie hung there as if suspended in mid-air. He turned and saw some guys staring at Leon and him. Staring at him! Archie Costello humiliated by this snivelling bastard of a teacher. His sweet moment of triumph spoiled by this nut and his ridiculous chocolate sale!

58

He watched Leon storming away, pushing his way through the tumultuous corridor, disappearing into the swarming stream of boys. Archie massaged his shoulder, gingerly feeling the spot where Leon's fingernails had bitten deep. Then he thrust himself into the crowd, pushing aside the guys gathered near the doorway. He stood at the entrance, drinking in the beautiful debris of Room Nineteen—his masterpiece. He saw Brother Eugene still standing there in the midst of the shambles, tears actually running down his cheeks.

Beautiful, beautiful.

Screw Brother Leon.

12

"*T*RY it again," the coach bellowed, his voice hoarse. The danger point—his voice always got hoarse when he lost his patience, when he was in danger of blowing his top.

Jerry picked himself up. His mouth was dry and he tried to suck spit into it. His ribs hurt, his entire left side was on fire. He stalked back to his position behind Adamo who played center. The other guys were already lined up, tense, waiting, aware that the coach wasn't happy with them. Not happy? Hell, he was furious, disgusted. He had arranged this special practice, giving his freshmen a chance to scrimmage against a few members of the varsity, to show off all he had taught them and they were doing lousy, rotten, terrible.

There was no huddle. The Coach barked the number of the next play, a play designed to suck in Carter, the big beefy varsity guard who looked as if he could chew freshmen up and spit them out. But the Coach had said, "We'll have some surprises for Carter." It was tradition at Trinity to toss star players against the Freshmen and to build plays designed to stop the stars. This was the only reward the Freshman team reaped because most of them were too young or too small to play varsity.

Jerry crouched behind Adamo. He was determined to

make this play work. He knew that the previous play hadn't worked because his timing was off and because he hadn't seen Carter come crashing out of nowhere. He had expected Carter to blitz and instead the big guard had pulled back and skirted the line, annihilating Jerry from behind. What infuriated Jerry was that Carter toppled him gently, lowering him to the ground almost tenderly as if to prove his superiority. I don't have to murder you, kid, it's easy enough this way, Carter seemed to be saying. But this was the seventh consecutive play and the damage of being tackled play after play was taking its toll.

"All right, guys, this is it. Make or break."

"It's all over, fellas," Carter taunted.

Jerry called the signals, hoping his voice sounded confident. He didn't feel confident. And yet he hadn't given up hope. Every play was a new beginning and even though something always seemed to go wrong he felt that they were on the verge of clicking. He had confidence in guys like Goober and Adamo and Croteau. Sooner or later, they had to click, all the work had to pay off. That is, if the coach didn't cut them all off the squad first.

Jerry's hands were joined like a duck's bill waiting to swallow the ball. At his signal, Adamo slapped the ball into his palms and Jerry began to fade at the same instant, to the right, slanted, swift, his arm already coming up, ready to be cocked, ready for the pass. He saw Carter snaking through the line again, like some monstrous reptile in his helmet, but suddenly Carter became all arms and legs tossing and turning in the air, hit devastatingly low by Croteau. Carter collapsed on Croteau and both of them fell in a tangle of bodies. Jerry felt a sudden sense of freedom. He continued to fade, fade, easy, easy, stalling until he could spot The Goober, tall and rangy, downfield where he'd be waiting if he had managed to elude the safety-man.

Suddenly Jerry spotted Goober's waving hand. Jerry avoided fingers that tore at his sleeve and he unloosed the ball. Someone brushed his hip but he shrugged off the blow. The pass was beautiful. He could tell it was beautiful, straight on target, even though he couldn't watch its progress, because he was dumped violently to the ground by Carter who had somehow recovered after being demolished. As he hit the ground, Jerry heard the yells and the cheers that told him The Goober had caught the pass and gone on to score.

"Good, good, good, good." The coach's voice, raucous in triumph.

Jerry struggled to his feet. Carter slapped him on the ass, signaling his approval.

The coach lumbered toward them, still scowling. But then he never smiled.

"Renault," the coach said, all hoarseness gone. "We just might make a quarterback out of you yet, you skinny little son of a bitch."

With the fellows standing all around him and his breath coming in gasps and Goober arriving with the ball, Jerry knew a moment of absolute bliss, absolute happiness.

There was a legend in the school that the Coach hadn't accepted you as a player until he'd called you a son of a bitch.

The guys lined up again. Jerry was sweet poetry and music as he waited for the ball to be slapped into his hand.

When he returned to the school after practice, he found a letter scotch-taped to the door of his locker. A summons from The Vigils. Subject: Assignment.

13

"**A**DAMO?"

"Yes."

"Beauvais?"

"Yes."

"Crane?"

"Yo." Crane, the comedian. Never a straight answer.

"Caroni?"

"Yes."

Everyone could see that Brother Leon was enjoying himself. This is what he liked—to be in command and everything going smoothly, the students responding to their names smartly, accepting the chocolates, showing school spirit. The Goober was depressed, thinking about school spirit. Ever since Room Nineteen had collapsed, he had lived in a state of mild shock. He awoke each morning depressed, knowing even before he opened his eyes that something was wrong, something had gone askew in his life. And then he'd remember: Room Nineteen. The first day or two had been kind of exciting. Word had gotten around that the destruction of Room Nineteen was the result of his assignment by The Vigils. Although no one mentioned the subject to him, he found himself a kind of underground hero. Even the seniors looked at him with awe and respect. Guys patted him on the ass when he passed by, an old Trinity mark of distinction. But as the days went on, an uneasiness stole across the campus. There were rumors. The place was always filled with rumors but this time they grew out of the Room Nineteen incident. The chocolate sale was postponed for a week and Brother Leon, speaking at chapel, gave a weak explanation. The Head was hospitalized, there was a lot of paperwork involved, etc. etc. There were also rumors that Leon was carrying on a quiet investigation of Room Nineteen. Poor Brother Eugene had not been seen since that devastating morning. He'd had a nervous breakdown, someone said. Others reported that there had been a death in his family and he'd been called away. Anyway, it all heaped itself upon The Goober and he found it hard to sleep at night. Despite the adulation of the guys at school, he felt as if there was some kind of distance between him and the fellows. They admired him, sure, but didn't want to get too close in case something backfired. One afternoon, he'd met Archie Costello in the corridor and Archie had pulled him aside. "If they call you in for questioning, you know nothing," Archie said. Goober had no way of knowing this was the kind of thing Archie loved to do—intimidate someone, get him worrying. Since then, The Goober had walked around in a state of apprehension, expecting to see his name on a Wanted sign on the bulletin board, for crying out loud. He didn't want the adulation of the fellows anymore—he simply wanted to be The Goober, to play football and to run in the morning. He dreaded a summons from Brother Leon, wondering if he could stand up under questioning, whether he could look into those moist eyes of Brother Leon's and actually lie to him.

"Goubert?"

He realized that Brother Leon had been calling his name, two or three times.

"Yes," The Goober replied.

Brother Leon paused, looking at him questioningly. The Goober shriveled.

"You don't seem to be entirely with us today, Goubert," Leon said. "At least, not in spirit."

"I'm sorry, Brother Leon."

"Speaking of spirit, Goubert, you realize, don't you, how this chocolate sale goes beyond a mere sale or routine project, don't you?"

"Yes, Brother Leon." Was Leon baiting him?

"The most beautiful part of the sale, Goubert, is that it's a project completely by students. The students sell the chocolates. The school merely administers the project. It's *your* sale, *your* project."

Bullshit, someone whispered, out of Leon's hearing.

"Yes, Brother Leon," Goober said, relieved, realizing that the teacher was too much involved with the chocolates to be assessing Goober's innocence or guilt.

"Then you accept the fifty boxes?"

"Yes," Goober said with eagerness. Fifty boxes was a lot of chocolates but he was glad to say yes and get out of the spotlight.

Leon's hand moved ceremoniously as he wrote down Goober's name.

"Hartnett?"

"Yes."

"Johnson?"

"Why not?"

Leon accepted this small hint of mockery from Johnson because he was in such a good mood. The Goober wondered whether he himself would ever be in a good mood again. And he was puzzled. Why should he be feeling so lousy about Room Nineteen? Was it the destruction? Actually, the desks and chairs had been put back together again in one day. Leon had thought he was inflicting punishment on the fellows selected to do the job but the discipline backfired. Each screw, each piece of furniture was a reminder of that marvelous event. Fellows even volunteered for the job. Then, why this terrible guilt? Because of Brother Eugene? Probably. Whenever Goober walked by Room Nineteen now, he couldn't resist glancing in.

The room would never be the same again, of course. The furniture creaked weirdly, as if it would collapse again without warning. The various teachers who used the room were uneasy—you could tell they were apprehensive. Once in a while, some guy would drop a book just to see the teacher flinch or leap in panic.

Immersed in his thoughts, The Goober didn't realize that a terrible silence had enveloped the classroom. But he became aware of the stillness when he glanced up to see Brother Leon's face, paler now than ever, and the eyes glistening like sun-splashed pools.

"Renault?"

The silence continued.

The Goober glanced toward Jerry three desks away. Jerry sat stiffly, elbows resting on the desk, staring straight ahead, as if he were in a trance.

"You *are* here, aren't you, Renault?" Leon asked, trying to turn the moment into a joke. But his effort had the opposite effect. No one laughed.

"Last call, Renault."

"No," Jerry said.

The Goober wasn't sure he'd heard correctly. Jerry had spoken so quietly, barely moving his lips, that his answer had been indistinct even in that utter quiet.

"What?" From Leon.

"No."

Confusion now. Someone laughed. A classroom joke was always appreciated, anything to fracture the dullness of routine.

"Did you say *no*, Renault?" Brother Leon asked, his voice testy.

"Yes."

"Yes, what?"

The exchange delighted the classroom. A giggle from somewhere and then a snort, followed by the strange mood that took hold of a classroom when the unusual occurred, the way students sensed a difference in the climate, an alteration of atmosphere, like the seasons changing.

"Let me get this straight, Renault," Brother Leon said and his voice brought the room under his command again. "I called your name. Your response could have been either *yes* or *no*. *Yes* means that like every other student in this school you agree to sell a certain amount of chocolates, in this case fifty boxes. *No*—and let me point out that the sale is strictly voluntary, Trinity forces no one to participate against his wishes, this is the great glory of Trinity—*no* means you don't wish to sell the chocolates, that you refuse to participate. Now, what is your answer? Yes or no?"

"No."

The Goober stared at Jerry in disbelief. Was this Jerry Renault who always looked a little worried, a little unsure of himself even after completing a beautiful pass, who always seemed kind of bewildered—was this him actually defying Brother Leon? Not only Brother Leon but a Trinity tradition? Then, looking at Leon, Goober saw the teacher as if in technicolor, blood beating in his cheeks, his moist eyes like specimens in laboratory test tubes. Finally, Brother Leon inclined his head, the pencil moving in his hand as he made some kind of horrible mark beside Jerry's name.

The silence in the class was the kind Goober had never heard before. Stunned, eerie, suffocating.

"Santucci?" Leon called out, his voice strangled but struggling to be normal.

"Yes."

Leon looked up, smiling at Santucci, blinking away the flush on his cheeks, a smile like the kind an undertaker fixes on the face of a corpse.

"Tessier?"

"Yes."

"Williams?"

"Yes."

Williams was the last. There was no one in this class with a name beginning with *X*, *Y*, or *Z*. Williams' *yes* lingered on the air. No one seemed to be looking at anyone else.

"You may pick up your chocolates in the gym, gentlemen," Brother Leon said, his eyes bright—wet bright. "Those of you who are true sons of Trinity, that is. I pity anyone who is not." That terrible smile remained on his face. "Class dismissed," Leon called although the bell had not sounded.

14

*L*ET'S see, he knew he could count on his Aunt
Agnes and Mike Terasigni whose lawn he cut every week
in the summer, and Father O'Toole at the rectory (although
his mother would massacre him if she knew he had Father
O'Toole on the list) and Mr. and Mrs. Thornton who weren't
Catholic but always willing to help a good cause, and, of
course, Mrs. Mitchell the widow whose errands he did every
Saturday morning and Henry Babineau the bachelor with
his awful breath that almost knocked you down when you
opened the door but who was pointed out by all the mothers
in the neighborhood as the kindest, most gentlest of men . . .

John Sulkey liked to make out the lists whenever there
was a sale at the school. Last year, as a junior, he had won
first prize for selling the most chances in a school raffle—
one hundred and twenty-five books, twelve tickets in each
book—and received a special pin at the Awards Assembly
at the end of the school year. The only honor he had ever
won—purple and gold (the school colors), shaped like a
triangle, symbolizing the trinity. His parents had beamed
with pride. He was lousy at sports and a squeaker at
studies—just barely squeaking by—but, like his mother
said, you did your best and God took care of the rest. Of
course, it took planning. That's why John made out his

lists ahead of time. Sometimes he even visited his regular customers before a sale began to let them know what was coming. He liked nothing better than getting out there on the street and ringing the doorbells and seeing the money pile up, money he would turn in the next day at roll call, and how the Brother in the homeroom would smile down on him. He remembered with a glow when he went up to the stage for his award last year and how the Headmaster had talked about Service To The School, and how "John Sulkey exemplified these special attributes" (the exact words which still echoed in John's mind, especially when he saw those undistinguished rows of C's and D's on his report card every term). Anyway. Another sale. Chocolates. Double last year's price but John was confident. Brother Leon had promised to put up a special honor roll on the bulletin board in the main first-floor corridor for those who made their quota or exceeded it. A quota of fifty boxes. Higher than ever before, which made John happy. It would be harder for the other guys to meet the quota—already they were groaning and moaning—but John was supremely confident. In fact, when Brother Leon had told them about the special honor roll, John Sulkey could have sworn he was looking directly at him—as if Brother Leon was counting personally on him to set a good example.

So, let's see, the new housing development on Maple Terrace. Maybe he should make a special campaign in that neighborhood this year. There were nine or ten new homes there. But first of all, the old faithfuls, the people who had become regular customers: Mrs. Swanson who sometimes smelled of liquor but was always eager to buy anything although she kept him talking too long, rambling on about people John Sulkey didn't even know; and good old reliable Uncle Louie who was always simonizing his car although simonizing cars seemed part of the Dark Ages these days;

and then the Capoletti's at the end of the street who always invited him in for something to eat, cold pizza that John wasn't exactly crazy about and the smell of garlic that almost knocked you down but you had to make sacrifices, big and small, for the sake of Service To The School . . .

"Adamo?"
   "Four."
   "Beauvais?"
   "One."
Brother Leon paused and looked up.
   "Beauvais, Beauvais. You can do better than that. Only one? Why, last year you set a record for the number of boxes sold in a week."
   "I'm a slow starter," Beauvais said. He was a good-natured kid, not exactly a whiz in his studies but likeable, without an enemy in the world. "Check me next week," he said.
   The class laughed and the Brother joined in the laughter. The Goober laughed, too, grateful for the small relaxation of tension. He found that in recent days the kids in class had a tendency to laugh at things that weren't really funny, simply because they seemed to be looking for something to divert them for a few moments, to prolong the roll call, prolong it until the *R*'s were reached. Everyone knew what would happen when Renault's name came up. It was as if by laughing they could ignore the situation.
   "Fontaine?"
   "Ten!"
   A burst of applause led by Brother Leon himself.
   "Wonderful, Fontaine. True spirit, a wonderful display of spirit."
   Goober found it hard to resist looking at Jerry. His friend sat stiff and tense, his knuckles white. This was the fourth

day of the sale and Jerry still called out *no* in the morning, staring straight ahead, rigid, determined. Forgetting his own troubles for a moment, Goober had tried approaching Jerry as they left the field after practice the day before. But Jerry pulled away. "Let me alone, Goob," he said. "I know what you want to ask—but don't."

"Parmentier?"

"Six."

And then the gathering of tension. Jerry was next. Goober heard a weird sound, almost as if the class had sucked in its breath all at once.

"Renault?"

"No."

Pause. You'd think Brother Leon would have gotten used to the situation by now, that he'd skip quickly over Renault's name. But each day, the teacher's voice sang out with hope and each day the negative response was given.

"Santucci?"

"Three."

The Goober exhaled. So did the rest of the class. Strictly by accident, Goober happened to look up as Brother Leon marked down Santucci's report. He saw Leon's hand trembling. He had a terrible feeling of doom about to descend on all of them.

The short fat legs of Tubs Casper carried him through the neighborhood in what for him was record time. He'd have made better time if one of his bicycle tires wasn't flat, not only flat but definitely beyond repair and he didn't have money to buy a new tire. In fact, it was a desperate need for money that sent Tubs scurrying around town like a madman, from one house to another, lugging the chocolates, knocking at doors and ringing doorbells. He also had to do it furtively, afraid that his father or mother might see him.

Small chance his father would come across him—he was at work at the plastic shop. But his mother was another thing altogether. She was a nut about the car, like his father said, and couldn't bear to stay home and was always driving around.

Tubs' left arm began to ache from the weight of the chocolates and he shifted his burden to his other arm, taking a moment to pat the reassuring bulge of his wallet. He had already sold three boxes—six dollars—but that wasn't enough, of course. He was still desperate. He needed a hell of a lot more by tonight and nobody but nobody had bought any chocolates at the last six houses he'd visited. He had saved every cent he could from his allowance and had even sneaked a folded and greasy dollar bill from his father's pocket last night when he arrived home, half-drunk and wobbly. He hated doing that—stealing from his own father. He vowed to return the money to him as soon as possible. When would that be? Tubs didn't know. Money, money, money had become the constant need of his life, money and his love for Rita. His allowance barely made it possible for him to take her to the movies and for a coke afterward. Two-fifty each for the movies, fifty cents for two cokes. And his parents hated her for some reason. He had to sneak out to meet her. He had to make phone calls from Ossie Baker's house. She's too old for you, his mother said, when actually Tubs himself was six months older. All right, she *looks* old, his mother said. What his mother should have said was, she looks beautiful. She was so beautiful that she made Tubs all shaky inside, like an earthquake going on. At night in bed, he could have one without even touching himself, just thinking of her. And now her birthday was tomorrow and he had to buy her the present she wanted, the bracelet she'd seen in the window of Black's downtown, that terrible and beautiful bracelet all sparkles and radiance, terrible

73

because of the price tag: $18.95 plus tax. *"Hon,"*—she never called him Tubs—"that's what I want most in all the world." Jesus—$18.95 plus the 3 per cent sales tax which Tubs figured out would make a grand total of $19.52, the sales tax amounting to fifty-seven cents. He knew that he didn't have to buy her the bracelet.

She was a sweet girl who loved him for himself alone. She walked along the sidewalk with him, her breast brushing his arm, setting him on fire. The first time she rubbed against him he thought it was an accident and he pulled away, apologetic, leaving a space between them. Then she brushed against him again—that was the night he'd bought her the earrings—and he knew it wasn't an accident. He'd felt himself hardening and was suddenly ashamed and embarrassed and deliriously happy all at the same time. Him—Tubs Casper, forty pounds overweight which his father never let him forget. Him—with this beautiful girl's breast pushed against him, not beautiful the way his mother thought a girl was beautiful but beautiful in a ripe wild way, faded blue jeans hugging her hips, those beautiful breasts bouncing under her jersey. She was only fourteen and he was barely fifteen but they were in love, love dammit, and it was only money that kept them apart, money to take the bus to her house because she lived on the other side of town and they'd made plans to meet tomorrow, her birthday, at Monument Park, a picnic sort of, she'd bring the sandwiches and he'd bring the bracelet—he knew the delights that awaited him but he also knew deep down inside that the bracelet was more important than anything else . . .

All of which rushed him along now, out of breath and out of shape, trying to raise money that he knew dimly would lead him eventually only to trouble. Where would he raise enough money to pay it all back when the returns were due at school? But what the hell—he'd worry about it later. Right now he needed to raise the money and Rita loved him—tomorrow she'd probably let him get under her sweater.

He rang the doorbell of a rich-looking house on Sterns Avenue and prepared his most innocent and sweetest smile for whoever opened the door.

The woman's hair was damp and askew, and a little kid, maybe two or three years old, was tugging at her skirt. "Chocolates?" she asked, laughing bitterly as if Paul Consalvo had suggested the most absurd thing in the world. "You want me to buy chocolates?"

The baby, wearing a soggy-looking droopy diaper, was calling, "Mommy . . . mommy . . ." And another kid was howling somewhere in the apartment.

"It's for a good cause," Paul said. "Trinity School!"

Paul's nose wrinkled at the smell of pee.

"Jesus," the woman said. "Chocolates!"

"Mommee . . . mommee . . ." the kid squalled.

Paul felt sorry for older people, stuck in their houses and tenements with kids to take care of and housework to do. He thought of his own parents and their useless lives—his father collapsing into his nap every night after supper and his mother looking tired and dragged-out all the time. What the hell were they living for? He couldn't wait to get out of the house. "Where're you going all the time?" his mother asked as he fled the place. How could he tell her that he hated the house, that his mother and father were dead and didn't know it, that if it wasn't for television the place would be like a tomb. He couldn't say that because he really loved them and if the house caught fire in the middle of the night he'd rescue them, he'd be willing to sacrifice his own life for them. But, jeez, it was so boring, so deadly at home—what did they have to live for? They were too old for sex

75

even, although Paul turned away from the thought. He couldn't believe that his mother and father ever actually . . .

"Sorry," the woman said, shutting the door in his face, still shaking her head in wonder at his sales pitch.

Paul stood in the doorway, wondering what to do. He'd had rotten luck this afternoon, hadn't sold a single box. He hated selling them anyway, although it gave him an excuse to get out of the house. But he couldn't really put his heart in it. He was just going through the motions.

Outside the apartment house, Paul considered his choices: pressing on with the sale despite his luck today or going home. He crossed the street and rang the doorbell of another apartment building. In an apartment house, you could knock off five or six families at one time even though the places all seemed to smell of pee.

Brother Leon had "volunteered" Brian Cochran for the position of Treasurer of the Chocolate Sale. Which meant that he'd looked around the classroom, pinned those watery eyes on Brian, pointed his finger and, *voila*, as Brother Aimé said in French class, Brian was treasurer. He hated the job because he lived in fear of Brother Leon. You never knew about Leon. Brian was a senior and he'd had Leon as either a classroom teacher or as homeroom supervisor for four years and he was still uncomfortable in his presence. The teacher was unpredictable and yet predictable at the same time, which reasoning confused Brian because he wasn't exactly a hotshot in the psychology department. It was this: you knew that Leon would always do the unexpected— wasn't that being both predictable and unpredictable? He loved to toss surprise exams at a class—and he also could suddenly be the nice guy, not giving a test for weeks or giving a test and then throwing away the results. Or con- cocting a pass-fail test—he was famous for that type—

76

where he threaded together questions that could throw a guy for a loss, with what seemed like a million possible answers. He was also quite a man with the pointer although he usually confined that kind of stuff to freshmen. If he ever pulled the pointer antics with, say, somebody like Carter, there'd be hell to pay. But not everybody was John Carter, president of The Vigils, All-Star Guard on the football team, and president of the Boxing Club. How Brian Cochran would love to be like John Carter, with muscles instead of glasses, quick with boxing gloves instead of figures.

Speaking of figures, Brian Cochran began double-checking the sales totals. As usual, there was a discrepancy between the amount of chocolates reported as sold and the actual money received. The guys were notorious for holding back some of the money until the last minute. Ordinarily, nobody got excited about it—it was human nature. A lot of the guys sold chocolates, spent the money on a big date or a big night, and then put in the money when they got their allowance or their pay at their part-time jobs. But this year, Brother Leon acted as if every dollar was a matter of life and death. In fact, he was driving Brian Cochran up a wall.

The job of treasurer called for Brian to check every homeroom at the end of the day and write down the returns the boys had reported. How many boxes sold. How much money turned in. Brian then went to Brother Leon's office and totaled all the figures. Then Brother Leon would come along and check Brian's report. Simple, right? Wrong. The way Brother Leon was carrying on this year made every day's report seem like a major headline event. Brian had never seen the Brother so edgy, so nervous. At first he'd gotten a kick out of the teacher's apprehension, the way the sweat poured off him like he had a special pump inside producing all that perspiration. When he came into the

77

office and took off the black suit coat he was required to wear in the classroom during all seasons, sweat stains darkened his armpits, and he smelled as if he'd just gone ten rounds in the ring. He fidgeted and fussed around, double-checking Brian's figures, chewing on a pencil, pacing the floor.

Today, Brian was more puzzled than ever. Leon had passed around a report to all the homerooms listing total sales thus far at 4,582. Which was wrong. The kids had sold exactly 3,961 boxes and had made returns on 2,871. Sales were definitely lagging behind last year and so was the money. He couldn't understand why Leon had issued a false report. Did he think he could hype them up that way?

Brian shrugged, tabulating his own totals once more to be sure that Brother Leon wouldn't blame him for any discrepancies. He'd hate to have Leon for an enemy, which was one reason he'd accepted the job of treasurer without making waves. Brian was a member of Leon's algebra class and he didn't want to take any chances with extra homework or sudden unexplained *F*'s on exams.

Looking at the summary once again, Brian saw the zero next to the name of Jerome Renault. He chuckled. That was the freshman who refused to sell any choloclates. Brian shook his head—who'd want to buck the system? Hell, who'd want to buck Brother Leon? The kid must be some kind of madman.

"LeBlanc?"

"Six."

"Malloran?"

"Three."

The pause. The intake of breath. It had gotten to be a game now—this roll call, this fascinating moment in Brother Leon's homeroom. Even Goober couldn't help but get caught up in the tension although the entire situation made him slightly sick to his stomach. Goober was a peaceful figure. He hated strain, contention. Peace, let's have peace. But there was no peace in Brother Leon's room in the morning as he called the roll of chocolate sales. He stood tense at the desk, those watery eyes blinking in the morning light, while Jerry Renault sat as usual at his desk, without emotion, frigid, elbows resting on the surface of the desk.

"Parmentier?"

"Two."

Now—

"Renault."

Inhale.

"No."

Exhale.

The color spreading on Leon's face, like his veins had turned into scarlet neon signs.

Santucci?"

"Two."

The Goober couldn't wait for the bell to ring.

15

"**H**EY, Archie," Emile Janza called.

"Yes, Emile."

"You still got the picture?"

"What picture?" Suppressing a smile.

"You know what picture."

"Oh, *that* picture. Yes, Emile, I still have it."

"I don't suppose it's for sale, Archie."

"Not for sale, Emile. What would you want with that picture, anyway? To tell the truth, Emile, it's not the greatest picture ever taken of you. I mean, you're not even smiling or anything. There's this funny look on your face. But you're not smiling, Emile."

There was a funny look on Emile Janza's face right at this moment and he wasn't smiling now either. Anyone else but Archie would have been intimidated by that look.

"Where do you keep the picture, Archie?"

"It's safe, Emile. Very safe."

"That's good."

Archie wondered, should I tell him the truth about the picture? He knew that Emile Janza could be a dangerous enemy. On the other hand, the photograph also could be used as a weapon.

"Tell you what, Emile," Archie said. "Someday you might be able to get the photograph all for yourself."

Janza flipped his cigarette against a tree and watched the butt ricochet into the gutter. He withdrew a package from his pocket, discovered it was empty and tossed it away, watching the breeze move it along on the sidewalk. Emile Janza didn't care about keeping America beautiful.

"How can I get the photograph, Archie?"

"Well, you won't have to buy it, Emile."

"You mean you'd give it to me? There must be a catch, Archie."

"There is, Emile. But nothing you can't handle when the time comes."

"You let me know when the time comes. Okay, Archie?" Emile asked, giggling his foolish giggle.

"You'll be the first to know," Archie said.

The tone of their conversation had been light, bantering, but Archie knew that Emile was deadly serious underneath. Archie also knew that Janza would be willing to practically murder him in his sleep to get his hot hands on the picture. And the terrible irony—there was no picture after all. Archie had merely taken advantage of a ridiculous situation. What happened was this: Archie had cut a class and glided through the corridor, evading the brothers. Moving past an open locker, he'd spotted a camera dangling from one of the coat hooks. Automatically, Archie had taken the camera. He wasn't a thief, of course. He figured he'd merely abandon it somewhere so that the owner, whoever he was, would have to chase around the school looking for it. Stepping into the men's room to grab a quick smoke, Archie had pulled open the door to one of the stalls and confronted Janza sitting there, pants dropping on the floor, one hand furiously at work between his legs. Archie lifted the camera and pretended to take a picture, yelling, "Hold it."

"Beautiful," Archie had called.

Janza had been too shocked and surprised to react quickly. By the time he had recovered, Archie was at the doorway, poised to flee if Janza made a move.

"Better hand over that camera," Janza called.

"If you're going to jack off in a toilet, at least lock your door," Archie taunted.

"The lock's broken," Emile replied. "All the locks are broken."

"Well, don't worry, Emile. Your secret is safe with me."

Now Janza turned from Archie and spotted a freshman hurrying across the street, evidently worried because he was afraid of being late for classes. It took a year or two to develop the timing that allowed you to linger until the last possible moment at the dorway.

"Hey, freshman," Janza called.

The kid looked up, panic-stricken, when he saw Janza.

"Afraid you're going to be late?"

The kid gulped, nodding his head.

"Have no fear, freshman."

The final whistle blew. Exactly forty-five seconds to make it to homerooms.

"I'm all out of cigarettes," Emile declared, patting his pockets.

Archie smiled, knowing what Janza planned. Janza considered himself a candidate for The Vigils and he was always trying to impress Archie.

"What I'd like, kid, is for you to run over to Baker's and buy me a pack of cigarettes."

"I haven't got any money," the boy protested. "And I'll be late for school."

"That's life, kid. That's the way it goes. Heads I win, tails you lose. If you haven't got the money, steal the smokes. Or borrow the money. Just meet me at lunch with the cigarettes. Any brand. Emile Janza's not fussy." Tossing in his name so that the kid would know who he was dealing with in the event he hadn't been tipped off about Emile Janza.

Archie lingered, knowing he was flirting with a tardy rap. But he was fascinated by Janza, crude and gross as he was. The world was made up of two kinds of people—those who were victims and those who victimized. There was no doubt about Janza's category. No doubt about himself, either. And no doubt about the kid, taking off down the hill, tears spilling onto his cheeks as he turned away.

"He's got the money, Archie," Emile said. "Don't you figure he's got the money and was lying through his teeth?"

"I'll bet you also kick old ladies down the stairs and trip cripples on the street," Archie said.

Janza giggled.

The giggle chilled Archie who himself was considered capable of hurting little old ladies and tripping cripples.

16

"SUCH a terrible mark, Caroni."

"I know, I know."

"And you are usually such a splendid scholar."

"Thank you, Brother Leon."

"How are your other marks?"

"Fine, Brother, fine. In fact, I thought . . . I mean, I was aiming for high honors this term. But now, this F . . ."

"I know," the teacher said, shaking his head sorrowfully, in commiseration.

Caroni was confused. He had never received an F before in his life. In fact, he had seldom received a mark lower than an A. In the seventh and eighth grades at St. Jude's, he had received straight A's for two years except for a B-plus one term. He had scored so high on the Trinity entrance exam that he had been awarded one of the rare Trinity scholarships—one hundred dollars contributed toward his tuition, and his picture in the paper. And then this terrible F, a routine test turning into a nightmare.

"The F surprised me as well," Brother Leon said. "Because you are such an excellent student, David."

Caroni looked up in sudden wonder and hope. Brother Leon seldom called a student by his first name. He always kept a distance between himself and his pupils. "There is an invisible line between teacher and student," he always said, "and it must not be crossed." But, now, hearing him pronounce "David" in such friendly fashion and with such gentleness and understanding, Caroni allowed himself to hope—but for what? Had the *F* been a mistake, after all?

"This was a difficult test for several reasons," the teacher went on. "One of those exams where the wrong, subtle interpretation of the facts made the difference between pass and fail. In fact, that was it exactly—a pass-fail test. And when I read your answer, David, for a moment I thought it was possible that you had passed. In many respects you were correct in your assertions. But, on the other hand . . ." His voice trailed away, he seemed deep in thought, troubled.

Caroni waited. A horn blew outside—the school bus lumbering away. He thought of his father and mother and what they would do when they learned of the *F*. It would drag down his average—it was almost impossible to overcome an *F* no matter how many other *A*'s he managed to make.

"One thing students don't always realize, David," Brother Leon went on, speaking softly, intimately, as if there were no one in the world except them, as if he had never talked to anyone in the world the way he was talking to David at this moment, "one thing they don't grasp is that teachers are human too. Human like other people." Brother Leon smiled as if he had made a joke. Caroni allowed himself a small smile, unsure of himself, not wanting to do the wrong thing. The classroom was suddenly warm, it seemed crowded although there were just the two of them there. "Yes, yes, we are all too human. We have our good days and our bad days. We get tired. Our judgment sometimes becomes impaired. We sometimes—as the boys say—goof. It's possible even for us to make mistakes correcting papers,

85

especially when the answers are not cut and dried, not one thing or another, not all black nor all white . . ."

Caroni was all ears now, alert—what was Brother Leon driving at? He looked sharply at Brother Leon. The teacher looked as he always did—the moist eyes that reminded Caroni of boiled onions, the pale damp skin, and the cool talk, always under control. He held a piece of white chalk in his hand like a cigarette. Or maybe like a miniature pointer.

"Did you ever hear a teacher admit that it's possible for him to make a mistake, David? Ever hear that before?" Brother Leon asked, laughing.

"Like an umpire saying he made the wrong call," Caroni said, joining in the teacher's little joke. But why the joke? Why all this talk of mistakes?

"Yes, yes," Leon agreed. "No one is without error. And it's understandable. We all have our duties and we must discharge them. The Headmaster is still in the hospital and I take it as a privilege to act in his behalf. Besides this, there are the extra-curricular activities. The chocolate sale, for instance . . ."

Brother Leon's grip was tight on the piece of chalk. Caroni noticed how his knuckles were almost as white as the chalk itself. He waited for the teacher to continue. But there was only silence. Caroni watched the chalk in Brother Leon's hands, the way the teacher pressed it, rolled it, his fingers like the legs of pale spiders with a victim in their clutch.

"But it's all rewarding," Leon went on. How was it that his voice was so cool when the hand holding the chalk was so tense, the veins sticking out, as if threatening to burst through the flesh?

"Rewarding?" Caroni had lost the thread of Brother Leon's thought.

"The chocolate sale," Leon said.

And the chalk split in his hand.

"For instance," Leon said, dropping the pieces and opening the ledger that was so familiar to everyone at Trinity, the ledger in which the daily sales were recorded. "Let me see—you have done fine in the sale, David. Eighteen boxes sold. Fine. Fine. Not only are you an excellent scholar but you possess school spirit."

Caroni blushed with pleasure—it was impossible for him to resist a compliment, even when he was all mixed up as he certainly was at the moment. All this talk of exams and teachers getting tired and making mistakes and now the chocolate sale . . . and the two pieces of broken chalk abandoned on the desk, like white bones, dead men's bones.

"If everyone did his part like you, David, the sale would be an instant success. Of course, not everyone has your spirit, David . . ."

Caroni wasn't sure what tipped him off. Maybe the way Brother Leon paused at this point. Maybe the entire conversation, all of it off-key somehow. Or maybe the chalk in Brother Leon's hands, the way he had snapped it in two while his voice remained cool and easy—which was the phony thing: the hand holding the chalk, all tense and nervous, or the cool, easy voice?

"Take Renault, for instance," Brother Leon continued. "Funny thing about him, isn't it?"

And Caroni knew. He found himself staring into the moist watchful eyes of the teacher and in a blinding flash he knew what this was all about, what was happening, what Brother Leon was doing, the reason for this little conversation after school. A headache began to assert itself above his right eye, the pain digging into his flesh—migraine. His stomach lurched sickeningly. Were teachers like everyone else, then? Were teachers as corrupt as the villains you read about in books or saw in movies and television? He'd always worshiped his teachers, had thought of becoming a teacher himself someday if he could overcome his shyness. But now—this. The pain grew in intensity, throbbing in his forehead.

"Actually, I feel badly for Renault," Brother Leon was saying. "He must be a very troubled boy to act this way."

"I guess so," Caroni said, stalling, uncertain of himself and yet knowing really what Brother Leon wanted. He had seen Brother Leon every day in the classroom calling out the names and had watched him recoil as if from a blow when Jerry Renault continued to refuse the chocolates. It had become a kind of joke among the fellows. Actually, Caroni had felt badly for Jerry Renault. He knew that no kid was a match for Brother Leon. But now he realized that Brother Leon had been the victim. He must have been climbing the walls all this time, David thought.

"Well, David."

And the echo of his name here in the classroom startled him. He wondered if he still had aspirins left in his locker. Forget the aspirins, forget the headache. He knew now what the score was, what Leon was waiting to hear. Yet, could he be sure?

"Speaking of Jerry Renault . . ." Caroni said—a safe beginning, a statement he could draw back from, depending on Brother Leon's reaction.

"Yes?"

The hand had picked up one of the pieces of chalk again, and that "Yes?" had been too quick, too sudden to allow any doubt. Caroni found himself hung up between choices and the headache didn't help matters. Could he erase that F by telling Brother Leon simply what he wanted to hear? What was so terrible about that? On the other hand, an F could ruin him. And how about all the other *F*'s it was possible that Leon could give him in the future?

"Funny thing about Jerry Renault," Caroni heard himself saying. And then instinct caused him to add, "But I'm sure you know what it's all about, Brother Leon. The Vigils. The assignment . . ."

"Of course, of course," Leon said, sitting back, letting the chalk fall gently from his hand.

"It's a Vigil stunt. He's supposed to refuse to sell chocolates for ten days—ten school days—and then accept them. Boy, those Vigils, they're really something, aren't they?" His head was killing him and his stomach was a sea of nausea.

"Boys will be boys," Leon was saying, nodding his head, his voice a whisper—it was hard to tell whether he was surprised or relieved. "Knowing Trinity's spirit, it was obvious, of course. Poor Renault. You remember, Caroni, that I said he must be troubled. Terrible, to force a boy into that kind of situation, against his will. But it's all over then, isn't it? The ten days—why they're up, let's see, tomorrow." He was smiling now, gaily, and talking as if the words themselves didn't matter but that it was important to talk, as if the words were safety valves. And then Caroni realized that Brother Leon had used his name but this time he hadn't said *David* . . .

"Well, I guess that's it then," Brother Leon said, rising, "I've detained you too long, Caroni."

"Brother Leon," Caroni said. He couldn't be dismissed at this point. "You said you wanted to discuss my mark . . ."

"Oh yes, yes, that's right, my boy. That *F* of yours."

Caroni felt doom pressing upon him. But he went on anyway. "You said teachers make mistakes, they get tired . . ."

Brother Leon was standing now. "Tell you what, Caroni.

At the end of the term, when the marks close, I'll review that particular test. Perhaps I'll be fresher then. Perhaps I'll see merit that wasn't apparent before . . ."

Now it was Caroni's turn to feel relief from the tension, although his headache still pounded and his stomach was still upset. Worse than that, however, he had allowed Brother Leon to blackmail him. If teachers did this kind of thing, what kind of world could it be?

"On the other hand, Caroni, perhaps the *F* will stand," Brother Leon said. "It depends . . ."

"I see, Brother Leon," Caroni said.

And he did see—that life was rotten, that there were no heroes, really, and that you couldn't trust anybody, not even yourself.

He had to get out of there as fast as possible, before he vomited all over Brother Leon's desk.

17

"**A**DAMO?"

"Three."

"Beauvais?"

"Five."

The Goober was impatient for the roll call to be over. Or, rather, for the roll call to reach Jerry Renault. Like everyone else, the Goober had finally learned that Jerry was carrying out a Vigil assignment—that's why he had refused to take the chocolates day after day, that's why he didn't want to talk about it with Goober. Now, Jerry could become himself again, human again. His football had suffered. "What the hell is the matter with you, Renault?" the coach had asked in disgust yesterday, "do you want to play ball or not?" And Jerry had answered, "I'm playing ball." All the kids knew the double meaning his answer conveyed because it was public knowledge now. He and Goober had had only one brief conversation about the assignment—in fact, it wasn't really a conversation. Leaving football practice yesterday, Goober had whispered, "When does the assignment end?" And Jerry had said, "Tomorrow I take the chocolates."

"Hartnett?"

"One."

"You can do better than that, Hartnett," Leon said, but there was no anger, not even disappointment in his voice. Brother Leon was buoyant today and his mood had spread throughout the class. That's the way Leon's classes were— he set the mood and the temperature. When Brother Leon was happy everybody was happy, when he was miserable everybody was miserable.

"Johnson?"

"Five."

"Good, good."

Killelea . . . LeBlanc . . . Malloran . . . the roll call went on, the voices shouting out their sales and the teacher checking the names off on the sheet. The names and the responses sounded almost like a song, a melody for a classroom, a tune for many voices. Then Brother Leon called out "Parmentier." And there was tension in the air. Parmentier could have called out any number and it wouldn't have mattered, it wouldn't have created any impact at all. Because the next name was Renault.

"Three," Parmentier called out.

"Right," Brother Leon answered, making the check against the name. Looking up, he called, "Renault."

The pause. The damn pause.

"No!"

The Goober felt as if his eyes were the lens for a television camera in one of those documentaries. He swung around in Jerry's direction and saw his friend's face, white, mouth half-open, his arms dangling at his sides. And then he swiveled to look at Brother Leon and saw the shock on the teacher's face, his mouth forming an oval of astonishment. It seemed almost as if Jerry and the teacher were reflections in a mirror.

Finally Brother Leon looked down.

"Renault," he said again, his voice like a whip.

92

"No. I'm not going to sell the chocolates."

Cities fell. Earth opened. Planets tilted. Stars plummeted. And the awful silence.

18

*W*HY *did you do it?*
I don't know.
Have you gone crazy?
Maybe I have.
It was a crazy thing to do.
I know, I know.
The way that "No" popped out of your mouth—why?
I don't know.

It was like the third degree, only he was both interrogator and suspect, both tough cop and hounded prisoner, a cruel spotlight pinning him in a blinding circle of light. All of this in his mind, of course, as he tossed in his bed, the sheet twisted around him like a shroud, suffocatingly.

He fought the sheet, filled suddenly with the terror of claustrophobia, being buried alive. Aware of his mortality, he turned over again, entangled in the bedclothes. His pillow fell off the bed, hitting the floor with a dull thud, like a small body landing there. He thought of his mother dead in the coffin. When did death arrive? He had read a magazine article about heart transplants—even the doctors couldn't agree on the exact moment that death occurred. Listen, he told himself, no one can be buried alive these days, not like in the olden times when there was no embalming fluid and stuff. Now they removed all your blood and pumped in chemicals and stuff. To make certain you were dead. But suppose, let's just suppose that some small spark in your brain remained alive, and knew what was going on. His mother. Himself, someday.

He leaped from the bed in terror, flinging the sheet away. His body was moist, oozing perspiration. He sat on the edge of the bed, trembling. Then his feet touched the floor and the cool kiss of the linoleum established reality. The specter of suffocation vanished. He made his way through the darkness to the window, and pulled back the drape. The wind came up, scattering October leaves which fluttered to the ground like doomed and crippled birds.

Why did you do it?

I don't know.

Like a broken record.

Was it because of what Brother Leon does to people, like Bailey, the way he tortures them, tries to make fools of them in front of everybody?

More than that, more than that.

Then what?

He allowed the drape to fall back into place and surveyed the bedroom, squinting into the half-darkness. He padded over to the bed, shivering in the kind of coolness that can only be found in the middle of the night. He listened for night sounds. His father snored in the next room. A car gunned along the street outside. He'd love to be gunning along the street, going someplace, anywhere. *I'm not going to sell the chocolates.* Boy.

He hadn't planned to do any such thing of course. He'd been happy to have the terrible assignment all over with, the assignment completed and life normal once again. Every morning he dreaded the roll call, the necessity of facing Brother Leon, saying *No* and watching Leon's reaction—how the teacher tried to pass off Jerry's rebellion as if it didn't matter, putting on a pathetic pretense of indifference but a pretense that was so transparent, so phony. It had been funny and terrible at the same time, watching Leon call the roll and waiting for his name to be called, and finally his name blazing in the air and the defiant *No*. The teacher might have been able to carry off his act successfully, except for his eyes. His eyes gave him away. His face was always under control but his eyes showed his vulnerability, gave Jerry a glimpse into the hell that was burning inside the teacher. Those moist eyes, the white eyeballs and the diluted blue of his pupils, eyes that reflected everything that went on in the class, reacting to everything. After Jerry had learned that the secret of Brother Leon lurked in his eyes, he became watchful, seeing the way the eyes betrayed the teacher at every turn. And then there came a time when Jerry was tired of it all, tired of watching the teacher, disgusted with the contest of wills that wasn't really a contest because Jerry had no choice. Cruelty sickened Jerry—and the assignment, he realized after a few days, was cruel, even though Archie Costello had insisted that it was only a stunt that everyone would get a kick out of later. And so he had finally waited, impatient for the assignment to come to an end, eager for that silent battle between Brother Leon and himself to be over with. He wanted life to be normal again—football, even his homework, without that daily burden weighing him down. He had felt isolated from the other fellows, separated by the secret he was forced to carry. He'd been tempted once or twice to talk it over with The Goober. In fact, he'd almost done so once when Goob tried to start a conversation. Instead, he'd cautioned himself to hold on for the two weeks, to carry it off, secrecy and all, and be done with it for good. He had met Brother Leon in the corridor late one afternoon after football practice and had seen hate flashing in the teacher's eyes. More than hate: something sick. Jerry had felt soiled, dirty, as if he should run to confession and bare his soul. And he'd consoled himself: when I accept the chocolates and Brother Leon realizes I was only carrying out a Vigil assignment then everything will be fine again.

Then why had he called *No* this morning? He'd wanted to end the ordeal—and then that terrible *No* had issued from his mouth.

In bed once more, Jerry lay without moving, trying to summon sleep. Listening to his father's snores, he thought of how his father was actually sleeping his life away, sleeping even when he was awake, not really alive. And how about me? What was it the guy on the Common had said the other day, his chin resting on the Volkswagen like some grotesque John the Baptist? *You're missing a lot of things in the world.*

He turned over, dismissing his doubts and calling to mind the figure of a girl he'd seen downtown the other day. Her sweater had bulged beautifully, her schoolbooks pressed against her rounded breasts. If my hands were only those books, he'd thought longingly. His hand now curled between his legs, he concentrated on the girl. But for once, it was no good, no good.

19

THE next morning Jerry found out how a hangover must feel. His eyes burned with fire, fueled by lack of sleep. His head throbbed with shooting pains. His stomach was sensitive to the slightest movement and the lurching of the bus caused strange reactions in his body. It reminded him of when he was a kid and got carsick sometimes on trips to the beach with his parents so that they'd have to stop the car by the side of the road while Jerry either vomited or waited for the storm in his stomach to subside. What added to his troubles this morning was the possibility of a test in geography and he hadn't studied at all last night, so wrapped up had he been in the chocolate sale and what had happened in Leon's class. Now, he was paying the penalty for too little sleep and no study—trying to read a lousy geography lesson on a lumbering lurching bus, the morning light dazzling on the white page.

Somebody slipped into the seat beside him.

"Hey, Renault, you got guts, know that?"

Jerry looked up, blinded momentarily as his eyes shifted from the page to the face of the kid who'd spoken to him. He knew him vaguely from school—a junior, maybe. Lighting a cigarette the way all the smokers did despite the "No Smoking" signs, the kid shook his head. "Boy, you really let Leon that bastard have it. Beautiful." He blew out smoke. Jerry's eyes stung.

"Oh," he said, feeling stupid. And surprised. Funny, all this time he had thought of the situation as a private battle between Brother Leon and himself, as if the two of them were alone on the planet. Now, he realized that it had gone beyond that.

"I'm so sick of selling the frigging chocolates," the kid said. He had a terrible case of acne, his face like a relief map. And his fingers were stained with nicotine. "I've been at Trinity two years—I transferred from Monument High when I was a freshman—and Christ I'm getting tired of selling stuff." He tried to blow a smoke ring but failed. Worse than that—the smoke blew back in Jerry's face, stinging his eyes. "If it isn't chocolates, it's Christmas cards. If it isn't Christmas cards, it's soap. If it isn't soap, it's calendars. But you know what?"

"What?" Jerry asked, wanting to get back to his geography.

"I never thought of just saying no. Like you did."

"I've got some studying to do," Jerry said, not knowing what to say, really.

"Boy, you're cool, know that?" the kid said admiringly.

Jerry blushed with pleasure despite himself. Who didn't want to be admired? And yet he felt guilty, knowing that he was accepting the kid's admiration under false pretenses, that he wasn't cool at all, not at all. His head pounded and his stomach moved menacingly and he realized he had to face Brother Leon and the roll call again this morning. And all the mornings to come.

The Goober was waiting for him at the school's entrance, standing tense and troubled among the other fellows waiting for school to start, like prisoners resigned to execution, taking their final drags from cigarettes before the bells began to ring. The Goober motioned Jerry aside. Jerry followed him guiltily. He realized that Goober wasn't the cheerful, happy-go-lucky kid he'd known when school first started. What had happened? He'd been so wrapped up in his own concerns that he hadn't bothered about Goob.

"Jeez, Jerry, what did you do it for?" Goober asked, drawing him away from the others.

"Do what?"

But he knew what Goober meant.

"The chocolates."

"I don't know, Goob." Jerry said. It was no use faking out Goober the way he had faked out that kid on the bus. "That's the truth—I don't know."

"You're asking for trouble, Jerry. Brother Leon spells trouble."

"Look, Goob," Jerry said, wanting to reassure his friend, wanting to wipe that look of concern from his face. "It's not the end of the world. Four hundred kids in this school are going to sell chocolates. What does it matter if I don't?"

"It's not that simple, Jerry. Brother Leon won't let you get away with it."

The warning bell sounded. Cigarettes were flipped into the gutter or mashed into the sand-filled receptacle near the door. Last drags were inhaled lingeringly. Guys who'd been sitting in cars listening to rock on the radio switched them off and slammed the doors behind them.

"Nice going, kid," somebody said, hurrying by, the pat on the ass Trinity's traditional gesture of friendship. Jerry didn't see who it was.

"Keep it up, Jerry." This, a corner-of-the-mouth whisper from Adamo, who hated Leon with a vengeance.

"See how the word is spreading?" Goober hissed. "What's

more important—football and your marks or the lousy chocolate sale?"

The bell rang again. It meant two minutes left to get to your locker and then to your homeroom.

A senior by the name of Benson approached them. Seniors were trouble for freshmen. It was better to be ignored by them than to be noticed. But Benson was clearly headed in their direction. He was a nut, known for his lack of inhibitions, his complete disregard of the rules.

As he neared Jerry and Goober, he began a Jimmy Cagney imitation, shooting his cuffs and hunching his shoulders. "Hey, there, guy. I wouldn't . . . I wouldn't be in your shoes . . . I wouldn't be in your shoes for a thou, boy, a mill . . ." He punched Jerry playfully on the arm.

"You couldn't fit those shoes anyway, Benson," somebody yelled. And Benson danced away, Sammy Davis now, wide grin, feet tapping, body whirling.

Walking up the stairs, Goober said, "Do me a favor, Jerry. Take the chocolates today."

"I can't, Goob."

"Why not?"

"I just can't. I'm committed now."

"The goddam Vigils," Goober said.

Jerry had never heard Goober swear before. He'd always been a mild kind of kid, rolling with the punches, loose and carefree, running around the track while the other kids sat uptight during practice sessions.

"It's not The Vigils, Goob. They're not in it anymore. It's me."

They stopped at Jerry's locker.

"All right," Goober said, resigned, knowing it was useless to pursue the subject any further at the moment. Jerry felt sad suddenly because Goober looked so troubled, like an old man heaped with all the sorrows of the world, his thin face drawn and haggard, his eyes haunted, as if he had awakened from a nightmare he couldn't forget.

Jerry opened his locker. He had thumbtacked a poster to the back wall of the locker on the first day of school. The poster showed a wide expanse of beach, a sweep of sky with a lone star glittering far away. A man walked on the beach, a small solitary figure in all that immensity. At the bottom of the poster, these words appeared—*Do I dare disturb the universe?* By Eliot, who wrote the Waste Land thing they were studying in English. Jerry wasn't sure of the poster's meaning. But it had moved him mysteriously. It was traditional at Trinity for everyone to decorate the interior of his locker with a poster. Jerry chose this one.

He had no time now to ponder the poster any longer. The final bell rang and he had thirty seconds to get to class.

"Adamo?"

"Two."

"Beauvais?"

"Three."

It was a different roll call this morning, a new melody, a new tempo, as if Brother Leon were the conductor and the class the members of a verbal orchestra, but something wrong with the beat, something wrong with the entire proceedings, as if the members of the orchestra were controlling the pace and not the conductor. No sooner would Brother Leon call out a name than the response came immediately, before Leon had time to make a notation in the ledger. It was the kind of spontaneous game that developed in classes without premeditation, everyone falling into a sudden conspiracy. The quickness of the responses kept Brother Leon busy at his desk, head bent, pencil furiously scribbling. Jerry was glad that he wouldn't have to look into those watery eyes.

"LeBlanc?"

"One."

"Malloran?"

"Two."

Names and numbers sizzled in the air and Jerry began to notice something curious about it. All the ones and twos, and an occasional three. But no fives, no tens. And Brother Leon's head still bent, concentrating on the ledger. And finally—

"Renault."

It would be so easy, really, to yell, "Yes." To say, "Give me the chocolates to sell, Brother Leon." So easy to be like the others, not to have to confront those terrible eyes every morning. Brother Leon finally looked up. The tempo of the roll call had broken.

"No," Jerry said.

He was swept with sadness, a sadness deep and penetrating, leaving him desolate like someone washed up on a beach, a lone survivor in a world full of strangers.

20

"**A**T this period of history, man began to learn more about his environment—"

Suddenly, pandemonium reigned. The class exploded in frantic motion. Brother Jacques looked aghast. The boys leaped from their chairs, performed an insane jig, jumping up and down as if to the beat of unheard music, all of this in complete silence—although the sound of their jogging feet was noisy enough—and then sat down again, frozen-faced, as if nothing had happened.

Obie watched the teacher sourly. Brother Jacques was obviously bewildered. Bewildered? Hell, he was on the edge of panic. The ritual had been going on for a week now and it would continue until the cue was heard no more. In the meantime, the class would suddenly erupt into a confusion of waving arms and jogging legs, unsettling poor Brother. Of course, Brother Jacques was easy to unsettle—he was new and young and sensitive, raw meat for Archie. And he evidently didn't know what to do about it and so he didn't do anything, figuring apparently that the thing would run its course and why risk a futile showdown when it was obviously a prank. What else could it be? Funny, Obie thought, how everybody—the kids as well as the teachers—knew these stunts were planned or carried out by The Vigils and yet they still maintained that air of mystery, refusing to acknowledge it all. He wondered why. Obie had been involved in so many Vigil assignments that he'd lost count of them and he was continually amazed at how they got away with it all the time. In fact, he'd been getting tired of the assignments, of playing nursemaid for Archie and his trigger man as well. He was tired of being the fixer, making certain the assignment went off on schedule in order to maintain Archie's big-shot reputation. Like the Room Nineteen assignment when he'd had to creep in there and help the kid Goober take the place apart—all that work so that Archie and The Vigils would look good. Even this particular assignment involved him—if Brother Jacques failed to come up with the cue, then Obie had to find a way to feed it to him.

The cue was the word "environment." As Archie had said when he announced the assignment, "The world today is concerned with ecology, the environment, our natural resources. We at Trinity also ought to get involved in this environment thing. You guys," he said, indicating the fourteen students of Grade Twelve Class II, of whom Obie was a member, "will carry on our environmental campaign. Let's say Brother Jacques' U.S. History class—history should be concerned with environment, shouldn't it? Now, whenever Brother Jacques says the word 'environment,' here's what happens . . ." And Archie had outlined the instructions.

"Suppose he doesn't use the word?" someone asked.

Archie looked toward Obie. "Oh, Brother Jacques will use the word. I'm sure somebody—Obie, maybe—will ask a question that will produce the word. Won't you, Obie?"

Obie had nodded, disguising his disgust. What the hell was Archie involving him in an asignment at this stage of the game for? He was a senior, for crying out loud. He was

105

secretary of the goddam Vigils, for crying out loud. Jesus, how he hated Archie, that bastard.

A new kid, a transfer from Monument High, asked, "What happens when Brother Jacques finds out we're putting him on? When he finds out that the key word is environment?"

"Then he stops using it," Archie said. "Which is the point of the whole damn thing. I'm getting sick and tired of all this environment crap—and at least we'll have one teacher in the frigging school who'll cross it off his vocabulary list."

For his part, Obie was getting sick and tired of Archie, of picking up the pieces behind him, of performing those little services—like Room Nineteen or cueing in Brother Jacques, feeding him a question that could only lead to the word "environment" in the answer. Anyway he was getting fed up with the entire deal. And he was also biding his time, waiting for Archie to overreach himself, to make a mistake. The black box was always there and who could tell when Archie's luck would run out?

"In any discussion of the environment . . ."

Here we go again, Obie thought in disgust as he found himself leaping up and down like a madman, jogging his heart out, hating every minute of the damn thing. And his energy was wearing down.

Brother Jacques used the word "environment" five more times in the next fifteen minutes. Obie and the other guys were practically wiped out from all that jumping up and down, weary, out of breath, their legs beginning to ache.

When Brother Jacques used the word a sixth time and a weary battalion of students struggled to their feet to perform their task, Obie saw a small smile play on the lips of the teacher. And he knew immediately what had happened. Archie, that bastard, must have tipped Brother Jacques off, anonymously, of course, to what was going on. And the teacher had turned the tables. It was now the teacher who was in command, making the guys jump up and down until they almost collapsed in exhaustion.

When they left the classroom, there was Archie leaning against the wall, that smirk of triumph on his face. The other guys didn't realize what had happened. But Obie did. He gave Archie a look that would shrivel anybody else, but Archie just kept that silly smile on his face.

Obie stalked off, insulted, injured. You bastard, he thought, I owe you for that.

21

KEVIN Chartier had gone to seven houses after
school and hadn't sold a box. Mrs. Connors next to the dry
cleaners had told him to come back at the end of the month
when her Social Security check came from the government
but he didn't have the heart to tell her that it would probably
be too late by then. A dog chased him halfway home. It
was like one of those terrible dogs the Nazis used for hunt-
ing down concentration camp prisoners who escaped in
those old TV pictures. At home, disgusted, he telephoned
his best friend, Danny Arcangelo.

"How'd you make out, Danny?" Kevin asked, trying to
ignore his mother who stood near the phone making sounds
at him. Kevin had learned long ago to translate whatever
she was saying into gibberish. She could talk her head off
now and the words reached his ears without meaning. A
wild trick.

"I made out terrible," Danny whined. He always
sounded like he had to blow his nose. "I sold one box—to
my aunt."

"The one with diabetes?"

Danny howled. One thing about Danny, he was a great
audience. But not Kevin's mother. She was still chattering
away. Kevin knew what was bugging her. She never wanted

him to eat when he was on the telephone. His mother didn't realize that eating wasn't something you did *separately*. Eating went along with whatever you happened to be doing at the time. You could eat doing anything. Well, almost anything. It's not polite to be on the phone with your mouth full of food, she always said. But right this minute, Danny also had *his* mouth full of food at the other end of the line. So who the hell was being impolite to who? Or whom? Screw it.

"I think maybe that Renault kid's got the right idea, after all," Kevin said, his mouth thick with peanut butter which, he wished he could explain to his mother, gave his words more resonance, like a disc jockey's.

"The freshman who's giving Brother Leon a hard time?"

"Yeah. He came flat out and said he wasn't going to sell the junk."

"I thought it was a Vigils thing," Danny said tentatively.

"It *was*," Kevin said, leering in triumph as his mother gave up and went into the kitchen. "But now it's something else." He wondered whether he was saying too much. "He was supposed to take the chocolates a couple of days ago. The assignment was over. But he still refused to take them."

Kevin could hear Danny chewing like a madman.

"What're you eating, anyway? Sounds delicious."

Danny howled again. "Chocolates. I bought a box myself. The least I could do for good old Trinity."

An awkward silence fell between them. Kevin was in line to become a member of The Vigils next year when he became a junior. No one could be sure, of course, but there had been some hints from the guys. His best friend, Danny, knew about the possibility—and he also knew that there was a certain secrecy about The Vigils that had to be

109

maintained. They usually avoided Vigil talk although Kevin often had inside information about assignments and stuff and he often fed it to Danny in bits and pieces, finding it hard not to show off a bit. Yet he was always afraid that Danny might say something about The Vigils to some other guys, strictly by accident, and screw up the whole situation. They had reached that point now in their conversation.

"What happens now?" Danny asked, still unsure about poking his nose in but made reckless by curiosity.

"I don't know," Kevin said truthfully. "Maybe The Vigils will take some action. Maybe they don't give a hell. But I'll tell you one thing."

"What?"

"I'm getting sick of selling stuff. Jeez, my father's starting to call me 'my son, the salesman.'"

Danny guffawed again. Kevin was a natural mimic. "Yeah, I know what you mean. I'm getting tired of this selling crap. The kid's probably got the right idea."

Kevin agreed.

"For two cents, I'd stop," Danny said.

"Got change for a nickel?" Kevin said, all in fun, of course, but thinking how beautiful—bee-yoo-tee-full—it would be not to have to sell anything anymore. He looked up to find his mother approaching him again, her mouth moving and sounds coming out, and he sighed, tuning her out, like shutting off the sound on television while the picture remained.

"Know what?" Howie Anderson asked.

"What?" Richy Rondell answered, lazily, dreamily. He was watching a girl approach. Fantastic looking. Tight sweater, clinging, low-slung jeans. Jesus.

"I think the Renault kid is right about the chocolates,"

110

Howie said. He'd seen the girl too, as she moved along the sidewalk in front of Crane's Drug Store. But it didn't break his train of thought. Watching girls and devouring them with your eyes—rape by eyeball—was something you did automatically. "I'm not going to sell them anymore, either."

The girl paused to look at newspapers in a metal rack outside the store. Richy gazed at her with wistful lust. Suddenly he realized what Howie had said. "You're not?" he asked. Without taking his eyes off the girl—her back was turned now and he feasted himself on her rounded jeans—he pondered the meaning of what Howie had said, sensing the importance of the moment. Howie Anderson wasn't just another Trinity student. He was president of the junior class, an unusual guy. High honor student and varsity guard on the football team. He could also hold his own in the ring and almost knocked out that monster Carter in the intramural matches last year. His hand could shoot up in class to show he had the answer to a tough question. But that same hand could also shoot out and floor you if you screwed around with him. An intellectual roughneck—that's what one teacher had called him a while back. A freshman-nobody like Renault not selling chocolates—that was nothing. But Howie Anderson—that was *something*.

"It's the principle of the thing," Howie went on.

Richy plunged his hand in his pocket, grabbing shamelessly, something he couldn't resist whenever he got excited, about a girl or anything else.

"What principle, Howie?"

"This is what I mean," Howie said. "We pay tuition to go to Trinity, don't we? Right. Hell, I'm not even a Catholic, a lot of guys aren't, but they sell us a bill of goods that Trinity is the best prep school for college you can find around here. There's a case full of trophies in the auditorium—debating, football, boxing. And what happens? They turn us into salesmen. I have to listen to all this religious crap and even go to chapel. And sell chocolates on top of it all." He spat and a beautiful spray hit a mailbox, dripping down like a teardrop. "And now along comes a freshman. A *child*. He says no. He says 'I'm not going to sell the chocolates.' Simple. Beautiful. Something I never thought of before—just stop selling them."

Richy watched the girl drifting away.

"I'm with you, Howie. As of this moment, no more selling of chocolates." The girl was almost out of sight now, blocked from view by other people walking by. "Want to make it official? I mean, call a meeting of the class?"

Howie pondered the question.

"No, Richy. This is the age of do your thing. Let everybody do his thing. If a kid wants to sell, let him. If he doesn't, the same thing applies."

Howie's voice rang with authority, as if he was delivering a pronouncement to the world. Richy listened with a kind of awe. He was glad that Howie let him hang around—maybe some of Howie's leadership qualities would rub off on him. His eyes went to the street again, looking for another girl to enjoy.

The odor of sweat filled the air—a gym's sour perfume. Even though the place was deserted, the aftermath of that final period of calisthenics lingered, the stink of boy sweat; armpits and feet. And the rotten smell of old sneakers. That was one of the reasons why Archie had never been attracted to sports—he hated the secretions of the human body, pee or perspiration. He hated athletics because it speeded up the process of sweat. He couldn't stand the sight of greasy, oozing athletes drenched in their own body fluids.

At least football players wore uniforms, but boxers wore only the trunks. Take a guy like Carter, bulging with muscles, every pore oozing sweat. Put him in boxing trunks and the sight was almost obscene. That's why Archie avoided the gym. He was a legend in the school for dreaming up ways of avoiding Phys. Ed. But he was here now waiting for Obie. Obie had left a note in Archie's locker. *Meet me in the gym after last period.* Obie loved dramatics. He also knew that Archie despised the gym and yet asked to be met here. Oh, Obie, how you must hate me, Archie thought, undisturbed by the knowledge. It was good to have people hate you—it kept you sharp. And then when you put the needle in them, the way he did constantly to Obie, you felt justified, you didn't have to worry about your conscience.

But at this minute he was getting annoyed with Obie. Where the hell was he? Sitting down on one of the bleacher seats, Archie found a sudden and unexpected peace in the deserted gymnasium. His moments of peace were becoming less frequent all the time. The Vigils—those assignments, the constant pressure. More assignments due and everybody waiting for what Archie would come up with. And Archie hollow and empty sometimes, no ideas at all. And his lousy marks. He was certain to flunk English this term, simply because English was mostly reading and he didn't have time anymore to spend four or five hours every night reading a lousy book. Anyway, between The Vigils and worrying about his marks, he didn't seem to have any time to himself anymore, not even time for girls, no time to hang around Miss Jerome's, the girls' high school across town where, when school let out for the day, you could let your eyes devour some luscious sights and usually talk one of them into the car, for a ride home. With detours. Instead, here he was every day, involved with assignments and homework,

113

juggling all this activity and then getting stupid notes from Obie. Meet me in the gym . . .

Finally, Obie made his entrance. He didn't just walk in. He had to make a production out of it. He had to peek around the door and sniff the air and act like he was the spy coming in from the cold, for Christ's sake.

"Hey, Obie, I'm over here," Archie called dryly.

"Hi, Archie," Obie said as his leather heels clicked on the gym floor. There was a rule in the school—only sneakers on the gym floor but everybody ignored it except when there was a brother around.

"What do you want, Obie?" Archie asked, getting down to business without preliminaries, keeping his voice flat and dry as the Sahara. The fact that he had showed up for the meeting had been an admission of curiosity. Archie didn't want to overdo it by acting too eager for Obie's company and whatever he had to say. "I haven't much time. Important things await."

"This is important too," Obie said. Obie had a thin sharp face with a permanent worried look. That's why he was such an obvious stooge, an errand boy. The kind of kid you couldn't help kicking when he was down. And you also knew this—that he would get up again and vow revenge and never have the nerve or the know-how to take that revenge. "Remember that kid Renault? The chocolate assignment?"

"What about him?"

"He's still not selling the chocolates."

"So?"

"So—remember? His orders were not to sell them for ten school days. Okay. So the ten days came and went and he's still staying no."

"So what?"

This is what infuriated Obie—the way Archie tried so

hard not to be impressed, to always play it cool. You could tell him that The Bomb was going to be dropped and he'd probably say, "So what?" It got under Obie's skin, mostly because he suspected that it was an act, that Archie wasn't as cool as he pretended to be. And Obie was awaiting his chance to find out.

"Well, there's all kinds of rumors around the school. First of all, a lot of kids think that The Vigils are in on the deal, that Renault still isn't selling them because he's still carrying out the assignment. Then there are some kids who know the assignment is over and think that Renault is leading some kind of revolt against the sale. They say Brother Leon is climbing the wall every day . . ."

"Beautiful," Archie said, showing reaction to Obie's news at last.

"Every morning Leon calls the roll and every day this kid, a freshman, sits there, and won't sell the goddam chocolates."

"Beautiful."

"You said that."

"Continue," Archie said, ignoring Obie's sarcasm.

"Well, I understand that the sale is going lousy. Nobody wants to sell the chocolates in the first place and it's turned into a kind of farce in some classes."

Obie sat down on the bleacher seat beside Archie, pausing to let the report sink in.

Archie sniffed the air and said, "This gymnasium stinks." Pretending indifference to Obie's report but his thoughts racing, pondering the possibilities.

Obie poured it on. "The eager beavers, the brown nosers are out selling chocolates like madmen. So are Leon's pets, his special boys. So are the kids who still believe in school spirit." He sighed. "Anyway, there's a lot going on."

Archie was busy contemplating the far side of the gym,

as if something interesting was going on over there. Obie followed his gaze—nothing. "Well, what do you think, Archie?" he asked.

"What do you mean—what do I think?"

"The situation. Renault. Brother Leon. The chocolates. The kids out there taking sides . . ."

"We'll see, we'll see," Archie said. "I don't know whether The Vigils should get involved or not." He yawned.

That phony yawn irritated Obie. "Hey, look, Archie. The Vigils are involved whether you know it or not."

"What are you talking about?"

"Look, you told the kid to refuse the chocolates in the first place. That's what started all this stuff. But the kid went beyond that. He was supposed to start selling after the assignment was over. So, now he's defying The Vigils. And a lot of guys know that. We are involved, Archie, whether we want to be or not."

Obie could see that he had scored. He saw something flash in Archie's eyes, like looking at a blank window and observing a ghost peeking out.

"Nobody defies The Vigils, Obie . . ."

"That's what Renault's doing."

". . . and gets away with it."

Archie had that dreamy look again and his lower lip drooped. "Here's what to do. Arrange to have Renault appear before The Vigils. Check up on the sale—get the totals, facts and figures."

"Right," Obie said, writing in his notebook. As much as he hated Archie, he loved to see him when he was swinging into action. Obie decided to add more fuel to the flames. "Another thing, Archie. Didn't The Vigils promise Leon way back they'd back him in the chocolate sale?"

Obie had scored again. Archie turned to him, surprise

scrawled on his face. But he recovered quickly. "Let me worry about Leon. You just run your errands, Obie."

God, how Obie hated the son of a bitch. He snapped his notebook shut and left Archie sitting there in the polluted atmosphere of the gymnasium.

22

BRIAN Cochran couldn't believe his eyes. He went through the totals again, double-checking, making sure he hadn't screwed up. Frowning, biting the pencil, he pondered the results of his arithmetic—sales were dropping at an alarming rate. For a week now, they'd been going steadily downward. But yesterday, the sharpest drop of all.

What would Brother Leon say? That was Brian's main concern. Brian hated the job of treasurer because it was such a drag but mostly because it brought him into personal contact with Brother Leon. Leon gave Brian the chills. The teacher was unpredictable, moody. He was never satisfied. Complaints, complaints—your sevens look like nines, Cochran. Or, you spelled Sulkey's name wrong—it's Sulkey with an *e*, Cochran.

Brian had been lucky recently. Brother Leon had stopped checking the totals on a daily basis, almost as if he anticipated the bad news the figures contained and wanted to avoid finding out about it definitely. Today was zero hour, however. He had told Brian to prepare the totals. Now Brian waited for the teacher to show up. He'd go ape when he saw the figures. Brian shivered, actually shivered! He'd read how in historic times they killed the bearer of bad news. He had the feeling that Brother Leon was that kind of character, that he would need a scapegoat and Brian would be closest at hand. Brian sighed, tired of it all, wishing he were outside on this beautiful October day, gunning around in the old Chevy his father had bought him when school started. He loved the car. "Me and my Chevy," Brian hummed to the tune of a song he'd heard on the radio.

"Well, Brian."

Brother Leon had a way of sneaking up on you. Brian leaped and almost came to attention. That's the kind of lousy effect the teacher had on him.

"Yes, Brother Leon."

"Sit, sit," Leon said, and took his place behind the desk. Leon was sweating, as usual. He had removed his black jacket and his shirt was stained with wetness at the armpits. A faint smell of perspiration reached Brian.

"The totals are bad," Brian said, plunging, wanting to get it over with, wanting to get out of the school, this office, Leon's suffocating presence. And feeling simultaneously a twist of triumph—Leon was such a rat, let him have some bad news for a change.

"Bad?"

"The sales are down. Below last year's. And last year, the quota was half of what has to be sold this year."

"I know, I know," Leon said sharply, swiveling away in his desk chair as if Brian weren't important enough to be addressed directly. "Are you sure of your figures? You're not exactly a whiz at adding and subtracting, Cochran."

Brian flushed with anger. He was tempted to throw the master sheet at the Brother but held back. Nobody defied Brother Leon. Not Brian Cochran, anyway, who only wanted to get out of here.

"I double-checked everything," Brian said, keeping his voice even.

Silence.

The floor vibrated under Brian's feet. The boxing club working out in the gym, maybe, doing calisthenics or the other stuff boxers did.

"Cochran. Read off the names of the boys who have reached or surpassed their quota."

Brian reached for the lists. A simple task because Brother Leon insisted that all kinds of cross-indexed lists be kept so that you could tell at a glance just where students stood.

"Sulkey, sixty-two. Maronia, fifty-eight. LeBlanc, fifty-two—"

"Slower, slower," Brother Leon said, still facing away from Brian. "Begin again and slower."

It was spooky but Brian began again, pronouncing the names more exactly, pausing between names and figures.

"Sulkey . . . sixty-two . . . Maronia . . . fifty-eight . . . Le-Blanc . . . fifty-two . . . Caroni . . . fifty . . ."

Brother Leon was nodding his head, as if listening to a beautiful symphony, as if lovely sounds filled the air.

"Fontaine . . . fifty . . ." Brian paused. "Those are the only ones who either made the quota or topped it, Brother Leon."

"Read the others. There are many students who sold over forty. Read those names . . ." His face still turned away, his body slouched in the chair.

Brian shrugged and continued, calling out the names in singsong fashion, with measured pauses, letting his voice linger over the names and numbers, a weird litany here in the quiet office. When he ran out of the sales in the forties, he continued into the thirties and Brother Leon did not tell him to halt.

". . . Sullivan . . . thirty-three . . . Charlton . . . thirty-two . . . Kelly . . . thirty-two . . . Ambrose . . . thirty-one . . ."

Once in a while Brian looked up to see Brother Leon's head nodding, as if he were communicating with someone

unseen or only himself. While the recitation went on—
from the thirties into the twenties.

His eyes running ahead, Brian saw that he was in for
trouble. After he was through with the twenties and the
teens, there was a big leap. He wondered how Brother
Leon would react to the small returns. Brian began to grow
warm and his voice turned hoarse. He needed a drink of
water, not only to relieve the dryness of his throat but to
ease the tension of his neck muscles.

". . . Antonelli . . . fifteen . . . Lombard . . . thirteen . . ."
He cleared his throat, breaking the rhythm, interrupting
the flow of the report. A deep breath and then, "Cartier
. . . six." He shot a look at Brother Leon but the teacher
hadn't moved. His hands were clasped together, resting in
his lap. "Cartier . . . he only sold six because he's been out
of school. Appendicitis. He's been in the hospital . . ."

Brother Leon waved his hand, a gesture that said, "I
understand, it doesn't matter." At least, that's what Brian
figured it meant. And the gesture also seemed to mean
"Continue." He looked at the last name on the list.

"Renault . . . zero."

The pause. No names left.

"Renault . . . zero," Brother Leon said, his voice a sibilant
whisper. "Can you imagine that, Cochran? A Trinity boy who
has refused to sell the chocolates? Do you know what's happened, Cochran? Do you know why the sales have fallen off?"

"I don't know, Brother Leon," Brian said lamely.

"The boys have become infected, Cochran. Infected by
a disease we could call apathy. A terrible disease. Difficult
to cure."

What was he talking about?

"Before a cure can be found, the cause must be discovered. But in this case, Cochran, the cause is known. The
carrier of the disease is known."

Brian knew what he was getting at now. Leon figured that Renault was the cause, the carrier of the disease. As if reading Brian's mind, Leon whispered, "Renault ... Renault ..."

Like a mad scientist plotting revenge in an underground laboratory, for crying out loud.

23

"**I**'M quitting the team, Jerry."

"Why, Goob? I thought you liked football. We're just starting to click. You made a sensational catch yesterday."

They were headed for the bus stop. Today was Wednesday—no practice on Wednesday. Jerry was looking forward to arriving at the bus stop. There was a girl, beautiful, with hair like maple syrup. He'd seen her there a few times and she'd smiled at him. One day he'd gotten close enough to read her name on one of the schoolbooks she held in her arms. Ellen Barrett. Someday he'd get up the courage to speak to her. *Hi, Ellen.* Or call her on the telephone. Today maybe.

"Let's run," Goober said.

Off they went on a mad and awkward sprint. Their books prevented them from running with grace and abandon. But the mere act of running cheered up The Goober.

"Are you serious about quitting the team?" Jerry asked, his voice higher than usual, strained from the running.

"I've got to quit, Jerry." He was glad that his own voice was normal, unaffected by the running.

They turned into Gate Street.

"Why?" Jerry asked, launching himself into Gate Street with a burst of speed.

Their feet pounded on the pavement.

How can I tell him, Goob wondered.

Jerry had shot ahead. He glanced back over his shoulder, his face crimson with effort. "Why, damn it?"

The Goober caught up to him with a slight acceleration of his pace. He could easily have slid past him.

"Did you hear what happened to Brother Eugene?" The Goober asked.

"He got transferred," Jerry answered, squeezing the words out of himself like toothpaste from a tube. He was in good shape because of football but he wasn't a runner and didn't know the tricks.

"I heard he's gone on sick leave," Goober said.

"What's the difference?" Jerry replied. He took a deep sweet breath. "Hey, my legs are okay but my arms are killing me." He carried two books in each hand.

"Keep running."

"You're some kind of nut," Jerry said, humoring him.

They were approaching the intersection of Green and Gate. Seeing Jerry's discomfort, The Goober slackened his pace. "They say Brother Eugene's never been the same since Room Nineteen. They say he's all broken up over it. Can't eat or sleep. The shock."

"Rumors," Jerry gasped. "Hey, Goob, my lungs are burning up. I'm in a state of collapse."

"I know how he feels, Jerry. I know how a thing like that can drive somebody up a wall." Shouting the words into the wind. They had never discussed the destruction of Room Nineteen although Jerry knew about Goober's involvement. "Some people can't stand cruelty, Jerry. And that was a cruel thing to do to a guy like Eugene . . ."

"What's Brother Eugene got to do with not playing football?" Jerry asked, really gasping now, really sweating, his

124

lungs threatening to burst and his arms aching from the burden of the books.

Goober put on the brakes, slackening his pace, coming finally to a halt. Jerry blew air out of his mouth as he collapsed on the edge of someone's front lawn. His chest rose and fell like human bellows.

The Goober sat on the curbstone, his legs jackknifed, his feet in the gutter. He studied the leaves clustered beneath his feet. He was trying to find a way to explain to Jerry the connection between Brother Eugene and Room Nineteen and not playing football anymore. He knew there was a connection but it was hard to put into words.

"Look, Jerry. There's something rotten in that school. More than rotten." He groped for the word and found it but didn't want to use it. The word didn't fit the surroundings, the sun and the bright October afternoon. It was a midnight word, a howling wind word.

"The Vigils?" Jerry asked. He'd lain back on the lawn and was looking at the blue sky, the hurrying autumn clouds.

"That's part of it," The Goober said. He wished they were still running. "Evil," he said.

"What did you say?"

Crazy. Jerry would think he'd flipped. "Nothing," Goober said. "Anyway, I'm not going to play football. It's a personal thing, Jerry." He took a deep breath. "And I'm not going out for track next spring."

They sat in silence.

"What's the matter, Goob?" Jerry finally asked, voice troubled and loaded with concern.

"It's what they do to us, Jerry." It was easier saying the words because they weren't looking at each other, both staring ahead. "What they did to me that night in the classroom—I was crying like a baby, something I never thought

125

I'd do again in my life. And what they did to Brother Eugene, wrecking his room, wrecking *him* . . ."

"Aw, take it easy, Goob."

"And what they're doing to you—the chocolates."

"It's all a game, Goob. Think of it as fun and games. Let them have their fun. Brother Eugene must have been on the borderline, anyway . . ."

"It's more than fun and games, Jerry. Anything that can make you cry and send a teacher away—tip him over the borderline—that's more than just fun and games."

They sat there for a long time, Jerry on the lawn and Goober on the curb. Jerry knew he'd be too late now to see the girl—Ellen Barrett—but he felt that Goober needed his presence at this moment. Some of the guys from school passed by and called to them. A bus came along and halted. The driver was disgusted when The Goober shook his head that they didn't want a ride.

After a while, Goober said, "Sell the chocolates, Jerry, will you?"

Jerry said, "Play football."

Goober shook his head. "I'm not giving anything more to Trinity. Not football, not running, not anything."

They sat in sadness. Finally, they gathered their books, got up, and walked in silence to the bus stop.

The girl wasn't there.

24

"**Y**OU'RE in trouble," Brother Leon said.

You're in trouble, not me, Archie wanted to answer. But didn't. He had never spoken to Leon on the telephone before and the disembodied voice at the other end of the line had caught him off balance.

"What's the matter?" Archie asked cautiously, but knowing, of course.

"The chocolates," Leon said. "They're not selling. The entire sale is in jeopardy." Leon's breath filled in the gaps between the words as if he'd been running a long distance. Was he on the edge of panic?

"How bad is it?" Archie asked, relaxing now, stalling. He knew how bad it was.

"It could hardly be worse. The sale is more than half finished. The initial push is over. There is no momentum. Half the chocolates haven't been sold yet. And the sales are virtually at a standstill." Leon paused in the recital. "You're not being very effective, Archie."

Archie shook his head in grudging admiration. Here was Leon with his back to the wall and still he was on the offensive. *You're not being very effective, Archie.*

"You mean the finances are bad?" Archie taunted, launching his own offensive. To Leon, it may have sounded like a shot in the dark but it wasn't. The question was based on information Archie had received that afternoon from Brian Cochran.

Cochran had stopped him in the second-floor corridor and motioned Archie into an empty classroom. Archie had been reluctant. The kid was Leon's bookkeeper and probably his stooge. But the information revealed that Cochran was no stooge for Leon.

"Listen, I think Leon's in deep trouble. There's more than chocolates involved here, Archie."

Archie resented Cochran's familiarity, the use of his name. But he didn't say anything, curious about what the kid had to say.

"I overheard Leon talking with Brother Jacques. Jacques was trying to back him into a corner. He kept mentioning something about Leon abusing his power of attorney. That he'd overextended the school's finances. That was his exact word, 'overextended.' The chocolates came into it. Something about twenty thousand boxes and Leon paying cash in advance. I didn't hear all of it . . . I got out of there before they could find out I was around . . ."

"So what do you think, Cochran?" Archie asked, although he knew. Leon needed at least twenty thousand dollars to draw even with the school.

"I think Leon bought the chocolates with money that he wasn't supposed to use. Now, the sale's going lousy and he's caught in the middle. And Brother Jacques smells a rat . . ."

"Jacques is sharp," Archie said, remembering how Jacques had acted on Archie's anonymous tip about the word "environment"—making the class look ridiculous, Obie among them. "Good job, Cochran."

Cochran beamed at the praise. Encouraged, he drew some sheets of paper out of a book he was carrying. "Take a look at this stuff sometime, Archie. It's facts and figures about this year's sale and last year's. And it's all bad. I think Leon's on the run . . ."

But Cochran really didn't know Leon, Archie realized now as the teacher's voice came vibrantly over the line. Leon had ignored Archie's taunt about finances and had resumed his offensive.

"I thought you had influence, Archie. You and your . . . friends."

"It's not my sale, Brother Leon."

"It's your sale in more ways than you realize, Archie," Leon said, sighing. It was his phony sigh, his usual act. "You played games at the beginning, Archie, with that freshman Renault and got yourself involved. Now, the game has backfired."

Renault. Archie thought of the kid's refusal to sell, his ridiculous defiance. He remembered the triumph in Obie's voice when he'd told him of Renault's action—it's your move, Archie baby. But it was always Archie's move anyway.

And he moved now. "Just a minute," he told Brother Leon. He put down the phone and went to the den, where he removed Cochran's data from his U.S. History textbook. Returning to the phone, he said, "I've got some figures here about last year's sale. Do you know they barely sold all the chocolates last year? Kids are getting tired of selling stuff. Last year, it took a lot of prizes and bonuses to get the kids to sell only twenty-five boxes at one dollar a box. And this year they're stuck with fifty boxes at two dollars each. That's why the sale is falling apart—not because of games being played."

Brother Leon's breathing filled the line, as if he were some kind of obscene phone caller.

"Archie," he said, whispering, menace in the whisper, as if the information he had to impart was too terrible to be spoken aloud. "I don't care about fun and games. I don't care whether it's Renault or your precious organization or the state of the economy. All I know is that the chocolates aren't being sold. And I want them sold!"

"Any ideas about how?" Archie said, fighting for time again. Funny, he knew Leon was in a precarious position and yet there was always the danger of underestimating him. He still had the authority of the school behind him. Archie had only his wits and a bunch of guys who were all big zeroes without him.

"Perhaps you should begin with Renault," Leon said. "I think he should be made to say 'yes' instead of 'no.' I'm convinced, Archie, that he's become a symbol to those who would like to see the sale defeated. The malingerers, the malcontents—they always rally around a rebel. Renault must sell the chocolates. And you, The Vigils—yes, I'm saying the name aloud—The Vigils must throw their full weight behind the sale . . ."

"That's quite an order, Brother."

"You've spoken the correct word, Archie. Order—it is an order."

"I don't know what you mean, Brother."

"I'll make it clear, Archie. If the sale goes down the drain, you and The Vigils also go down the drain. Believe me . . ."

Archie was about to respond, tempted to let Leon know that he had learned about the financial trouble, but he didn't get the chance. Leon, that bastard, had already hung up and the dial tone exploded in Archie's ear.

25

THE summons looked like a ransom note—letters cut out of a newspaper or magazine. *vIgiL MeEtinG tWO-THirTy*. The wackiness of the note, those crazy letters, made it seem childish and ridiculous. But that same touch of the childish also gave it an air of something not quite rational, faintly threatening and mocking. That was the special quality of The Vigils, of course, and Archie Costello.

Thirty minutes later, Jerry stood before The Vigils in the storage room. The nearby gym was occupied by fellows either practicing basketball or boxing calisthenics and the walls echoed with thuddings, bouncings and whistles blowing, like a grotesque sound track. Nine or ten Vigil members were present, including Carter who was getting tired of this Vigil crap, especially when it meant he had to miss boxing, and Obie who looked forward to the meeting with pleasure, wondering how Archie would proceed. Archie sat behind the card table. The table was covered with a scarf of purple and gold—the school colors. In the exact center of the table: a box of chocolates.

"Renault," Archie said softly.

Instinctively, Jerry came to attention, squaring his shoulders, sucking in his stomach, and immediately disgusted with himself.

"Have a chocolate, Renault?"

Jerry shook his head, sighing. He thought wistfully of the guys out on the football field in the sweet fresh wind, tossing the ball around before practice began.

"They're good," Archie said, opening the box and taking out a chocolate. He inhaled its flavor and popped it into his mouth. He chewed slowly, deliberately, smacking his lips in exaggerated fashion. A second chocolate followed the first. And a third followed the second. His mouth was crammed with the candy now and his throat rippled as he swallowed. "Delicious," he said. "And only two dollars a box—a bargain."

Somebody laughed. A short bark that was instantly cut off as if a needle had been lifted from a record.

"But you wouldn't know about the price, would you, Renault?"

Jerry shrugged. But his heart began to beat wildly. He knew there had to be a showdown. And this was it.

Archie reached for another chocolate. Into his mouth. "How many boxes have you sold, Renault?"

"None."

"None?" Archie's gentle voice curled in surprise and wonder. He swallowed, shaking his head in mock puzzlement. Without taking his eyes from Jerry, he called, "Hey, Porter, how many boxes have you sold?"

"Twenty-one."

"Twenty-one?" Archie's voice was now filled with awe. "Hey, Porter, you must be one of those hustling, eager-beaver freshmen, huh?"

"I'm a senior."

"A senior?" More awe. "You mean to tell me you're a big-shot senior and you've still got enough spirit left to get out there and sell all those chocolates? Beautiful, Porter." The voice full of mockery—or was it? "Anybody else here sell chocolates?"

A chorus of numbers filled the air as if The Vigil members were calling bids at a weird auction.

"Forty-two."

"Thirty-three."

"Twenty."

"Nineteen."

"Forty-five."

Archie raised his hands and silence fell. Someone in the gym fell against the wall and shouted an obscenity. Obie marveled at the way Archie ran the meetings and how The Vigils quickly took his cues. Porter hadn't sold ten boxes, if any at all. Obie himself had only sold sixteen but had called out forty-five.

"And you, Renault, a freshman, a new student who should be filled with the spirit of Trinity, you haven't sold any? Zero? Nothing?" His hand reached for another chocolate. Actually, he loved them. Not as good as Hershey with almonds but an acceptable substitute.

"That's right," Jerry said, his voice small, a wrong-end-of-the-telescope kind of voice.

"Do you mind if I ask why?"

Jerry pondered the question. What should he do? Play a game? Tell it straight? But he wasn't sure if it would make sense if he told it straight, especially to a roomful of strangers.

"It's personal," he said finally, feeling like a loser, knowing he couldn't win. It had all been going so beautifully. Football, school, a girl who had smiled at him at the bus stop. He had edged close to her and seen her name written on one of her books—Ellen Barrett. She had smiled at him two days in a row and he'd been too shy to speak to her but had looked up all the Barretts in the phone book. Five of them. Tonight he was planning to call them up, track her down. It seemed to him that he'd be able to talk to her on the phone. Now, for some reason, he had the feeling he would never talk to her, never play football again—a crazy feeling but one that he couldn't shake.

Archie had been licking his fingers, one at a time, letting the echo of Jerry's response linger in the air. It was so quiet that he heard someone's stomach growl intimately.

"Renault," Archie said, friendly, his voice conversational. "I'll tell you something. Nothing's personal here in The Vigils. No secrets here, understand?" He took a final suck at his thumb. "Hey, Johnson."

"Right," a voice called behind Jerry.

"How many times you jack off every day?"

"Twice," Johnson replied quickly.

"See?" asked Archie. "No secrets here, Renault. Nothing personal. Not in The Vigils."

Jerry had taken a shower this morning before school but now he smelled his own perspiration.

"Come on," Archie said, a good friend now, encouraging, coaxing. "You can tell us."

Carter blew air out of his mouth in exasperation. He was losing patience with Archie's cat-and-mouse crap. He had sat here for two years watching Archie play his silly games with kids, having Archie act the big shot as if he ran the show. Carter carried the responsibility for the assignments on his shoulders. As president, he also had to keep the other guys in line, keep them psyched up, ready to help make Archie's assignments work. And Carter wasn't crazy about this chocolate stuff. It was something beyond the control of The Vigils. It involved Brother Leon and he didn't trust Leon as far as he could throw him. Now, he watched the kid Renault, looking as if he was ready to faint with fright, his face pale and eyes wide with dread, and Archie having fun with him. Jesus. Carter hated this psychological crap. He loved boxing, where everything was visible—the jabs, tho hooks, the roundhouse swings, the glove in the stomach.

"Okay, Renault, play time is over," Archie said. The gentleness was gone from his voice. No chocolates in his mouth. "Tell us—why aren't you selling the chocolates?"

"Because I don't want to," Jerry said, still stalling. Because—what else could he do?

"You don't want to?" Archie asked, incredulous.

Jerry nodded. He'd bought time.

"Hey, Obie."

"Right," Obie answered, stung. Why the hell did Archie have to pick on him all the time? What the hell did he want now?

"Do you want to come to school every day, Obie?"

"Hell, no," Obie responded, knowing what Archie wanted and giving it to him but resentful as well, feeling like a stooge, as if Archie was the ventriloquist and Obie the dummy.

"But you *come* to school, don't you?"

"Hell, yes."

Laughter greeted the answer and Obie allowed himself a smile. But a quick look from Archie wiped the smile away. Archie was dead serious. He could tell that by the way his lips were tight and thin and his eyes flashing like neon signs.

"See?" Archie said, swiveling back to Renault. "Everybody has to do things in this world they don't want to."

A terrific sadness swept over Jerry. As if somebody had died. The way he felt standing in the cemetery that day they buried his mother. And nothing you could do about it.

"Okay, Renault," Archie said, a finality in his voice.

You could feel the room tense. Obie sucked in his breath. Here it comes, the Archie touch.

"Here's your assignment. Tomorrow at the roll call, you

take the chocolates. You say, 'Brother Leon, I accept the chocolates.'"

Stunned, Jerry blurted out, "What?"

"Something wrong with your hearing, Renault?" Turning aside, he called, "Hey, McGrath, did you hear me?"

"Hell, yes."

"What did I say?"

"You said the kid should start selling chocolates."

Archie returned his attention to Jerry. "You're getting off easy, Renault. You've disobeyed The Vigils. That calls for punishment. Although The Vigils don't believe in violence, we have found it necessary to have a punishment code. The punishment is usually worse than the assignment. But we're letting you off cheap, Renault. We're just asking you to take the chocolates tomorrow. And sell them."

Jesus, Obie thought in disbelief. The great Archie Costello is running scared. The word "asking" was the tipoff. A slip of the lip, maybe. But as if Archie was trying to bargain with the kid, *asking*, for crying out loud. I've got you, Archie, you bastard. Obie had never known such sweet victory. The goddam freshman was going to screw Archie up, at last. Not the Black Box. Not Brother Leon. Not his own cleverness. But a skinny freshman. Because Obie was certain of one thing as if it was a natural law, like gravity— Renault wasn't going to sell the chocolates. He could tell by looking at the kid, standing there scared, like he could shit his pants, but not backing down. While Archie was *asking* him to sell the chocolates. Asking.

"Dismissed," Archie called out.

Carter was surprised at the sudden dismissal and he banged the gavel too hard, almost splitting the crate he used as a desk. He had a feeling that he had missed a beat somewhere, had missed a crucial moment. Archie and all his subtle crap. What the kid Renault needed was a stiff

136

jab to the jaw and another to the belly. That'd make him sell the frigging chocolates. Archie and his stupid *let's not have any violence*. Anyway, the meeting was over and Carter felt like working out, like working up a sweat with the gloves and the big bag.

He banged the gavel again.

26

"*H*ELLO."

His mind went blank.

"Hello?"

Was it her? But it had to be—this was the last Barrett in the book and the voice was fresh and appealing, the kind of voice that went with all that beauty he had seen at the bus stop.

"Hello," he managed, his voice emerging as an ugly croak.

"Is this Danny?" she asked.

He was instantly, insanely jealous of Danny, whoever Danny was.

"No," he croaked again, miserably.

"Who is this?" she asked, annoyance now in her voice.

"Is this Ellen? Ellen Barrett?" The name was strange on his tongue. He had never said it aloud although he had whispered it silently a thousand times.

Silence.

"Look," he began, his heart beating desperately. "Look, you don't know who I am but I see you every day . . ."

"Are you some kind of pervert?" she asked, not horrified at all but good-naturedly curious, like, "Hey, Ma, I've got a pervert on the line."

"No. I'm the fellow at the bus stop."

"What follow? What bus stop?" Her voice had lost all its demureness. It had become a wise-guy, show-me kind of voice.

He wanted to say, you smiled at me yesterday, the day before that, last week. And I love you. But couldn't. He suddenly saw how futile, how ridiculous the situation was. A fellow didn't call up a girl on the evidence of a smile and introduce himself this way. She probably smiled at a hundred guys a day.

"I'm sorry for bothering you," he said.

"Are you sure this isn't Danny? Are you trying to put me on, Danny? Look, Danny, I'm getting tired of you and your crap . . ."

Jerry hung up. He didn't want to hear anymore. The word "crap," echoing now in his mind, had destroyed all illusion about her. Like meeting a lovely girl and having her smile reveal rotten teeth. But his heart was still beating wildly. *Are you some kind of pervert?* Maybe I am. Not a sexual pervert but another kind. Wasn't refusing to sell the chocolates a kind of perversion? Wasn't it crazy to go on refusing to sell the chocolates, particularly after that last warning yesterday by Archie Costello and The Vigils? And yet this morning, he had stood his ground and fired a level and positive *No* at Brother Leon. For the first time, the word brought exultancy to him, a lifting of the spirit.

With that latest *No* resounding in his ears, Jerry had expected the school building to fall or something dramatic to happen. Nothing. He had seen Goober shake his head in dismay. But Goober didn't know about this new feeling, the sense that his bridges were burning behind him and for once in his life he didn't care. He was still buoyant when he arrived home, otherwise he wouldn't have had the courage to call all those Barretts and to actually talk to the girl.

It had been a miserable failure, of course. But he had made the call, taken a step, broken the routine of his days and nights.

He went into the kitchen, suddenly ravenous, and dumped some ice cream from the freezer into a dish.

"My name is Jerry Renault and I'm not going to sell the chocolates," he said to the empty apartment.

The words and his voice sounded strong and noble.

27

THEY shouldn't have picked Frankie Rollo for an assignment, of course. A junior, Rollo was insolent, a troublemaker. He was a non-participant, refusing to take part in athletics or extra-curricular activities that were so important in the Trinity scene. He seldom opened a book and never did any homework, but he managed to survive because he possessed a native and cunning intelligence. His major talent was cheating. He was also lucky. Under ordinary circumstances, he was the kind of guy Archie took pleasure in assigning, watching him bend or break. All these so-called rough characters melted into ninety-seven-pound weaklings when confronted by Archie and The Vigils. The scorn and the swagger evaporated as they stood ill-at-ease in the storage room. But not Frankie Rollo. He stood loose and easy, unintimidated.

"Your name?" Archie asked.

"Come on, Archie," Rollo replied, smiling at all this foolishness. "You know my name."

The silence was awesome. But before that silence, a gasp from someone in the room. Archie was careful to keep his poker face, intent on not betraying an emotion. But he was shaken inside. No one had ever reacted this way before. No one had ever challenged Archie or an assignment.

"Let's not have any crap, Rollo," growled Carter. "Let's hear your name."

A pause. Archie swore silently. It was irritating to have Carter step in that way, as if he was coming to Archie's rescue. Ordinarily, Archie ran the meetings his way, not anybody else's way.

Rollo shrugged. "My name is Frankie Rollo," he announced in sing-song fashion.

"You think you're a big shot, don't you?" Archie asked.

Rollo didn't respond but the smirk on his face was an eloquent answer.

"A big shot," Archie repeated, as if savoring the word, but stalling, playing for time, shifting his thoughts, knowing it would be necessary to improvise, to turn this insolent bastard into a victim.

"You said it, not me," Rollo said smugly.

"We like big shots here," Archie said. "In fact, that's our specialty—turning big shots into little shots."

"Cut the shit, will you, Archie?" Rollo said. "You're not impressing anybody."

Again that terrible silence, like a shock wave, stunning the room, an invisible blow. Even Obie, who had looked forward to the day when a victim would defy the great Archie Costello, blinked in disbelief.

"What did you say?" Archie asked, biting off every word and spitting it at Rollo.

"Hey, you guys," Rollo said, swiveling away from Archie and addressing the entire assembly. "I'm not a scared kid who pees his pants because the big bad Vigils call him to a meeting. Hell, you guys can't even scare a punk freshman into selling a few lousy chocolates . . ."

"Look, Rollo," Archie began.

But he didn't have a chance to finish as Carter leaped to his feet. Carter had been waiting for a moment like this for months, his hands itching for action in the storage room instead of sitting there week by week as Archie played his little cat-and-mouse games.

"That's enough out of you, Rollo," Carter said. Simultaneously, his hand shot out and struck Rollo on the jaw. Rollo's head snapped back—*snap* like a knuckle cracking—and he bellowed with pain. As Rollo lifted his hands to his face in tardy defense, Carter's fist sank sickeningly into his stomach. Rollo groaned and retched, doubled over, clutching himself in disbelief, gasping for breath. He was shoved from behind, and dropped to the floor, coughing and spitting, crawling on all fours.

A muffled roar of approval rose from The Vigils. At last, action, physical action, something you could see with your own eyes.

"Get him out of here," Carter said.

Rollo was picked up by two Vigil members and half-carried, half-dragged toward the doorway. Archie had watched Rollo's swift demolition in dismay. He resented Carter's quick move into the spotlight, the way the guys had cheered Carter on. It had placed Archie at a disadvantage for the first time as assigner because Rollo had only been the curtain raiser, a bit of amusement Obie had arranged to enliven the proceedings. Actually, the meeting had been called to discuss Renault and what could be done about the stubborn freshman who refused to fall into line.

Carter called for order, banging his gavel on the table. In the developing silence, they could hear Rollo being dumped onto the gymnasium floor outside and then the sound of vomiting like a toilet being flushed.

"Okay, quiet," Carter demanded, as if he were yelling at Rollo to quit throwing up. Then he turned to Archie. "Sit down," he said. Archie recognized the command in Carter's voice. For a moment, he was tempted to challenge him but he realized that The Vigils had approved Carter's action against Rollo. This was no time to have a showdown with Carter, it was time to play it cool, cool. Archie sat.

"We've arrived at the moment of truth, Archie," Carter said. "And here's how I read it—tell me if I'm wrong. When a gross creep like Rollo comes in here and challenges The Vigils, then there's something wrong. Very wrong. We can't afford to have guys like Rollo thinking they can screw around with us. The word will spread and The Vigils fall apart." Carter paused to let them imagine the dissolution of The Vigils. "Now, I said that something is very wrong. And I'll tell you who's wrong. We are."

His words were greeted with surprise.

"How come *we're* wrong?" Obie, the perennial straight man, called out.

"First of all, because we let our name get connected with the goddam chocolate sale. Like it's our baby or something. Second of all, like Rollo said, we let a punk freshman make fools out of us." He turned to Archie. "Right, Archie?" The question was loaded with malice.

Archie didn't say anything. He was suddenly in a roomful of strangers and he decided to do nothing at all. When in doubt, play the waiting game. Watch for an opening. It would be ridiculous to disagree with Carter, of course. Word had been spreading throughout the school—the kid had refused to sell the chocolates in direct defiance of The Vigils. That's why they had assembled here this afternoon.

"Obie, show us what you found this morning on the bulletin board," Carter said.

Obie was eager to comply. Reaching under his chair he withdrew a poster that he had folded in two. Unfolded, the poster was about the size of an ordinary kitchen window. Obie held it up for all to see. The poster proclaimed in scrawled, scarlet letters—

SCREW THE CHOCOLATES
AND
SCREW THE VIGILS

"I saw the poster because I was late for math," Obie explained. "It was on the bulletin board in the main corridor."

"Do you think many guys saw it?" Carter asked.

"No. I'd shot by the bulletin board a minute before on the way to my locker for my math book. And the poster wasn't there. Chances are, hardly anybody saw it."

"You think Renault put it up?" someone asked.

"No," Carter snorted. "Renault doesn't have to go around putting up posters. He's been saying screw The Vigils and the chocolates for weeks now. But this shows what's happening. The word is spreading. If Renault can get away with defying us, other people are gonna try." Finally, he turned to Archie. "Okay, Archie. You're the brains of the outfit. And you also got us into this mess. Where do we go from here?"

"You're pushing panic buttons for nothing," Archie said, voice quiet and casual. He knew what he must do—regain his previous status, wipe away the memory of Rollo's defiance and prove that he, Archie Costello, was still in command. He had to show them that he could take care of both Renault and the chocolates. And he was ready for them. While Carter had been making speeches and Obie flashing his poster around, Archie's mind had been racing, probing, testing. He always worked better under pressure, anyway. "First of all, you can't go around beating up half the kids in school. That's why I usually lay off the strong-arm stuff in the assignments. The brothers would close us down in no time and the kids would really start sabotaging if we started hurting people." Noticing Carter's frown, Archie decided to throw him a bone—Carter still ran the meetings and as Vigils president he could be a dangerous adversary. "All right, Carter, I'll admit you did a beautiful job on Rollo and he had it coming. But nobody gives a damn about Rollo. He can lay in his vomit till kingdom come and nobody'd care. But Rollo's an exception."

"Rollo's an example," Carter said. "Let the word spread about Rollo and we won't have to worry about other kids acting wise or putting up posters."

Anticipating a deadlock on that topic, Archie changed directions. "But that doesn't sell chocolates, Carter," Archie said. "You told us The Vigils are linked up with the sale. Then the solution is simple. Let's get the goddam sale over with as soon as possible. Let's sell the chocolates. If Renault's turning into some kind of rebel hero because he's not selling the chocolates, how the hell is he going to look when everybody in the school is selling, except him?"

Murmurs of assent came from the members, but Carter appeared doubtful. "And how do we get everybody in the school to start selling the chocolates, Archie?"

Archie allowed himself the indulgence of a quiet, confident laugh, but closed his fists to hide his moist palms. "Simple, Carter. Like all great schemes and plans, it has the beauty of simplicity." The guys waited, spellbound as always when Archie began to outline assignments and plans. "We make selling chocolates popular. We make it cool to sell the things. We spread the word. We organize. We bring in the class officers, the homeroom officers, the student council, the kids with influence. Do or die for good old Trinity! Everybody sells!"

"Not everybody will want to sell fifty boxes, Archie," Obie called out, disturbed because somehow Archie had taken charge again—he had them eating out of his hand.

"They will, Obie," Archie predicted, "they will. Do your

thing, they say, Obie, do your thing. Well, we're going to make selling chocolates the thing to do. And The Vigils will come out on top as usual. The school will love us for it— getting rid of their chocolates. We'll be able to write our own ticket with Leon and the brothers. Why do you think I pledged support to Leon in the first place?" Archie's voice was gentle with assurance, the old gentleness they all recognized as Archie's hallmark when he was sailing high, wide and handsome. They admired the way Carter had employed his fists to demolish Rollo but they felt more secure with Archie in command, Archie who was capable of surprise after surprise.

"How about Renault?" Carter asked.

"Don't worry about Renault."

"But I do, I worry about him," Carter said, sarcastically. "He's making patsies out of us."

"The Renault thing will take care of itself," Archie said. Couldn't Carter and the others see? Were they so blind to human nature, to developing situations? "Let me put it this way, Carter. Before the sale is over, Renault will be wishing with all his heart that he had sold the chocolates. And the school will be glad he didn't."

"Okay," Carter said, banging the gavel. He always banged the gavel when he was unsure of himself. The gavel was an extension of his fist. But feeling that Archie had somehow eluded him, had somehow won a victory, Carter said, "Look, Archie, if this backfires, if the sale doesn't work, then you've screwed yourself up, do you understand? You'll be all done and it won't take the Black Box."

Blood stung Archie's cheeks and a pulse throbbed dangerously in his temple. No one had ever talked to him that way before, not in front of everyone like this. With an effort he made himself stay loose, kept that smile on his lips like a label on a bottle, hiding his humiliation.

"You'd better be right, Archie," Carter said. "As far as I'm concerned, you're on probation until the last chocolate's sold."

The final humiliation. Probation.

Archie kept that smile on his face until he felt his cheeks would crack.

28

*H*E handed the ball off to Guilmet, slapping it into his belly, and then hung in there, waiting for Carter to lunge through the line. The play called for Jerry to hit Carter low and send him toppling, an assignment Jerry didn't relish. Carter was easily fifty pounds heavier and he was used by the Coach to keep the freshmen squad on their toes. But the Coach always said, "It doesn't matter how big the body, it's what you do with it." Now, Jerry waited for Carter to emerge from the jungle of skirmishing bodies as Guilmet plunged off tackle. And there he was, like a freight train on the loose, out of control, rampaging wildly, trying to career toward Guilmet but too late, too late. Jerry leaped toward him, low, aiming for that vulnerable territory of the knees, the target pinpointed by the Coach. Carter and Jerry collided like a street accident. Colored lights whirled— Fourth of July on an October afternoon. Jerry felt himself lunging toward the ground, arms and legs askew, all mixed up with Carter's arms and legs. There was exhilaration in the collision, the honest contact of football, not as beautiful maybe as a completed pass or a fake that threw your opponents off balance but beautiful nevertheless and manly, prideful.

The good damp smell of the grass, the earth, rushed into

Jerry's nostrils and he let himself be carried on the waves of the sweet moment, knowing he'd carried out his assignment: get Carter. He glanced up to see Carter raising himself in astonishment, shaking his head. Jerry grinned as he got to his feet. Suddenly, he was struck from behind, a vicious blow to his kidneys, sickening in its impact. His knees caved in and he sank to the ground again. As he attempted to turn around to find out who had attacked him, another blow landed, some place, and Jerry felt himself hurtling off-balance to the ground. He felt his eyes watering, tears spilling onto his cheeks. He looked around and saw the fellows getting into position for the next play.

"Come on, Renault," the Coach called.

He got to one knee, then managed to stand on both feet. The pain was subsiding, translated now into a dull spreading ache.

"Come on, come on," the Coach urged, irritable as usual.

Jerry made his way tenderly toward the lineup. He thrust his head and shoulders into the huddle, considering what play he should call next, but a part of him was not concerned with the play or the game. He lifted his head and scanned the field, as if he were figuring out what to do next. Who had assaulted him that way? Who hated him so much that he'd racked him up so viciously?

Not Carter—Carter had been in full view. But who else? Anybody. It could have been anybody. From his own team, maybe.

"You okay?" somebody inquired.

Jerry plunged into the huddle again. Called his own number—a run-keep. At least if he carried the ball, he'd be in full view of everyone and not as vulnerable to a sneak attack.

"Let's go," he said, putting juice into the words, letting

them all know that he was fine, great, ready for action. He found that his rib cage ached when he walked.

Lined up behind the quarterback, Jerry raised his eyes again, sweeping the players. Somebody was trying to wipe him out.

Give me eyes behind my head, he prayed, as he barked the signals.

The telephone rang as he inserted the key in the front door. Turning the key swiftly, he flung the door open and tossed his books on the chair in the hallway. The ringing went on unendingly, a lonely sound in the empty apartment.

Finally, he grabbed it off the wall.

"Hello."

Silence. Not even a dial tone. Then out of the silence, a faint sound, from a distance, getting closer, like someone chuckling, privately, at a secret intimate joke.

"Hello," Jerry said again.

The chuckle was louder now. An obscene phone call? Only girls got those, didn't they? Again that chuckle, more defined and louder but still somehow intimate and suggestive, a chuckle that said, I know something you don't know.

"Who is this?" Jerry asked.

And then the dial tone, like a fart in his ear.

That night at eleven o'clock the telephone rang again. Jerry figured it was his father—he was working the late shift at the drugstore.

He lifted the receiver and said hello.

No response.

No sound at all.

He wanted to hang up but something made him hold the instrument to his ear, waiting.

The chuckle again.

151

It was weirder than three o'clock this afternoon. The night, the darkness outside, the apartment riddled with lamplight shadows seemed more menacing. Forget it, Jerry told himself, it always seems worse at night.

"Hey, who is this?" he asked, the sound of his voice restoring normalcy.

Still the chuckle, almost evil in its quiet mockery.

"This some creep? Some flaky nut? Some stupid jerk?" Jerry asked. Draw him out, make him angry.

The chuckle turned into a hoot of derision.

Then the dial tone again.

He seldom kept anything of value in his locker. The school was notorious for "borrowers"—kids who weren't exactly thieves but walked off with anything that wasn't nailed down or locked up. No sense buying a lock—it would be busted the first day. Privacy was virtually non-existent at Trinity. Most of the kids didn't give a damn or have any respect for the rights of others. They rummaged desks, pried lockers open, sifted through books on a perennial search for loot—money, pot, books, watches, clothing—anything.

The morning after that first night phone call, Jerry opened his locker and shook his head in disbelief. His poster had been smeared with ink or some kind of blue paint. The message had been virtually obliterated. *Do I dare disturb the universe?* was now a grotesque jumble of unconnected letters. It was such a senseless, childish act of vandalism that Jerry was more awed than angered. Who'd do such a crazy thing? Looking down, he saw that his new gym sneakers had been slashed, the canvas now limp shreds, rag-like. He'd made the mistake of leaving them here overnight.

Ruining the poster was one thing, a gross act, the work of the animal—and all schools had animals, even Trinity.

But there was nothing prankish about ruining the sneakers. That was deliberate, somebody sending him a message.

The telephone calls.

That attack on the football field.

Now this.

He closed the locker quickly so no one would see the damage. For some reason, he felt ashamed.

He'd been dreaming of a fire, flames eating unknown walls, and the siren sounded, and then it wasn't a siren but the telephone. Jerry scrambled from his bed. In the hallway, his father was slamming the receiver down on the hook. "Something funny's going on around here." The grandfather clock chimed twice.

Jerry didn't have to blink the sleep from his eyes. He was wide awake, chilled, the floor cold beneath his feet.

"Who was it?" he asked. Although he knew, of course.

"Nobody," his father answered, disgusted. "Same thing happened last night about this time. But it didn't wake you up. Some nut on the other end of the line, laughing away like it's the biggest joke in the world." He reached out and tousled Jerry's hair. "Go back to bed, Jerry. There are all kinds of nuts running around loose."

It was hours before Jerry fell into a strange dreamless sleep.

"Renault," Brother Andrew called.

Jerry looked up. He'd been immersed in his new art project—copying a two-storey house in order to learn perspective. A simple exercise but he loved the ordered lines, the neatness, the stark beauty of planes and angles.

"Yes, Brother?"

"Your watercolor. The landscape assignment."

"Yes?" Puzzled. The watercolor which was a major

153

project had taken a week of painstaking work, simply because Jerry was not at his best in free art. He was more at ease with formal or geometric designs where the composition was well-defined. But the watercolor would account for fifty percent of his mark this semester.

"Today's the final day for handing it in," the Brother said. "I don't find yours here."

"I put it on your desk yesterday," Jerry said.

"Yesterday?" Brother Andrew asked, as if he'd never heard of yesterday. He was a fastidious, precise man who ordinarily taught math but had been filling in for the regular art teacher.

"Yes, sir," Jerry said firmly.

Eyebrows arched, the Brother looked through the pile of drawings on the desk.

Jerry sighed quietly, in resignation. He knew that Brother Andrew wouldn't find the drawing there. He wanted to turn, to scan the faces of the kids in the class, to find that one kid who'd be gloating in satisfaction. Hey, you're getting paranoid, he told himself. Who'd sneak in here and remove your drawing? Who'd watch so close that they'd even know you submitted the drawing yesterday?

Brother Andrew looked up. "To use a cliché, Renault, we are locked on the horns of a dilemma. Your landscape is not here. Now, either I have lost it and I do not make a habit of losing landscapes . . ." the teacher paused here as if, incredibly, he expected a laugh, and, incredibly, the laugh did come ". . . or your memory is faulty."

"I handed it in, Brother." Firmly. Without panic.

The teacher looked steadily into Jerry's eyes. Jerry saw the honest doubt there. "Well, Renault, perhaps I *do* make a habit of losing landscapes, after all," he said, and Jerry felt a rush of camaraderie for the teacher. "At any rate, let me check further. Perhaps I left it in the teachers' lounge."

For some reason, this remark also provoked laughter and even the teacher joined in. It was late in the period and late in the day and everyone needed to relax, let down, take it easy. Jerry wanted to look around, to see whose eyes gleamed with triumph over the missing watercolor.

"Of course, Renault, as sympathetic as I am, if I do not find the landscape, then I must fail you this semester."

Jerry opened his locker.

The mess was still there. He hadn't torn down the poster or removed the sneakers, letting them remain there as symbols. Symbols of what? He wasn't certain. Looking wistfully at the poster, he pondered the damaged words: *Do I dare disturb the universe*?

The usual corridor pandemonium surrounded him, slammed locker doors, wild yells and whistles, pounding feet as the guys hurried to the after-school activities, football, boxing, debating.

Do I dare disturb the universe?

Yes, I do, I do. I think.

Jerry suddenly understood the poster—the solitary man on the beach standing upright and alone and unafraid, poised at the moment of making himself heard and known in the world, the universe.

29

*B*EAUTIFUL.

Brian Cochran added the totals again and again, toying with them, playing with them, as if he were a juggler and they were fascinating figures of delight. He couldn't wait to report the totals to Brother Leon.

In the past few days, the volume of sales had risen staggeringly. Staggeringly was the correct word. Brian felt as if he were drunk on the statistics, the figures like liquor, making him light-headed, giddy and dizzy.

What had happened? He wasn't certain. There was no single reason for the sudden turnabout, the surprising upswing, the unexpected rash of sales. But the proof of the change was not only here in the figures before him but everywhere in the school itself. Brian had witnessed the feverish activity and how the chocolates had suddenly become a vogue, a fad, the way hula hoops had caught on when they were kids in the first or second grade, the way demonstrations had been the big thing a few years ago. Rumors indicated that The Vigils had adopted the sale as a special crusade. And that was possible, although Brian hadn't made any inquiries—he always steered clear of The Vigils. However, he'd seen some of the more prominent Vigil members waylaying kids in the corridors, checking on

156

their sales, whispering menacingly to those who had sold only a few boxes. Each afternoon, teams of fellows left the school, loaded down with chocolates. They piled into automobiles and drove off. Brian heard that the teams drove to various sections of town and invaded neighborhoods, ringing doorbells, banging on doors, a massive sales effort as if they were all encyclopedia salesmen on commission, for crying out loud. Brian heard reports that someone had gotten permission to solicit at one of the local factories— four guys had circulated through the place and sold three hundred boxes in a couple of hours. The feverish activity kept Brian hopping, maintaining the records and then rushing down to the big boards in the assembly to post the results. The hall had become the school's focal point. "Hey, look," a kid had yelled out during the last posting. "Jimmy Demers sold his fifty boxes."

That was the creepy aspect of the sale, the way the credit was being distributed among all the students. Brian didn't know whether this was fair or not but he didn't argue about methods—Brother Leon was interested in results and so was Brian. And yet Brian was made uncomfortable by the situation. A few minutes ago, Carter had walked into the office with a fistful of money. Brian treated Carter with utmost care—he was head of The Vigils.

"Okay, kid," Carter had said, flinging the money, bills and change, on the desk. "Here's the returns. Seventy-five boxes sold—one hundred fifty dollars. Count it."

"Right." Brian leaped to the task under Carter's watchful gaze. His fingers trembled and he cautioned himself to make no mistakes. Let it be one-fifty exactly.

"Right on the nose," Brian reported.

And then came the weird part.

"Let me see the roster," Carter said.

Brian handed over the list of names, each name with

boxes beside it in which returns were noted as they arrived, corresponding to the master list on the big boards in the assembly hall. After studying the roster for a few minutes, Carter told Brian to credit various students with sales returns. Brian made the entries as Carter called them out: Huart, thirteen . . . DeLillo, nine . . . Lemoine . . . sixteen. And so on, until the entire seventy-five boxes had been distributed among seven or eight students.

"Those guys worked hard selling the chocolates," Carter said, a silly smile on his face. "I want to make sure they get credit."

"Right," Brian said, not making waves. He knew, of course, that none of the fellows chosen by Carter had sold the chocolates. But that was not his business.

"How many guys reached the fifty quota today?" Carter asked.

Brian consulted his figures. "Six, counting Huart and LeBlanc. Those sales they just made put them over the top." Brian actually was able to keep a straight face.

"Know what, Cochran? You're a bright boy. You're cool. You catch on fast."

Fast? Hell, they'd been juggling the sales all week long and Brian hadn't caught on for two entire days. He was tempted now to ask Carter if the campaign had turned into a Vigils project—like one of Archie Costello's assignments—but decided to hold down his curiosity.

Before the afternoon had ended, the sale of four hundred and seventy-five boxes had been received—cold, cold cash—as the teams returned to school with horns blowing, high with the hilarity of success.

When Brother Leon arrived, they totaled the sales together and discovered that fifteen thousand and ten boxes of chocolates had been sold thus far. Only five thousand to go—or four thousand, nine hundred and ninety to be exact, as Brother Leon pointed out in that fussy meticulous way of his. But Leon wasn't a problem today. He, too, seemed giddy, high, his wet eyes sparkling with the success of the sale.

He actually called Brian by his first name.

When Brian went to the assembly hall to post the latest figures, a cheering bunch of fellows applauded as he made the entries. No one had ever applauded Brian Cochran before and he felt like a football hero, of all things.

30

HERE was no necessity for the chocolate roll call now because most of the students were bringing their returns directly to Brian Cochran in the office. But Brother Leon persisted anyway. The Goober noticed that the teacher now took a delight in the process, making a big deal of it. He read off the latest sales as reported to Brian Cochran, reciting them to the class in detail, lingering over the names and the totals, wringing as much drama and satisfaction out of the situation as possible. And he had stooges or frightened kids like David Caroni who sang out their reports in the classroom as Leon basked in the totals.

"Let's see, Hartnett," Leon said, shaking his head in pleased surprise. "The report says you sold fifteen boxes yesterday, bringing your total to forty-three. Wonderful!" And he'd glanced slyly at Jerry.

It was all ridiculous, of course, because Hartnett hadn't sold any chocolates at all. The sales had been made by the teams of fellows who went out every afternoon. The school had become chocolate crazy. But not Goober. As a show of sympathy to Jerry, he had decided to stop selling the chocolates altogether and his total had remained unchanged for the past week at twenty-seven. It was little enough to do.

"Mallan," Leon was calling out.

"Seven."

"Let me see now, Mallan. Why, that brings your total to forty-seven. Congratulations, Mallan. I'm sure you'll be selling those three remaining boxes today."

Goober shriveled in his seat. Next would be Parmentier. And then Jerry. He glanced toward Jerry, saw him sitting erect in his chair as if he was looking forward to having his name called.

"Parmentier."

"Seven."

"Parmentier, Parmentier," Leon marveled. "That makes your total, yes, by George, fifty! You've made the quota, Parmentier. Good boy, good boy! A round of cheers, gentlemen."

Goober faked his cheer—little enough.

The pause. And then Leon's voice sang out, "Renault!" That was the exact description—sang. His voice exultant, lyrical. Goober realized Leon didn't care now whether Jerry sold chocolates or not.

"No," Jerry answered, his own voice clear and forceful, ringing with a triumph of its own.

Maybe both of them could win. Maybe a showdown could be averted, after all. The sale was winding down. It could end in a stalemate and eventually be forgotten, absorbed by other school activities.

"Brother Leon."

All eyes turned to Harold Darcy who had spoken.

"Yes, Harold."

"May I ask a question?"

A frown of annoyance from the teacher. He'd been having such a great time that he resented the interruption.

"Yes, yes, Darcy."

"Would you ask Renault why he isn't selling the chocolates like everybody else?"

The sound of a car horn could be heard from two or three blocks away. Brother Leon's face was guarded. "Why do you want to know?" he asked.

"I figure it's my right to know. The right of everybody to know." He looked around for support. Somebody called out, "Right on." Darcy said, "Everybody else is doing his part, why isn't Renault?"

"Would you care to answer that, Renault?" the teacher said, the moist eyes flashing, the malice unmistakable.

Jerry paused, face flushed. "It's a free country," he said, words which touched off a ripple of laughter. Someone snickered. Brother Leon looked positively joyous and Goober felt nauseous.

"I'm afraid you'll have to be more original than that, Renault," Brother Leon said, playing to his audience, as usual.

Goober could see the color rising to Jerry's cheeks. He was also aware of a change in the class, a subtle alteration of mood and atmosphere. Until this particular roll call, the class had been neutral, indifferent toward Jerry's position, maintaining a live-and-let-live attitude. Today, however, the air was filled with resentment. More than resentment—hostility. Take Harold Darcy. Ordinarily he was a regular kid, minding his own business with no tinge of the crusader or fanatic about him. And suddenly here he was challenging Jerry.

"Did you say this sale was voluntary, Brother Leon?" Jerry asked.

"Yes," the teacher said, hanging back as if he were trying to fade into the background, letting Jerry betray himself with his own words.

"Then I don't feel that I have to sell the chocolates."

A ripple of resentment across the classroom.

"You think you're better than we are?" Darcy shot out.

162

"No."

"Then who do you think you are?" Phil Beauvais asked.

"I'm Jerry Renault and I'm not going to sell the chocolates."

Damn it, Goober thought. Why didn't he bend a little? Just a little.

The bell rang. For a moment, the boys sat there, waiting, knowing that the issue hadn't been settled, something ominous in the waiting. Then the moment broke and the boys began to push back their chairs, rising from the desks, shuffling as usual. No one looked at Jerry Renault. By the time Goober got to the door, Jerry was walking swiftly to his next class. A crowd of boys, Harold Darcy among them, stood sullenly in the corridor, watching Jerry's progress down the hallway.

Later that afternoon, The Goober wandered to the assembly hall, attracted by cheers and hoots. He stood in the rear of the hall, watching as Brian Cochran posted the latest returns. There were probably fifty or sixty guys in the place, unusual for that time of day. Every time Cochran wrote in new sales, the fellows burst forth in cheers, led by, of all people, big bruising Carter who probably hadn't sold any chocolates at all but had others do his dirty work.

Brian Cochran consulted a sheet of paper he held in his hand and then went to one of the three big boards. Beside the name Roland Goubert, he wrote down the number fifty.

For a moment, it didn't occur to The Goober who Roland Goubert was—he watched, fascinated, unbelieving. And then—hey, that's me!

"Goober sold his fifty boxes," someone called.

Cheers, applause and ear-splitting whistles.

The Goober started to step forward in protest. He had only sold twenty-seven boxes, damn it. He had stopped at

163

twenty-seven to show that he was supporting Jerry, even though nobody knew, not even Jerry. And now the whole thing evaporated and he found himself sinking back in the shadows, as if he could shrivel into invisibility. He didn't want trouble. He'd had enough trouble, and he had held on. But he knew his days at Trinity would be numbered if he walked into that group of jubilant guys and told them to erase the fifty beside his name.

Out in the corridor, The Goober's breath came fast. But otherwise he felt nothing. He willed himself to feel nothing. He didn't feel rotten. He didn't feel like a traitor. He didn't feel small and cowardly. And if he didn't feel all these things, then why was he crying all the way to his locker?

31

"**W**HAT's your hurry, kid?"

It was a familiar voice—the voice of all the bullies in the world, Harvey Cranch who used to wait for Jerry outside the third grade at St. John's, and Eddie Herman at summer camp who delighted in the small tortures he inflicted on the younger kids, and the complete stranger who knocked him down at the circus one summer and tore the ticket from his hand. That was the voice he heard now: the voice of all the bullies and troublemakers and wise guys in the world. Mocking, goading, cajoling and looking for trouble. *What's your hurry, kid?* The voice of the enemy.

Jerry looked at him. The kid stood before him in defiant posture, feet planted firmly on the ground, legs spread slightly apart, hands flat against the sides of his legs as if he wore two-gun holsters and was ready to draw, or as if he was a karate expert with hands waiting to chop and slice. Jerry didn't know a thing about karate, except in his wildest dreams when he demolished his foes without mercy.

"I asked you a question," the kid said.

Jerry recognized him now—a wise guy named Janza. A freshman-baiter, somebody to stay away from.

"I know you asked me a question," Jerry said, sighing. He knew what was coming.

"What question?"

And there it was. The taunt, the beginning of the old cat-and-mouse game.

"The question you asked me," Jerry countered but knowing the futility of it. It didn't matter what he said or how he said it. Janza was looking for an opening and he'd find it.

"And what was it?"

"You wanted to know what was my hurry."

Janza smiled, having won his point, gained his little victory. A smug superior smile spread across his face, a knowing smile, as if he knew all of Jerry's secrets, a lot of dirty things about him.

"Know what?" Janza asked.

Jerry waited.

"You look like a wise guy," Janza said.

Why did the wise guys always accuse other people of being wise guys?

"What makes you think I'm a wise guy?" Jerry asked, trying to stall, hoping someone would come along. He remembered how Mr. Phaneuf had rescued him once when Harvey Cranch had cornered him near the old man's barn. But there was nobody around now. The football practice had been miserable. He hadn't completed a pass and the Coach had finally dismissed him. *This ain't your day, Renault, take an early shower.* Turning away from the Coach, Jerry had seen the secret smirks, the quick smiles on the faces of the players and had realized the truth. They'd dropped his passes purposely, had refused to block. Now that Goober had quit the team, there was no one he could trust. More paranoia, he chided himself, trudging along the pathway that led from the football field to the gym. And had encountered Janza who should have been out there practicing but had been waiting for him.

166

"Why do I think you're a wise guy?" Janza asked now. "Because you put on a big act, kid. You try to get by with a sincerity act. But you're not kidding me. You live in the closet." Janza smiled, a knowing, this-is-just-between-us smile, intimate, creepy.

"What do you mean—closet?"

Janza laughed, delighted, and touched Jerry's cheek with his hand, a brief light touch, as if they were old friends engaged in friendly conversation on an October afternoon, leaves whirling around them like giant confetti as the wind rose. Jerry figured he knew the meaning of Janza's light tap—Janza was aching for action, contact, violence. And he was getting impatient. But he didn't want to start the fight himself. He wanted to provoke Jerry into beginning— that's the way bullies worked so they could be held blameless after the slaughter. *He started it*, they'd claim. Strangely enough, Jerry felt as though he could actually beat Janza in a fight. He could feel a gathering of outrage that promised strength and endurance. But he didn't want to fight. He didn't want to return to grammar school violence, the cherished honor of the schoolyard that wasn't honor at all, the necessity of proving yourself by bloody noses and black eyes and broken teeth. Mainly, he didn't want to fight for the same reason he wasn't selling the chocolates—he wanted to make his own decisions, do his own thing, like they said.

"This is what I mean by *closet*," Janza said, his hand flicking out again, touching Jerry's cheek, but lingering this time for the fraction of a second in faint caress. "That you're hiding in there."

"Hiding what? Hiding from who?"

"From everybody. From yourself, even. Hiding that deep dark secret."

"What secret?" Confused now.

167

"That you're a fairy. A queer. Living in the closet, hiding away."

Vomit threatened Jerry's throat, a nauseous geyser he could barely hold down.

"Hey, you're blushing," Janza said. "The fairy's blushing . . ."

"Listen . . ." Jerry began but not knowing, really, how to begin or where. The worst thing in the world—to be called queer.

"*You* listen," Janza said, cool now, knowing he had struck a vulnerable spot. "You're polluting Trinity. You won't sell the chocolates like everybody else and now we find out you're a fairy." He shook his head in mock, exaggerated admiration. "You're really something, know that? Trinity has tests and ways of weeding the homos out but you were smart enough to get by, weren't you? You must be creaming all over—wow, four hundred ripe young bodies to rub against . . ."

"I'm not a fairy," Jerry cried.

"Kiss me," Janza said, puckering his lips grotesquely.

"You son of a bitch," Jerry said.

The words hung on the air, verbal flags of battle. And Janza smiled, a radiant smile of triumph. This is what he'd wanted all along, of course. This had been the reason for the encounter, the insults.

"What did you call me?" Janza asked.

"A son of a bitch," Jerry said, measuring out the words, saying them deliberately, eager now for the fight.

Janza threw back his head and laughed. The laughter surprised Jerry—he'd expected retaliation. Instead, Janza stood there utterly relaxed, hands on his hips, amused.

And that was when Jerry saw them. Three or four of them emerging from bushes and shrubbery, running, crouched, keeping themselves low. They were small, pigmy-like, and they moved so swiftly toward him that he couldn't get a good look at them, saw only a smear of smiling faces, smiling evilly. More coming now, five or six others, slipping into view from behind a cluster of pine trees, and before Jerry could gird himself for a fight or even raise his arms in defense, they were swarming all over him, hitting him high and low, tumbling him to the ground as if he was some kind of helpless Gulliver. A dozen fists pummeled his body, fingernails tore at his cheek and a finger clawed at his eye. They wanted to blind him. They wanted to kill him. Pain arrowed in his groin—somebody had kicked him there. The blows rained upon him without mercy, with no let-up, and he tried to curl up and make himself small, hiding his face, but somebody was pounding his head furiously, *stop*, *stop*, another kick in his groin and he couldn't hold down the vomit now, it was coming and he tried to open his mouth to let it spray forth. As he threw up, they let him go, someone yelled "Jesus" in disgust and they withdrew. He could hear their gasps, their running feet receding although somebody stayed behind to kick him again, this time in his lower back, the final sheet of pain that drew a black curtain over his eyes.

32

SWEET, sweet in the dark, safe. Dark and safe and quiet. He dared not move. He was afraid that his body would come loose, all his bones spilling out like a building collapsing, like a picket fence clattering apart. A small sound reached his ears and he realized it was himself, crooning softly, as if he were singing himself a lullaby. Suddenly, he missed his mother. Her absence formed tears on his cheeks. He hadn't cried at all from the beating, had lain there on the ground for a few moments after the brief blackout, and then had dragged himself up and made it agonizingly to the locker room at school, walking as if on a tightrope and one misstep would send him hurtling into depths below: oblivion. He'd washed himself, cold water like liquid fingernails inflaming the scratches on his face. I won't sell their chocolates whether they beat me up or not. And I'm not a fairy, not a queer. He had stolen away from the school, not wanting anyone to witness his painful passage down the street to the bus stop. He kept his collar up, like a criminal, like those men in newscasts being herded into court. Funny, somebody does violence to you but you're the one who has to hide, as if you're the criminal. He shuffled to the back of the bus, grateful that it wasn't one of the crowded school buses but a maverick bus that appeared at odd hours. The bus was full of old people, old women with blue hair and big handbags and they pretended not to see him, sailing their eyes askew from him as he stalked to the rear of the bus, but their noses wrinkled as they caught the smell of vomit when he passed. Somehow, he'd made it home on the jolting bus, made it to this quiet room where he now sat, sun bleeding low in the sky and spurting its veins on the den window. Dusk moved in. After a while, he took a warm bath, soaking in the water. Then he sat in the dark, quiet, letting himself mend, not stirring, feeling a dull ache settle in his bones now that the first waves of pain had moved away. The clock struck six. He was glad that his father was on the evening shift, at work until eleven. He didn't want his father to see him with these fresh cuts on his face, the bruises. Make it to the bedroom, he urged himself, undress, curl into cool sheets, tell him I came home sick, must be a virus, twenty-four-hour flu, and keep my face hidden.

The telephone rang.

Oh no, he protested.

Let me alone.

The ringing continued, mocking him the way Janza had mocked him.

Let it be, let it be, like the Beatles sang.

Still ringing.

And he saw suddenly that he must answer. They didn't want him to answer this time. They wanted to think that he was incapacitated, injured, unable to make it to the phone.

Jerry lifted himself from the bed, surprised at his mobility, and made his way through the living room to the phone. Don't stop ringing now, he said, don't stop ringing. I want to show them.

"Hello." Forcing strength into his voice.

Silence.

"I'm here," he said, shouting the words.

Silence again. Then the lewd chuckle. And the dial tone.

"Jerry . . . oh Jerry . . ."

"Yoo hoo, Jerree . . ."

The apartment Jerry and his father occupied was three floors above street level and the voices calling Jerry's name reached him faintly, barely penetrating the closed windows. That distant quality also gave the voices a ghostly resonance, like someone calling from the grave. In fact, he hadn't been certain at first that his name was being called. Slouched at the kitchen table, forcing himself to sip Campbell's Chicken Broth, he heard the voices and thought they were the sound of kids playing in the street. Then he heard distinctly—

"Hey, Jerry . . ."

"Whatcha doing, Jerry?"

"Come on out and play, Jerry."

Ghostly voices from the past recalling when he was a little boy and the kids in the neighborhood came to the back door after supper calling him to go out and play. That was in the sweet time when he and his parents lived together in the house with the big backyard and a front lawn his father never got tired of mowing and watering.

"Hey, Jerry . . ."

But these voices calling now were not friendly after-supper voices but nighttime voices, taunting and teasing and threatening.

Jerry went into the living room and looked down cautiously, careful not to be seen. The street was deserted except for a couple of parked cars. And still the voices sang.

"Jerree . . ."

"Come out and play, Jerry . . ."

A parody of those long ago childhood pleadings.

Peering out again, Jerry saw a shooting star in reverse. It split the darkness and he heard the dull plunk as a stone, not a star at all, hit the wall of the building near the window.

"Yoo hoo, Jerree . . ."

He squinted at the street below but the boys were well hidden. Then he saw a spray of light sweeping the trees and shrubs across the street. A pale face flared in the darkness as the ray of a flashlight caught and held it for a moment. The face disappeared in the night. Jerry recognized the plodding gait of the building custodian who evidently had been drawn out of his basement apartment by the voices. His flashlight swept the street.

"Who's there?" he shouted. "I'm gonna get the police . . ."

"Bye, bye, Jerry," a voice called.

"See you later, Jerry." Fading into the dark.

The telephone ruptured the night. Jerry groped upward from sleep, reaching for the sound. Instantly awake, he glanced at the alarm clock's luminous face. Two-thirty.

Painfully, his muscles and bones protesting, he lifted himself from the mattress and poised, on one elbow, to thrust himself from the bed.

The ringing persisted, ridiculously loud in the stillness of night. Jerry's feet touched the floor and he padded toward the sound.

But his father was already at the phone. He glanced toward Jerry and Jerry drew back into the shadows, keeping his face hidden.

"Madmen loose in the world," his father muttered, standing there with his hand on the phone. "If you let it ring, they get their kicks. If you answer, they hang up and still get their kicks. And then start all over again."

173

The harassment had taken toll on his father's face, his hair disheveled, purple crescents under his eyes.

"Take the phone off the hook, Dad."

His father sighed, nodded assent. "That's giving in to them, Jerry. But what the hell. Who are *them*, anyway?" His father lifted the receiver, holding it to his ear for a moment, then turned to Jerry. "The same thing, that crazy laugh and then the dial tone." He placed the receiver on the table. "I'll report it to the telephone company in the morning." Peering in at Jerry, he said, "You okay, Jerry?"

"Fine. I'm just fine, Dad."

His father rubbed his eyes, wearily.

"Get some sleep, Jerry. A football player needs his sleep." Trying to keep it light.

"Right, Dad."

Compassion for his father welled in Jerry. Should he tell his father what it was all about? But he didn't want to involve him. His father had given in, taken the receiver off the hook, and that was defeat enough. He didn't want him to risk more.

In bed once more, small in the dark, Jerry willed his body to loosen, to relax. After a while, sleep plucked at him with soft fingers, soothing away the ache. But the phone rang in his dreams all night long.

33

"J ANZA, can't you do anything right?"

"What the hell are you talking about? By the time we got through with him, he'd been willing to sell a million boxes of chocolates."

"I mean those kids. I didn't tell you to make it a gang bang."

"That was a stroke of genius, Archie. That's what I thought it was. Let him get beat up by a bunch of kids. Psychological—isn't that what you're always talking about?"

"Where'd you get them? I don't want outsiders involved in this."

"Some animals from my neighborhood. They'd beat up their own grandmothers for a quarter."

"Did you use the queer pitch on him?"

"You were right, Archie. You called it beautiful. That really spaced him out. Hey, Archie, he isn't queer, is he?"

"Of course not. That's why he blew up. If you want to get under a guy's skin, accuse him of being something he isn't. Otherwise, you're only telling him something he knows."

The silence on the phone indicated Emile's appreciation of Archie's genius.

"What's next, Archie?"

"Let's cool it, Emile. I want to keep you in reserve. We've got some other stuff going now."

"I was just starting to enjoy myself."

"You'll have other chances, Emile."

"Hey, Archie."

"Yes, Emile."

"How about the picture?"

"Suppose I told you there was no picture, Emile? That there was no film in the camera that day . . ."

Wow, that Archie. Full of surprises. But was he kidding around? Or telling the truth?

"I don't know, Archie."

"Emile, stick with me. All the way. And you can't go wrong. We need men like you."

Emile swelled with pride. Was Archie talking about The Vigils? And was there really no photograph after all? What a relief that would be!

"You can count on me, Archie."

"I know that, Emile."

But after he'd hung up, Emile thought: Archie, that bastard.

34

SUDDENLY, he was invisible, without body, without structure, a ghost passing transparently through the hours. He'd made the discovery on the bus going to school. Eyes avoiding his. Looking away. Kids giving him wide berth. Ignoring him, as if he wasn't there. And he realized that he really wasn't there, as far as they were concerned. It was as if he were the carrier of a terrible disease and nobody wanted to become contaminated. And so they rendered him invisible, eliminating him from their presence. All the way to school he sat alone, his wounded cheek pressed against the cool glass of the window.

The chill of morning hurried him up the walk to the school entrance. He spotted Tony Santucci. Purely from instinct, Jerry nodded hello. Tony's face was usually a mirror, reflecting back whatever greeted him—a smile for a smile, a frown for a frown. But now he stared at Jerry. Not really stared. Actually, he wasn't looking at Jerry but *through* him as if Jerry were a window, a doorway. And then Tony Santucci fled the scene, into the school.

Jerry's progress through the corridor was like the parting of the Red Sea. Nobody brushed against him. Guys stepped out of his path, giving him passage, as if reacting to some secret signal. Jerry felt as though he could walk through a wall and emerge untouched on the other side.

He opened his locker—the mess was gone. The desecrated poster had been removed and the wall scrubbed clean. The sneakers were gone. The locker had an air of absence, of being unoccupied. He thought, maybe I should look in a mirror, see if I'm still here. But he was still here, all right. His cheek still stung with pain. Staring at the inside of the locker, like looking into an upright coffin, he felt as though someone was trying to obliterate him, remove all traces of his existence, his presence in the school. Or was he becoming paranoid?

In the classrooms, the teachers also seemed to be part of the conspiracy. They let their eyes slide over him, looking elsewhere when Jerry tried to catch their attention. Once, he waved his hand frantically to answer a question but the teacher ignored him. And yet it was hard to tell about teachers—they were mysterious, they could sense when something unusual was going on. Like today. The kids are giving Renault the freeze so let's go along with it.

Resigning himself to the freeze, Jerry drifted through the day. After a while, he began to enjoy his invisibility. He was able to relax. There was no longer any need to be on his guard, or afraid of being attacked. He was tired of being afraid, tired of being intimidated.

Between classes, Jerry searched for The Goober but didn't find him. Goober would have established reality once again, planted Jerry solidly in the world once more. But Goober was absent from school and Jerry figured it was just as well. He didn't want anybody else getting involved in his trouble. It was enough that the phone calls had involved his father. He thought of his father standing at the phone last night, haunted by the persistent ringing, and he thought,

I should have sold the chocolates, after all. He didn't want his father's universe to be disturbed and he wanted his own to be put in order again.

After the last class that morning, Jerry walked freely down the corridor, headed for the cafeteria, swinging along with the crowd, enjoying his absence of identity. Approaching the stairs, he felt himself pushed from behind and he pitched forward, off balance. He began to fall, the stairs slanting dangerously before him. Somehow, he managed to grab the railing. He held on, pressing his body against the wall. As the stream of guys thudded past, he heard someone snicker, someone else hiss.

He knew he wasn't invisible any longer.

Brother Leon entered the office at the moment Brian Cochran finished his final tabulation. The end. The last total of them all. He looked up at the teacher, delighted with the timing of his arrival.

"Brother Leon, it's all over," Brian announced, triumph in his voice.

The teacher blinked rapidly, his face like a cash register that wasn't working. "Over?"

"The sale." Brian slapped down the sheet of paper. "Finished. Done with."

Brian watched the information sinking in. Leon took a deep breath and lowered himself into his chair. For an instant, Brian observed relief sweeping the teacher's face, as if a huge burden had been lifted from him. But it was only a brief glimpse. He looked at Brian sharply. "Are you sure?" he asked.

"Positive. And listen, Brother Leon. The money—it's amazing. Ninety-eight percent has been turned in."

Leon stood up. "Let's check the figures," he said.

Anger surged through Brian. Couldn't the teacher let

down for one minute? Couldn't he say "good job?" or "thank God?" Or something? Instead, "Let's check the figures."

Leon's rancid breath—didn't he ever eat anything else but bacon, for crissakes—filled the air as he stood beside Brian looking over the tabulations.

"There's only one thing," Brian said, hesitating to bring the subject up.

Leon caught the boy's doubt. "What's the matter?" he asked, more angry than curious, as if he anticipated an error on Brian's part.

"It's the freshman, Brother Leon."

"Renault? What about him?"

"Well, he still hasn't sold his chocolates. And it's weird, really weird."

"What's so weird about it, Cochran? The boy's obviously a misfit. He tried in his small ineffectual way to damage the sale and he succeeded in doing the opposite. The school rallied against him."

"But it's still weird. Our sales total comes to exactly nineteen thousand, nine hundred fifty boxes. Right on the nose. And that's practically impossible. I mean, there's always some spoilage, some boxes get lost or stolen. It's impossible to account for every single box. But this comes out right on the dot. With exactly fifty boxes missing— Renault's fifty."

"If Renault didn't sell them, then obviously they are not sold. And that's why there are fifty missing boxes," Leon said, his voice slow and reasonable, as if Brian were five years old.

Brian realized that Brother Leon didn't want to see the truth. He was only interested in the results of the sale, knowing that his previous nineteen thousand, nine hundred fifty boxes had been sold and he was off the hook. He'd probably be promoted, become Headmaster. Brian was glad he wouldn't be here next year, particularly if Leon became permanent Headmaster.

"You see what's important here, Cochran?" Leon asked, assuming his classroom voice. "School spirit. We have disproven a law of nature—one rotten apple does not spoil the barrel. Not if we have determination, a noble cause, a spirit of brotherhood . . ."

Brian sighed, looking down at his fingers, tuning Leon out, letting the words fall meaninglessly on his ears. He thought of Renault, that strange stubborn kid. Was Leon right, after all? That the school was more important than any one kid? But weren't individuals important, too? He thought of Renault standing alone against the school, The Vigils, everybody.

Ah, the hell with it, Brian thought as Leon's voice droned on sanctimoniously. The sale was over and his job as treasurer was over. He wouldn't be involved with Leon or Archie or even Renault anymore. Thank God for little favors.

"You got the fifty boxes set aside, Obie?"

"Yes, Archie."

"Beautiful."

"What's it all about, Archie?"

"We're having an assembly, Obie. Tomorrow night. A special assembly. To report on the chocolate sale. At the athletic field."

"Why the athletic field, Archie? Why not the school?"

"Because this assembly is strictly for the student body, Obie. The brothers are not involved. But everybody else will be there."

"Everybody?"

"Everybody."

"Renault?"

"He'll be there, Obie, he'll be there."

"You're really something else, Archie, you know that?"

"I know that, Obie."

"Pardon me for asking, Archie . . ."

"Ask away, Obie."

"What do you want Renault there for?"

"To give him a chance. A chance to get rid of his chocolates, old buddy."

"I'm not your old buddy, Archie."

"I know that, Obie."

"And how's Renault going to get rid of his chocolates, Archie?"

"He's going to raffle them off."

"A raffle?"

"A raffle, Obie."

35

A raffle, for crying out loud.

But what a raffle!

A raffle like no other in Trinity's history, in any school's history.

Archie, the architect of the event, watched the proceedings—the stadium filling up, the kids streaming in, the slips of paper being sold, passed back and forth, the lights dispelling some of the cool of the autumn evening. He stood near the improvised stage that Carter and The Vigils had erected that afternoon under Archie's direction—an old boxing ring resurrected from the bowels of the bleachers and restored to its former use except for the absence of ropes. The platform stood directly at the fifty-yard line close to the stands so that each kid would see everything and wouldn't miss any of the action. That was Archie. Give them their money's worth.

The athletic field was at least a quarter of a mile from the school and the residence where the brothers lived. But Archie had taken no chances. He had disguised the event as a football rally, strictly for students, without the inhibition of the teachers being present. They had arranged for the sweet-faced kid, Caroni, to ask for permission—Caroni who looked like a choir boy. What teacher could refuse him?

And now the moment was at hand, the kids arriving, the air crisp and cool, excitement shivering through the crowd—and Renault and Janza there in the ring, glancing uneasily at each other.

Archie always marveled at things like this, things he had arranged and manipulated. For instance, all these guys tonight would be doing something else except for Archie who had been able to alter their actions. And all it took was a little bit of Archie's imagination and two phone calls.

The first call had been to Renault, the second to Janza. But Janza's call had been simply routine. Archie knew he could shape Janza's actions the way he could shape a piece of clay. But the call to Renault had required the right moves, resourcefulness and a little touch of Archie in the night. Shakespeare yet, Archie chuckled.

The phone must have rung, oh, fifty times and Archie hadn't blamed the kid for not rushing to lift the receiver. But persistence paid off and finally there was Renault on the line, the quiet *hello*, the calm voice but something else, something else. Archie had detected another quality in the voice—a deadly calm, determination. Beautiful. The kid was ready. Archie had soared with triumph. The kid wanted to come out and fight. He wanted action.

"Want to get even, Renault?" Archie goaded. "Strike back? Get revenge? Show them what you think of their goddam chocolates?"

"How do I do that?" The voice was guarded but interested. Definitely interested.

"Easy, easy," Archie responded, "if you're not chicken, that is." The needle, always the needle.

Renault was silent.

"There's a guy named Janza. He's really a rotten kid, no class at all. He's not much more than an animal. And word has gotten around that he needed the help of a bunch of

184

kids to make you fall in line. So I figure we ought to settle the matter. At an assembly at the athletic field. Boxing gloves. Everything under control. Here's a way to get even with everybody, Renault."

"With you too, Archie?"

"Me?" The voice innocent and sweet. "Hell, why me? I was only carrying out my job. I gave you an assignment—don't sell the chocolates—and then I gave you another—sell them. You did the rest, kid. I didn't beat you up. I don't believe in violence. But you touched off the fireworks . . ."

Silence on the line again. Archie pressed on, softening his voice, cajoling, leading him on. "Look, kid, I'm giving you this choice because I believe in fair play. Here's a chance to end it all and get on with other things. Christ, there's more to life than a lousy chocolate sale. You and Janza alone in the ring, facing each other fair and square. And that's it, finished, the end, all done. I guarantee it. Archie guarantees it."

And the kid had fallen for it, hook, line and sinker, although the conversation had gone back and forth for a while. Archie had been patient. Patience always paid off. And he had won, of course.

Now, surveying his handiwork, the crowded bleachers, the frantic comings and goings as the raffle tickets were bought and sold and the directions scrawled on the tickets, Archie exulted quietly. He had successfully conned Renault and Leon and The Vigils and the whole damn school. I can con anybody. I am Archie.

Pretend you're a spotlight, Obie told himself, a spotlight sweeping the place, stopping here and there, and lingering at other places, picking up the highlights of the thing, this momentous occasion. Because, let's admit it, this *is* an important event and Archie, that bastard, that clever clever bastard, has done it again. Look at him down there near the fight ring, like he's king of all he surveys. And he is, of course. He's got Renault there, pale and tense as if he's facing a firing squad, and Janza, the animal, a chained animal waiting to spring loose.

Obie, the spotlight, concentrated on Renault. Poor dumb doomed kid. He can't win and he doesn't know it. Not from Archie. Nobody wins from Archie. Archie, who'd been going down to defeat—what a great scene that had been, the last Vigils meeting when he'd stood there humiliated—but now he was on top again, all the chocolates sold, in charge once more, the entire school in the palm of his hand. All of which proves that the meek don't inherit the earth. Not very original. Archie must have said it at one time or another.

Don't move. Not a muscle. Just wait. Wait it out, wait and see.

Jerry's left leg had fallen asleep.

How can your leg fall asleep when you're standing up?

I don't know. But it's asleep.

Nerves, maybe. Tension.

At any rate, small darts stung his legs and he had to fight to keep from moving. He didn't dare move, afraid he would fall apart if he moved.

He knew now that it had been a mistake coming here, that Archie had faked him out, tricked him. For a few moments while Archie's voice whispered enticingly of sweet revenge, suggesting the fight as a way of ending it all, Jerry had actually believed it was possible, possible to beat Janza and the school and even Archie. He had thought of his father and the terrible look of defeat when he had listened on the phone the other night and finally placed the receiver on the table, giving up. I'm not giving up, Jerry had pledged, listening to Archie's goading voice. He also ached for a chance to confront Janza. Janza who had called him a fairy.

So, he had agreed to meet Janza in a fight and already Archie had doublecrossed him. Had doublecrossed Janza as well. He'd allowed them to be led onto the platform, stripped to the waist, shivering slightly in the evening air, given boxing gloves. And then Archie, his eyes sparkling with triumph and malice, had explained the rules. Those rules!

Jerry had been about to protest when Janza opened his mouth. "It's okay with me. I can beat this kid any way you want."

And Jerry saw, to his dismay, that Archie had counted on Janza's reaction, had counted on the guys filing into the stadium. He had known that Jerry couldn't back away now—he had come too far. Archie had bestowed one of his sickly sweet smiles on Jerry. "What do you say, Renault? Do you accept the rules?"

What could he say? After the phone calls and the beating. After the desecration of his locker. The silent treatment. Pushed downstairs. What they did to Goober, to Brother Eugene. What guys like Archie and Janza did to the school. What they would do to the world when they left Trinity.

Jerry tightened his body in determination. At least this was his chance to strike back, to hit out. Despite the odds Archie had set up with the raffle tickets.

"Okay," Jerry had said.

Now, standing here, one leg half asleep, nausea threatening his stomach, the night chilling his flesh, Jerry wondered if he hadn't lost the moment he had said *okay*.

The raffle tickets were selling like dirty pictures.

Brian Cochran was amazed but he shouldn't have been—he was getting used to being amazed where Archie Costello was concerned. First the chocolate sale. And now

187

this—this wacky raffle. Never anything like it at Trinity. Or anywhere. And he had to admit that he was kind of enjoying himself even though he had protested when Archie approached him this afternoon, asking him to take charge of the raffle. "You did great with the chocolates," Archie said. The compliment melted Brian's opposition. Besides, he was scared stiff of Archie and The Vigils. Personal survival, that's what Brian believed in.

He had been seized by doubt again when Archie explained how the fight and the raffle would work. How are you going to get Renault and Janza to do it? That's what Brian wanted to know. Easy, Archie assured him. Renault's looking for revenge and Janza's a beast. And they can't back down with the whole school looking on. Then Archie's voice had gone cold again and Brian had shriveled inside. "You just do your job, Cochran, sell the tickets. And leave the details to me." So Brian had lined up a bunch of kids to do the selling. And Archie had been right, of course, because there they were, Renault and Janza up there on the platform, and the tickets were selling like there was no tomorrow.

Emile Janza was tired of being treated like one of the bad guys. That's the way Archie made him feel. "Hey, animal," Archie would say. Emile wasn't an animal. He had feelings like everybody else. Like the guy in the Shakespeare thing in English I, "Cut me, do I not bleed?" All right, so he liked to screw around a little, get under people's skin. That was human nature, wasn't it? A guy had to protect himself at all times. Get them before they get you. Keep people guessing—and afraid. Like Archie with his rotten picture that didn't even exist. Archie had convinced him that there was no picture, after all. How could there be a picture, Emile, Archie'd reasoned. Remember how dim it was in the john that day? And I didn't have a flash. And there wasn't any film in the camera. And if there had been, I didn't have time to focus. The truth had both relieved Emile and made him mad as hell. But Archie had pointed out that Emile should be mad at people like Renault. Hell, Emile, guys like Renault are your enemy, not guys like me. They're the squares, Emile, they're the ones who screw it up for us, who blow the whistle, who make the rules. Then Archie had provided the climax, the door-slammer—besides, the guys are starting to talk about how Renault was beaten up, how you needed the help of others and couldn't do it yourself . . .

Emile looked across the stage at Renault. He longed for combat. To prove himself in front of the whole school. The hell with that psychology crap Archie had made him use— telling Renault he was a fairy. He should have used his fists, not his mouth.

He was impatient to get started. To wreck Renault in front of everybody, no matter what was written down on the raffle tickets.

And in a corner of his mind, there still lurked the doubt— did Archie have that picture of him in the john, after all?

36

THOSE raffle tickets.

Wow! Terrific!

Archie hadn't seen any that had been filled out yet and he stopped one of the guys who'd been recruited as a salesman by Brian Cochran.

"Let's see," Archie said, holding out his hand.

The kid was quick to comply and Archie was pleased at his submissiveness. I am Archie. My wish becomes command.

The sound of the restless audience in his ears, Archie scrutinized the paper. Scrawled there, the words

Janza
Right To Jaw
Jimmy Demers

That was the simple, stunning beauty of the raffle, the unexpected twist that Archie Costello was famous for, what they always knew Archie could do—top himself. In one stroke, Archie had forced Renault to show up here, to become part of the chocolate sale, and he also placed Renault at the mercy of the school, the students. The fighters on the platform would have no will of their own.

They would have to fight the way the guys in the bleachers directed them. Everybody who bought a ticket—and who could refuse?—had a chance to be involved in the fight, to watch two guys battering each other while they were at a safe distance, with no danger of getting hurt. The risky part had been getting Renault here tonight. Once he was on the platform Archie knew he could not refuse to go on, even when he heard about the tickets. And that's the way it worked out. Beautiful.

Carter approached. "They're really selling, Archie," he said. Carter appreciated the fight concept. He loved boxing. He had, in fact, bought two tickets and had gotten a kick out of deciding which blows he would call for. He'd finally decided on a right cross to the jaw and an uppercut. At the last moment, he'd almost assigned the blows to Renault— give the kid a break. But Obie was standing nearby, Obie who stuck his nose in everybody else's business. So Carter had written in Janza's name. Janza, the beast, always ready to jump when Archie said jump.

"Looks like a beautiful night," Archie said now, smugly, that know-it-all attitude Carter hated. "You see, Carter, I told you everybody was pushing panic buttons for nothing."

"I don't know how you do it, Archie," Carter was forced to admit.

"Simple, Carter, simple." Archie reveled in the moment, basking in Carter's admiration, Carter who had humiliated him at The Vigils meeting. Someday he'd get even with Carter but at the moment it was satisfying enough to have Carter regarding him with awe and envy. "You see, Carter, people are two things: greedy and cruel. So we have a perfect set-up here. The greed part—a kid pays a buck for a chance to win a hundred. Plus fifty boxes of chocolates. The cruel part—watching two guys hitting each other, maybe hurting each other, while they're safe in the bleachers. That's why it works, Carter, because we're all bastards."

Carter disguised his disgust. Archie repelled him in many ways but most of all by the way he made everybody feel dirty, contaminated, polluted. As if there was no goodness at all in the world. And yet Carter had to admit that he was looking forward to the fight, that he himself had bought not one but two tickets. Did that make him like everybody else—greedy and cruel, as Archie said? The question surprised him. Hell, he'd always thought of himself as one of the good guys. He had often used his position as president of The Vigils to keep control of Archie, to prevent him from going overboard on assignments. But did that make him one of the good guys? The question bothered Carter. That's what he hated about Archie. He made you feel guilty all the time. Christ, the world couldn't be as bad as Archie said it was. But hearing the shouts of the kids in the bleachers, impatient for the fight to get underway, Carter wondered.

Archie watched Carter drift away, looking troubled and perplexed. Great. Burning with jealousy. And who wouldn't be jealous of someone like Archie who always came out on top?

Cochran reported. "All sold out, Archie."

Archie nodded, assuming the role of the silent hero.

The moment was here.

Archie lifted his head toward the bleachers and it seemed to be some kind of signal. A ripple went through the crowd, a quickening of tempo, a sweep of suspense. All eyes were directed to the platform where Renault and Janza stood at diagonal corners.

In front of the platform stood a pyramid of chocolates— the last fifty boxes. The stadium lights burned bright.

Carter, gavel in hand, walked to the center of the

192

platform. There was nothing to bang the gavel on so he simply raised it in the air.

The audience responded with applause, impatient shoutings, catcalls. "Let's go," someone yelled.

Carter gestured for silence.

But the silence had already fallen.

Archie, walking toward the platform for a close view of the proceedings, sucked in his breath, as if he were sipping this sweetest of all events. But he exhaled in surprise and stopped in his tracks as he saw Obie walk on the platform carrying the black box in his hands.

Obie smiled maliciously when he caught Archie standing there in surprise, his mouth wide open in astonishment. No one ever surprised the great Archie that way, and Obie's moment of triumph was a thing of beauty. He nodded toward Carter who was on his way to escort Archie to the platform.

Carter had been doubtful about using the black box, pointing out that this was not a Vigils meeting. How can we make Archie try for the marbles?

Obie had the answer, the kind of answer Archie himself would have given. "Because there are four hundred kids out there yelling for blood. And they don't care whose blood it is anymore. Everybody in the school knows about the black box—how can Archie back down?"

Carter pointed out that there was no guarantee that Archie would pull out the black marble. The black would mean he'd have to take on the position of one of the fighters. But there were five white marbles and only one black marble in the box. Archie's luck had held up throughout his career as the assigner—he had never drawn the black one.

"The law of averages," Obie had said to Carter. "He's

going to have to draw two marbles—one for Renault, the other for Janza."

Carter had gazed steadily at Obie. "We couldn't . . . ?" His voice curled into a question mark.

"We can't fix it, no way. Where could I find six black marbles, for crying out loud? Anyway, Archie is too smart—we could never con him. But we can throw one hell of a scare into him. And who knows? Maybe his luck has run out."

Thus, the agreement. Obie would emerge with the black box at the moment before the drawings and the fight began. And that's exactly what he was doing now, crossing to the center of the platform as Carter went down to meet Archie.

"You guys are really something else, aren't you?" Archie said, pulling away from Carter's grip. "I can walk up there alone, Carter. And I'll walk back again, too."

Archie's fury was a cold hard ball in his chest but he played it cool. As usual. He had a feeling nothing could go wrong. I am Archie.

The sight of the black box stunned the gathering into a silence more deep than before. Only members of The Vigils and their victims had seen it. In the garish stadium light, the box was revealed as worn and threadbare, a small wooden container that might have been a discarded jewelry box. And yet it was a legend in the school. For potential victims, it was possible deliverance, protection, a weapon to be used against the might of The Vigils. Others doubted its existence: Archie Costello would never allow that sort of thing. But here was the black box now. Out in the open. In front of the whole frigging school. And Archie Costello looking at it, reaching out his hand to draw the marble.

The ceremony took only a minute or so because Archie insisted on getting it over quickly before anyone knew what was going on. The less drama, the better. Don't let Obie and Carter build it up. Thus, before any protest could be made, Archie had shot his hand out and pulled a marble from the box. White. Obie's jaw dropped in surprise. Things were moving too fast. He'd wanted Archie to squirm; he'd wanted the audience to realize what was going on here. He'd wanted to prolong the ceremony, get as much of the drama and suspense out of the situation as possible.

Archie's hand shot out again and it was too late for Obie to prevent the action. He drew in his breath.

The marble was hidden in Archie's closed fist. He held the fist out, toward the audience. Archie held his back stiff. The marble had to be white. He hadn't come this far to be denied at the last moment. He let a smile play over his lips as he faced the audience, gambling everything in his show of confidence.

He opened his palm and held up the marble for all to see.

White.

37

THE Goober arrived at the last moment and made his way through the turmoil to the top of the bleachers. He'd been reluctant to come. He had washed his hands of the school and its cruelties and hadn't wanted to witness Jerry's daily humiliations. The school also reminded him of his own betrayals and defections. For three days, he'd been home in bed. Sick. He wasn't at all sure whether he'd really been sick or whether his conscience had revolted, infecting his body, leaving him weak and nauseous. At any rate, the bed had become his private world, a small safe place without people, without The Vigils, without Brother Leon, a world with no chocolates to sell, no rooms to destroy, no people to destroy. But one of the guys called up and told him about the fight between Jerry and Janza. And how the raffle tickets would control the fight. The Goober had moaned in protest. The bed had become unbearable. He had tossed and turned all day, prowling the bed like an animal seeking sleep, oblivion. He didn't want to go to the fight—Jerry couldn't possibly win. But he couldn't stay in bed, either. Finally, desperate, he had gotten out of bed, and dressed hurriedly, ignoring the protests of his parents. He had taken the bus across town and walked half a mile to the stadium. Now, he huddled in the seat, looking down at the platform, listening to Carter explaining the rules of the crazy fight. Terrible.

"... and the kid whose written blow is the one that ends the fight, either by knockout or surrender, receives the prize ..."

But the crowd was impatient for the action to begin. Goober looked around. These fellows in the stands were known to him, they were classmates, but suddenly they'd become strangers. They stared feverishly down at the platform. Some of them were yelling. "Kill 'em, kill 'em ..." The Goober shivered in the night.

Carter advanced to the center of the platform where Obie held a cardboard carton. Carter reached in and pulled out a piece of paper. "John Tussier," he called. "He's written down Renault's name." Murmurs of disappointment, a few scattered boos. "He wants Renault to hit Janza with a right to the jaw."

Silence fell. The moment of truth. Renault and Janza faced each other, an arm's reach away. They had been standing in the traditional pose of fighters, gloves raised, ready for battle but a pathetic parody of professional fighters. Now, Janza followed the rules. He lowered his arms, prepared to take Jerry's blow without resistance.

Jerry hunched his shoulders, cocked his fist. He had been waiting for this moment, ever since Archie's voice had taunted him on the telephone. But he hesitated now. How could he hit anyone, even an animal like Janza, in cold blood? I'm not a fighter, he protested silently. Then think of how Janza let those kids beat you up.

The crowd was restless. "Action, action," someone called. And the cry was taken up by others.

"What's the matter, fairy?" Janza taunted. "Afraid you might hurt your little hand hitting great big Emile?"

Jerry sent his fist sailing toward Janza's jaw, but he had

swung too quickly, without sufficient aim. The blow almost missed its target, finally brushing Janza's jaw ineffectually. Janza grinned.

Boos filled the air. "Fix," someone called.

Carter motioned to Obie to bring the box out quickly. He sensed the impatience of the crowd. They had paid their money and they wanted action. He hoped Janza's name would be on this slip. And it was. A kid named Marty Heller had ordered Janza to hit Renault with a right uppercut to the jaw. Carter sang out the command.

Jerry planted himself, like a tree.

Janza got ready, insulted by the cries of *fix*. Just because Renault was chicken. I'm not chicken, I'll show them. He had to prove that this was a genuine contest. If Renault wouldn't fight, then at least Emile Janza would.

He struck Jerry with all the force he could summon, the impact of the blow coming from his feet, up through his legs and thighs, the trunk of his body, the power pulsing through his body like some elemental force until it erupted through his arm, exploding into his fist.

Jerry had girded himself for the blow but it took him by surprise with its savagery and viciousness. The entire planet was jarred for a moment, the stadium swaying, the lights dancing. The pain in his neck was excruciating—his head had snapped back from the impact of Janza's fist. Sent reeling backward, he fought to stay on his feet and he somehow managed not to fall. His jaw was on fire, he tasted acid. Blood, maybe. But he pressed his lips together. He shook his head, quick vision-clearing shakings and established himself in the world once more.

Before he could gather himself together again, Carter's voice cried out, "*Janza, right to the stomach*," and Janza struck without warning, a short sharp blow that missed Jerry's stomach but caught him in the chest. His breath

198

went away, like it did in football, and then came back again. But the blow had lacked the power of the uppercut. He crouched again, fists erect, waiting for the next instructions. Dimly, he heard the crowd both cheering and booing but he concentrated on Janza, who stood before him, that idiot smile on his face.

The next raffle ticket gave Jerry his chance to strike back at Janza. A kid Jerry had never heard of—someone named Arthur Robilard—called for a right cross. Whatever that was. Jerry had only a vague idea but he wanted to hit Janza now, to repay him for that first vicious blow. He cocked his right arm. He tasted bile in his mouth. He let his arm go. The glove struck Janza full face and Janza staggered back. The result surprised Jerry. He had never struck anyone like that before, in fury, premeditated, and he'd enjoyed catapulting all his power toward the target, the release of all his frustrations, hitting back at last, lashing out, getting revenge finally, revenge not only against Janza but all that he represented.

Janza's eyes leaped with surprise at the strength behind Jerry's blow. His immediate reaction was to counterpunch but he held himself in control.

Carter's voice. "Janza. Left uppercut."

Again, the quick jolting neck-snapping pain as Janza, without pause or preparation, struck out. Jerry back-pedaled weakly. Why should his knees give way when the blow struck his jaw?

The guys were shouting from the bleachers for more action now. The noise chilled Jerry. "Action, action," came the shouts from the audience.

That was when Carter made the mistake. He took the slip of paper Obie handed him and read the instructions without pausing. "Janza, low blow to the groin." As soon as the words were out of his mouth, Carter realized his error.

They hadn't warned the crowd about illegal punches—and there was always a wise guy out there ready to pull a fast one.

At the words, Janza aimed for Jerry's pelvic area. Jerry saw the fist coming. He raised his fists and looked toward Carter, sensing that something was wrong. Janza's fist sank into his lower stomach but Jerry had deflected part of the force of the blow.

The crowd didn't understand what had happened. Most of them hadn't heard the illegal instruction. They only saw that Jerry had tried to defend himself, and that was against the rules. "Kill 'im, Janza," a voice cried from the crowd.

Janza, too, was puzzled, but only for a moment. Hell, he'd followed instructions and here was Renault, the chicken, breaking the rules. The hell with the rules, then. Janza let his fists fly in a flurry of violence, hitting Renault almost at will, on the head, the cheeks, once in the stomach. Carter withdrew to the far side of the platform. Obie had fled the scene, sensing disaster. Where the hell was Archie? Carter couldn't see him.

Jerry did his best to build defenses against Janza's fists but it was impossible. Janza was too strong and too fast, all instinct, sensing a kill. Finally, Jerry covered his head and face with the gloves, letting the blows rain on him, but waiting, waiting. The crowd was in a turmoil now, shouting, jeering, urging Janza on.

One more shot at Janza, that's what Jerry wanted. Crouching, absorbing the attack, Jerry waited. There was something wrong with his jaw, the pain was intense, but he didn't care if he could hit Janza again, renew that earlier beautiful punch. He was being hit everywhere now and the crowd noises leaped to life as if someone had turned up the volume on a monstrous stereo.

Emile was getting tired. The kid wouldn't go down. He

drew back his arm, pausing a moment, seeking true aim, wanting to come up with the final devastating blow. And that was when Jerry saw his opening. Through the pain and his nausea, he saw Janza's chest and stomach unprotected. He swung—and it was beautiful again. The full force of all his strength and determination and revenge caught Janza unguarded, off balance. Janza staggered backward, surprise and pain rampant on his face.

Triumphantly, he watched Janza floundering on weak, wobbly knees. Jerry turned toward the crowd, seeking— what? Applause? They were booing. Booing him. Shaking his head, trying to reassemble himself, squinting, he saw Archie in the crowd, a grinning, exultant Archie. A new sickness invaded Jerry, the sickness of knowing what he had become, another animal, another beast, another violent person in a violent world, inflicting damage, not disturbing the universe but damaging it. He had allowed Archie to do this to him.

And that crowd out there he had wanted to impress? To prove himself before? Hell, they wanted him to lose, they wanted him killed, for Christ's sake.

Janza's fist caught him at the temple, sending Jerry reeling. His stomach caved in as Janza's fist sank into the flesh. He clutched at his stomach protectively and his face absorbed two stunning blows—his left eye felt smashed, the pupil crushed. His body sang with pain.

Horrified, The Goober counted the punches Janza was throwing at his helpless opponent. Fifteen, sixteen. He leaped to his feet. Stop it, stop it. But nobody heard. His voice was lost in the thunder of screaming voices, voices calling for the kill . . . *kill him, kill him.* Goober watched helplessly as Jerry finally sank to the stage, bloody, opened mouth, sucking for air, eyes unfocused, flesh swollen. His body was poised for a moment like some wounded animal and then he collapsed like a hunk of meat cut loose from a butcher's hook.

And the lights went out.

Obie would never forget that face.

A moment before the lights went out, he turned away from the platform, disgusted with the scene, the kid Renault being pummeled by Janza. The sight of blood always sickened him, anyway.

Looking away from the bleachers, he glanced up at a small hill that looked down at the field. The hill was actually a huge rock imbedded in the landscape, partially covered with moss and also with scrawled obscenities that had to be scrubbed off almost daily.

A movement caught Obie's eye. That's when he saw the face of Brother Leon. Leon stood at the top of the hill, a black coat draped around his shoulders. In the reflection of the stadium lights, his face was like a gleaming coin. The bastard, Obie thought. He's been there all the time, I'll bet, watching it all.

The face vanished as the darkness fell.

The darkness was sudden and deep.

Like a giant ink blot poured over the bleachers, the platform, the entire field.

Like the world suddenly wiped out, devastated.

Goddam it, Archie thought, as he stumbled away from the bleachers toward the small utility building where the electrical controls were located.

He tripped, fell down, and groped to his feet.

Someone brushed past him. The noise from the bleachers was awesome, kids screaming and shouting, guys tumbling from the seats. Small flames tore at the darkness as matches and cigarette lighters were lit.

Stupid, Archie thought, they're all stupid. He was the only one here with the presence of mind to check the cause of the power failure at the control building.

Tripping over a fallen body, Archie swiveled his way to the building, arms extended in front of him. As he reached the door, the lights went on again, blinding in their intensity. Dazed, blinking, he flung the door open and encountered Brother Jacques whose hand was on the switch.

"Welcome, Archie. I imagine you are the villain here, aren't you?" His voice was cool but his contempt was unmistakable.

38

"JERRY."

Wet darkness. Funny, darkness shouldn't be wet. But it was. Like blood.

"Jerry."

But blood wasn't black. It was red. And he was surrounded by black.

"Come on, Jerry."

Come on where? He liked it here, in the darkness, moist and warm and wet.

"Hey, Jerry."

Voices outside the window calling. Shut the window, shut it. Shut the voices out.

"Jerry . . ."

Something sad in the voice now. More than sad—scared. Something scared in the voice.

Suddenly the pain verified his existence, brought him into focus. Here and now. Jesus, the pain.

"Take it easy, Jerry, take it easy," The Goober was saying, cradling Jerry in his arms. The platform was brilliantly lit again, like an operating table, but the stadium was almost empty, a few curious stragglers still hanging around. Bitterly, Goober had watched the guys leaving, chased away by Brother Jacques and a couple of other faculty members.

The guys had vacated the place as if leaving the scene of a crime, strangely subdued. Goober had struggled toward the ring in the darkness and had finally reached Jerry as the lights went on. "We better get a doctor," he had yelled at the kid called Obie, Archie's stooge.

Obie had nodded, his face pale and ghostlike in the floodlights.

"Take it easy," Goober said now, drawing Jerry closer. Jerry felt broken. "Everything will be all right . . ."

Jerry raised himself toward the voice, needing to answer it. He had to answer. But he kept his eyes shut, as if he could keep a lid on the pain that way. But it was more than pain that caused an urgency in him. The pain had become the nature of his existence but this other thing weighed on him, a terrible burden. What other thing? The knowledge, the knowledge: what he had discovered. Funny, how his mind was clear suddenly, apart from his body, floating above his body, floating above the pain.

"It'll be all right, Jerry."

No it won't. He recognized Goober's voice and it was important to share the discovery with Goober. He had to tell Goober to play ball, to play football, to run, to make the team, to sell the chocolates, to sell whatever they wanted you to sell, to do whatever they wanted you to do. He tried to voice the words but there was something wrong with his mouth, his teeth, his face. But he went ahead anyway, telling Goober what he needed to know. They tell you to do your thing but they don't mean it. They don't want you to do your thing, not unless it happens to be their thing, too. It's a laugh, Goober, a fake. Don't disturb the universe, Goober, no matter what the posters say.

His eyes fluttered open and he saw Goober's face all askew, like on a broken movie film. But he was able to see the concern, the worry on his face.

Take it easy, Goober, it doesn't even hurt anymore. See? I'm floating, floating above the pain. Just remember what I told you. It's important. Otherwise, they murder you.

"Why did you do it to him, Archie?"

"I don't know what you're talking about."

Archie turned away from Brother Jacques and watched the ambulance making its careful progress out of the athletic field, the rotating blue light casting emergency flashings all over the place. The doctor said that Renault may have sustained a fracture of the jaw and there may be internal injuries. X-rays would tell. What the hell, Archie thought, those were the risks of the boxing ring.

Jacques swung Archie around. "Look at me when I talk to you," he said. "If someone hadn't come to the Residence and told me what was going on here, who knows how far it might have gone? What happened to Renault was bad enough, but there was violence in the air. You could have had a riot on your hands, the way those kids were stirred up."

Archie didn't bother to answer. Brother Jacques probably considered himself a hero for putting out the lights and stopping the fight. As far as Archie was concerned, Jacques had merely spoiled the evening. And Jacques had arrived too late anyway. Renault had already been beaten. Too fast, much too fast. Leave it to that stupid Carter to screw things up. Low blow, for crying out loud.

"What have you got to say for yourself, Costello?" Brother Jacques persisted.

Archie sighed. Bored, really. "Look, Brother, the school wanted the chocolates sold. And we got them sold. This was the payoff, that's all. A fight. With rules. Fair and square."

Leon was suddenly there with them, one arm clapped around Jacques' shoulder.

"I see you have everything under control, Brother Jacques," he said, heartily.

Jacques turned a cold face toward his fellow teacher. "I think we barely averted a disaster," he said. There was rebuke in his voice but a gentle, guarded rebuke, not the hostility he had revealed to Archie. And Archie realized that Leon was still in command, still in the position of power.

"Renault will get the best of care, I assure you," Leon said. "Boys will be boys, Jacques. They have high spirits. Oh, once in a while they get carried away but it's good to see all that energy and zeal and enthusiasm." He turned to Archie and spoke more severely but not really angrily. "You really didn't use your best judgment tonight, Archie. But I realize you did it for the school. For Trinity."

Brother Jacques stalked away. Archie and Leon watched him go. Archie smiled inside. But he masked his feelings. Leon was on his side. Beautiful. Leon and The Vigils and Archie. What a great year it was going to be.

The ambulance's siren began to howl in the night.

39

"SOMEDAY, Archie," Obie said, a warning in his voice, "someday . . ."

"Cut it out, Obie. Enough preaching tonight. Brother Jacques already delivered a sermon to me." Archie chuckled. "But Leon came to the rescue. Good man, that Leon."

They were sitting in the bleachers, watching some of the guys cleaning up the place. This was where they had first seen Renault that afternoon Archie had selected him for the assignment. The night had grown cold and Obie shivered slightly. He looked at the goal posts. They reminded him of something. He couldn't remember.

"Leon is a bastard," Obie said. "I saw him on the hill over there—watching the fight, enjoying the whole thing."

"I know," Archie said. "I tipped him off. An anonymous phone call. I figured he would enjoy himself. And I also figured that if he was here and part of the proceedings, he'd also be protection for us if anything went wrong."

"Someday, Archie, you'll get yours," Obie said but the words were automatic. Archie was always one step ahead.

"Look, Obie, I'm going to forget what you did tonight— you and Carter and the black box. What the hell, it was a dramatic moment. And I understand how you felt. My understanding of you and guys like Carter is a marvel to behold." He had lapsed into his phony way of speaking when he wanted to be fancy or sarcastic.

"Maybe the black box will work the next time, Archie," Obie said. "Or maybe another kid like Renault will come along."

Archie didn't bother to answer. Wishful thinking wasn't worth answering. He sniffed the air and yawned. "Hey, Obie, what happened to the chocolates?"

"The guys raided the chocolates in the confusion. As far as the money's concerned, Brian Cochran has it. We'll have some kind of drawing next week at assembly."

Archie barely listened. He wasn't interested. He was hungry. "You sure all the chocolates are gone, Obie?"

"I'm sure, Archie."

"You got a Hershey or anything?"

"No."

The lights went off again. Archie and Obie sat there awhile not saying anything and then made their way out of the place in the darkness.

CORMIER

Beyond the Chocolate War

TO MARILYN E. MARLOW
with thanks for always believing in me

PART ONE

Ray Bannister started to build the guillotine the day Jerry Renault returned to Monument.

There was no connection between the two events. In fact, Ray Bannister didn't even know Jerry Renault existed. The truth of the matter is that Ray began to construct the guillotine out of sheer boredom. More than boredom: loneliness, restlessness. He was a newcomer to Monument and to Trinity High. He hated both—well, maybe hate was too strong a word, but he had found Monument to be a dull and ugly mill town of drab tenement houses and grim factories, with no class at all, a terrible contrast to Caleb, the resort village on Cape Cod where he'd grown up with beach sand between his toes and salt spray stinging his cheeks. Trinity was a suffocatingly small school, filled with guys who were suspicious of strangers or, at the very least, unfriendly. The Headmaster and the teachers were brothers, those strange people who wore stiff white collars but weren't quite priests and yet weren't quite like ordinary men. Ray's father insisted that brothers made the ideal teachers, dedicated and loyal to education. They have nothing to distract them, his father said. They don't have to worry about earning a big salary—the Order takes care of all their needs—and they don't have wives or children to support, except maybe a girl friend or two in these crazy, liberal times. That last remark was supposed to pass for wit: Ray Bannister's father was renowned for his wit at cocktail parties, but Ray, frankly, didn't find him amusing at all. Particularly since he'd accepted the company promotion that meant a transfer from the Cape to this rotten city in the middle of New England.

Ray had always been a loner, even on the Cape, where he had spent long hours roaming the beaches and dunes or sailing his beloved skiff in the warm waters south of Caleb. In a fit of disgust and disillusionment, he'd practically given his boat away, sold it for a quarter of its worth to Joe Scerra, his best friend in Caleb. Ray had built the boat himself, lovingly, knew every section and area of its surface just as he knew the tone and texture of his own body.

Monument looked as if sailing weather didn't exist. Snow melted on the Cape as soon as it kissed the land; Ray was dismayed to find Monument covered with the dirty rags of old snow when he arrived in February. The landscape of city streets was bleak and forbidding, like a movie set from one of those old late-night films about the Depression. Lonely, unable to make friends at Trinity and not really trying very hard, Ray pursued his interest in magic. His father, who had been an amateur magician years ago, had given him a magic kit for Christmas as a kind of bribe to compensate for the transfer to Monument. At first Ray had only gone through the motions of showing interest. But, bored and restless, he began to fool around with the kit and found, to his surprise, that the tricks were not merely kid stuff but sophisticated and challenging, almost professional. He discovered the Stripper Deck and the Cups and Balls and the Silk Scarves and soon found himself adept at sleight of hand. With no one to entertain, he performed before the mirror in his bedroom.

As winter changed into spring or, rather, as the grayness of February and March yielded to the soft yellow of April, Ray grew bored with the simple finger tricks. He rummaged around the cellar, remembering that his father had all kinds of paraphernalia left over from his days as an entertainer at club and organization parties when Ray himself was just a kid. His father had carefully packed the stuff away when they had moved to Monument. During his search, Ray came across an old cardboard box that contained complicated tricks and effects he couldn't do anything with because there were no directions. Then he discovered an old leather-bound book, copyright 1922, that provided instructions for hundreds of magic effects. The book included plans and illustrations for various stage illusions, like levitation and disappearances. Ray was disappointed to learn the secrets of the illusions, how mechanical they were. He thought: There's no magic, really, anywhere in the world. It was like finding out there was no Santa Claus.

The plans for the guillotine attracted his immediate attention, however. The secret was so simple and yet so effective. He imagined himself on the stage in the Trinity auditorium, performing for the student body—"May I have a volunteer from the audience?"—and hearing the guys gasp with astonishment as the blade fell, seeming to penetrate the volunteer's neck. Ray's hands itched to build the guillotine, just as they had itched to build his skiff. He'd always been clever with his hands. In fact, his father had said that he hated the idea of squandering money on Ray's college education when he'd probably do better as a carpenter—and a carpenter didn't need a college degree.

At any rate, lonely, indifferent to both Monument and Trinity, tired of the perennial gray clouds that haunted the early days of spring, wistful for those bikini girls who would be emerging on Caleb's beaches any day now, Ray Bannister assembled his tools and the lumber required to build the guillotine. He bought the blade at a magic store in Worcester. And, as he told Obie later: Honest, he'd never heard of Jerry Renault or Archie Costello or any of the others.

Obie was in love. Wildly, improbably, and wonderfully in love. The kind of thing he thought happened only in the movies. *Can't eat, can't sleep* love. *Daydream in class* love. *Can't concentrate on your studies* love. *The hell with doing homework* love. Her name was Laurie Gundarson and she was beautiful. Obie's legs dissolved at the sight of her, and he felt as though he would sink into the earth and disappear. He had never known such happiness or such sweet torture. He lived his days and nights in a rosy haze and went around with a stunned and radiant expression on his face. Which disgusted Archie Costello, of course.

Like at this moment when the Vigils had gathered to put the finishing touches on the new assignment. The other members, plus the three sophomores, awaited in tense and silent anticipation, a little nervous about what was going to happen. Archie always kept them on edge, springing his small surprises now and then to keep them alert and on their toes. But Obie sat there with that stupid expression on his face. That's why Archie turned to Bunting, the sophomore.

"Okay, Bunting," Archie said, "bring us up to date."

The selection of Bunting to present the report didn't immediately register on Obie. Obie wasn't actually here in the stupid storage room near the gym where the Vigils held their meetings. He was off somewhere with Laurie Gundarson. They were driving on the freeway toward Mount Wachusum. They were climbing the mountain on a sparkling spring day. He assisted her over the rough terrain, allowing his hands to roam across the marvelous geography of her body. He couldn't get enough of touching her, caressing her, although she kept that kind of stuff down to a minimum. Only on special occasions would she allow those intimate caresses for which Obie lived, to which he had dedicated his every waking moment.

"Are you with us, Obie?" Archie asked, his voice cool as always, never allowing an emotion to show, making it seem as if he was doing you a favor by using your name.

"I'm here, Archie," Obie said, reluctant to leave the warmth and softness of Laurie's flesh.

"Go on, Bunting," Archie said.

At that moment Obie saw the notebook in Bunting's hands. Startled, he checked his jacket pocket to make certain that his current notebook was safe and intact. Obie's notebooks were legend on the Trinity campus. Not only did they contain the assignments Archie dreamed up, but they had information about every student at Trinity, stuff that didn't show up in the school's official records. Observing Bunting now with his own notebook, Obie felt some surprise, but he wasn't as disturbed as he might have been if this had occurred before he'd met Laurie Gundarson. Laurie made all the difference: let Bunting have his notebook.

Bunting stood there with the cheerful insolence that was the hallmark of being a sophomore. Obie hated sophomores; most seniors did. Sophomores had lost the timidity of freshmen and hadn't attained the casualness of the juniors or the coolness of the seniors. Sophomores were feeling the first stirrings of arrogance, and believed that the school—and the world—existed for them alone. They barged into places nobody in his right mind would go. One example: Bunting now throwing a glance of triumph and superiority at Obie, smirking maliciously. Obie summoned a small smile to his own lips, a smile that was supposed to communicate to Bunting that he didn't give a damn who gave the report. But despite the sweetness of Laurie's presence in his life, he felt a flicker of jealousy. Not jealousy, exactly. Who could be jealous of a sophomore, for crying out loud? Hate, maybe. But not really for Bunting. A renewal of his hatred for Archie. Or was it hatred, after all? He wasn't sure. He was never sure of anything about Archie. Nobody was.

"Plans are proceeding according to schedule," Bunting sang out. "Every guy has been contacted, either directly or indirectly. A lot of guys don't know what it's all about. Nobody gave us any shit, though."

"Bunting, Bunting," Archie said, chiding, like a father scolding an errant son.

"What's the matter?" Bunting asked, puzzled.

"Your language."

"What language?" Not only puzzled but uneasy now.

"That word you used."

"What word?" Voice going up half an octave.

Archie didn't reply, regarding Bunting with utter contempt.

"You mean *shit?*" Bunting asked, incredulous.

Archie nodded. "You broke the rule, Bunting. You used profane language. A no-no. Taboo."

Obie shook his head in reluctant admiration. That Archie. Leave it to him. There was, of course, no rule about language. That's what was intriguing about Archie—you never knew what was coming next. Obie relaxed now, prepared to enjoy the game, whatever it was, that Archie was playing with Bunting. And he also alerted himself to be on his guard, knowing that he would inevitably become a part of it.

"You mean there's a rule against swearing?" Bunting asked, his confidence rapidly deteriorating.

"That's right, Bunting. The rule—no profane language, no more swearing at Vigil meetings. No taking the name of the Lord in vain." Archie and that mocking voice. Archie shaking his head in simulated disappointment with Bunting. "Hey, Obie, how long has the rule been in effect?"

"Six days," Obie responded automatically.

"See, Bunting? You're ambitious. You want to scale the heights of the Vigils. But you missed out on a new rule."

The other two sophomores—a skinny kid with bulging eyes named Harley and a brooding, sullen kid with an acne-ravaged face called Cornacchio—sat immobilized. They had never seen Archie in action before, and they obviously felt threatened. The Vigil veterans watched the proceedings with amusement, having instantly recognized along with Obie another Archie improvisation.

"Tell Bunting why we adopted the new rule, Carter."

Carter hated this sort of thing. As president of the Vigils, he usually didn't participate in the games but enforced the rules, wielding the gavel, slamming it down on the wooden crate that served as a desk to provide exclamation points to

Archie's commands. Carter didn't approve of Archie's psychological games. He liked stuff you could see, something you could hit. The tragedy of Carter's senior year was the ban on boxing imposed by Brother Leon. Carter had been captain of both the boxing team and the football squad. With the boxing team disbanded and the football season a distant memory, he was now captain of exactly nothing. His simple claim to distinction these days was his presidency of the Vigils. And as president he had to respond to Archie, play his games, shadowbox with words.

"We instituted the rule because of the need to clean up the atmosphere," Carter said, the words issuing easily and glibly. The fact that he was a boxer didn't mean he was stupid. "It's impossible to clean up the crap and junk that gets tossed out of cars. But at least we can keep the air pure of profanity."

Archie smiled at him, pleased, and Carter hated himself for responding so quickly to one of Archie's gimmicks.

"And the penalty for anyone who swears, Obie?"

"Whoever breaks the rule," Obie said, mind racing as he pondered all the possibilities, "has to stand naked for one hour at the bus stop downtown at Monument Square." He squirmed, knew instantly by Archie's dour expression that it was a rotten punishment.

"That's right," Archie said, looking at Obie with disgust. "A mild-enough punishment, Bunting, you must admit. That's because we're saving the real good stuff for the second offense. It'll be a nice surprise for whoever swears a second time."

Bunting nodded, abashed, confused, wondering what had happened, how he had become so quickly a victim instead of a perpetrator, realizing, simultaneously, Archie's power and unpredictability. A small part of his brain had also registered the antagonism developing between Archie and Obie, and he tucked it away for future reference.

"Okay,"Archie said. "We'll excuse your error this time, Bunting. Next time, though, you get the penalty." His eyes swept the gathering. "That goes for everybody else. No more swearing at Vigil meetings." Again to Bunting: "Go on with your report, please."

Bunting plunged ahead without waiting for any more instructions. But he chose his words carefully.

"Like I said, it looks as if there'll be no trouble. Almost everybody has been alerted. Some of the guys are organizing parties and stuff. A bunch are going to the beaches, Hampton, some to the Cape. Other guys are hitching to Boston. We gave them the word: If you stay in town, stay out of sight. We don't give a sh— We don't care what you do. Just don't come to school, and lay low. . . ." Bunting couldn't resist glancing at his notebook, knowing this would get a rise out of Obie. "We expect some stragglers, but we're about ninety percent organized."

"I don't want stragglers," Archie said. Deadly, in command, the Archie who ruled the school. "I want one hundred percent."

Bunting nodded. And so did everyone else.

This latest assignment wasn't really an assignment but one of Archie's entertainments, something to break up the boredom that always settles over a school in that no-man's-land of time between spring and summer vacations, when the days seem endless and pointless, when even the teachers are caught in the lethargy and boredom of the stagnant hours. The seniors had lost interest in school and now had their sights set on the coming year; most had already been accepted at colleges. The juniors meanwhile were caught in an in-between stage, almost finished with the junior year and not officially seniors. Even the freshmen were straining a bit, tired of their role as lowly underclassmen, eager to confront the new batch of freshmen arriving in the fall. The school was not really as placid or lethargic as it seemed; there was an undercurrent of restlessness.

Sensing all of this, knowing that only the sophomores were content (but sophomores were a breed apart), Archie had responded with a perfect solution: a day off from school. But not a day arranged through subtle blackmail of Brother Leon. No, this day would have an Archie Costello sting. Every student at Trinity—and there were almost four hundred of them—would simply stay away from class on a certain designated day. They would vanish. No one would be able to find them. When the brothers began frantically to call the various homes—absenteeism was always checked with a telephone call to the student's home—they would learn that Jimmy or Joey or Kevin or whoever had gone off to school as usual. Thus, the scheme would have a double impact: on the school, and on the homes of the students. And then Archie had gone one step further. He had learned, in advance, the date of the Bishop's visit to Trinity. The traditional annual visit always began before classes with a high mass and holy communion in the school auditorium, which was converted into a chapel for the occasion. This year, the auditorium would be without students.

Carter had been horrified at the thought of humiliating the Bishop, an act that could have serious repercussions. But he had said nothing. Like everyone else, he had learned not to oppose Archie's schemes. Play along and go along. He felt helpless, wishing he had the courage to make a protest. He had courage enough on the football field and in the boxing ring. But that was different. He felt alone these days, an exile in this school he loved. Everybody thought he was only bone and muscle. Didn't see that a jock could be sensitive. And his sensitivities told him that the Bishop's visit would spell disaster. He didn't want to be a part of that disaster, not at this point, so near to graduation when he'd be rid of Archie Costello once and for all time.

"I've got a suggestion," Bunting said.

Obie looked at the sophomore with new respect, the way he was bouncing back after the earlier attack by Archie and risking another with a suggestion. Ordinarily, only Archie made suggestions. And they weren't suggestions, they were orders, more or less.

"Let's hear it," Archie said. "But watch the language, right?" Almost primly, lips pursed.

Bunting nodded.

"What I figure is this," he said, gathering confidence. "Why not have everybody stay out of school except one kid? I mean, if everybody's absent, there's no . . ." He was at a loss for a word.

Archie grabbed one out of the air. "No contrast." Then another: "No emphasis." He regarded Bunting with admiration, or what passed for admiration coming from Archie because he still maintained his coolness, the distance he managed to keep between himself and everyone else. "Beautiful, Bunting. I can see it now. The Bishop and Brother Leon and all the faculty up there on the stage, near the altar. And one kid sitting in the audience, right in the middle of the place, surrounded by all those empty seats, not another kid in sight."

"We have to pick the right kid," Bunting went on, really rolling now. "He'll be part of the plot, with orders to act normal, like he's not alone in the audience. As if everything is happening as usual."

Archie lifted his hands, palms downward, almost as if he were about to bless the congregation, but the Vigils had come to know that the gesture meant he wanted instant silence. Suddenly the gathering seemed to be holding its collective breath, a stillness pervading the room. Obie marveled at Archie's ability to take command of all situations, the way he was able now to take the spotlight away from Bunting effortlessly and bring all eyes in the place to himself. Archie's eyes were mere slits: he was thinking, concentrating. Or pretending to be thinking and concentrating. Obie had seen him perform this stunt a thousand times. Or was it a stunt?

The heat in the storage room had grown almost unbearable, heat saturated with the smell of boys' bodies. Vigil meetings were always brief, because Archie couldn't stand the smell of perspiration, couldn't stand the sight of sweat on flushed skin. Obie surreptitiously surveyed the boys as they sat there immobile, focused on Archie, not daring to move. Nobody wanted to be noticed or singled out by Archie. Bunting alone seemed at ease, sure of himself, his black curly hair glistening in the harsh glow of the unshaded bulb hanging from the ceiling. He looked as if he'd just stepped from a shower: cool and refreshed. Obie almost shuddered. He knew that Archie was grooming Bunting to be the new Assigner, the student who would take Archie's place next year. Although Bunting was short and dark and muscular in contrast to Archie's tall and slender blondness, there was a similarity between them, something Obie could not pin down precisely. Maybe ruthlessness.

"Okay," Archie said, coming out of his trance or whatever it was. Voice crackling. Blue eyes flashing. "What we need is one more touch. The kid who's coming to school that day." He shot a glance toward Obie. "I want a new kid. Somebody who hasn't been involved in anything yet."

As if by reflex, Obie flipped his notebook open. And hated himself for leaping to action at Archie's slightest wish. "There's a kid who came to Trinity for the second term. His family moved here from the Cape. His name is Raymond Bannister. He's a sophomore. *B*-minus average student but got a *D* in chemistry. He's a loner."

"Why haven't we heard about him before?" Archie asked, a mild rebuke in his voice as he used the editorial *we*, as if he was the Pope, for crying out loud. *We.*

Obie shrugged an answer. New kids were always Vigil bait. Archie loved nothing better than putting a new kid through the hoops.

"Did you slip up, Obie?" Archie asked. Slyly, tauntingly.

Obie felt the color creep into his face, like a stain of guilt. Archie was a master at this, humiliating someone in front of others.

"I didn't think it was the right time psychologically," Obie replied. "Ray Bannister is a loner, like I said." He looked meaningfully at Archie, wondering if he was getting the message. The message of the chocolates.

Something flickered in Archie's eyes, as if an invisible branch had snapped across his face. Pause. But only for a beat. "Maybe it's time to get around to him," he said, looking directly at Obie. "Get to this Bannister kid. If he's a loner, he'll love sitting there all by himself. Fill him in. Tell him the part he has to play. Impress upon him the importance of his role. How we don't put up with failure."

The Vigils murmured their approval.

Archie turned to Bunting, swiveling away from Obie as if dismissing him.

"Nice work, Bunting."

Bunting glowed and couldn't resist shooting another glance of triumph at Obie.

"Any other business?" Archie asked, addressing nobody in particular.

Silence, as Archie looked around the room, inspecting each of them in turn, studying them with those cold, intelligent eyes and managing as usual to look superior to them.

"What about Fair Day?" Bunting asked.

A shadow crossed Archie's face. Obie thought with glee: Bunting has pushed his luck too far.

"What about Fair Day?" Archie's voice held a hint of cool mockery.

What Bunting didn't know: Archie was less than enthusiastic about Fair Day. Bored, in fact. Fair Day was a family fun day at Trinity, the last social event before graduation, a day of hot dogs and hamburgers, booths and merry-go-rounds and other rides for the kid brothers and sisters of Trinity students. The Vigils always kept a low profile during the day except, of course, for the Fool. The Vigils even maintained a hands-off policy during Skit Night (which some guys called Shit Night), the evening of Fair Day. All of which Bunting should have known. But Bunting was the classic sophomore: Act now, think later.

"Let's get the visit over with first," Carter growled, exercising his privilege as Vigils president. Wanting to end the meeting, tired of all this crap.

Archie chuckled, looking with feigned exasperation at Bunting, the father now indulging the favorite son. "Slow down, Bunting," he said. Then nodded at Carter.

Carter banged the gavel and stood up. The atmosphere

became tense, like an elastic band stretched to the breaking point. Carter drew a black box from a shelf within the crate. He held it in his hands as if it contained all the crown jewels of Europe.

Archie sighed, wearily, resignedly. He turned to Harley and Cornacchio, the two sophomores who had watched the proceedings with awe and wonder and maybe a bit of fear.

"Your first meeting, right?" Archie asked them, kindly, gently. The master actor, Obie thought, turning facets of his personality on and off to suit his purposes.

The sophomores nodded in unison, gulping, as if they had rehearsed their response.

Archie nodded toward the black box.

"This is what I have to face after every assignment," Archie said. Then, wryly: "To keep me honest." Looking at Bunting now. "This is what you'll have to put up with, Bunting, if you step into my shoes."

The sophomores regarded the box warily. The box was legendary at Trinity and had been seen in public on only one occasion.

As Carter held the box reverentially aloft now, Archie said: "Whenever an assignment is given out, I have to face the box. There are six marbles in there, five of them white, one black. If I pull out a white marble, no sweat. The assignment stands. But if I pull out the black, I have to take on the assignment myself. Some creep years ago came up with this concept. It's supposed to keep an Assigner from getting too fancy, too dangerous, if he knows there's a chance he'd be carrying out the assignment."

Carter and Obie approached Archie, Carter extending the box, Obie holding the key. The box was an old jewelry container some nameless student years ago had stolen from his mother's bedroom.

"In this particular case"—Archie continued his explanation to the sophomores—"if I draw the black marble, I have to take Bannister's place in the audience. Which isn't bad at all. There have been worse risks."

Archie laughed again, this time with obvious delight. Obie wondered, as usual, what kind of blood ran in Archie's veins. Or was it blood at all?

"Look at Obie," Archie said.

Obie almost dropped the key. Uncanny, as if Archie could reach into his mind.

"Obie's hoping the black marble will turn up. He never used to hope that. But now he does." As he spoke he reached up and shoved his hand into the box, swiftly, without hesitation. In almost the same motion, he withdrew his hand and tossed a white marble in the air, the whiteness glinting in the bulb's stark glow, and caught it effortlessly as it came down. In all his time as the Assigner, Archie had never drawn the black marble.

"Sorry, Obie," he said, laughing.

Obie realized that somehow he and Archie had become enemies. He didn't know when it had happened or why. He knew only that something existed between them now that hadn't been there before. As Carter banged the gavel, adjourning the meeting, Obie shivered in the heat of the storage room and realized that he had just gone five minutes without thinking of Laurie Gundarson.

Everything had been going along smoothly, life returning to normal, the horror and the betrayal receding and diminishing—and then the telephone call came.

He had started running again, flying over the streets, up and down the hills, moving with easy, fluid grace, invigorated by the chilly morning air, eyes dazzled by the sun setting fire to eastern windows. A collie that belonged to someone on Spruce Street had taken to running beside him, and he felt a sense of kinship with the animal. Often he and the collie were the only living things on the streets at that hour.

His father was happy to see him running again. "Good, Roland, good," his father said, meeting him at the end of the run as he departed for work.

Drawing up beside his father, breathing deeply, the air sweet in his lungs, his moist body cooling in the morning breeze, the Goober felt great.

"You see, Roland? Time heals all things," his father said, waving the lunch pail as he made off down the street.

His father was a very formal man. He didn't believe in

nicknames; he never called his son the Goober or Goob as others did. The Goober watched him walking off to work, erect, head held high, and was overcome with an emotion he could not identify. Love? Affection? He wasn't quite certain. Maybe it's what a son felt for his father when the father had helped the son through a bad time of his life. Time heals all things. . . .

The Goober lived five miles from Trinity, too far to run, especially with books and other stuff to carry. He ran part of the way, though, passing up the bus stop nearest his home and boarding a bus downtown near the library. This bus didn't carry as many Trinity students as the other, which was fine with Goober. He still planned to transfer to Monument High next fall; his father had frowned at a mid-year transfer and had asked him to stick it out until June. But although he felt much better about Trinity these days, the Goober still didn't mix much with the other guys. No problem: He was a freshman and hardly knew anybody. Trinity drew students not only from Monument but from the entire area, and only a few had enrolled from St. Jude's Parochial School, where Goober had gone. Anyway, he had decided to play it cool until June. The fourteen-year-old heart is a marvelous thing, his father had said. It can be ruptured but it does not really break, no matter what the poets say.

The Goober wasn't sure whether his heart had ruptured or broken completely during those terrible chocolate days last fall. All he knew was that a numbness had finally seeped through him, like a novocaine of the spirit. But time and the running had also helped him emerge from the bad days. He still felt like a traitor, however, and he avoided, whenever possible, Archie Costello and Obie and the other Vigils. He also avoided Room Nineteen, even though it sometimes meant a long detour through the halls and stairways. Room Nineteen and Brother Eugene. The chocolate days and Jerry Renault. Under control now, he passed his hours at school without undue panic or depression. He could do nothing about Brother Leon, of course, and had learned to live with his presence. Leon popped into the classrooms now and then, turning up when he was least expected, substituting for teachers on occasion or observing the class and teacher from the rear of the room. The Goober felt he had scored a personal triumph recently: He had met Leon in the corridor and was able to look into those milky moist eyes without feeling nausea gathering in his stomach.

And then the telephone call.

He was alone in the house when the phone rang: his father at work, his mother out shopping. He picked up the receiver.

"Roland?"

For a moment he thought his father was on the line. And panicked slightly. His father never called from work. An accident? No one else but his father called him Roland.

"Yes," he said, warily, tentatively.

"This is Jerry Renault's father."

The words echoed in the Goober's ears as if they'd been shouted, bellowed.

"Oh, yes," Goober heard himself say. He had met Jerry's father only once. The night they had admitted Jerry to Monument Hospital. His memory of the man had been blurred by the incidents of that night, plus the tears that kept welling in his eyes. "How's Jerry?" the Goober asked now. Forced himself to ask. Afraid of the answer. Am I being a traitor again? he wondered.

"Well, he's home," Mr. Renault said, voice quiet and subdued, as if he were speaking from a sickroom where the patient must not be disturbed.

"Oh," the Goober said. Stupid, unable to say anything more. He felt the old November panic again, the novocaine wearing off, the pain coming back.

Jerry Renault had spent several weeks at Monument Hospital before being transferred to a hospital in Boston. A few weeks later Mr. Renault had called to report that the boy had gone to Canada to recuperate with relatives. "I think the change of scene will do him good," Mr. Renault had said. And then had added: "I hope," his voice filled with a tone of impending doom. The Goober had not seen Jerry since those first days at the hospital.

"I think it might do Jerry some good to see old friends," Mr. Renault said now. "He always spoke very warmly of you, Roland." Pause, then: "The Goober, isn't it?" Then hurried on: "At any rate, I'm hoping that seeing some of his friends, people like yourself, will help him."

"You mean he's not okay?" Goober asked. And thought: Don't answer that. He didn't want to hear the answer.

"I think he needs to get adjusted after being away so long. He has to pick up the pieces of his life." Was he choosing his words carefully? "That's why I think a friend like yourself can help."

But what kind of friend am I?

"When would be a good time to visit?" Goober asked, hating the thing in him that hoped Mr. Renault would say, Forget it, this is a mistake, Jerry's not home, he's still in Canada, he'll be there forever.

"Anytime. We're just getting settled. How about tomorrow afternoon? After school?"

"Fine," Goob said. But it was as if somebody else was using his voice.

He held the receiver at his ear a long time after Jerry's father had hung up, the dial tone like a warning signal of disaster.

The Stripper Deck is a trick deck, but its secret is simple: The cards are tapered at one end. Thus, if a particular card is turned around and slipped back into the deck, it can be detected by touch because it sticks out from the other cards. The object of the trick is to locate the projecting card with fingertips or thumb tip. This is called "stripping the deck."

When Ray first tried the trick he was instantly discouraged. He picked up the cards at odd moments, however, and as he fooled around with them, shuffling and reshuffling, his fingertips developed sensitivity. After a few weeks he was able to locate the reversed card without hesitation. The Stripper Deck was a good time-killer, blunting the edge of his loneliness.

As spring burst into vivid life without warning, Ray became aware for the first time of the beauty of an inland spring. Weeping willow trees that he had never noticed before wore halos of soft yellow as the buds came to life. He grudgingly admitted that Monument was not as gray and ugly as it had been at first sight. Sweet fragrances filled the air, and the hills surrounding Monument, while not exactly alive with the sound of music, were beautiful in their sweep and radiant in their colors.

Lounging in the shade of a maple tree in front of Trinity, inhaling the zesty spring air, Ray manipulated the deck as he waited for the school bus to take him home. He watched the other guys coming and going, ignoring him as usual. Screw them all, Ray thought.

He removed the ace of spades from the deck, reversed it, and riffled the cards. As he blew on his fingertips, he looked up to see a kid standing nearby, hands on his hips, watching him with small, squinting eyes.

Ray waved a greeting.

The kid ignored the greeting but advanced toward him, face neutral, neither friendly nor unfriendly.

"You a card sharp?" the kid asked, hovering over him now.

Feeling suddenly vulnerable, Ray scrambled to his feet. "No, I just like to fool around with cards," he said.

"What do you mean, fool around?" the kid asked. Ray changed his mind: The kid's face wasn't neutral. The small eyes were watchful, challenging. His lips were thick, poised on the edge of a sneer. He wasn't particularly big or muscle-bound, but he gave an impression of strength. Brute strength, maybe.

"Tricks. I do tricks," Ray said, putting the cards in his pocket, shuffling his feet, looking away, searching the distance for the bus.

"Do one," the kid said quietly. His hands were still on his hips. He barely moved his lips when he talked. Like a ventriloquist.

Ray hesitated, having only performed before a mirror. He knew he would goof it up if he attempted to strip the deck before an audience. A hostile audience of one, at that.

"Well, I'm not too good yet," he said lamely, feeling his heart quicken. "I'm still at the practicing stage."

"Do one," the kid said, lips still not moving, voice still quiet except for a slight demand, a slight menace in the words. A caricature of a tough guy. But still menacing.

"Look, when I really get good at it, I'll do one." Keep it light. "In fact, I'll see that you get a complimentary ticket for opening night. . . ."

No response from the kid except that aura of menace his presence created.

"Hello, Emile."

Both Ray and the kid turned at the greeting.

"Hi, Obie," the kid said, disgust in his voice, his menace evaporating. He was suddenly just a slightly overweight guy.

"Introducing yourself to the new student?" the kid called Obie inquired.

A kind of secret signal seemed to pass between them, an unspoken understanding. Ray looked away, kicking at a stone on the grass. Sometimes Trinity gave him the creeps. Something in the air, in the attitude of the kids, something he couldn't pin down or put his finger on. A mood, a sense of mysterious goings-on. Like now: the kid called Obie intervening as if challenging the kid called Emile. And Emile backing off, backing down although he looked as if he could pick up Obie and throw him against a wall. "Hell, I was just curious, Obie. I saw him playing with those cards and thought he might do a trick or two. I thought he might be a magician. . . ." Voice trailing off.

Obie ignored him, turning away as if he hadn't heard his words or, if he had heard them, didn't consider them worthy of attention. "You're Ray Bannister, aren't you?" he asked. As if Ray was a long-lost friend.

"That's me." Surprised and trying not to appear surprised.

"I'm Obie." Extending his hand. Ray took it.

"I'd like to see those tricks sometime," Emile called, lingering at a distance, directing his remarks to Ray, the menace back in his voice. Ray felt as though he had made an enemy. Cripes, he thought, I was better off when nobody paid any attention to me.

As Emile finally left the scene, Obie chuckled. "You've just encountered the one and only Emile Janza," he said.

"I'm glad he's the one and only," Ray replied. "Two of him would be too much."

"He's an animal," Obie said. "He thinks the world is out to put the screws to him. So he tries to put the screws to everyone else." Shifting gears: "How are things going, Ray?"

"How do you know my name?"

Obie pulled out a small frayed spiral pad, flipped the pages. "Ray Bannister. From Caleb on the Cape. Height, five ten. One hundred forty-two pounds. Father an insurance executive. Doesn't make friends easy. Likes to play with cards."

"You seem to know a lot about me," Ray said, feeling positively spooky, as if somebody had been spying on him all this time. "This school is weird."

"Not really," Obie said. Suddenly Obie hated what he was doing and wanted to turn on his heel and get the hell away from Trinity and everybody here. He had approached guys like this too many times. For Archie. Setting up yet another assignment. Carrying out orders. Like some . . . stooge. He hadn't always felt this way: he used to enjoy Archie's schemes and strategies. Now other things seemed more important. All because of Laurie, of course. But more than Laurie. A name surfaced from the depths of his brain and memory. He denied the name, concentrating on the notebook and then looking up at Ray Bannister. The name came anyway—Renault.

"Look, Ray. Trinity isn't as weird as it seems. We had a rough first term—hell, our football team lost more games than it won, and our boxing squad—boxing used to be the big thing here—folded up. And then the Headmaster got sick and retired and somebody new took over—"

"Brother Leon?" Ray asked. Leon gave him the willies.

"Right." Obie seemed about to say something about Leon but didn't. After a pause: "Anyway, it's been a tough year. Actually, Trinity is a great place, a great school." He tried to inject enthusiasm, heartiness, into the words, but they sounded unconvincing to his ears, and he wondered if Ray Bannister heard the phoniness in his voice. Ray merely nodded as if his real thoughts were elsewhere.

"You waiting for a bus?" Obie asked, knowing that he had to stop acting like a press agent for Trinity and get down to business.

Ray nodded.

"I'll drive you home. My car's in the parking lot."

Suspicion ran like a chill through Ray's bones. After weeks of being ignored, why this sudden attention?

"Come on," Obie said, plastering his friendliest smile on his face. Like a label, he felt, on a stick of dynamite.

Ray shrugged and picked up his books. What the hell. He'd been alone too long. Maybe he was getting paranoid about the school. Actually he should be grateful for this kid called Obie. Trudging behind him now, Ray thought wistfully of Caleb and the Cape, and the sea lapping the shore like the tongue of an old and friendly dog. No sea here, no benevolent sun. No girls lounging on the beach. He'd better make do with what he had: at the moment, a ride home with a guy who might become a friend.

Obie was properly impressed by Ray Bannister's manipulation of the Stripper Deck, watching in awe as the card Obie had selected, the queen of hearts, appeared magically before him, unerringly drawn from the deck although Ray had not known its identity. Ray did it again—although magicians should never repeat their tricks, he said—with the three of diamonds and the ace of clubs, and Obie was fooled each time.

"The hand is quicker than the eye, to coin a cliché," Ray said, laughing, obviously delighted with the effect on Obie. He had been hesitant about performing for Obie at first, but the kid had seemed so genuinely interested and friendly that he had taken a chance. His nervousness had disappeared as he shuffled the deck. He was pleasantly surprised to see his fingers behaving so beautifully.

"Wow," Obie said, sincere in his admiration. But his mind was also working. Here was a kid with an obvious talent: how could it be used for the Vigils? "Do you do anything else?" he asked.

Ray hesitated once more. He was not as skilled with the Cups and Balls, but the effects were simpler to attain. Frowning, studying Obie, trying to judge if Obie was really being sincere, Ray thought: Why not give it a whirl?

So he took out the cups, balls, and a small table and was amazed once more at his performance, making the red balls appear, it seemed, at will from under the cup of his choice. Palming one ball, he passed it swiftly to his other hand and then appeared to be taking it out of Obie's ear.

Obie looked thunderstruck, his mouth open in astonishment.

"What's the matter?" Ray asked, puzzled. Hadn't Obie ever seen the ball trick before?

"Will you do that again, Ray? I mean, make the ball disappear in your hand and then appear someplace else?"

"I'm not supposed to do it twice," Ray said. But did it anyway, because he liked the challenge. Obie would be watching him closely now, anticipating his every move. And anticipation was fatal to illusion, making it difficult for Ray to use misdirection, a magician's most powerful tool. He wondered if he should tell him about the guillotine.

The red ball, no larger than a marble, flashed in the air. Obie watched closely. Ray's hands moved, open-palmed; fingers wiggled and then nothing—the ball vanished. Ray reached out with his right hand—Obie could swear the hand was empty—and popped the ball into view, as if he had removed it from Obie's shirt pocket.

Turning away, blinking into the sunlight that slanted into the bedroom, Obie whistled softly, thinking of Archie. Had Archie all these years used sleight of hand when he drew the white marble from the box? Was that how he had avoided the assignments he would have had to take on if the black marble had appeared in his hand? The possibility dazzled Obie. Nothing was beyond Archie. Archie was always one step ahead of everybody else. The members of the Vigils had always been amazed at Archie's luck, resented, in fact, the way he laughed mockingly when the white marble appeared in his hand time after time. Archie had been taken by surprise only once, last fall during the chocolate fracas. That time Archie had also pulled out the white marble, but sweat had danced on his forehead—Archie, who never perspired—and he had looked apprehensive.

Obie regarded Ray Bannister once more. "Great, Ray," he said, "simply great." Then, carefully: "How long did it take to learn the ball trick?" Trying to sound only casually interested.

"Not long. A few weeks. I've had time on my hands," Ray said. "Frankly, Obie, Trinity isn't the friendliest place on earth." Rolling the red ball between thumb and forefinger as Obie watched fascinated. "In fact, the school is kind of spooky. Is there something wrong with the place?"

Obie snapped out of his contemplation of the ball, wondering how much he should tell Ray Bannister about Trinity.

"Like I said, we've had a tough year," he began. A perception formed itself in his mind: Ray Bannister and his sleight of hand, something Archie didn't know about, a secret weapon Obie might be able to employ in the future. Maybe he should level with Bannister, let him know what was really going on at Trinity. What had gone on. . . .

"It's like this," Obie said. "We had our usual chocolate sale last fall. Our biggest fund-raiser. And a kid by the name of Jerry Renault, a freshman for crissake, refused to sell any. The only kid in school who refused to participate . . ."

Ray Bannister lifted both hands in a *so what?* gesture.

"The problem is that one rotten apple can spoil the barrel. And this kid became a kind of symbol. Other kids started to follow his lead. Everybody hates school sales to begin with. Brother Leon was ready to have a nervous breakdown. The Headmaster was in the hospital, Leon was in charge of the place . . ."

"All over chocolates?"

"It was twenty thousand boxes of chocolates."

Ray whistled.

"Right," Obie went on. "Leon bought them on the cheap. They were left over from Mother's Day. He bought them for a dollar a box. Which sounds okay except that means he spent twenty thousand dollars of school money—which he wasn't authorized to spend—for the chocolates. Which also means that each kid had to sell fifty boxes at two dollars to make a killing."

Obie was reluctant to say more, had been avoiding thoughts about the chocolate sale and Jerry Renault for months, sorry he had started to tell Ray Bannister the story. But he couldn't stop now.

"Anyway. The school was in an uproar. The guys were in an uproar. And the Vigils—"

"The Vigils?" Ray asked. "What's the Vigils?"

"Oh, boy." Obie sighed. How do you begin to explain the Vigils? The word was seldom spoken aloud on the Trinity campus. The brothers knew the organization existed but preferred to ignore it, allowing it to function because it served a purpose: kept peace at Trinity during a time when unrest and violence were sweeping the nation's schools and colleges. How to explain all that to a newcomer, someone who didn't know of the long tradition of the Vigils?

"Well, the Vigils is, like, a secret organization at Trinity. A guy by the name of Archie Costello is the Assigner. The Vigils has officers like any club—a jock named Carter is president and I'm secretary—but the Assigner is the key officer. In fact, the Assigner, Archie Costello, *is* the Vigils."

Ray turned away, puzzled. He didn't like this kind of stuff. Secret organizations. Assigners . . . "What the hell is an assigner?" he asked. And had a feeling that he really didn't want to know.

"Well, he assigns kids to certain . . . duties," Obie said, his words limping as if on crutches. "They have to perform certain acts—"

"Like in a college fraternity? Staying all night in the woods, stuff like that? Pranks? Stunts?"

Obie nodded, knowing that Archie would be furious to hear his meticulous assignments described as fraternity pranks and stunts. But he let the description stand. He couldn't tell Ray everything about the Vigils: in fact, he had probably told him too much already.

"Anyway, Brother Leon asked the Vigils to support the chocolate sale," Obie went on. "The first time Leon or any other faculty member acknowledged the existence of the club. That's how the Vigils got mixed up in it. . . ."

"What about that kid? Jerry What's-his-name?" Ray asked.

"Renault," Obie supplied. As if he could ever forget that name or that kid. "Renault still refused to sell the chocolates. Despite . . . pressure."

"What kind of pressure?"

"The usual," Obie said. How to describe Archie's methods to a stranger? "Archie Costello doesn't like physical violence. But in this case—"

"Violence was used, right?" Ray said, dismayed, head in a whirl. A couple of hours ago he hadn't known anything about Trinity, was a complete outsider. And now this kid named Obie was here in his home, telling him crazy things about the place.

Obie shrugged. "A kind of violence. A boxing match. Between Renault and Emile Janza—"

"The animal I just met at school?" Ray asked. Mimicking Janza's tight-lipped delivery: "Show me a card trick, kid."

"Right," Obie said, a flicker of amusement in his eyes.

"And the Renault kid got beat up, right?" Ray asked.

"Right," Obie said reluctantly. "Look, the kid was hurt, but he survived. Actually, he was a tough little character. They say he went to Canada to recuperate." Obie paused. "Anyway, that's all over now. The chocolate sale was a success. The Headmaster retired. And Brother Leon became top man. . . ."

"All's well that ends well," Ray Bannister said, wondering if Obie detected the sarcasm in his voice.

"Right," Obie said heartily, slapping his hands against his sides. Then frowned. "But . . ."

"But what?" Ray prompted.

"The thing rocked the school," Obie said, putting into words what he had avoided for so long. "That night. The kids calling for blood. Renault's blood. The chocolates became more important than anything else, more important than a kid's blood. . . ."

I wish we had stayed in Caleb, Ray Bannister thought.

"And now," Obie continued, "it's as if those chocolates exploded last fall and we're walking around in the leftovers, the crap. See what I mean? Everybody being careful, playing it cool."

"Like you've all got a guilty conscience?" Ray offered.

"Right," Obie agreed. But uncomfortable now, wondering if he had said too much.

"How about that club—the Vigils? They still playing it cool?"

"Well, not exactly," Obie said.

Which brought him to his reason for being here in Ray Bannister's house. To introduce him to the Vigils and how it worked.

Poor Jerry Renault, Obie thought suddenly.

And now poor Ray Bannister. About to learn the facts of life at Trinity High School.

In this corner, Archie Costello, five feet nine and a half inches tall, one hundred forty pounds, unchallenged champion of Trinity High School. Champion of what? Of all he surveyed—the classrooms, the corridors, the campus, his power extending even into the residence where Brother Leon and the other faculty members lived.

In *that* corner, the opposite corner, Brother Leon, formerly Assistant Headmaster of Trinity High School, now full-fledged Headmaster, ruler of the school, the faculty, the curriculum, the extracurricular activities, responsible for (and ruling) 387 students between the ages of thirteen and eighteen (with the exception of Richard O'Brien, who had turned nineteen on the fourth of April). Brother Leon of the pale face, the quick and sudden classroom movements in which a student was usually the loser, struck with a teacher's pointer or a piece of chalk flying across the room faster than a speeding bullet. Brother Leon. Whose eyes could flash with malice or quicken with a cold intelligence in which there wasn't an ounce of pity or mercy. Brother Leon of the swift short steps, who had gone moderately mod these days. His thinning hair threatened to cover his collar at the back. Sideburns dropped to his earlobes. He wore a silver chain, from which dangled a cross so fancy that you had to squint to make certain it was a cross. Brother Leon, who sometimes seemed a bit ridiculous to Archie. Which didn't deny the fact that Leon could also be dangerous.

And now, gentlemen, step to the center of the ring. . . .

There was no ring, of course, except in Archie's mind. He often thought about Brother Leon as he strolled the grounds of Trinity and stopped at the far end of the parking lot, from which point he could inspect the rear of the brothers' residence. Leon's private study, to which students were summoned occasionally, looked out on the parking lot. Archie enjoyed standing there, sensing that Leon was hidden behind the stiff white curtain drawn across the window pane. In his mind he was the champion and Leon the challenger, although on the surface one would suppose that Leon had the upper hand. Archie, a student; Leon, the Headmaster. In any contest, the Headmaster would be sure to emerge victorious, wouldn't he? Wouldn't he? Ah, but not according to Archie. Not according to the gospel of Trinity as written by Archie Costello.

Now he stood at that particular spot, glancing up at the residence, not knowing what he was looking for. Certainly not a confrontation with Leon. Archie realized that he and Leon had not talked or even run into each other for weeks. Leon was famous for surprise visits to classrooms, but he either avoided or did not happen to enter any of Archie's classes. Once in a while Archie saw Leon at a distance, across the campus or on the stage of the assembly hall or getting into a car. But their paths never crossed. Accident or design? Archie didn't know and didn't care. He kept his emotions under control, in cold storage, in neutral. He allowed himself measures of enjoyment—for instance, in the car with one of the girls from Miss Jerome's School across town—but always holding a part of himself aloof, never letting go completely. He enjoyed what he saw in the eyes of the other students when he directed his attention to them—fear, apprehension, resentment. He was aware of how others felt about him, but frankly, he paid only passing attention, preferred not to think about other people. People thought too much, anyway. Or talked too much.

Once in a while he expressed his thoughts to Obie. Obie was the only person he allowed into his privacy. But not recently. He and Obie had grown apart. No, that was wrong, not grown apart. They had been pulled apart by that girl, all that nonsense of Obie being in love. Love, for crissakes. Obie of all people. Although he hated to admit it to himself, Archie missed the talks with Obie. He could bounce ideas off Obie although Obie was unaware of what Archie was doing. Obie was so normal, so regular, so average, so typical of what a high school guy was like, that Archie, by being close to Obie, knew all the time what the school was thinking. Okay, so he used Obie. But wasn't that what life was all about? Using? Just as Obie, no doubt, used him, used his proximity to the Assigner of the Vigils to set him apart from, probably above, the other students.

The afternoon was dying, turning the campus into long shadows, hidden doorways, bushes and shrubbery hugging the residence, many places now for people to hide. Archie always envisioned lurkers, predators, watchers in the shadows or around corners, peeking out of windows, waiting behind closed doors. That was why he always stood tense, alert, at the ready, keen, eyes shifting, on guard under his exterior of coolness. It was a rotten world, full of treachery and evil, and you had to be on your toes at all times, ready for combat, to outfox, outwit, outdeal everybody else. Archie endorsed the graffiti he had once seen scrawled on a downtown brick wall: *Do Unto Others, Then Split.*

He heard the footsteps behind him at the same moment the voice reached his ears.

"Are you expecting an apparition, Costello?"

Archie didn't turn but winced slightly, instantly humiliated by allowing Brother Leon to creep up and surprise him. He didn't like to be surprised, particularly by Leon. He remained still, waiting for Leon to swing around and come into his view. Which Leon did, a satisfied look on his face, as if he had gained some kind of advantage. Leon was dressed in his black and whites, black suit, stiff white collar.

The campus was still. A car with a ruptured muffler violated the air far down the street.

"You're lurking late here, aren't you, Costello?" Leon asked.

Lurking and *Costello.* Leon had a trick of choosing certain words and pronouncing them so as to make them seem sinister, unsavory. As if Archie by *lurking* here was doing something illegal, dirty, shameful. And *Costello.* Since assuming the authority of Headmaster, Brother Leon called all students by their last names, kept a strict formality with them. He had never been the buddy-buddy type anyway; now he treated the students as if they were underlings, mere subjects in the kingdom of his royal highness, Leon the First.

Archie shrugged, didn't bother to answer Leon's question; it didn't require an answer, in fact. To Leon, the question itself was important, not the answer. The question and how he asked it, with that faint smirk, the suggestive curl of his lips. But Archie knew Leon's methods—and Leon *knew* he knew—so Archie permitted himself a smile at Leon, a smile that told Leon exactly how he felt about it all. And then Archie decided to answer, seeing an opportunity to level his own shaft at Leon.

"Just checking the premises," Archie said. "Some of the neighbors have been complaining about a child molester—wearing a white collar—lurking in the area."

A glitter in Leon's eyes, a quickening, like a sudden touch of cold sunlight on the surface of a lake. His face was expressionless, but Archie sensed a tension in the flesh of Leon's cheeks. He and Leon had always dueled this way, tossing veiled barbs at each other, in a game that wasn't quite a game.

Leon waved his right hand, almost limply, dismissing Archie's barb, showing that he recognized it for what it was, verbal retaliation.

"The campus has been quiet for some time," Leon said, his tone now more conversational, as if some prologue had ended and he could get on with the business at hand. "You have been holding them in check."

Archie knew who he meant by *them.*

"I must express my admiration, Costello. For you. Your methods. I know that your odd activities go on, but you have been discreet. And life has been kind, hasn't it?"

They had made a pact months ago, after the chocolates and immediately after Leon had assumed the Headmastership of Trinity. "Life at Trinity can be very pleasant, Costello, for both of us," Leon had said. "My desire is to continue the fine traditions of Trinity, to make it the best preparatory school in New England. And this takes faculty working together with the student body. Our dear retired Headmaster was a wonderful man but did not comprehend the ways of students, Costello. He was not vigilant." *Vigilant.* Leon had caressed the word with his tongue, his lips, his voice, giving it a special meaning, the word leaping into the air and hanging there. Archie had nodded. Knew Leon's meaning. "I, however, am vigilant. Will continue to be. I also know that boys must be allowed their games, their sports, must indulge their idiosyncrasies on occasion. This I understand and allow. But within limitations. Without obstructions to the lofty goals and purposes of Trinity. And its administration."

Words, of course. Bullshit. The administration of the school was under the strict control of Brother Leon. In fact, he had arranged a transfer for Brother Jacques, the only member of the faculty who had ever showed signs of independence—Jacques had objected to the events surrounding the chocolate skirmish last fall—and Jacques was no longer on the scene at Trinity. So much for Leon's pretensions. But even though Leon's words were bullshit, the meaning came through straight and true to Archie. He and Leon spoke the same language, not the verbal language of ordinary communication but the between-the-lines language of conspirators and plotters. What Leon meant: Play your tricks, Archie, carry out the assignments, let the Vigils have their fun. But keep your distance from me. Don't do anything to embarrass me as Headmaster of the school. Otherwise . . .

"Incidentally, Costello, I have some bad news."

Not so incidentally, Archie figured. He knew now the

reason Brother Leon had sought him out, confronted him here on the campus as the sun began to droop. *I have some bad news.* He had never known Leon to bring good news.

"It's news from provincial headquarters. In Manchester, New Hampshire."

Get to the point, Brother Leon, and spare the geography.

"Brother Eugene—remember him?" Leon asked, guilelessly, innocently. But not so guileless, not so innocent.

Archie nodded, glad that he seldom perspired, whether under pressure or during heat waves, glad that beads of moisture on his forehead would not betray him.

"He is dead, Brother Eugene. He died yesterday in the infirmary at Manchester."

For a moment, in the shadows, Archie saw the soft, quizzical face of Brother Eugene superimposed on Leon's features, then shrugged it away.

"He never fully recovered," Leon said.

Archie knew what Leon wanted him to ask: Recovered from what? But Archie wouldn't give him the satisfaction. And, anyway, they both knew.

"The Order has lost a wonderful, sensitive teacher," Leon said. "Have you anything to say, Costello? Perhaps a tribute of your own? You had Brother Eugene in class, didn't you?"

"History," Archie said. "One semester."

"Room Nineteen?" Brother Leon asked, malice in his voice as he shifted his body suddenly so that the last flash of the sun's rays struck Archie's eyes, causing him to blink, to look away. Room Nineteen and its beautiful debris, a legend now at Trinity.

"I never had Brother Eugene in Room Nineteen," Archie said, holding his voice steady. "It was some other room in my freshman year." He squared off, changed position so that he could look Leon in the eye again.

Their gazes held for a moment, and it was Leon who broke the contact this time. Casting his eyes downward, he said: "We shall have a special memorial mass for Brother Eugene at assembly. But I think you should make a special visit to your church and offer up prayers for the repose of his soul."

Archie said nothing. He had not prayed for years. Went through the motions during the masses in assembly hall on special occasions. Attended mass with his parents when they insisted, and followed the rituals that pleased them. He didn't care whether he pleased them or not, but peace reigned in the house when he played the role of dutiful son.

"Have you nothing to say, Costello?" Leon said, anger showing through the words.

"Brother Eugene was a nice guy," Archie said. "I liked him." Having to say something. He spoke the truth, really. There had been nothing personal in the Room Nineteen assignment. There was never anything personal in the assignments.

"I don't want to dwell on the past, Costello," Leon said. "But prayer is always good for the soul. Your own, for instance."

Archie remained silent, and Leon seemed willing to accept his silence as acceptance, because he sighed expansively, as if he had just done his good deed for the day and could go on with his usual routine. He glanced around the darkening campus, the buildings shrouded in silence, the white clapboards of the residence gleaming like dinosaur bones.

44

"I love this school, Costello," Leon said.

Like a criminal loves his crime, Archie thought. That was the secret of the world's agony, and the reason crime—and, yes, sin—would always prevail. Because the criminal, whether a rapist or a burglar, loves his crime. That's why rehabilitation was impossible. You had to get rid of the love, the passion, first. And that would never happen.

Leon looked at Archie again, seemed about to speak, and then changed his mind.

"Carry on, Costello," he said, and padded away, in those short mincing steps the guys imitated so easily and frequently.

Archie allowed himself a moment of loathing as he watched Leon disappearing into the gloom. What a fake he was. All that phony concern about Brother Eugene. Leon had done nothing about Room Nineteen, too worried about his own career. Archie had always been able to depend on that. And that's what had made him and Leon allies. Which always bothered Archie, being linked with someone like Brother Leon. Then he remembered a surprise that awaited Leon—the day of the Bishop's visit. And maybe some others.

Walking toward his car at the parking space nearest the entrance, the choice space in the lot that no one else dared occupy, Archie sought the surge of satisfaction that usually filled him when he contemplated assignments.

The wind came up, trembling the limbs of trees, rattling a shutter on the residence. Archie was suddenly elated, knew he was apart from other people. It was a dark and beautiful secret he shared with no one.

Halting near his car, he pivoted, lifted his face to the rising wind, and whispered: "I am Archie." Heard his

voice withering away in the darkness. No response, no
echo. Which was what he wanted: to be alone, separate
from the others, untouchable except by the knowing hands
and mouths of the girls at Miss Jerome's.

"**T**oo far."

"No it isn't."

"Yes it is."

"Just once. Just this once."

"Once won't be enough."

"Yes it will."

"No it won't. It never is."

It was a game they played, a delicious delightful game that made every nerve end and something else stand up at attention. A cat-and-mouse game. An inch-here-and-inch-there game. Give a little, take a little. Squeeze here and caress there. A daring, terrific game that never moved beyond a certain agonizing point which, crazy, only made him love Laurie Gundarson more and more each time they played.

The game had become a ritual. They would drive to the Chasm and park in their favorite spot, an apron of land jutting out from the hillside. The lights of Monument winked below them like neon fireflies. Obie ignored the lights, Monument, Trinity, the Vigils, as he immersed himself in the marvel of Laurie's presence here in the car, in his life.

As he kissed her she moaned softly, low, husky, a slight tremor of her body betraying her own horniness. No, not horniness. He didn't want to think of her in those terms. She was more than a body to him, more than a girl to fondle and caress. Even this game was more than a game: it was a ritual in which they expressed their love, their desire for each other, the sweet, aching longing. But Laurie would let them go only so far. So far and no further. And he always complied. He complied because he had to proceed cautiously with Laurie, never knowing when she might turn away for good. Because of Trinity, for one thing.

The night they first met, at a dance, instantly attracted to each other, coming together beautifully in a slow number, she had stiffened and drawn away when she had learned he was a student at Trinity.

"What's the matter?" he had asked.

"That place is creepy," she said, wrinkling her nose.

"All schools are creepy," he retorted, trying to pull her against him again.

"I always hear weird things about it," she said, against the music, resisting his body.

"Rumors. Don't judge me by my school." He felt as though he was betraying Trinity but realized this girl in his arms was suddenly more important than Trinity. "Judge me by what I am."

"What are you?" she asked, looking directly into his eyes.

"One of the good guys," Obie said.

And she smiled.

But Trinity always stood between them. More than

Trinity, of course: the Vigils. Actually they seldom spoke of the school, continually skirting the subject, which often left gaps in their conversations. As a result, Obie was constantly on his guard with Laurie, fearful of losing her, of doing anything to make her draw away and grow distant as she had that first night on the dance floor.

She was not distant from him now, in the car, close to him in this delicious game, responding, throbbing until, breathless, she drew back.

"Obie, please . . ."

"One more minute," he whispered.

"It's for your own good," she said, but he could hear the huskiness in her voice that always betrayed her own desire.

"Let me count to sixty."

As he spoke he squeezed tenderly and delicately, his thumb and index finger moving as if he were playing some precious instrument.

After a few moments she put on the brakes again, wrenched her mouth from his, pulled away. "Too much, and too fast," she said. Strangely enough, he was relieved. Obie had always been terrified of going all the way. He had a feeling that he would somehow fail at the last minute, botch it all up, and leave himself humiliated in her eyes. He couldn't risk that. Thus, despite his passionate protests, he was grateful for Laurie's caution, the limits she had drawn.

Holding her tenderly, he whispered: "I love you. . . ." She cupped his cheek in her hand, an endearing gesture that almost brought tears to his eyes.

A sudden slash of headlights illuminated the interior of the car. Instinctively Obie and Laurie ducked their heads. As the favorite spot in town for parkers—fellows and girls making out, caressing, or maybe just shyly talking—the

Chasm was also a target for bushwhackers, wise guys who got their kicks out of driving into the area with swiveling spotlights and squealing tires, scaring hell out of everybody. Obie and Laurie clutched each other as the intruding car swept past, the spotlights spraying the air with brilliance. The only compensation was that Laurie was close to him again, her warm and pulsing body melting into his. Darkness enveloped them completely as the car roared away and his mouth sought hers. His hand also moved in the dark, feeling the soft flesh he loved.

The delicious game again.

"Now, Obie . . ." Warningly.

"Once more."

"Obie . . ."

"Please. A ten count."

"Obie."

God, how he loved her. Wanted her. *Needed* her.

"No," she said, finality in her voice, removing his hand in a swift, impatient motion.

It was at moments like this that doubts riddled him. Did she really love him? Was she really doing this for his own good? Theirs had been a whirlwind romance, four weeks of movies and burgers at McDonald's and these sweet tortures here at the Chasm. But he realized he knew very little about Laurie Gundarson. Had never met her mother and father, few of her friends. As if he was a secret part of her life. Plenty of time later for introductions, she'd said. Or was she afraid to bring him into her life? Obie drew comfort by telling himself that she wanted him exclusively for her own.

He watched lovingly as she tucked in her blouse, patted her hair. Thank God for Laurie. She balanced the lousy things in his life, like his visit to Ray Bannister this afternoon. Watching Ray's face collapse like a folded tent in the wind when Obie had told him about the role he must play in Archie's new assignment.

"It's getting late," Laurie said, hands folded in her lap.

"I know," he said, resigned.

She could be ardent and loving one moment, prim and practical the next.

He started the car, wishing they could drive away together and keep going, never stopping, away from Monument and Trinity, Archie Costello and the Vigils.

Carter hit the wall with his fist. Bare-knuckled, unprotected by the nineteen-ounce glove he wore in the boxing ring. The impact reverberated throughout his body like an earthquake, his head snapping a bit as his fist crashed against the plaster wall. The pain, however, was sweet and fulfilling. The action had responded to Carter's need to strike out. At something, someone. Until recently Carter had drifted with the Vigils, letting things happen, indifferent, because he'd had his boxing and football. There had been a time, in fact, when he had been amused by Archie's assignments. But no more. He knew that he would never forgive Archie for the chocolate assignment, the result of which had been Brother Leon's edict disbanding the boxing team. And now the Bishop's visit.

Carter looked around the gym, this place he'd always loved. The camaraderie of the boxing squad, the smell of the place—that sweet-sour aroma of liniment and sweat-soaked clothing—and the equipment, the big bag and all the beautiful paraphernalia of the sport. Gone now. Surveying the gym, the empty bleachers, the basketball nets hanging limply at either end, the absence of the boxing ring, dismantled and gone forever, Carter felt his anger returning, mixed with sadness. All gone because of Archie Costello.

He hit the wall again, despite his bruised knuckles, and the hit felt good. He was striking back at more than Archie. Striking at the entire world. Because the world looked at him and saw the jock, the rugged football guard, the slugger in the ring. Not only the world but the officials in charge of admissions at Daleton College, which specialized in physical education. Made to order for a guy like Carter. Carter had gunned for a scholarship but had been unsuccessful. He had not yet even received an acceptance. Which kept him dangling on a string. Okay, he was not a brain, but his SAT scores were adequate. He made the honor roll now and then. But nobody saw beyond his jock image. Was there anything else to see? Yes. There was. Had to be. He had to show people, had to show everybody he was more than just a jock, an ex-jock, in fact, who stood around and did nothing.

"I've got to call Obie," he said to no one in particular. Nobody in the gym at this time of day. Lately he'd fallen into the habit of talking aloud to himself when no one was around.

He called Obie from the telephone booth in the main corridor on the first floor across from Brother Leon's office. The phone book had long ago disappeared, and he had to call information for Obie's number. The door of the booth had been torn off and never replaced. As the phone rang, Carter glanced around the corridor, his eye coming to rest on the trophy case farther down the hall. Looking at the case always made him feel good.

When Obie answered, his voice sounded thin and reedy. Carter had never spoken to him on the phone before.

"What's up?" Obie asked.

"The Bishop's visit, that's what's up," Carter said, plunging in. "I think it's a mistake, Obie."

Silence at the other end of the line.

"Archie's going too far with this one," Carter went on. "It's too much, Obie."

"With Archie it's always too much," Obie said. "Haven't you gotten used to that by now?"

"It's okay when he confines it to the school. But this new deal involves the diocese, for crissake. And the priests in town who always come as guests. It's a mistake, Obie. Archie's setting out to humiliate the Bishop. It's big trouble. Heap big trouble."

"What do you want to do about it?" Obie asked.

"I don't know."

"You're not going to make Archie change his mind, that's for sure."

Carter paused, took a deep breath, wondering how far he could go with Obie but following his instincts, the instincts that told him Obie was not exactly buddy-buddy with Archie these days. Not like the old days.

Carter plunged again. "I wasn't thinking of changing *Archie's* mind."

"Who were you thinking of?"

"Brother Leon."

He heard Obie's sharp intake of breath. He looked around at the same time, as if invoking Leon's name could cause him to appear. But the corridor was deserted.

"We've got to get Leon to call off the Bishop's visit," Carter said.

More silence at the other end of the line. Finally Obie asked: "And how do we do that, Carter?" Sarcastically.

"That's what I want to talk to you about. I mean, two heads are better than one, right?"

"Sometimes."

"Sometimes?" Carter asked, worried suddenly. Maybe he had misjudged Obie. Maybe Obie's first loyalty was to Archie, after all. "Am I talking out of line, Obie? Do you agree with me that Archie's plan for the visit is a mistake?"

"Okay, okay," Obie said, impatient, anger in his voice. "Look, I'm sick and tired of Archie Costello and his assignments too. But leading a mutiny is something else."

"I'm not talking about a mutiny, for crissakes," Carter said. "I'm talking about a quiet little plan to stop the Bishop's visit."

He heard a long-drawn-out sigh.

"I don't know, Carter. I don't like getting mixed up with Leon. Maybe there's some other way—"

"Think about it," Carter said.

"I'll do that." Pause. "Look, I've got to go. I'll talk to you later." Hurried, as if he couldn't wait to hang up.

Carter frowned as he replaced the receiver on the hook. He listened to see if his coin would be returned. No luck. He knew now he could not depend on Obie. Obie had his own problems: he also had Laurie Gundarson. Carter realized that he could not depend on anyone. Only himself.

Stepping out of the booth, he was aware of the emptiness all around him. Enjoying the sense of aloneness, Carter walked toward the trophy case with the gleaming silver and gold statuettes testifying to Trinity's triumphs on the football field and in the boxing ring. His triumphs, really.

He was hypnotized by the glow of the trophies, which

almost shimmered as the corridor lights caressed them. Even if he never got to college, never won another championship, they would remain symbols of his accomplishment. Nothing, nobody, could ever take that away.

Not even Archie Costello.

The eyes, of course. Mostly it was the eyes. They followed him around the room, like those eyes in certain paintings that haunt the viewer. Jerry looked like a figure in a painting, his face expressionless, as if caught by an artist and frozen forever. After the first few minutes of sitting across from him, unnerved by the silence in the room and those terrible eyes, the Goober had started wandering around, glancing out the window, stooping to relace his sneaker, anything to avoid that terrible, empty stare.

But it really wasn't empty. It was like the difference between a vacant house where the windows are shuttered and boarded up and a house where someone might be peeking out of the windows when you're not looking, where a billowing curtain might hide prying eyes. Crazy, Goober thought, as he looked up from his sneakers, crouched on the floor. He told himself to cool it, take it easy, start from the beginning. This was his friend, Jerry Renault. They had played football together, had run the streets together after school although Jerry had had no interest in the track team. They had shared a lot of stuff. Like the chocolates. The goddam chocolates.

Goober was determined to try again.

"How about Canada, Jerry? Did you have a good time up there?" The question sounded stupid to Goober—Jerry had been sent to Canada to recuperate. How could he have had a good time up there?

"Yes," Jerry said. The word fell between them like a heavy stone.

That was the problem. Jerry wasn't mute or completely silent, but he answered Goober's questions in monosyllables, squeezing out one-word answers that left Goober dangling. How are you, Jerry? *Fine*. Glad to be back home? *Yes*. And asked no questions of his own. Did not seem at all interested in Goober. Looked at him, in fact, as if Goober was a stranger. At one point he was afraid that Jerry would lean forward and ask: Who the hell are you, anyway?

He wished Jerry's father had let him know what to expect when he'd arrived at the house. In response to Goober's inquiry—"How's he doing?"—Mr. Renault had merely shrugged, his face tightening as if his flesh had been drawn taut from behind his skull by invisible hands. Jerry's father was a mild, soft-spoken man who seemed to drift away even as you spoke to him. An air of sadness pervaded him and the apartment as well. More than sadness. The apartment seemed lifeless, like a museum. Goober knew without any doubt that the flowers on the dining-room table were artificial, fake. He had the feeling that Jerry and his father occupied the apartment the way mannequins inhabited rooms of furniture in a department store.

The Goober had forced himself to turn off the morbid thoughts as Jerry's father led him to a den at the far end of the apartment. At first glance Jerry looked fine. No signs of the beating he had absorbed, his skin pale but unblemished. Sitting in a rocking chair, he didn't look disabled but seemed fragile, sitting stiffly, as though he might fall apart if he relaxed.

"Hi, Jerry, good to see you," Goober said, hoping Jerry didn't catch the false heartiness.

Jerry smiled remotely, said nothing, offered nothing.

That's when the one-sided conversation began, Goober like an inquisitor and Jerry like a reluctant witness, answering grudgingly or not at all.

Settling down in a chair across from Jerry now, Goober thought: One last try and then I'll go. Actually he was eager to leave, to get out of Jerry's sight. He realized that Jerry's reluctance to talk or to communicate probably stemmed from Goober's betrayal last fall. He had betrayed Jerry, hadn't he? He had allowed Jerry to face Archie Costello and Emile Janza and the Vigils all by himself. Had gone, finally, to help his friend when it was too late, Jerry bloody and beaten and broken, urging the Goober in painful gasps not to defy the Vigils or anybody else. Don't disturb the universe, Jerry had whispered out of his agony. Don't make waves.

Okay, one last try:

"Trinity's still the lousy school it's always been," the Goober said, immediately disgusted with himself. He had vowed not to bring up Trinity unless Jerry specifically asked about the school. But, desperate, he found himself going on stupidly about the place, meaningless stuff about courses and report cards, avoiding certain topics, picking his way through the monologue like someone avoiding broken glass while walking barefoot.

Surprisingly, Jerry seemed interested, eyes a bit brighter, head tilted slightly, rocking gently, long fingers gripping the arms of the chair.

The Goober decided to take a chance, to say what he had waited all these months to say:

"I'm sorry, Jerry, about last fall." Taking a deep breath, plunging on. "I let you down. Let you face Archie Costello and Emile Janza and the Vigils by yourself."

Jerry's hands flew up as if holding off an attack. He began to shake his head, eyes troubled now, not vacant or staring but shining with—what? Sadness? More than that. Resentment, hate?

"Don't . . ." Jerry said. The word as if dredged up from deep inside of him. "I don't want to talk about that. . . ."

"I have to talk about it," the Goober went on.

Jerry began to shake his head furiously, rising from the chair as if in panic, as if the building had suddenly caught fire. Tears threatened his eyes.

"That's all done with now," he said. "It's got nothing to do with me now." He turned away, walked to the window, and the Goober sensed that he was making a tremendous effort to control himself. Jerry faced him again and Goober was struck once more by how pale and fragile he seemed.

"I didn't invite you here," Jerry said, in control again, no tears visible, chin tilted a bit, defiantly. "My father did." He seemed to be groping for words. "I . . ." And turned away again, shutting out Goober as he stared out the window.

"I'm still sorry," the Goober said. Having to say it all, like confession, not expecting absolution but needing to confess. "That was terrible. What I did last fall. I just wanted you to know."

Jerry nodded, without looking back at him, still concentrating on something outside the building, still unreach-able, still looking frail and vulnerable. Which heaped fur-ther guilt on the Goober.

"Better go now," Jerry said. Sounding weary, spent. He turned around, facing Goober, but avoided his eyes.

"Right," Goober said. "Don't want to tire you out." Pretending everything was normal. "I've got an appoint-ment with my dentist." Throwing in an easy lie—was that another betrayal? "I'll come back again sometime." Never in a million years.

Jerry's father appeared at the doorway as if summoned by a bell the Goober had not heard.

"Going already, Goober?" he asked, false, voice off key, fake.

Goober nodded, turned back to say good-bye to Jerry, hoping that Jerry might say: *Stay awhile, Goob, stick around.* But not really wanting him to say that. Hoping Jerry might also say: *You didn't betray me, Goober. And even if you did, I understand. I'm still your friend.* Know-ing those were impossible words for Jerry to say.

Jerry said nothing. Merely stood there, looking troubled and abandoned, as if wounded somehow, although there was no visible mark on him.

"I've got a dentist's appointment," Goober heard him-self say inanely to Mr. Renault.

"Of course, of course," Mr. Renault replied gently, un-derstandingly. "I'm sorry. . . ."

Sorry for what?

"So long, Jerry," Goober said.

Jerry lifted his hand in a limp salute, still avoiding his eyes, and looking somewhere beyond Goober.

The Goober got the hell out of there.

Later he ran the streets of Monument, pounding the

pavement, not the leisurely pace of his usual stride but a frantic tempo, not singing as he sometimes did, lungs bursting now, full of pain and hurt but accepting the pain and the hurt. Like a sacrifice. Like the psalm they recited at mass sometimes: I offer up myself as an evening sacrifice.

Hours later, safe in his bed, pulling the covers around his shoulders, eyes tightly shut, he saw only Jerry's face. Vowed never to go near him again. But he knew somehow he must. But would think about that later, next week, next year. He slept finally, a strange blank sleep, as if he had been erased from all existence.

The next morning at school he learned that Brother Eugene had died. Which was worse even than Jerry Renault's return to Monument.

"What's her name?"

"Laurie Gundarson."

"School?"

"Monument High. A senior. Interested in drama. Played one of the leads in the senior class play." Bunting paused, then added: "She's really built. Stacked, like they say."

Bunting hesitated, coughed, a bit nervous. He and Archie were alone on the front steps of the school, the entire student body and faculty inside at the special memorial mass for the soul of Brother Eugene. Bunting had approached Archie as the students had filed into the assembly hall, asking to speak to him later. Archie had motioned him outside.

"Now?" Bunting asked. "This minute?"

The odor of burning candles filled the air.

"Why not?" Archie asked, a dare in his voice. "They'll never miss us."

Bunting had followed, swaggering, unwilling to let Archie see his apprehension about skipping the mass. He sat uneasily now beside Archie, unable to fully enjoy giving his report about Obie and the girl.

"Old Obie," Archie mused. Was that fondness in his voice? "I knew he was hooked, had it bad." He said no more. He had dispatched Bunting to find out details about the girl, a test of Bunting's effectiveness as a gatherer of information. He was also curious about her.

Bunting studied Archie, wanting to play it cool: always had to play it cool with Archie. Archie was unpredictable, and Bunting had to always be on the alert, trying to stay one step ahead. You never knew whether Archie was pleased or pissed off. So Bunting walked a continuous thin line. But it was worth it, of course. His future was linked with Archie, for the remainder of the school year, anyway. His burning ambition was to succeed Archie as the Assigner of the Vigils, and he had the inside track on the job. Archie hadn't singled out anyone else for special attention, and he was relying more and more on Bunting. In fact, Bunting was slowly but surely taking Obie's place.

Bunting had always envied Obie's nearness to Archie, which meant being near the center of power. Now he had something else to envy Obie for—his involvement with Laurie Gundarson. She was too beautiful for somebody like Obie. The other night, while he and Harley and Cornacchio were bushwhacking, they had spotted Obie and Laurie clinging together in Obie's car. Bunting had started to burn with both lust and jealousy. He was a virgin, much to his dismay and disgust, except in wild dreams in the privacy of his bed or the bathroom. He dreamed of girls exactly like Laurie, went weak sometimes with desire and longing. Yet when he came within range of a girl, something went wrong. He was tongue-tied, blushed furiously, didn't know what to do with his arms and legs. So he kept his distance and, not wanting to betray himself with the guys, he maintained a sort of world-weary demeanor, as if he'd seen it all and done it all.

Bunting looked toward the doorway—was someone standing there? One of the brothers on the search for delinquents?

"They're all too busy praying," Archie said, intercepting Bunting's glance. "You're always safe when someone's praying for the dead. Go on. Give me some specifics about that Laurie Gundarson."

So Bunting gave him specifics, a routine he'd learned observing Obie at the Vigil meetings, flipping open the pages of his notebook.

"Laurie Gundarson, straight *A*'s, high honor roll, Honor Society, Debating Club, Drama Club."

Enough specifics. Looking up, he added, confidentially: "She's gone out with lots of guys, but I think she's one of those touch-me-not types." Bunting was improvising now, letting himself be carried away by his vision of Laurie Gundarson. "Stuck up, too. A teaser." Bunting had given her a big hello once at a dance, after a half hour of summoning up his courage, and she'd looked at him as if he was transparent. Made him feel like a pane of glass. "Under all that sweet stuff and the honor roll crap, she's a bitch."

"Stick to the facts," Archie said dryly.

"Hell, anybody can tell by just looking at her that she's a tease," Bunting said. "Stacked but acting like she doesn't know what she has, what it's all about. Poor Obie." He chortled. "She's probably driving him up a wall."

Archie took his attention away from Bunting. That described his action precisely. He didn't merely look away or become distracted. He had the ability to shut a door in people's faces, dismissing them immediately, indicating his boredom or disinterest or indifference by a slight movement of his head.

Bunting realized that Archie had shut him out, leaving him alone, exposed here on the school steps.

"We saw them the other night," Bunting said, needing to capture Archie's attention again. "Making out at the Chasm."

Interest flashed in Archie's eyes.

"How far did they go?"

Bunting shrugged. "I don't know. I recognized Obie's car—he hasn't washed it for like ten years. It's lousy with dirt. We got a quick glance. They were close, maybe kissing, arms around each other."

"That all?"

"Listen, for a tease like Laurie Gundarson, that's going a long way."

Long pause, Archie thinking, eyes far away.

"You want us to do something about Obie and the girl?" Bunting asked. Gently, tentatively.

"What would you do?" Archie asked.

"Whatever you want."

Archie chuckled, a sound as dry as rolling dice.

"An interesting offer," he said, looking at Bunting again, amused.

Bunting smiled. Was that a look of admiration on Archie's face? Approval? He wanted Archie to know that he was loyal, that there were no limits to what he would do for Archie and the Vigils.

The doorway behind them exploded with bodies. Trinity students never simply left a classroom or school building: they stampeded, jousting for position, using arms and elbows, knees and thighs, to best advantage. Guys now swarmed down the stairs, swiveling, braking to avoid Archie and Bunting. Bunting leaped aside, but Archie remained on the steps, calm, unruffled, letting the tide of bodies flow around him. "I'll see you later," Archie called to Bunting, mouthing the words so that the sophomore would understand the dismissal over the noise.

Archie watched Bunting fleeing into the mass of bodies, glad to be rid of him. Archie disliked his know-it-all attitude, his smirks and strutting walk, his eager display of willingness to carry out orders. Oh, Bunting was smart enough, but he lacked style. He was gross and obvious and superficial. Not subtle at all. Subtlety was an element Archie considered precious, the most important commodity of all for the Assigner. He had never bothered to tell Bunting that.

If Bunting had been a proper pupil, Archie would have been willing to share his secrets. To tell him, for instance, how to pick victims and about the secrets of passion. Find out a person's passion and you have him in the palm of your hand. Find out what a person loves or hates or fears, and you can play that person like a violin. Find someone who cares and what he cares about, and he is yours on a silver platter. So simple, so obvious. But some people never saw this. Particularly Bunting. Bunting also wanted to generate excitement by physical means—setting up fights, crowding people, looking for blood. He had once, for crissakes, suggested loosening a banister on the third-floor stairs so that a kid would go crashing through space. Stupid. Dangerous. Not worthy of Archie Costello. Not worthy of the Vigils. When physical combat entered the scene, trouble came with it. The chocolates, for instance, even though the violence had been controlled. Yet it could have been a disaster. He could have told Bunting to remember the chocolates. But hadn't. He gave no warnings to Bunting.

"How can you stand that little bastard?"

Carter spoke directly behind Archie. He had seen Archie and Bunting leaving the assembly hall before mass, not surprised at Archie's lack of respect, his lack of guilt. Knowing that Archie was invulnerable, he focused his anger on Bunting. Somebody should be angry about what had happened to Brother Eugene.

"Bunting serves a purpose," Archie replied, not turning, letting Carter do the approaching. Which he did, of course, sitting down beside Archie.

"Got a Hershey?" Archie inquired.

Carter shook his head impatiently. Some stooges always had Hershey bars in their pockets to keep Archie in supply. Thank God Archie didn't indulge in drugs.

"Bunting is such a bastard," Carter said, flexing his arms, opening and closing his fists. "He's another Janza, for crissake. A little smoother, maybe. Doesn't pick his nose or his ass. But another Janza, all right."

Archie didn't say anything and Carter brooded, resting his chin in his hands.

"I always wonder about guys like that, Archie. Guys like Bunting and Janza." He could have added: You too, Archie. But didn't. Hated himself for his cowardice but accepted it. "Know what gets me? They're bastards and it doesn't bother them. They enjoy it. They don't even think of themselves as bastards. They do lousy things and think it's great."

"You know what the secret is, Carter?" Archie asked in that superior tone of his.

"Tell me."

"This: Everybody likes the smell of his own shit," Archie said, looking away.

Carter frowned, looked about him at guys running for buses, cars roaring out of the parking lot with shrieking brakes and wheels, the frenzy of an improvised touch-football game on the lawn.

"That's the story of life, Carter, and why things happen the way they do." Pause. "You like the smell of yours, don't you?"

"Jesus, Archie . . ." Carter began to protest but he didn't know what words to use, didn't know what to say to a thing like that. A few minutes ago he had bowed his head in prayer for the soul of Brother Eugene. Felt guilty for some reason, although he had had no part in the Room Nineteen assignment. Prayer hadn't helped. He had felt a void within himself, an emptiness, couldn't wait for the mass to end, for a chance to escape. Escape to what? To Archie Costello and his terrible words.

"Think about it, Carter," Archie said, rising to his feet, stretching, yawning, moving off. Without saying good-bye. Archie never said hello or good-bye.

Archie walked across the lawn, passing easily through clusters of students, knowing they were all conscious of his presence and making way for him, stepping aside to allow him passage.

Everybody likes the smell of his own shit.

Archie's voice echoed in Carter's mind.

You like the smell of yours, don't you?

Okay, okay.

There had to be more than that.

Had to be.

But Carter couldn't say what it was.

David Caroni waited until he was alone in the house, his father still at work at the Hensen Transportation Company, where he was employed as traffic manager, and his mother downtown shopping with his brother, Anthony. Anthony was a terrific tennis player, a natural, and he was shopping for a new racquet. His mother, who couldn't resist a shopping trip, had left a note saying she'd run her own errands while Anthony cruised the sports stores. His mother liked to write notes and make lists. Anyway, David knew that it would be at least an hour, maybe an hour and a half, before anyone came home. That was enough time.

He had not known this morning when he emerged from sleep at the ringing of the alarm that this would be the day. Yet this act he contemplated now was not the result of a sudden decision. The knowledge that his life would end sometime this year, probably before summer arrived, had been with him for weeks, months. He wasn't quite certain when the knowledge had flowered within him, at which precise moment he knew that he must end this desperate, pointless thing his life had become. He knew only that it must happen, that he must terminate what had become not even a life, really. Then what was it? A sunless, airless desert in which he trudged wearily and purposelessly, like a being from an alien planet, out of place and out of touch, without appetite or desires. Blank, unreachable, friendless, loveless. Funny. Only the knowledge that he would end this life made it bearable. Until the right moment, the right time. Which was now, this afternoon, this hour.

He seemed lifted by a light breeze as he went upstairs, placed his books tidily on the table near his bed, looking at them lingeringly, knowing there would be no need to do homework tonight, that marks did not matter. This made him smile, but it was a smile without joy or warmth. All during these past weeks he had continued to do his homework, eat his meals, take showers, shampoo his hair, wait for the school bus, take notes in school, carry on conversations with his classmates and his family, and nobody but nobody could see that he wasn't really *there*, that he was contributing nothing of himself to conversations or classes or mealtimes, holding back the essential ingredient that was himself. Me. David Caroni, son, brother, student. But it didn't matter, really, it was merely amusing in an unfunny kind of way because it would all end soon. He was thankful for that knowledge, clung to it. Otherwise he might not have made it through the dry monotony of his days and evenings.

Yet there were moments of startling surfacings, as if he were emerging from deep waters into sunlight, and for a brief moment, suspended in time, he would see the ridiculous thing his life had become, making no sense. Just as the Letter made no sense. (Of course the Letter made no sense in itself—the use of the *word* Letter was a sly and furtive substitute for the real thing.) And then the burst of sunlight would end and he would be plunged again into the sterile, austere life that was the life he now knew, no sun, no sky, nothing. No place to go and no place to hide.

He surveyed his room for a final time, remembering a poem he had read once long ago:

> *Look thy last on all things lovely,*
> *Every hour.*

His stereo, which he had loved once and played now only as a cover, a disguise, pretending that the music had meaning. The books lined up on his shelves, well-thumbed paperbacks that he had not opened for weeks although he'd always had a compulsion to read and reread favorite passages time and again. He sighed, thinking of all the faking he'd had to do in order to act normal, protecting his family so that they would not know, would not suspect, talking, listening, *acting*, Academy Award stuff, but hugging all the time his little secret within him. His eyes encountered now the posters he had plastered to his walls. Stupid, they were, really. *After the Rain, the Rainbow.* Words. Meaningless. Vowels and consonants. Letters. Twenty-six letters in the alphabet. That one fatal deadly letter. But don't think about that now. *Look thy last . . .*

He began to undress. Removed his shirt and pants. Folded them neatly on the bed. Slipped off his socks, frowning at the faint smell of foot odor, his feet having a tendency to perspire even on the coldest winter day. Pulled off his blue-plaid boxer shorts and drew his T-shirt over his head, dropped socks and shorts and shirt into the hamper. Stood naked, a bit chilly, avoiding his reflection in the full-length mirror near the closet. He had avoided his reflection for months, grateful that he hadn't yet begun to shave.

He was strangely calm and almost lifted himself on tip-toe as he felt that pleasant rising wind again, but *within* him, not outside. He was more than calm: it was a sleep-walking kind of feeling, drift, as if he were being drawn by some invisible current to an inevitable destination. He had contemplated other forms of the act but had discarded them. Had read books at the library, studied statistics, looked up methods in an encyclopedia, pondered stories in newspapers—astonished but gratified by the frequency of the act—and had finally decided on the best way. For him.

He walked, seemed to glide, toward the bureau, still avoiding the mirror, and opened the bottom drawer. He shifted odds and ends of clothing around, then lifted the white lining paper. He withdrew two envelopes and held one in each of his hands for a moment, as if his hands were plates on a scale. One envelope contained a letter that would explain to his mother and father and Anthony why this act had become necessary. He had struggled long and hard with it, knowing they must not feel guilt or blame. He had written and rewritten the letter a hundred times, find-ing it, guiltily, the only act of any pleasure in the previous months. Now he placed the letter on the bureau, against the picture they had taken of him when he won highest honors at his graduation from St. John's Parochial School. All *A*'s for eight years. He stared at the picture, thinking of the Letter, and then turned away, eager to open the other envelope.

The other envelope contained a steel single-edged razor blade, gleaming lethally in the slant of afternoon sunlight. Pleasantly lethal. His friend, his deliverer. Carrying the blade delicately between the thumb and index finger of his right hand, he walked to the bathroom, placed the blade on the top of the toilet tank, and began to run water into the bathtub. After a few moments the hot water splashed steamily into the tub, vapors rising from the water's surface, clinging to the tile walls, fogging the mirror above the small sink. He looked at the turbulent water, feeling neither hot nor cold, feeling nothing, really. He tested the water with his right hand and then increased the flow of cold. He waited patiently, conscious of the blade nearby. He tested the water again and found it to be satisfactory. He shut off the faucets.

He placed the razor blade on the side of the tub and then slipped into the water from the end opposite the faucets, letting the warmth flow over him. He was grateful for once that he was a blank. Without thought or emotion. As if he were transparent, without weight. He realized he hadn't sat in a tub for years, showering instead each morning on arising. He sighed, felt the warmth of the water seeping into his pores, the steam forming rivulets on his forehead, cheeks, and chin. Beautiful here. Soon this terrible, ugly, desperate, despicable world would come to an end along with his utterly useless place in it. Kill yourself and you also kill the world, someone had said. He would always spare his family, but how he would love to obliterate Trinity and all it stood for. Brother Leon and the Letter. *Look thy last . . .*

He reached for the blade.

But could not touch it.

Stared at it, a small steel rectangle catching the ceiling light.

His finger touched the blade but remained there, as if pinning the blade to the tub.

74

He knew he couldn't do it, could not perform this act. Not now. Not today. Today was not the day, after all.

A small glimmer lit up a corner of the dark thing his mind had become. Brother Leon's face glowed in that glimmer. Why should he go alone, leaving Leon behind, sparing him?

He drew his hand back from the razor.

Weary, exhausted, knowing he must endure this bleak existence for a while more.

And remained in the tub, weeping, until the water grew cold.

During Vigil meetings or holding court on the school steps or simply walking around the campus, Archie was always in command, in control. The only place he was not in control—although he admitted this to no one—was in Leon's office. Leon never summoned Archie to a meeting without a solid reason for doing so, and Archie always went to the meetings with his guard up, a bit on edge. Not exactly nervous: Leon didn't have the power to make him nervous.

Archie admitted to a degree of uncertainty now, as he stepped into Leon's study, but he didn't allow it to show. In fact he sat down without invitation, slouched in the chair, assuming a don't-give-a-hell attitude.

Leon regarded him critically but said nothing. They stared at each other, the old game that always had to be played. This time Leon looked away first. He pulled open the center drawer of the desk and withdrew a white envelope. His slender, dainty fingers took a sheet of folded paper out of the envelope. He unfolded the paper, shot a glance at Archie.

"Do you know about this?"

"About what?" Archie asked, alert.

Leon handed the sheet of paper to Archie. Slowly Archie reached out and took it, the motion deliberate and unhurried. He stifled his curiosity, holding the paper in the palm of his hand for a moment. Then he read the words.

> *Brother Leon:*
> *It is imperative to cancel the Bishop's forthcoming visit to Trinity. Bad things will happen if he comes. This is friendly advice, not a warning.*

The letters were printed in blue ballpoint ink. Awkward letters, slanting both left and right as if the writer of the note were drunk or didn't have full control of his hands. Or wanted to disguise his handwriting. As Archie's eyes took in the message, slowly reading again each word, another word leaped to the forefront of his mind.

Traitor.

For the first time in his years at Trinity, a traitor had appeared. Oh, there had been the expected enemies, the stubborn kids (like Renault), the animals (like Janza). The reluctant guys, the timid ones, the protestors. But never a whistle-blower, a turncoat, a traitor. Never someone tipping off the Headmaster. The ultimate act of betrayal. Because even the students who feared and hated the Vigils realized that the Vigils were on their side. The common enemy was Trinity itself, the faculty, the Headmaster, whether Brother Leon or anyone else. By their very natures the faculty and the student body were enemies. And one did not consort with the enemy. This was the worst thing that someone could do, the most despicable act of all. Thinking of all this and also: Who could it be? Not just anybody. Not just any student. Most students had been delighted by the prospect of a day off. Most students didn't care whether the Bishop or the school would be embarrassed. Most students probably *wanted* something to happen, to end this boring school term. So who?

He looked up to see Leon glaring at him. More than a glare. A baleful look full of contempt.

"This I cannot condone, Archie. Your foolish pranks here at school have been one thing, along with your stupid adolescent behavior. If your fellow students are ignorant enough to indulge you, fine. As long as it concerns only them and not me." Leaning forward, he snatched the letter from Archie's hand. "But involving the Bishop in one of your pranks . . ." He let his voice die, but the snap and crackle of his words continued to echo in the room. "This is unforgivable and could threaten the school."

Archie was always at his best when he was under attack. That's when his blood seemed to sing as it coursed through his veins, when every fiber of his body was alert and standing ready, when his brain was clear and swift, not bogged down as sometimes happened during a test, particularly math. And so he felt himself responding to Leon's attack by cooling down, becoming calm, relaxed, forming his thoughts as if they were battalions of soldiers marshaling for a defensive maneuver. Go easy, slow and easy and cool. And play the ace up your sleeve when the time comes.

"I don't blame you for being upset, Brother Leon," Archie said, voice reasonable but dignified. Mustn't give any hint of apology, because that would indicate guilt. "I've always been careful to limit . . ." Groping for the word, impossible to use *assignment*. ". . . our activities to the school, the campus." Pausing, watching Leon intently—but not too intently, must remain cool and yet permit a bit of his own anger and outrage to emerge little by little. "This is the kind of thing I've warned the guys about. But there's a lot of jealousy among the students. This jealousy . . ."

Jealousy was the key word, of course. That's why he had repeated it. Jealousy was the hook Leon had to grab. And he grabbed. "Jealousy?" Puzzled, caught off guard for a split second.

"Yes. I've heard rumors that some of the students want to disrupt the school." He knew the words sounded phony—hadn't he, more than any other person, disrupted the school through the years?—but he had to convince Leon that the words weren't phony. "The Vigils, Brother Leon, have always worked *with* the school, never against, never destructive. Oh, we probably went overboard now and then, but all in the interest of school spirit."

Archie could tell his words were having an effect.

And knew why.

Because Leon *wanted* to believe him.

That was the card up Archie's sleeve.

The fact that he and Leon had to be allies. And if Leon couldn't trust Archie any longer to keep the students in check, then all hell could break loose.

And so Leon listened intently, nodding his head as Archie talked, selecting careful words, each designed to show Brother Leon that he was innocent of any scheme to embarrass the Bishop or the school or Brother Leon himself. He explained that one of his problems had always been jealous students who attempted to discredit what he tried to do. And what he had tried to do, of course, was keep peace on the campus. The Vigils had served a purpose, didn't Brother Leon agree? Monument High, for instance, had been ravaged by student misbehavior, bomb scares, vandalism. None of those things had occurred at Trinity. Because of the Vigils.

Leon listened, expressionless now, eyes impossible to read, the eyes of a fishlike creature in a tank. He cleared his throat and indicated the letter with an accusing index finger. "What about this? I have some questions. First, what do you think the plotters planned to do during the Bishop's visit? Secondly, do you know who the plotters are? Do you have any clues to go on?"

The important thing was to assure Leon that he was on top of everything. "I know who they are, Brother Leon. Believe me, I will take care of them."

Leon seemed to be measuring Archie's words. "With discretion? I want no civil wars on this campus, no revenge or retaliation."

"Don't worry. This is a minor matter."

"Do you know what they were up to? In what way could they embarrass the Bishop and the school?"

"I have some inkling, heard some rumors," Archie said, more careful now. "A demonstration before mass, on the Bishop's arrival." Improvising. "Some signs, like a picket line."

"What kind of signs?"

Archie knew he had him now. And this is what he loved, improvising and embellishing. "Signs asking for a shorter school day, more vacation time."

"That's impossible. We must operate under state law."

"The kids know that. A nuisance effect, that's all they're after."

Doubtful now, Leon regarded the note once more.

"*Bad things will happen.* That doesn't sound like a nuisance. That sounds suspiciously like a threat."

"Guys get carried away. Believe me, Brother Leon."

Actually, Brother Leon had no choice but to believe. Archie knew that Brother Leon could do nothing about the situation without embarrassing himself. Fighting the Vigils or what he believed to be a group of dissidents would be like fighting fog, impossible to grasp or penetrate. He had to depend on Archie, take Archie's word.

Leon sighed, frowned, tugged at his chin. Even from five or six feet away, Archie smelled his stale breath, rancid breath. Then a smirk developed on Leon's lips. Slowly Brother Leon opened the drawer once more, withdrew another sheet of paper, glanced at it and then at Archie.

"Whatever the conspirators planned was all in vain, at any rate," he said. "I received a letter from the diocese yesterday. It has been necessary for the Bishop to cancel his visit this year. The National Council of Bishops has called an important meeting in Chicago." He placed the letter on the desk, on top of the other, squared them off neatly, meticulously, the delicate fingers like insect legs.

Leon regarded Archie with triumph, smiling almost grotesquely, a caricature of a smile really. Leon was not accustomed to smiling. But something else was behind the smile, behind those icy cold eyes, the moisture frozen now, a smile that said Leon had not believed a word of what Archie had said. Which did not bother Archie in the least. The important thing is that Leon had chosen to pretend he had believed.

"Let me reiterate, Archie," Leon said, and the smile was gone now, so quickly that it might never have been there. "I want no embarrassments, no violence, no incidents here on the campus. We have less than two months to graduation. This has been a difficult year. A year with great triumphs—the most successful chocolate sale of all time, for instance—but a year of change and uncertainty. I want this year to end on a note of triumph."

Archie made ready to leave, didn't want to linger here any longer than necessary, never knowing what other surprises Leon had up his sleeve.

"You may go," Leon said, settling back, the smugness on his face as he fanned himself with the letter from the seat of the diocese.

Archie wasted no time getting out of there, rose from his chair without hesitation and made his way to the door. No good-bye, no thanks a lot, Brother Leon. Thanks for nothing.

Outside, Archie paused in the corridor as if to catch his breath, but it wasn't his breath he needed to catch, it was something else, *someone* else. His mind raced, zigzagging all over the place.

Who wrote that note?

Who was the traitor?

Their favorite spot at the Chasm was occupied by another car, so Obie steered toward an unfamiliar area at the far end and finally parked near a big old maple tree, with branches so low they scraped the roof of the car. He killed the motor and turned toward Laurie.

She sat in the far corner of the front seat, hunched up, her arms wrapped around her chest, shivering once in a while. She had a cold. Her nose was red. So were her eyes. One of those sudden spring colds that arrived overnight, without warning.

"I'm sorry," he said.

"About what?" Sniffing, voice nasal.

"About making you come out tonight, bringing you here." But he hadn't seen her for three nights: she'd been busy with a play rehearsal, homework, a shopping trip with her mother. Or had she been avoiding him for some reason?

She wiped her nose with a Kleenex, looked at him, eyes watery. "No fooling around, though, Obie. Besides, you'd probably catch a million germs."

I wouldn't mind, he thought, face warm with guilt. Despite how miserable she looked, he still felt a surge of desire, would love to kiss her, touch her, even if she were hot with fever. God, what a pervert I am, he thought. But you're not a pervert when you're in love, are you?

He reached out to touch her hand and she drew away. "Now, Obie . . ." she said.

Hey, I can't catch your cold by holding your hand, Obie thought. But didn't say anything. He pondered the terrible baggage of love: all the doubts, the jealousies, the questions he didn't dare ask. Like: Do you really love me?

Instead he asked another question: "Is something wrong?"

"I've got this cold," she answered, with a trace of impatience.

Instinct drove him on. He hated that instinct. "Sure it's not something else?"

"Lots of things. This cold. I missed the honor roll by one lousy C plus. . . ."

"I didn't know that. You never talk about school—"

"And Trinity," she said, the word like a bomb thrown in Obie's face. "What I keep hearing about Trinity. All my friends say—"

"What do your friends say?" he asked, trying for sarcasm but failing, his voice suddenly hoarse.

"Well, for one thing," she said, "they say there's a monster operating at Trinity. Archie What's-his-name. He's the head of a secret society and he's surrounded by a bunch of . . . stooges. Worse than stooges: They run his errands and do all kinds of gross things. . . ." The words tumbled out, as if she'd been saving them up and couldn't get rid of them fast enough.

Obie was at a loss for a reply.

She turned toward him. "Do you know this guy? This character? This Archie Whatever . . ."

He had a feeling that Laurie knew Archie's last name. Did she know everything else, too?

"Costello," he said. "His name is Archie Costello. And I know him. Hell, Trinity's not that big."

"They say he runs Trinity like some kind of Mafia gangster. Is that true, Obie?" Wiping her eyes as if weeping. But she wasn't weeping. She sounded like a lawyer in court, for crying out loud.

"There's no Mafia at Trinity," he said.

"Is there a secret society there?"

Damn it. He always had to proceed carefully with Laurie Gundarson, always in sweet agony, never certain of her feelings. Why did she have to bring Trinity up tonight? Because she felt miserable, because of the cold? Was she the kind of person who wanted to make other people feel rotten just because she felt rotten?

"Is there?" Laurie asked, wiping her nose like mad with the Kleenex.

"Okay," he said, sighing. "Yes, there's a secret organization at Trinity—"

"Are you a member of it? One of the . . . you know . . ."

He had to deny her words. Turning to her, he ached to tell her everything. He wanted to tell her that he had already defected from the Vigils—in spirit, at least—that he was merely going through the motions these days, that he and Archie were no longer friends. They'd never been friends, really. But he knew he couldn't say anything about that. What could he tell her, then?

He reached out and took her hand. It was cool, impersonal, like a piece of merchandise on a store counter. "Look, Laurie, every school has its traditions—some are okay, some are crazy. Stuff goes on all the time. Monument High's the same. I'll bet it has some weird traditions, too. So Trinity has the Vigils. But it's not all bad." He squeezed her hand to emphasize his words but there was no response: she could have been wearing surgical gloves. "The most important thing in the world for me now is you. You're the greatest thing that ever happened to me." He heard his voice crack, the way it used to when he was an eighth grader and his voice was changing. "I love you, Laurie. You're all that matters. Not the Vigils, not Trinity, nothing . . ."

That's when the spotlight caught him and Laurie in its glare, illuminating the entire front seat. Laurie's face was ghostly white in the harsh radiance. "Lock your door," he called to her, moving to do the same to the door on his side. But it was too late. The front door on Laurie's side was flung open and a lewd laugh rose out of the darkness behind the light. Obie squinted, trying to see beyond the burst of light, sensing that there was more than one person out there, felt as though he and Laurie were surrounded. He hoped it was all a joke, a prank. A sick prank but still a prank.

"Everybody out," a voice called. Muffled, a voice he did not recognize.

"She's juicy, right?" another voice said. "Can I be first?"

Obie knew instantly that this was not a prank. The door beside him swung open and at the same moment Laurie began to scream, a scream like a knife plunged into his heart. Rough hands gripped him, pulling him out of the car. Laurie's screaming was cut off abruptly, like someone snapping off a stereo.

And the sudden silence was even worse than the screaming.

PART TWO

I t hadn't been much of a rape, really.

Not a rape at all, in fact.

Archie, frankly, grew bored as Bunting again went into the details. He realized Bunting habitually repeated himself, making a statement, then stating it again, and sometimes a third time, as if you were too stupid to understand what he had said in the first place.

Yet Archie was secretly delighted as he listened to Bunting's lurid recital of events. He was delighted because he saw that Bunting was perfect for what he had planned for the future. The audacity, for crissake: a rape. And then the botching of it. Perfect.

Archie had enjoyed Bunting's discomfort as he listened to the details. But Bunting had not gone into all the details, of course. There were certain things Bunting kept to himself, would not share with Archie Costello. He told Archie about Harley and Cornacchio. How Cornacchio had taken care of Obie beautifully, seized him and dragged him from the car, held him in a fierce armlock, forced him to the ground, shoving his head under the car so that he couldn't see anything or anybody. That was important. Good job by

Cornacchio. Harley had also performed above expectations. He had yanked open the door on the passenger side of the car, reached for the girl, and then, as if acting from instinct or long practice, had grabbed at her sweater and pulled it up over her face, blinding her, keeping her from witnessing anything, her arms imprisoned above her head.

The part that he did not tell Archie: how the raising of the sweater had revealed her bra. White, full, heaving. Like in the movies or the magazines. Beyond Bunting's wildest dreams. He hadn't realized Laurie Gundarson's breasts were so large, concealed as they'd always been by blouses and sweaters. Bunting lunged toward her, wanting to fill himself with her, wanting to fill *her* with him, aching with desire, lust, the necessity to grab her, hold her close, caress those beauties. He pinned her down with his body as she struggled and squirmed, small mews of protest muffled in the sweater. For one sweet, throbbing moment he held her right breast in his hand, full and firm in the nylon bra, yet soft and yielding at the same time. He'd never touched a girl's breast before, and he throbbed with such ecstasy that his breath came in sharp bursts. Beautiful. But without warning Laurie Gundarson kicked out, her legs churning and thrashing, and at the same time she managed to scream, loud and piercing. Pain arrowed through Bunting's groin. All desire left him; he grew limp. He released her in revulsion. Realized suddenly and with blinding clarity what they—*he* was doing. Rape, for crissake. That was sick. Nausea swept his stomach. He shouted to Harley: "Christ, let's get out of here," thankful that his voice emerged hoarse, almost a grunt, unrecognizable to his own ears and, he hoped, to hers as well.

They abandoned the scene as quickly as they had struck,

withdrawing without pause, leaving the girl whimpering, face still covered, and Obie under the car, legs jutting out at a grotesque angle. They roared away, Hailey laughing like a madman while Bunting managed to bring himself under control. Take it easy. As they raced away from the Chasm, Bunting's thoughts also raced, reliving the incident to see if they'd left behind clues to their identities. Was certain they hadn't. Almost certain. But even if the girl or Obie had caught a glimpse of their faces, what could they do? Three against two. The couple's words against theirs. Still, an alibi would come in handy. And Bunting knew immediately who would provide that alibi.

"Okay, okay," Archie said now, letting his annoyance and distaste finally show. "Why are you telling me all this?"

They were sitting in Archie's car in the parking lot, a half hour before the start of classes. Bunting had called Archie early this morning, rousing him from sleep. Ordinarily, Archie would have bristled with anger—home and school were separate entities in his life—but the urgency in Bunting's voice had held his anger in check. Something else: a bad dream during the night, of snowflakes large as letter-sized papers covering the entire city of Monument. Soiled snowflakes, dirtied by scrawled words, falling suffocatingly on the world. Archie had leaped from sleep, glad to leave the nightmare behind.

"I had to tell someone, Archie. I mean, you've pulled a lot of stuff in the Vigils—"

"Never rape," Archie said quickly, contempt in his voice. "Never anything like that."

"We didn't rape her," Bunting protested. "I didn't even touch her." He knew he had to cling to that statement.

"Assault," Archie said. "I was going to say assault with a deadly weapon." He looked down at Bunting. "But I don't think the weapon's very deadly. . . ."

Bunting flushed but didn't reply, willing to take this abuse if he got what he wanted from Archie.

"Thing is," Bunting said after a pause, knowing the plunge he was taking, "we could use an alibi—"

"Alibi," Archie scoffed. "What is this—*Saturday Night at the Movies*?"

"I mean, in case they saw us. Caught a glimpse. I figure the Vigils could cover us. . . ."

"I thought you said they didn't see you. Or anything else. The girl's sweater over her head, Obie under the car. That you didn't touch her—"

"But just in case . . . I think it's better to be prepared," Bunting said stubbornly. Then played his ace. "In fact . . ." Letting the words dangle there.

"In fact what?" Archie asked, immediately suspicious. Until this moment, he had been half amused by Bunting's dilemma.

"I was thinking," Bunting said, choosing his words carefully, "that maybe Obie thinks this was a Vigil assignment."

"Are you crazy, Bunting? Obie is part of the Vigils. We always protect our members. Never touch them. He's at all the meetings. . . ."

Bunting sighed, then plunged.

"The other day when I told you about Obie and the girl at the Chasm—remember?"

"I remember."

"I asked if you wanted anything done about them."

"I didn't tell you to do anything."

"You didn't tell me *not* to do anything," Bunting said, speaking deliberately.

"Christ, Bunting, what are you saying?"

"I figured you *wanted* us to do something. That you were being . . . subtle." Subtle: a beautiful word, Bunting thought, ready and waiting when he needed it.

"I don't have to be subtle," Archie responded, voice cold. "When I want something done, I say: Do it."

"But you're a subtle guy, Archie," Bunting said, pressing on, knowing that if he could make Archie a part of what had happened last night, his troubles were over. "Last night we were driving around and went to the Chasm and I saw Obie's car there. Then I remembered our conversation. How you seemed to want something done about Obie. And the girl. And we figured we'd throw a little scare into them. Then . . ."

"Then what?" Archie asked, realizing how dangerous this little bastard was. Had to be cautious. This was not assignment stuff, or fun and games on campus. This was assault. Attempted rape. Suppose the girl went to the police?

"Then . . ." Bunting began. And halted. Because what had started out as a dare, a threat, a bit of fun, had turned into something else once he'd approached the car and seen Laurie Gundarson there. "Then . . . what happened, happened." A bit panicky now, he said: "But it wouldn't have happened at all, Archie, if I'd thought you didn't want it to happen."

Archie drew a deep sharp breath. Then sank inside himself, as he often did when he needed to pull back, think things through, assess a situation, make a decision. Bunting was apparently shrewder than he had thought, trying to make Archie an accessory both before and after the fact.

Obie, of course, was the key figure. All depended on what Obie and the girl had done after the attack, whether they had decided to remain quiet or report the incident. Archie didn't think they had gone to the police. That kind of news traveled fast, and all seemed peaceful this morning at Trinity: no police cruisers, no sign of unusual activity on the campus. With the police not involved, the case became much simpler. First of all, the assault did not have any Vigil trademarks. Obie knew that Archie did not operate on the level of assaults and rapes. Yet this stupid incident could have repercussions. The problem was that he did not know what effect the attack had had on Obie, what Obie was thinking at this minute, what he suspected. His first step was a confrontation with Obie. Obie had always been transparent to Archie, could hide no secrets.

"Bunting," he said, voice sharp and cold. "Here's the deal. A Vigil meeting today. The usual time . . ."

Doubt formed a frown on Bunting's face.

"Dig into your notebook and find somebody for an assignment. Pick a name from the list I gave you the other day."

"But Obie will be at the meeting," Bunting said. The last thing he wanted was to meet Obie face to face.

"Exactly."

Let Bunting stew awhile. Let him worry through the day.

"Problems are never solved by delay," Archie said in his best lecturing tone, enjoying Bunting's growing discomfort. "We have a problem here, and the best way to solve it is to take action. So we meet today. Bring everybody together. Business as usual. That's why we need a kid for an assignment. Everything must look normal. And then let me read between the lines." This is what Archie loved. Showdowns, sixguns at sunset, adversaries coming face to face. To see what would happen, what explosions would be touched off or, if not explosions, what emotional collisions would occur.

There was an even more important reason for calling a meeting, however. The Obie-Bunting showdown was only a screen for Archie's real purpose—searching for the traitor. He suspected that the traitor was a member of the Vigils. More than suspected. Few kids outside the Vigils knew that the day off from school was to have coincided with the Bishop's visit. And the letter to Leon had focused on the visit. Thus, the meeting was a place to begin his pursuit of the traitor, and instinct—instinct that never failed him—dictated that he would find his betrayer there.

He turned again to Bunting, saw his troubled countenance, the beads of sweat dancing on his upper lip.

"And Bunting . . ."

"Yes?"

"Forget the alibi. The Vigils don't provide alibis," Archie said. The words final, like a trapdoor slamming shut.

Notices for Vigil meetings were always posted on the main bulletin board in the first-floor corridor, directly across from the Headmaster's office. Archie was entertained by the location of the notice right under Leon's nose. The notice was simple, involving the words TRINITY HIGH SCHOOL at the top of the board. On the day of the meeting, the Y of Trinity was inverted: ⅄. Which made it look, as Archie said, like an upright finger. Thus, the Vigils giving the finger to the world while calling a meeting. That's what the upside-down Y was called: the Finger.

Bunting inverted the Y shortly before the bell sounded for the start of classes. Stepping away from the bulletin board, he pondered his next move: delivering the invitation, without being spotted, to the victim selected for today's meeting. The invitation was usually a crudely written note left in the victim's desk in his homeroom, or in his locker, sometime during the day. Bunting delivered the note without difficulty a few minutes later—the victim's homeroom was empty, and he slipped the sheet of paper into the desk without risk of being seen.

As he headed for his first class, Bunting's mind was dark with doubts and forebodings. He wondered whether his confession to Archie this morning had been a mistake. He knew he could control Cornacchio and Harley. But Archie was different, so different that Bunting sometimes woke up in a cold sweat in the middle of the night, almost sorry that he had ever gotten involved with Archie and the Vigils.

Obie had gotten into the habit of checking the bulletin board for a possible Vigil meeting ever since Bunting had come on the scene. There had been a time, only a short while ago, when Obie had controlled the meetings and inverted the Y. But Archie had been carrying on his own relationship with Bunting for a few weeks, obviously grooming him for the role of Assigner, and Obie had accepted the situation. Because Laurie had become more important than calling Vigil meetings.

Now he was like all the other Vigil members, at Archie's mercy, unable to plan what to do after school until he learned whether a meeting was scheduled. This morning, like all mornings, he headed for the board before going to his locker. Did it automatically. Still numb from the events of the night before, he trudged wearily down the corridor, feeling dull, eyes burning from lack of sleep, an anger he had never known before smoldering within him, consuming him, taking away his appetite, making him sleepless, feeding his thoughts—and his thoughts were agonizing as he played over in his mind last night's events.

Laurie. Her cries. The assault upon her body. The devastation to her—her *being*. As if they had violated the thing that made her a person, a girl, a woman. When he finally confronted her after scrambling to his feet, the echo of the departing car deafening in his ears, she had looked at him with such an expression of—what? Fear, loathing, revulsion. Eyes wide with panic, injury, and the most terrible thing of all—accusation. As if he himself had been the attacker.

In short hysterical bursts, she told him what had happened while he had been a helpless prisoner under the car. She had not been raped. It took her a long time to get the words out, and Obie winced as he saw how hard it was for her to talk. She was like a child crying in the dark, horrified, in the middle of the night. Not raped, no, but he, whoever he was, had touched her. *Touched.* As she said the word, the sobs began again. Obie was unable to comfort her. All the time that she was telling him what had happened, she kept herself shriveled away from him, huddled pathetically against the door. And then silence, snifflings, a sigh now and then. She refused to speak after that first outburst, sat silent and immobile as Obie drove her home. He felt hopeless, helpless.

In an attempt to provide reassurance, he reached out to touch her, hold her hand, caress her shoulder. She shrank away from him, shuddered a bit. He tried to apologize for what had happened, felt responsible, guilty, knew that he had failed to protect her. Christ, he thought as he drove carefully through the darkened streets, if only he'd had some warning. If only he was the macho type, knew karate, how to defend himself instead of being so easily, effortlessly subdued.

His arm still ached from the way the guy had pushed it far up his back. Would ache forever, it seemed. But it was not as bad as the ache he felt in his soul, his spirit, whatever it was in him that had suddenly come into existence in order to hold his anguish.

Now, in the corridor, he saw in dismay the Finger on the

bulletin board. Could he face a meeting today? He only wanted to get through the classes somehow and then drive to Laurie's house this afternoon.

She had sent him away last night in silence. She was calm by the time they reached her house, in control, but a deadly calm, a part of her elsewhere, not in the car, out of his reach, beyond his presence.

"You okay?" he asked, frowning, emotions in a whirl, wanting to say *something*, the right thing, but confused, not knowing what to do or say.

"Yes," she answered. But the *yes* was unconvincing.

"Sure?"

"I'm sure."

They agreed to do nothing about the assault, decided not to report it to the police. After all, there had been no rape and no injuries inflicted: they had not really seen the assailants, had no evidence, no clues to their identities. What's more, Laurie said she did not want to talk about the attack, not to the police, not to anybody.

"Talking about it makes me feel dirty," she said. After a long pause: "I don't feel clean anymore."

He kissed her lightly on the cheek, not daring anything else. She didn't flinch but did not respond. "I'll call you tomorrow after school," he whispered. She did not reply. Then she went into the house, walking slowly, robotlike. Watching her go up the steps, he dreaded the possibility that he had somehow lost her, that things would never be the same again. And told himself: Tomorrow everything will be different, will be better. He clung to that thought. That's all he had.

Now, on top of all that, a Vigil meeting. The last thing in the world he needed.

•　　•　　•

Carter saw the Finger and swore.

He'd avoided Archie this morning, feared somehow that Archie would look into his eyes and know immediately that he had sent the letter to Brother Leon. Carter knew his strengths and weaknesses, knew what he was good at and what he lacked. Confident about his prowess as an athlete, he was no great shakes when it came to Archie's specialties: intimidation, outguessing people, anticipating their thoughts and actions. Archie was always one step ahead.

Frowning at the bulletin board, as if the X would disappear if he stared long enough, he wondered whether he had made a mistake. He'd taken a terrible chance when he'd decided to tip off Brother Leon about the visit. That kind of thing was outside his experience. He had painstakingly written the letter in fourth-period study, printing with his left hand. Delivering it to Leon had been easy—he had merely slipped it into the letter box inside his office door. The agony came after the letter had been delivered. The realization of what he had done. The possibility that Leon would know through some shrewdness who had written it. And would inform Archie. Leaving the school, looking over his shoulder, feeling as if unseen watchers were stalking him, Carter was filled with regret. He should have minded his own business, let the Bishop come, let the chips fall. Jeez. Head down, moving in his muscular, athletic way—movements that always kept people out of his path—Carter began hours of torment. Found it hard to concentrate on his homework. Pushed his food around on his plate at supper. Finally plunged into dreamless sleep. But didn't feel rested or refreshed when he woke up.

He turned away from the bulletin board, blinking away the afterimage of the inverted Y that remained printed on his brain. He spotted Archie Costello heading in his direction, surrounded by stooges, as usual. Carter looked around in panic, spotted the door to the janitor's storage room. He stepped into the room, closed the door softly behind him, didn't turn on the light. Listening to the hammering of his heart, he waited, picturing Archie passing by in all his swagger and insolence. What's happened to me? he thought.

Ah, but he knew what had happened to him. Why he was hiding here in the storage room among the mops and brooms and buckets.

Writing the letter had been the action of a rat.

An informer.

A traitor.

He had become one of the things he'd always hated, a thing hiding in the dark now, afraid to face the world.

And all because of Archie Costello.

A German shepherd sat, silent and still, beneath a hovering tree on the sidewalk in front of the white cottage with black shutters on Hale Street, watching the Goober's progress with baleful yellow eyes. He had seen the dog before, and always hurried past. He felt that someday the dog would strike, attacking him swiftly and viciously, without barking, without warning.

This morning he had more than the German shepherd to worry about, however. As he left the dog behind on Hale Street and turned into George Street, he felt as if he were running away from a ghost, the ghost of Brother Eugene, and he shivered in the morning air even though his body pulsed with the exertion of running. He had still not fully absorbed the fact of Brother Eugene's death, although the announcement over the intercom and the memorial mass had taken place days ago. Leon's voice on the intercom was still fresh in his mind. *Death, after a lengthy illness.* How long was lengthy? As long as the time between last fall's destruction of Room Nineteen and the moment Brother Eugene took his last breath?

Cut it out, he told himself now, as he almost twisted his ankle on a corner of sidewalk jutting slightly higher than the rest of the pavement. You had nothing to do with Eugene's death. It's a coincidence, that's all. Okay, a terrible coincidence, but a coincidence all the same. He had shouted the word *coincidence* in his mind a thousand times in the last few days. The scene in Brother Eugene's classroom, the clutter of collapsed desks and chairs, and Eugene in the middle of the rubble, tears streaming down his cheeks, his chin wobbling like an infant's, was burned into the Goober's mind.

The Goober had been the student assigned to take Brother Eugene's room apart. Archie Costello had given the orders: to loosen the screws in the chairs and desks—including Eugene's chair and desk—to the point where the furniture would collapse at the slightest touch. He was assisted in the job by masked members of the Vigils during the long night he spent in the classroom. The next morning he had witnessed the destruction of Brother Eugene, a shy and sensitive teacher who often read poetry aloud in the final moments of class, despite certain snickers and smirks. Brother Eugene had stood devastated in the midst of the classroom's debris, unable to believe the assault on his beloved room. Shocked, crying—the Goober had never before seen a grown man crying—shaking his head in a refusal to believe what his eyes told him must be so. He had immediately gone on sick leave. Had never returned to Trinity after that shambles of a day. He had died last week in New Hampshire, but the Goober knew that his death had really taken place last fall. And the Goober was responsible, as if he had held a gun to the teacher's temple and pulled the trigger. No, it wasn't like that at all, a small

103

voice within him protested. A collapsing classroom is not fatal, doesn't bring on a heart attack or whatever physical illness caused Eugene's death. But who knows? He repeated the words now, gasping them out of the depths of his guilt and despair, as he ran blindly through the morning. *Who knows?*

I know. I should have refused the assignment from the Vigils. But nobody refused Vigil assignments, nobody denied whatever Archie Costello demanded.

He found himself on Market Street, with its rows of high-rise apartment buildings and condominiums. His arrival here was not accidental. Jerry Renault lived in one of the apartment buildings. The Goober refused to look up at the building, kept his eyes riveted on the pavement. The ghost of Brother Eugene following him down the street was bad enough; he didn't need another ghost joining the pursuit. Jerry Renault wasn't dead, of course. Yet something of him had died. Although he looked like the friend he had known last year, that Jerry Renault was now gone. The guy who had been subdued and distant the other day was someone else altogether. Which was just as well. He had betrayed that other Jerry Renault. Just as he had betrayed Brother Eugene. . . .

He looked down the street toward Jerry's apartment building. He searched the facade, the rows and rows of windows, fastening finally on the fourth floor. Wondering if Jerry was standing behind the curtain at one of the windows, staring out.

Aw, Jerry, he thought. Why did things have to turn so rotten? Life at Trinity could have been so beautiful. He and Jerry on the football team, the quarterback and the long end, linked by the beautiful passes Jerry threw, linked even more by a budding friendship. All of it gone now. Brother Eugene dead and Jerry Renault maimed. And him, Roland Goubert, the Goober, dogged with guilt, almost afraid to look at his hands, afraid he'd see bloodstains.

Stupid, he told himself. You were stupid. Acting that way when the Goober came. Stupid. The word was a theme weaving its way through his thoughts, and he got up from the chair, threw down the magazine he'd been holding for ten minutes without reading a word of it, and went to the window. Pulled the curtain and looked out at the street. Everything gray outside: the street, the cars, the buildings, the trees. Glancing back at the room, the drabness of the beige walls and the nondescript furniture, he wondered whether he was the one at fault, had gone color-blind, would forever see the world in muted tones.

All of which was evading the question, of course.

What question?

The question of the Goober and why he'd acted so stupidly when the Goober visited him.

I should have stayed in Canada, he thought, turning from the window. I shouldn't have come back.

After those bruised weeks of pain and desolation in the Boston hospital, he had accepted without protest or any emotion at all his father's decision to send him to Canada, to spend a few months with his uncle Octave and aunt

Olivine. They lived in the small parish of St. Antoine on the banks of the Riviere Richelieu, where his mother had lived as a child. His small Canadian world had three focal points: the modest farm operated by his uncle and aunt; the village, which consisted of a few stores, a post office, and a Sunoco service station; and the ancient church, a small white frame building overlooking the aimless river. He spent a lot of time in the church, although he found it spooky at first, creaky, buffeted by stiff river winds. The winds breathed life into the old building, made the floors squeak, the walls buckle, the windows rattle. He didn't pray; not at first, anyway. Merely sat there. The winter had been mild by Canadian standards but the wind was relentless, blowing away the snow that fell almost every day. The church was a good resting place after his daily walk from the farm to the village. He picked up a few groceries, checked the post office for mail (his father wrote at least once a week, brief, keep-in-touch letters that said nothing, really), and began to look forward to the church visits.

The wind made the church talk. The Talking Church. The small hum of the boiler addressing the hiss of the steam pipes. The walls and windows chattering to each other, and the creaking floor contributing to the conversation. He smiled as he listened to the small whispering, chatting sounds. His first smile in ages. As if the church had induced his smile. After a while he knelt and prayed, the old French prayers his mother had taught him long ago—"Notre Père"; "Je Vous Salue, Marie"—the words meaningless but comforting somehow, as if he and the church had joined each other in a kind of companionship.

His aunt and uncle treated him with gruff tenderness and affection. A childless couple, farmers, at the constant mercy of the elements, they were patient, quiet people. His uncle's only vice was television, and he watched it continuously when he wasn't out in the fields or the barn, marveling at the succession of programs on the glowing tube, uncritical, amused, whether watching a soap opera in French or a hockey game with his beloved Canadiens from Montreal. His aunt was a small peppy woman whose hands were never empty and fingers never still as she knitted, crocheted, sewed, cooked, dusted, swept, bustled around the modest house. She did all this in silence. The television provided the soundtrack to their lives.

Jerry spoke a bit of French, enough to get by, but he too enjoyed the absence of conversation, learned to accept the sounds of television. He immersed himself in the daily routine of chores, going to the village and the church, reading late at night, blocking from his mind all thoughts of Monument and Trinity, as if by some magic he was able to turn his mind into a blank screen at will.

More and more drawn to the church, he found comfort there, despite the chilled atmosphere. He had read somewhere of contemplatives, priests or brothers or monks, who spent their days and nights in solitude, praying, musing, contemplating, and Jerry could understand the peace these men must attain. The afternoon sun would lose its warmth, the church growing colder, the pipes rattling, and Jerry would shiver himself back to the warmth of the farmhouse.

So the winter passed, a succession of peaceful days and evenings, Monument and Trinity existing in another world, another time, having nothing to do with him. Until his father telephoned to say it was time to come home. "I miss you, Jerry," he said. And Jerry felt tears stinging his eyes. *I miss you, Jerry.* Although he was reluctant to leave the peace and serenity of St. Antoine, he felt a leap of gladness at his father's words.

Once back in Monument, however, he longed to return to Canada, to see the spring season bursting in the fields, wondering what kind of conversation the church would be carrying on with the windows open to the outside world. But knew that was impossible. He had to resume his life here in Monument. Enter Monument High in the fall. Live according to the rules he had established for himself after the chocolate sale. Don't make waves, go with the flow. Pretend the world wore a sign like the kind hanging on doorknobs in motels: DO NOT DISTURB. But the Goober's visit had upset his balance, taking him by surprise.

"I really acted stupid this afternoon. Right, Dad?" he had asked as they sat at the supper table that evening.

"I wouldn't say stupid," his father replied. "Besides, it was my fault. I didn't realize you weren't ready for that kind of thing. . . ."

"But I should be. And I should tell the Goober that he didn't double-cross me last year. Cripes, he acts like he was a traitor or something. And he wasn't."

Silence in the dining room. Their lives were filled with silences, but not the comfortable kind that existed in the farmhouse in St. Antoine. Because his father was quiet and reserved by nature, they had never talked at length, communicated mostly in brief conversations with many stumblings. The death of Jerry's mother a year before had stunned them into a deeper silence, his father moving as in a trance through his days and evenings while Jerry had been immersed in his own troubles. Entering Trinity. Football and making the freshman team. The chocolate sale. And everything that followed. Which Canada had helped him forget. Until the Goober showed up.

"I should call him, right?" Jerry asked.

"Not if it hurts you, son. You're the important one. The Goober can always wait. . . ."

Again the silence. In the silence, Jerry was grateful for his father's words. Let the Goober wait. He felt bad for his old friend, but he had to make certain that he himself was back to normal again, restored and repaired, before he worried about others.

And yet. And yet.

Later, after his father had gone to work, Jerry found himself at the telephone, looking at the phone book under the instrument. Could almost recall the Goober's number, not certain of the last digit—6 or 7? Reached for the telephone book but, finally, didn't pick it up. Some other time.

He went to the window, glanced out at the dark street, and withdrew into the room. He knew that he had to get out of this apartment, pick up the pieces of his life. Walk the streets, drop in at the library, check the record store, breathe some spring air into his lungs. And call the Goober.

Maybe tomorrow.

Or the next day.

Or never.

Tubs Casper had sworn off girls forever. But the result of that decision was agonizing. He hadn't realized it would be this way when he broke up with Rita, said good-bye forever, stalked off in anger and desperation and, yes, pain. Jeez, what pain. Pain in his heart and in his groin. He felt wounded, as if he'd been through a war in the trenches like the soldiers in World War I—the War to Make the World Safe for Democracy, they had called it in Social Science—trudging through his days and nights like the walking wounded, trying to keep himself from feeling anything, which was impossible, of course. Worst of all, he was eating like a madman and had gained nine pounds, which meant he was now forty-five pounds overweight. Found it hard to breathe going up the stairs, sweated all the time, perpetually moist, oozing. And on top of all that, the Vigils.

He was bubbling with sweat now as he stood in the small storage room in the gym. He had to blink to get rid of the perspiration gathering in his eyes. He knew that he looked as if he was crying. But he wasn't. He didn't want anybody to think he was a weeper. Underneath this terrible fat that he couldn't get rid of or disguise, he was brave and strong and durable. As he stood before the members of the Vigils, he was determined to put up a good front, despite the fat and the sweat. He recognized some of the guys who sat in the room's dimness, knew their names but had never talked to any of them. Freshmen like Tubs kept out of the way of upperclassmen. He looked around for the kid called Obie but did not see him here. Obie was the only Vigil member he had talked with, and he preferred not to think about their association, because it had to do with Rita and the chocolates.

There was an attitude of waiting in the room, the guys talking together in low tones, acting as if Tubs didn't exist. Tubs knew who they were waiting for. Archie Costello. He dreaded Archie Costello's arrival. He knew all about him, his power and his assignments.

The door swung open, admitting a shaft of light. Without looking, Tubs knew that the great Archie Costello was now on the scene. All conversation ceased and the guys became alert, tension developing as if somebody had lit a fuse and everyone was waiting for an explosion to occur.

"Hello, Ernest," Archie said.

Caught off guard by the use of his real name (he really hated "Tubs" but had learned to accept the nickname), Tubs swiveled toward him.

A smile on his face, Archie regarded Tubs with something like affection. Tubs wasn't exactly put at ease, but his sense of doom and foreboding diminished a bit.

"Too bad about Rita," Archie said, after pausing a moment, speaking casually as if they were continuing a conversation begun earlier.

Tubs was caught off guard again. First, he'd expected the meeting to be called to order. Second, nobody was supposed to know about Rita and what had happened. But the kid called Obie knew about her. *Too bad about Rita.* Tubs's heart began to thud in his chest.

"Remember Rita?" Archie prompted, the smile still on his face, a fake smile, Tubs realized now, like the smile painted on a clown's face. But Archie was no clown.

"Yes, I remember," Tubs said, his voice small and squeaky. He hated his voice, couldn't control it, never knew when it would come out high and squeaky or low and rumbling. Either like a belch or like a fart. Embarrassing him, either way.

"Beautiful girl, Rita," Archie said, tilting his head a bit, voice soft, as if he'd known Rita and his memories were fond and gentle. "Isn't she?"

Tubs nodded, dumbfounded. How much did Archie know about Rita? Rita, his pride and his agony, his throbbing love, his ultimate betrayer. Hell, he'd almost gone to jail for her. Well, probably not jail but district court, at least. That's what Obie had threatened. Tubs had loved her, hated her now, of course, but still wanted her, still feverish for her, that body of hers, the only girl he'd ever touched, caressed, held. Those breasts. Willing to die for those breasts. Willing to keep the money from the stupid chocolate sale. Not stealing, as Obie had accused him of doing. Merely borrowing. Going into debt to buy her that birthday present, the bracelet she loved. $19.52 including tax. The amount was seared into his heart, his brain.

"You still believe in love, Ernest?" Archie asked.

Somehow, Archie didn't act like the bastard he was supposed to be. Maybe it was his soft voice, the *Ernest* on his tongue, the sympathetic eyes.

"Do you?" Archie asked gently.

It seemed as if they were alone in the room, just the two

of them, the members of the Vigils receding, his heart beating almost normally now.

"Yes," Tubs said. He believed in love, believed in Rita, even now. In a small and secret place in his overweight and perspiring body, he harbored a belief that somehow there had been a mistake and Rita would come into his life again, apologetic, loving him, offering herself to him.

Obie chose that moment to arrive at the meeting.

Obie was late for the meeting because he'd been trying, without success, to call Laurie Gundarson. Her line had been busy. He'd waited in the corridor, stalling, placing the call again and again, greeted by the busy signal that taunted him agonizingly. It occurred to him that her line might not be busy at all. Laurie had once confessed that she often took the phone off the hook when she wanted to avoid certain people. Did she want to avoid Obie now? The possibility filled him with anguish.

His first impulse when classes ended for the day was to dash out of school and drive to her house. But the inverted *Y* on the bulletin board detained him. The Vigils meeting. He realized that the meeting might in some way be connected with last night's attack. He had not anticipated a meeting today, knew no reason why Archie should have suddenly called one. He also knew that news spreads quickly in a school like Trinity. Was the attack already common knowledge? Depositing the dime again, dialing, then hearing the blurt of the busy signal once more, Obie hung up and made his way downstairs, miserable and confused. He nodded to Jimmy Saulnier, who kept guard outside the meeting room, and entered to find Tubs Casper the center of attention. Poor blubber of a kid who looked as if he might faint at any moment. Obie flushed with guilt at the sight of the kid. Hell, one more lousy thing on the lousiest day of his life.

Obie winced as he listened to the exchange between Archie and Tubs.

"Yes, what?" Archie was asking.

"Yes, I believe in love," Tubs said, his voice an agonized whisper.

Obie swore under his breath. He'd hoped that Archie had forgotten all about Tubs Casper. He should have known better: Archie never forgot. Archie, in fact, had goaded Obie into giving him Tubs's name, back in January, half a lifetime ago. Archie had been taunting Obie about his lack of proposed victims. *Running on empty, Obie? Losing your touch?* Obie had winced because Bunting and Carter and some other guys were present, gathered on the front steps of the school. *Or maybe you just lack imagination.* Obie's pulse throbbed in his temple; his cheeks grew warm. *You haven't come up with a decent name in weeks.* A decent name meant a victim, someone vulnerable Archie could use in an assignment.

Like Tubs.

Obie had learned about Tubs Casper's existence as a Trinity student in the final frantic days of the chocolate sale last fall. Checking the sales roster for delinquents— guys who had not sold their quotas—he had seen Tubs's name listed as having made two sales. Preposterous. It had taken Obie three days to track him down. Tubs had proved elusive, staying a few steps ahead of Obie, quite a feat when you considered Tubs and all that fat. Somehow, Tubs always seemed to have left a room moments before Obie got there. Or stepped on the school bus just as it drove away. Obie finally caught up with Tubs Casper at Cogg's Park one evening, spotting him with a girl, the girl clinging to Tubs the way ivy clung to the south-side wall of Trinity. Obie knew immediately what had been going on, knew that Tubs had been selling chocolates all along and not making returns, spending the money on the girl: typical. Sitting in his car, he watched Tubs and the girl cavorting as they strolled along, feeding the pigeons, pausing on a bench. The girl couldn't keep her hands off Tubs. She brushed him continually with her breasts. She was built beautifully, tight sweater, tighter jeans. Obie felt himself swelling with envy and lust (this was before Laurie, of course), and knew he had Tubs Casper exactly where he wanted him.

Obie had confronted Tubs later that night, waiting for him at his doorstep.

"But what about Rita?" Tubs had cried. "She's in love with that bracelet."

"That's the point, Casper," Obie had said. "She's in love with the bracelet. Not you. Figure it as a test. Make those returns tomorrow morning at school. Then see what happens with Rita. If she loves you, it won't make any difference to her if you don't buy the bracelet. . . ."

Confused, riddled with guilt, exhausted from lack of sleep, Obie shrank back into the shadows of the storage room wondering: What the hell am I doing here, anyway? But knew that he couldn't leave, not yet, not until he found out the real reason for the meeting.

"Do you know the procedure here?" Archie asked Tubs.

Obie watched Tubs Casper nodding his head eagerly. He had never intended to nominate Tubs for an assignment: The kid had enough troubles with his weight and with Rita, the teenage sexpot. Because Rita had broken up with Tubs when he hadn't bought the bracelet. Obie had met him on the street a few days later. "What happened?" he'd asked Tubs.

And Tubs, defeated looking, his pudgy face like that of an old man suddenly, said: "You know what happened." No resentment in his voice, no anger, only a heavy, weary acceptance of what life is.

"That's the way it goes, kid," Obie had said, strolling away, walking away from the temptation to tell the kid: Look, be happy, I'm not turning you in for an assignment. See the favor I'm doing you? Yet, taunted by Archie—and, yes, manipulated—he had eventually handed over Tubs Casper as a victim to save his own reputation as a selector of victims.

Archie's voice reached him again.

"You know, Ernest, there is nothing personal in these assignments?"

Tubs nodded, resigned, wanting to get it over with.

"Okay," Archie said, pausing.

This was the beautiful moment Vigil members looked forward to, the moment when Archie revealed his latest assignment, his newest caper, some of the beauty coming from the fact they were not victims, like the moment you are plunged into grief when a rotten thing happens to someone else and that small spurt of guilty relief when you tell yourself: It's not me.

"How much do you weigh, Ernest?" Archie asked.

Tubs squirmed, hated to talk about his weight. But knew he could not deny Archie any information he wanted.

"One hundred and seventy-five."

"Exactly?"

Tubs nodded disgustedly. "I weighed myself this morning."

"That's not so fat, Ernest," Archie said.

Again, Tubs had the sensation that he and Archie were alone in this place, that Archie was his friend.

"In fact," Archie said, "I think you could use a bit of weight. Say, like, twenty pounds. Give you more . . . stature. Make you more of an imposing figure . . ."

"Twenty pounds?" Tubs said, disbelief making his voice squeak.

"Right."

Someone sighed, the kind of sigh that comes with comprehension, and a slight shudder rippled through the room.

"That's the assignment, Ernest. Put on twenty pounds. In the next, say, four weeks. That will bring us almost to the end of school. Eat to your heart's content, Ernest. You love to eat, don't you? And four weeks from now we'll meet here. We'll have a scale."

Tubs opened his mouth. Didn't know why he opened his mouth. Certainly not to protest. Nobody protested an assignment. Stood there gaping, the prospect of more weight staggering to his mind. His life was dedicated to trying to lose weight, despite the fact that he was always hungry, always starved, and always lost the battle. But gaining purposely?

"Close your mouth, Tubs, and get out of here," Archie said, no longer the gentle Archie, the tender Assigner.

Tubs did just that. Hurried his ponderous body out of that terrible place, tripping on somebody's foot as he made his way to the door.

"Beautiful," someone called out. But certainly not Obie, who felt small and cheap as he watched Tubs stumbling out the door.

Archie called for the black box with a snap of his fingers,

wasted no time as he thrust his hand inside and withdrew the white marble, looked at it with amusement, and tossed it back.

The members of the Vigils rustled in their seats, preparing for departure. But Archie held up his hand.

"I have an announcement to make," he said, his words as cold as ice cubes rattling in a tray.

He glanced at Carter, waiting for him to bang the gavel.

The gavel was an important part of Vigil meetings.

And Carter had become the master of its use.

Carter banged the gavel to emphasize Archie's words and actions, the way a drummer underscores the movements of a juggler or a magician on the stage. He'd hit the desk to prod some poor quivering kid into an answer. Or to provide impact for Archie's pronouncements.

Archie waited for attention to focus completely on him once more. Carter tensed himself.

"I've received word," Archie said, "that the Bishop's visit to Trinity has been canceled."

Carter dropped the gavel.

Archie looked at Carter with contempt, waited for him to pick it up, then spoke again.

"Which means that there will be no day off. It's canceled."

Quick intakes of breath, stirrings among the Vigils, a whispered *"Aw, shit"* from someone.

Archie searched the room with those cold and merciless eyes, assessing the impact of his news.

Obie caught Archie's questioning scrutiny, the intensity of his search. He knew the great Archie Costello intimately enough to realize that something had gone askew.

Carter's hand seemed welded to the handle of the gavel. Blood raced under the surface of his flesh, pounding its way to his face.

"But it also means something else," Archie said, drawing the words out slowly, and all the time studying his audience, looking at them as if he had never seen them before.

Obie frowned, puzzled, glad that he was standing in the shadows, virtually unseen.

Ah, but Archie saw everything, and he turned his eyes now on Obie.

"What do you think that something else is, Obie?"

Stymied, Obie shrugged.

"I don't know."

"Bunting?"

Bunting leaped with surprise as if someone had goosed him, one of the more ordinary pastimes at Trinity. He had been uncomfortable about Obie's presence in the room, had barely followed Archie's conversation with Tubs Casper. Hearing Obie's voice now, he gained confidence. Obie certainly wouldn't be answering Archie's questions so normally if he suspected that one of the guys who had attacked him and his girl was in the room.

"I don't know either," Bunting said.

"Carter?"

The blood was pounding a tom-tom beat in Carter's head now, but he tried to keep his features in control.

"You've got me," he said, giving his voice the proper amount of disdain. Acting as if it didn't matter.

But it did matter. He dreaded Archie's next move. The announcement that someone had tipped Leon off about the visit.

Silence as Archie's eyes swept the room again. Inscrutable eyes that revealed nothing, told no secrets. Did his eyes linger on me a moment longer than anyone else? Carter wondered, knowing the secret of that "something else." He was relieved to hear Bunting interrupt Archie's scrutiny.

"Can't we still arrange a day off from school?" Bunting asked. "Everybody's going to be . . . teed off." He'd almost said *pissed off*, which would have landed him in trouble again. "We put a lot of work into the arrangements."

"The project is canceled," Archie said flatly. "Without the Bishop, it's pointless."

Carter didn't know what to do with the damn gavel. Was Archie about to end the meeting?

"Anybody know what the something else is?" Archie asked, not belligerent, seeming to be genuinely interested in a possible response.

No response. Everybody wanted simply to get out of there.

Archie glanced at Carter.

"The gavel, Carter," Archie reminded. "The meeting's over."

The gavel struck the desk like a hammer driving a nail through wood into flesh.

Although he hated the smell of the storage room, the stench of boy sweat and overripe socks and sneakers, Archie remained behind after everyone had gone.

To add up the score.

He hadn't managed a confrontation between Obie and Bunting, but none had been necessary. He knew Obie intimately, could almost read his mind, could certainly read his expressions, Obie's face like a relief map with nothing hidden. He had seen a stunned and subdued Obie, obviously still reeling from the events of the night before, but not suspicious, not ready to spring into action. Obie had barely glanced at anyone in the room, had not sought out Bunting in any way. Archie was willing to bet his reputation on the fact that Obie did not know who had attacked him and his girl in the car.

The other result of the meeting was even more obvious to Archie. And more satisfying.

Carter was the traitor, of course. Carter, who had showed no enthusiasm for the Bishop's visit from the start. Carter, who obviously hated his role as gavel wielder. Carter had stumbled through the meeting as if in a trance, missing his cues with the gavel. Dropping it, for crissakes. Guilt had spread on Carter's face like a coat of paint. Paint the color of blood. Carter the jock, lost without his stupid sports. Carter, who had suddenly developed a conscience. From the moment the meeting started, Archie had been aware of Carter's haunted eyes, pale face, the jock turned jellyfish, turned stool pigeon.

Carter was the traitor.

Further proof would be needed, of course, to eliminate any doubt. But Archie would get that proof.

He stood in the foul, fetid air of the storage room and thought:

Poor Carter.

Carter's life would never be the same again.

Laurie wasn't home.

Or maybe she wasn't responding to the doorbell, just as she might have been refusing to answer the telephone.

He pressed the button again, heard the faint echo of the bell—ding, ding, ding—within the house. But no activity. Somehow, the house *felt* empty. Laurie's presence had always been blazingly immediate to him, charging the air, alerting his senses. Now: nothing. Her mother's VW wasn't in the driveway either.

He rapped on the door, not expecting a response now, but having to do something.

Damn it. He ached to see her. Was filled with guilt and loneliness and longing. Felt hounded, his thoughts swirling around like the snowflakes in those glass globes people keep on mantelpieces.

Turning away, walking down the steps, feeling as though he was in retreat from a skirmish he had just lost, he plodded to his car. The merriment of the spring day mocked him. Brilliant sun, whiff of lilac in the air, all of it empty somehow.

This was his second visit to Laurie's house this afternoon. He had come here directly from Trinity, found no response, and driven to Monument High. The campus was deserted. Peering in the front door, he had seen a custodian pushing a mop down the corridor. He was an outsider at her school. As he walked back to his car, he realized how little he knew about her life, her daily existence. She talked sometimes of her girl friends and he had met two or three of them—but their faces were a blur and their names a vague litany of Debbies and Donnas.

Resting his chin on the steering wheel now, disconsolate, he stared at Laurie's house. His vigil seemed hopeless; the house wore an air of vacancy, abandonment.

His mind went to the Vigils meeting and Archie's strange performance. Under ordinary circumstances he would have been figuring out all the angles, pondering the potential meaning of Archie's behavior. But he couldn't concentrate on Archie now. Laurie and his anguish dominated everything else.

Fifteen minutes went by. More frustrated than ever, sighing almost to the point of hyperventilating—he often had trouble drawing a deep breath when he faced tough situations—he started the car, raced the motor. Couldn't stand doing *nothing* any longer.

There was only one bright spot in the day, not exactly bright but at least not as downbeat, grim, and depressing as everything else: Ray Bannister's deliverance from his assignment on the day of the visit. The project had been canceled and so had Ray's part in it all.

At least he could deliver a bit of good news to someone on this most rotten of all days.

A while later Ray Bannister's mother directed him to the cellar.

"He's working on his secret project, so he might not let you in," she said good-naturedly. She had the most astonishing tan Obie had ever seen. Deep and rich, like melted caramel. He followed her directions through the house and down the cellar stairs. "Don't forget to knock," she called after him.

The door at the bottom of the stairs was closed. Secret project? He knocked.

"Who's there?" Ray's voice was faint on the other side of the door.

"Obie."

A few moments later Obie confronted the secret project. It looked, for crying out loud, like a guillotine.

Which, as it turned out, was exactly what it was, Ray Bannister said. Then explained: "Well, not exactly a guillotine. It's an illusion. But one of the best."

"Did you build it yourself?" Obie asked, both attracted and repulsed by the apparatus, sensing a threat in its presence, ugly in the cellar's dim light.

Ray seemed shy suddenly. "I always liked working with my hands." Running his hand over the side of the blade, he said: "I was just about to test it. Want to help?"

Obie stepped back instinctively, wanted nothing to do with this lethal piece of machinery. Yet he had to admit that he was fascinated. His eyes kept straying to the crossblock with the carved-out groove on which the victim's neck would rest. *Victim* was the wrong word, of course. After all, this was only fun and games. Illusion, like Ray Bannister said.

Ray walked over to the workbench and picked up a shopping bag. Smiling wickedly at Obie, he pulled out a head of cabbage. "See, Obie? I'll give a demonstration, just like a regular magician. A real cabbage—my mother got it at the supermarket for forty-nine cents. She's a good egg, didn't even ask me what I needed a head of cabbage for."

Ray Bannister placed the cabbage in the curved groove, about three feet below the slanted blade. The blade looked menacing, extremely dangerous poised above the cabbage. Suppose it wasn't a head of cabbage but a real head? Obie recoiled from the thought.

"Watch," Ray Bannister said, drawing out the syllable, letting his voice trail off dramatically. He pressed a button near the top of the guillotine. The blade plummeted, flashing brilliantly for a moment as it caught a ray of light from the ceiling bulb, hitting the cabbage, exploding the vegetable into a thousand pieces of moist green and yellow leaves.

"Not as clean as slicing somebody's neck, but you get the idea, don't you, Obie?" Ray asked, chuckling.

"Messy," Obie said, hiding his queasiness. What a terrible day. And a guillotine demolishing a cabbage to top it all. "Now," Ray said, with a flourish, bowing toward the guillotine, assuming the role of Bannister the Great. "Be my guest."

"You're kidding," Obie said.

"Don't you trust me?"

Trust? Obie thought of Archie and Bunting and the attack at the Chasm and now Laurie unapproachable. "I don't trust anybody," Obie said.

"Hey, it's only a trick, an illusion," Ray said, frowning. Frankly, he was a bit nervous about this first demonstration. Knew it was foolproof, nothing to worry about, but edgy. He had been edgy ever since Obie had approached him, plunging him into the strange world of Trinity. "Look, I'll offer myself as the victim." Keeping his voice light. "I'll lay my neck on the line. Literally. And *you* press the button."

Obie eyed the deadly blade and the remnants of the demolished vegetable. The smell of raw cabbage filled the air. "I'd rather not," Obie said. Then, also trying to keep it light so that Ray Bannister wouldn't think he was chicken, "I can see the headlines if anything goes wrong: 'Student Loses Head Over Trick.'"

"Come on," Ray said, stepping smartly to the guillotine. He knelt down and bent over, placing his neck in the groove, facing the floor now. "All you have to do, Obie, is hit the button."

"Not me," Obie protested.

Ray craned his neck to look up at him. "There's no risk. Do you think I'd be crazy enough to take a chance like that?"

Obie wondered whether he was being ridiculous and paranoid.

"Let's go," Ray commanded, adjusting himself once more, wriggling his body a bit. "This isn't the most comfortable position in the world."

"Are you sure it's foolproof?" Obie asked.

"Is anything really sure in this world?" Ray asked. Then quickly: "Just fooling, Obie. Come on, push the damn button."

Obie sighed, accepting his fate, realizing that this was a day in which nothing could go right, and if the trick didn't work, then the hell with it. The hell with everything.

"Well, it's your neck, not mine," Obie said, stepping up to the guillotine. "And I'm not kidding." Glancing down at Ray, he said: "Ready?"

"Ready." A bit muffled. Was that a quiver in his voice?

Obie pressed the button.

Nothing happened. For an agonizing moment, the blade remained still, poised dangerously, of course, but unmoving. And then a sudden *swish*, so startling and unexpected, catching Obie as he drew breath, that he leaped back in surprise. The blade fell so quickly that his eyes could barely follow its descent. The most startling thing of all was the way the blade penetrated Ray's neck—or *seemed* to penetrate it—and yet did not. Ray's neck was undisturbed, no terrible rending, no blood. The blade now rested below the curved groove as if it had passed through Ray's flesh.

"Jesus," Obie said, awed.

Ray leaped from the kneeling position, smiling triumphantly, smirking really, immensely pleased with himself. *"Voilà,"* he pronounced, waving toward the guillotine and then bowing sweepingly, his arm moving as if doffing a hat.

Obie shook his head in wonder. "How the hell does that work?" Actually, he was shuddering inside, realizing that for a stunning moment he had wanted the blade to slice through human flesh, imagining that the neck on the block was the neck of whoever had assaulted Laurie, had *touched* her.

"A magician never tells his secrets," Ray Bannister said, a little breathless.

Obie narrowed his eyes as he regarded him. Had Ray somehow doubted, just a little bit, the effectiveness of the trick? Had there been a chance it might not have worked?

He'd never know, of course, because it was an impossible question to ask. Anyway, Ray Bannister was now basking in his triumph, running his hands across the walnut-stained wood and the gleaming blade.

Remembering the original purpose of his visit, Obie

said: "Listen, Ray, that assignment I told you about? The Bishop's visit?"

Ray nodded, remembering, his features twisted into a look of distaste.

"Well, it's canceled, called off. The Bishop can't make it that day. You're off the hook."

Ray gave a whoop of relief. "Great! I really didn't want to get mixed up in that Vigils business you told me about."

Obie didn't reply, feeling a small stab of pity for Bannister. He knew that Archie never forgot and that Bannister was doomed to become involved sooner or later.

Ray Bannister turned his attention to the guillotine again, eyes full of affection. Obie squinted, studying the apparatus, then turned his eyes to the remains of the cabbage strewn across the floor. He shivered for some reason.

When he arrived home a half hour later, he found a note from his mother.

At hairdresser's. Laurie's mother called. She and Laurie off to visit relatives in Springfield for a few days.

Obie's thoughts were insects chasing each other bewilderingly. Why hadn't Laurie herself called? Why her mother? And where in Springfield were they visiting? He crumpled the note and threw it into the wastebasket. A moment later he retrieved it, smoothed the paper out, read the words again. He sensed doom in the message.

His dreams were wild that night. Were they really dreams? Or simply thoughts and emotions racing just below the surface of his mind as he lay uncomfortably in bed, restless, heaving himself from one side of the mattress to the other? Images flooded his mind. Laurie, of course, beautiful, full lips, a teardrop of ketchup at the corner of her lips, in the car. The guillotine swishing down and splitting the cabbage, suddenly not the cabbage but a human neck, blood spattering around the room instead of cabbage leaves. The smell of blood in his nostrils. Did blood have a smell? He was helpless as the images continued, the slash of light in the car's interior, Laurie gasping, then screaming, the rough hands forcing him to the ground, holding him prisoner, the slashed loafer with the dangling buckle.

Loafer?

He saw the loafer distinctly. Scuffed brown, ripped or torn as if someone had slashed the instep with a knife.

And the dangling buckle, hanging by a thread, dull brass, never polished.

He burst awake as if flying into the air from the upper part of a seesaw while the lower part banged the earth violently. He sat up in bed, head aching, squinted at the digital alarm clock. 2:31. Throwing the blanket aside, he rubbed his forehead as if he could erase the ache like figures from a blackboard. Had he been dreaming? But the loafer did not seem like an image from a dream, receding as you come awake. The loafer had been real, not a manifestation of his weariness and frustration and disappointment, but a reality exploding out of memory.

This memory:

As the unknown assailant had held him prisoner on the ground, while somebody else had assaulted Laurie in the car, he had peered into the awful thing his life had suddenly become and had seen, a mere few inches from his eyes, the torn loafer worn by the bastard who held him captive.

Staring now into the night, eyes wide as if toothpicks held his lids open—something he had seen in a kung fu movie—he was wild with the knowledge of what his subconscious mind had uncovered.

A clue.

More than a clue.

A piece of evidence that could identify without any doubt one of the attackers at the Chasm that night. He saw himself unmasking the bastard, forcing a confession out of him, getting information about the others who had been involved, all of this while Laurie watched, her eyes shining with admiration and love.

He lay back, breathing deeply, exhausted, as if he had just completed a perilous mission, avoided a thousand pitfalls, escaped with his life . . . and he fell into a deep sleep in which an army of men wearing slashed and ruined loafers trampled across his body all night long.

When the telephone rang, Carter answered it immediately, his hand shooting out to pick up the receiver. In the past few days he had become jumpy, nervous, glancing over his shoulder occasionally to check if he was being followed (which was paranoid, of course). Ordinarily Carter did not admit to nerves. He'd always been able to nap minutes before a big football game, always fell asleep instantly at night when his head hit the pillow. Not these days, however, not anymore. He walked around as if a great cloud of doom hung over him and would collapse upon his head at any moment. Thus, when the telephone rang, he acted as if it were a summons. To a trial by jury.

"Hello," he said, snapping the word, using the old gusto of the jock.

Silence on the line. But a sense of someone there. The hint of a person quietly breathing.

"Hello," he said again, trying to keep the wariness out of his voice. "Got the wrong number, chum?" Beautiful: keeping it jaunty. But a bead of perspiration traced a cold path as it ran down Carter's leg from his crotch.

Still nothing.

Carter thought, The hell with it, summoning bravado. He decided to hang up.

The caller's timing was perfect, speaking just as Carter was about to remove the receiver from his ear.

"Why did you do it, Carter?"

"Do what?" he asked, responding automatically but groaning inside. Archie knew. Knew what he had done.

"You know...."

"No, I don't know." Stall, admit nothing. And for cris-sake try to control your voice. His voice sounded funny to his ears.

"I don't want to have to spell it out," the voice said.

Was it Archie's voice? He couldn't be sure. Archie was an expert actor and mimic. Carter had observed his talents at a thousand Vigil meetings.

"Look, I don't know what you're talking about—"

"It will be much easier on you if you confess, Carter."

"Confess what?"

A pause on the line. Then the chuckle. The all-knowing, lewd chuckle, the kind of chuckle someone might utter during an obscene phone call.

"Actually, we don't need your confession. But it might ease your conscience a bit if you confessed. Make you feel better. Let you sleep better at night...."

Carter recoiled, told himself to keep in control. He knew Archie's tactics. Knew how Archie prided himself on his insights, always taking shots in the dark and winning. Like now. Guessing that Carter had trouble sleeping nights. So, beware. Don't let him talk you into giving yourself away.

"Still there, Carter? Still thinking it over, Carter?"

"Thinking what over?" In command a bit now, calming down, feeling ready and able to handle the phone call.

Like in the ring. Feinting and faking. Sizing up an opponent. The first thrusts and advances and retreats as you felt out the adversary.

"Oh, Carter, oh, Carter . . ." The voice tender, full of understanding, suddenly.

"What's all this *oh, Carter* bullshit?" Strong, firm. Feeling good.

"Don't you see, you poor bastard? If you hadn't done it, you'd have hung up right away. Slammed the phone down. Christ, Carter, you've got guilt written all over you."

Carter knew he had somehow walked into a trap just by talking on the phone. He should have hung up right away. Should hang up right now. But couldn't.

"Look," Carter said. "I know who you are. And I know what you're trying to do. Intimidation. I've seen you do it a thousand times, Archie. But it won't work this time. I didn't write that letter. You don't have any proof, couldn't have any proof, because I didn't write it."

Big silence on the line.

Then the laughter.

Carter told himself: Hang up. Hang up now while you're ahead.

But couldn't. Caught and held there by the laughter. Something in the laughter that wouldn't let him go, had him snared.

"You pathetic sucker, Carter. Nobody ever mentioned a letter. Nobody knows about any letter. . . ."

Carter's mind raced, his thoughts tumbling wildly. He knew the fatal mistake he had made. Had to backpedal somehow.

"At the Vigils meeting, when the Bishop's visit was called off . . ." he began.

"The letter was never mentioned. Nobody knows about

the letter, Carter. Except Brother Leon and Archie Costello and the guy who wrote it. You, Carter."

Carter tried to prevent the moan that escaped his lips.

"You're going to pay for it, Carter," the voice that Carter knew *had* to be Archie Costello threatened. "Pity on traitors. Pity on you, Carter."

Carter opened his mouth to call back the groan, to deny the accusation, to shout his innocence, to denounce Archie, to—

But the connection was broken.

And above the sound of the dial tone, he heard the echo of that hideous, insinuating voice:

Pity on you, Carter....

Brother Leon reached for the parcel that had been left on his desk—special delivery—a few moments before. Afternoon sunlight filled the office with radiance.

Curious, Brother Leon inspected the package, touching it gingerly. The size of a shoe box, wrapped in plain brown paper, tied with white string. His name and the address of Trinity were printed on the package. Blue, by a Flair pen. In the upper left-hand corner, the name of the sender: *David Caroni.*

It was important that Brother Leon should know David Caroni's identity; that was essential to the plan.

Frowning, puzzled but pleasantly mystified, identifying Caroni in his mind as the quiet, sensitive student who seldom met anyone's eyes, Brother Leon drew his trusty red Swiss knife from his pocket. He cut the taut string, and it collapsed like a fatally wounded snake. He gently unwrapped the package, careful not to tear the paper. Brother Leon was fastidious, precise in his movements, never a wasted motion.

He removed the cover.

The explosion was tremendous. The blast blew off

Leon's head, shattered his body into a thousand pieces of flesh and blood and tissue that spattered the walls and floors of the office.

His head left a bloody trail as it bounced across the floor. . . .

Or:

Brother Leon stood on the stage of the auditorium, addressing the student body. Berating the students. Criticizing some kind of activity. He was never satisfied, never happy, never content with student behavior, always finding fault.

Suddenly a small angry red hole appeared in the center of his forehead. Blood spilled from the hole, spreading in two streams on either side of his nose, down his cheeks. Dark, ugly blood.

Brother Leon pitched forward as if trying to flee some unspeakable horror behind him. But striking an invisible stone wall. The echo of the sniper's rifle shot reverberated off the walls of the assembly hall, startlingly magnified in the stunned silence.

The sniper, smiling as he watched Leon's body plunging to the floor of the stage with an enormous thud, was, of course, David Caroni.

Or:

But David Caroni was tired of the game of killing Brother Leon. Tired of himself as well. Tired of this charade he was living. He longed for action, for the moment of decision, but had to wait. Wait for what? He would know *what* when the moment arrived, when the command was given. What command? Ah, but he knew what command. And knew that his duty was to wait. He was allowed to indulge in visions and fantasies—Brother Leon blown apart or mortally wounded with a rifle shot—but these were only small diversions to pass the time while he waited patiently for orders.

Sitting in the chair in the kitchen, he held himself erect, back straight, chin tucked in, at attention. Had to be alert. Had to be silent and still. Speak only when spoken to. So that he would be ready and able when the command came.

May I have a glass of water? he asked nobody in particular. (Knew *who* he was asking, of course, but must not acknowledge that presence. Not yet.)

Yes. Drink the water.

He drew water from the faucet, drank mechanically, wasn't really thirsty but had found the secret of killing time by filling up the minutes and hours of his life with little actions. That was the secret. To keep doing, moving, eating, talking, fighting the desire for drift, for going limp. Had to play the many roles his life demanded now. Had to do anything to keep them from knowing. Them: his mother and father and Anthony. Them: his classmates, teachers, people on the bus, in stores, on the sidewalks. Had to hide from the world, had to be clever. The best way to hide, he had learned in his cleverness, was to use camouflage, protective coloration. Hey, Mother, everything's fine. School was good today. A nice day, Mother. What he didn't say: I stood at the guardrail on the bridge over the railroad tracks today but did not jump. Wanted to jump but did not. Could not. Because the command did not come. When would the command come?

He left the kitchen, walked through the dining room, conscious of his movements, arms and legs working together, and paused at the French doors leading to the parlor. After a moment's hesitation he opened the doors and stepped into the room, like going from one century to another, the musk of the past engulfing him like ancient perfume.

The parlor was only used for special occasions, major holidays, family gatherings (like when relatives from Italy visited), graduations, first communions, and such. Thick carpet, gleaming furniture that his mother kept polished despite its lack of use, the upright piano with closed lid. Nobody had played the piano since the death of his grandmother a year ago. David had taken lessons at St. John's Parochial School from a forbidding, tone-deaf nun who delighted in rapping his fingers with a ruler when he struck a wrong note. His mother played "by ear"—terrible chords, everything in the key of C.

He lifted the lid now, like opening a coffin, looked at the grinning keyboard, hideous grin, yellowing teeth. His finger touched middle C, the sound surprisingly deep and full here in the room. He was held immobile by the sound.

C. A piano note but also another Letter, like the Letter that had ruined his life. Brother Leon's Letter.

David closed the piano lid, cutting off the horrible grin of the keyboard. Then stood there for a moment. Would the command come from an inanimate object, like a piece of furniture or the piano, or from a person? He didn't know. Yet he knew he would recognize the command as soon as he heard it. And what he must do. To himself. To Brother Leon.

He carefully shut the French doors and went to the dining-room window, looked out at the backyard. A bird cried piercingly, as if wounded. The soil that his father had turned over in preparation for planting the garden lay in turmoil, like a new grave.

Problem: finding a brown loafer with slashed instep and a dangling brass buckle among hundreds, hell, thousands of pairs of shoes worn by guys everywhere in Monument. Impossible? But he had to make it seem possible. Had to take action. Make the search. Start somewhere—and the somewhere was Trinity. Then go on from there.

Trinity's dress code was not overly strict. It required students to wear shirts, ties, jackets, and trousers of no particular color. Banned were sneakers (except during gym classes), boots, and jeans. The most popular footwear on Trinity's campus were loafers and buckled shoes.

Think positively, Obie told himself as he dressed for school, having trouble as usual knotting his tie so that the two ends came out even. He could not allow himself to be pessimistic. With pessimism would come utter futility and desperation. And, finally, defeat. He couldn't let that happen. He felt that his entire life was in danger of collapsing, and he couldn't just stand there and let it happen.

Somewhere, right this minute, some guy in his own

home was probably putting on that damaged shoe just as Obie was slipping into his own loafers.

Obie inspected his reflection in the mirror. He looked terrible. Bloodshot eyes. Yellow flecks in the corners of his eyes that always showed up when he was tired. A new colony of acne on his chin. Hair lusterless, like dried grass. As if his body—even his *hair*, for crying out loud—was giving up, giving in. Something that must not happen, that he couldn't let happen.

He felt like bawling, saw the corners of his mouth drooping. Time for a pep talk, Obie. You've got a clue. Follow it up. Find the shoe and find the kid. Then go on from there. It was better than doing nothing, better than just waiting for Laurie to get back and having nothing to offer her when she did return.

He had mapped out his strategy on awakening. Had decided not to drive his car to school but to take the bus. This would give him access to the other students, on the sidewalks, in the bus, as he searched for the loafer. He hated the thought of riding the bus—have I become that much of a snob?—but knew that the search was more important than driving to school. He would have to mingle with the mob, eyes sharp and probing.

He hurried out of the house, but his steps were those of an old man, legs heavy, feet dragging as if in winter boots. At the bus stop down the street, he stood apart from a cluster of waiting students. They were frisky and impatient in the morning air, stamping their feet, hitting each other with elbows, hips. Obie's eyes went to their shoes. Three kids wore faded, beat-up sneakers: Monument High kids, no dress code at MHS. Some other pairs of shoes: two pairs of loafers, black and brown, with buckles intact; high black boots; two pairs of laced shoes.

Obie felt like a derelict walking through life with head down, searching for lost coins, cigarette butts, whatever bums look for on the ground.

In the next few hours—on the bus, in the school yard, in the classrooms, in the corridors—Obie encountered a bewildering jungle of footwear, an eye-boggling array of shoes of all shades and styles and conditions. Clean shoes, scuffed shoes, mud-encrusted shoes. Brown, black, mottled gray. Buckles of all kinds. Fancy, plain, brass, silver. Silver? No, not silver but a silvery kind of dull metal. You could tell that the school year was drawing to a close. No shoes sparkling with newness, no fresh articles of clothing. Instead, faded shirts, limp ties, threadbare trousers thin at the seat. Scuffed shoes that no polish could revitalize. Occasionally he spotted a loafer with a buckle that was broken or missing or askew, and a pulse would beat in his throat, but he looked in vain for the slash across the instep. False alarm. A day filled with false alarms, frustration, weariness.

Waiting for the bus after classes were over for the day, hoping that Archie or any of his own friends would not spot him standing alone, he realized again the impossibility of his search. How could he hope to check every pair of shoes in the entire city? Suppose the attackers had come from out of town?

His shoulders sagged; his chin dropped to his chest.

Tears of frustration gathered in the corners of his eyes. He turned away in shame, not wanting the other guys to see him this way. He left the bus stop, wanted to be alone. The search, he knew, was futile. Not only the search but his entire life as well. Futile, empty, without any meaning at all.

What Archie liked about Morton was that she was both smart and dumb. But, before that, beautiful. Long and slender and blond. Compliant. Bending like the willow, as the song went. And so Archie usually came to Morton, his favorite of all the girls at Miss Jerome's, and she never failed him.

He told her everything. And nothing. She listened. But more than listened. She was attuned to his moods and his needs, needs he did not admit to anyone else, and her touch was deft and expert. He could also talk to her. Up to a point, of course. Ordinarily, he talked to her in riddles, and somehow she understood. Not the riddles, but the necessity for him to talk in riddles. Morton was fine. She sometimes got on his nerves, but most of the time she was just fine.

Like now, in his car, hushed in the darkness, Morton and her willingness to please and her knowing ways, and Archie relaxed, drifting, giving himself over to the pleasures of her touch.

"Do you like that, Archie?" Morton asked, her tone indicating that she already knew the answer.

Archie murmured indistinctly, no need for words, his reactions to her ministrations easily decipherable.

"You haven't been around for a while," Morton said, breathing the words into his ear, her breath warm.

"Busy," he said, touching her hair, caressing her cheek. He inhaled the subtle cologne she wore, a hint of lilac, but would have preferred a complete absence of scent.

"How busy?" Morton asked. Keeping busy herself, letting Archie know what came first.

He wondered what he could or should tell her, missing Obie, missing the way he could bounce ideas off Obie, gauging his future actions by Obie's reactions. Obie was the only person who knew how Archie's mind worked, had seen him come up with dozens of assignments, pulling the rabbit out of the hat at the last moment, walking the high wire, taking the risks, and never failing. Meanwhile, he had Morton. She gave him what Obie could never give him and he responded now to her touch. And to her question.

"There's this guy on the campus," Archie said, relieved to be talking about Carter, his thoughts always clearer when he verbalized them. "Football hero. Macho man. Lots of trophies. Tall, dark, and handsome . . ."

"Can I meet him?" Morton asked throatily. She was least sexy when she tried to be sexy, and Archie ignored the question, recognizing Morton's automatic response for what it was: automatic.

"This guy has a sense of honor, too. A social conscience," Archie said, thinking of the letter Brother Leon had waved in his face. "Respects his elders, the authorities. Willing to risk a lot to stick by his principles." His voice as dry as wood crackling in the cold.

"Sounds like the last perfect guy left in America," Morton said.

144

"That's where you're wrong, Morton," Archie said. "Nobody's perfect." Remembering Carter's shaky voice on the telephone.

"Jill," she said. "People call me Jill. Only teachers call me Morton. And then it's Mizz Morton."

"Okay, Jill," he said, giving her name such a twist of his tongue that she should be glad to be called Morton again. "But back to the point. And the point is nobody's perfect. There's always a flaw. A secret. Something rotten. Everybody has something to cover up. The nice man next door is probably a child molester. The choir singer a rapist. Look at all the unsolved murders. Which means the man standing in line next to you could be a murderer. Nobody's innocent."

She withdrew her hand. "God, Archie, you're really something, know that? You always make a person feel like a piece of shit. . . ."

"Don't blame me," he said, surprised at her reaction. "Blame human nature. I didn't make the world."

Morton pulled away from Archie and he let her go, immersed in his own thoughts and the pursuit of Carter's personality, probing for weaknesses. Some of Carter's weaknesses were not hidden at all. For instance, the pride he took in his athletic accomplishments, the way he checked the trophy case fifty times a day, the way he strutted around the school, his swinging shoulders and athletic gait an advertisement for his jock image. Honor and pride, the twin facets of Carter's personality, and also the chinks in his armor. The problem, of course, was to exploit those chinks.

He reached out and touched Morton, who was staring into the darkness, watching the car headlights splashing and clashing down on the highway. She hated the part of herself that always responded to Archie Costello. She was pretty and popular and intelligent. Had not missed a prom or Saturday-night dance since the seventh grade. Independent and self-possessed. But had this weakness for Archie, this response to his demands, a certain excitement springing to life when she heard his voice on the telephone. So maybe he was right, after all, when he said everybody had a touch of something rotten in their lives. Archie Costello was hers. She would never accompany him to a prom (but then, he had never asked her to one) and yet could not deny the pleasure, however guilty, she kept discovering and rediscovering whenever they were together. She did not let herself go like that with anyone else. And now she responded again as he caressed her.

She yielded . . . and for the next few moments Archie Costello and Jill Morton knew only the small sensual world of an ancient Chevy until the quick spurt, the sweet seizure, and an eruption of beauty and fury that left both of them shaken with delight, a moment they abandoned so swiftly that they barely had a memory of its existence a minute later.

They sat awhile in a drifting lassitude, all spent. Archie let himself go in the drift, enjoying these few moments of silence because he knew that eventually Morton would begin to talk. She always began to talk afterward. And he hid his irritation and impatience, knowing that she had a need for talking that was as strong as her need for something else had been a few moments earlier.

"What's bothering you about this all-American hero?" she asked lazily.

Archie recoiled, drawing away. "Nothing's bothering me," he said.

"Then why all that talk about him?"

Archie realized anew why he always kept himself distant from people. Let them approach a bit and they come too close, take too many liberties.

"Forget it," he said, turning the key in the ignition, the engine leaping to life.

"Hey, don't get mad," she said. "You brought up the subject, not me." She reached for the key and turned off the engine.

Archie did not answer, knew that Morton was right. Carter *was* bothering him. And he knew why. He needed to take special action against Carter, not some minor assignment that would be temporary or fleeting. Carter was a special case. He would begin by attacking that special honor of his, but must end elsewhere, something longer lasting.

Morton intruded on his thoughts again, Morton and her knowing, expert touch, hands busy, mouth open, tongue like a small, sweet, darting snake. And Archie let himself be drawn into her orbit, forgetting Carter and everything else, giving himself over to Morton, carried on waves of sensuality that he knew would erupt into a deep dark flower of ecstasy that was almost, almost but never, never quite happiness.

He completed dialing the Goober's number on the third try, having missed the first two times, his finger slipping from the rounded slot—a Freudian slip of the finger? he wondered, smiling grimly, but glad that he could make a bit of a joke at a moment like this—and then heard the phone ringing at the other end.

Bracing himself, planting his feet solidly on the floor, he felt as though he were about to face hurricane winds that would sweep him across the room. Crazy. He was merely making a phone call to his old buddy.

Three rings, four, the sound like an invisible strand of rope between this room where he stood and the living room at Goober's house. Where, apparently, no one was present to answer the phone.

Seven . . . eight.

Good, he thought, nobody home, I've done my part; some other time. Relieved, about to hang up, he heard someone say "Hello." Out of breath, exhaling the word. And again: "Hello."

Jerry gulped. Where do I begin?

"Hello?" The voice again, still out of breath, a question mark at the end of the word and a hint now of annoyance.

Jerry rushed in:

"Hello, Goober? How are you? This is Jerry Renault, just thought I'd call. . . ." Too much too fast, the words running together. "Been out running?" Cripes. Living in silence all this time and now I can't shut up.

"That really you, Jerry?" Goober asked, taking a deep breath, probably just ending a run, and Jerry envied him, wanted to run, jump, careen around in the spring air, realized how suffocating and deadly dull the apartment had been since his return.

"It's really me," Jerry said, wanting to sound normal, like the Jerry Renault that Goober knew and remembered.

"Great to hear your voice," the Goober said, but a bit guarded, the words fine and normal but his voice tentative.

Let's get this all out of the way as soon as possible, Jerry thought. And plunged again: Give me the ball and the hell with the signals.

"Look, Goob. Can I say something? A couple of things, in fact? First, I'm sorry about the other day. When you came here. I wasn't ready, I guess. I was really glad to see you but not ready for other things. I mean, not ready for Monument. I must have looked like a nut. . . ."

Goober's laugh was easy, almost grateful. "Well, it wasn't your everyday kind of hello-how-are-you. But you sound okay now, Jerry." And, after a slight pause: "Are you?"

"I think so. Yes." Having to make it clear: "I'm fine. Really."

"Great. And Jerry, let me say something too, okay? Something I've got to say before anything else—"

"Look, Goober, I know what you want to say ... and you don't have to. You're my friend."

"But I've got to say it, Jerry, and you have to listen and then you have to make a decision. Don't say anything yet. Let me. Let me tell you that I know that I betrayed you last fall. Stayed home as if I was sick when you were going through hell because of the chocolates, that beating from Janza ..."

"But you were there, Goob. I saw you. You helped me. ..." He almost said: You held me in your arms when I was all broken inside and out.

"But I got there too late, Jerry. Stayed home until the last minute. And was too late to help you. ... Okay, I've said it. It had to be said. And I don't blame you if you hate me."

"Cripes, Goober, I don't hate you. You're my friend."

"I didn't act like a friend that night. ..."

"Goober, Goober ..." Admonishing gently, as if Goober were a child to be soothed and reassured.

"Do I get another chance?"

"You don't need another chance, Goob. You're my friend—so what's all this about another chance?"

"I'll never let you down again, Jerry."

"Hey, look, Goob. Will you do me a big favor? As a friend forever?"

"Sure." The Goober's voice was easier now, lighter. "Name it—and consider it done."

"Okay. The favor is this: Don't talk about that night anymore, don't talk about letting me down or anything like that. That was last fall—this is now. Let's forget it ever happened."

"There's one thing I can't forget. What you told me that

night, Jerry. Because it's the truth. It's the way I live my life now. You said to play ball, play the game, sell the chocolates or whatever they want you to sell. That's what I'm doing, Jerry. What I'm always going to do . . ."

The words made Jerry uneasy. It was one thing to believe in them yourself: it was another to know that someone else, a friend, believed in them, too. Changing his life because of words you spoke. Jerry felt engulfed by sadness at the words, although he knew them to be true.

"Let's not talk about it anymore," he said, wondering if he had called too soon, whether he should have waited, whether he should never have called. Desperate to get away from the subject, he searched for another subject, seized one: "You still running, Goob? You were all out of breath when you answered the phone."

"Right. I didn't run for a long time, but I started again."

"I'd like to run," Jerry said, glancing around the room at the sterile furniture, not home, really, but like a waiting room in a doctor's office or air terminal.

"Hey, you always hated running," Goober chided.

Jerry responded to the Goober's good-natured jibe.

"I know—but it feels so good when you stop. Like hitting yourself on the head with a hammer. . . ."

They both exploded with laughter. His remark hadn't been *that* funny, but Jerry sensed that they needed to grab on to something to bring them together again. Like old times.

"Want to run again? With me?" Goober asked.

"Why not? I need the exercise."

"Tomorrow afternoon?"

"Sure . . ." Jerry hesitated. "On one condition, Goob. No more talk about what happened. No more of that stuff—"

"Okay, okay," Goober said. "I give up. But get ready for tomorrow, Jerry. I'll run you ragged. . . ."

"Tomorrow," Jerry said, hanging up, weak with relief, breathing his thanks. His thanks to whom? God, maybe, thinking of the Talking Church in Canada.

O bie spotted the slashed loafer with the dangling buckle at a moment when he was not looking for it. Climbing the stairs to the third floor for the final class of the day, forced along by the between-classes stampede of students, Obie was engrossed in his thoughts, barely aware of the press of bodies. About the two tests today he had either flunked or scored no higher than a *D* on, thus falling further behind in his studies. Angry thoughts. Angry at his parents and all grown-ups who thought that school life was a lark, a good time, the best years of your life with a few tests and quizzes thrown in to keep you on your toes. Bullshit. There was nothing good about it. Tests were daily battles in the larger war of school. School meant rules and orders and commands. To say nothing of homework.

The loafer appeared before his eyes without warning, so unexpected that his brain did not immediately register the sight. His brain was still concerned with this lousy life called high school, adolescence, the teen years. But then: the loafer. The cruel slash across the instep. He stopped in his tracks, one foot on the step above him, the other in midair as his brain intercepted what his eyes had recorded.

"Wait a minute," he said.

Nobody among the rampaging students coming and going up and down the stairs heard his words or paid attention.

Obie sprang into action. The guy wearing the loafer had been coming down the steps: At one point the shoe had been at his eye level. Turning, looking below, he spotted a familiar figure hurrying across the second-floor corridor, trying like everyone else to beat the final bell to the class. Torn between getting to his own class on time (he'd already been tardy once today) and tracking down his quarry, Obie threw caution aside. His life depended on that loafer: the hell with being late for class. The hell with everything else. He set off in pursuit, going against the mainstream now, darting in and out of the streaming students, getting jabs in his ribs from sharp elbows.

He caught up with the student (he was almost sure of his identity, had recognized him from behind but had to be absolutely certain, without a shadow of a doubt, because this was life and death now, not fun and games) at the doorway to Room Nineteen. Ironic, of course. Putting on the brakes, his own shoes skidding on the wooden floor, he almost crashed into the guy. Looking down, he confirmed the evidence. Yes, the loafer was slashed, the buckle was loose. He looked up again as the kid, perhaps sensing his scrutiny or hearing the skidding arrival of someone behind him, turned around and regarded him. Full face.

No doubt now. No doubt at all.

Cornacchio, the sophomore. Bunting's stooge.

The bell rang, splitting the air as Cornacchio, after a hurried, puzzled look at Obie (but was it puzzled or more like horrified?) jammed through the door, shouldering his way between two other students.

Obie remained alone as the corridor emptied and the doors slammed shut. Stood there, caught and held, his heart like the ticking of a bomb about to explode.

The fever that coursed through his body now made him sharp and alert. He had gone beyond fatigue and exhaustion into a kind of hyper state, senses sharp, body on the alert, a new energy pulsing with the beat of the fever. He used all the old strategies and methods that he had learned during his years as Archie's right hand, setting up the assignments, compiling his notes and data on students. His notebooks were filled with the names of students and the background details of their lives that had been valuable for the assignments. Hundreds of names. And, of course, Cornacchio among them.

Vincent Cornacchio. Sixteen years old. Height, five seven; weight, one sixty-five. Father, factory worker. *B*-minus average. Not stupid. In fact, did not live up to his potential. An underachiever. Hobbies, none. Unless you call hanging around downtown eyeballing the girls or reading dirty magazines in drugstores a hobby. Nickname: Corny. Which he hated. Worked after school at Vivaldi's Supermarket.

That night in bed, curled up fetuslike, still not sleeping but not wanting now to sleep, thoughts alive and sharp like needles pricking his consciousness, Obie plotted and schemed and mapped his strategy. Cornacchio had held him down and under the car. But somebody else had attacked Laurie, had *touched* her. Bunting, probably. Cornacchio was Bunting's stooge. Bunting, whom he already had reason to hate. But must be sure. And Cornacchio was the key.

He finally fell into a deep, dreamless sleep that was

more of a coma, a little death, than anything else. He awoke in the morning without any sense of having slept. Eyes still flaming, pulse still throbbing in his forehead, stomach still rejecting the thought of food. But his mind keen and knife-edged, eager for action, in a hurry for the day to pass until this evening, when he would confront Cornacchio. Cornacchio of the slashed loafer with the dangling buckle, who would lead him to the guy who had touched Laurie.

"Brother Eugene's dead."

"Oh, no. . . ."

They rounded the corner of State Street into Stearns Avenue past the Hilite Dry Cleaners (In by 9, Out by 5) and Rasino's Barber Shop, the wind assailing their bodies, brushing their cheeks, cool air on moist warm flesh.

"He died in New Hampshire," the Goober said, eyes straight ahead, back arched, legs pumping. "He never came back to Trinity after . . ."

His voice trailed off.

After.

The word lingered in the air as they ran. Cars and buses and people, young and old, flowed past them as if on movie screens, outside their own isolated world of running.

After Room Nineteen.

Propelled by guilt, the Goober left Jerry behind in a burst of speed. Not only running now but running away. But impossible to run away, of course. As he zoomed around a corner, he was back in Room Nineteen again, in the middle of the night, terrified, the screwdriver so tight in his hand that blisters exploded in his palm.

Jerry followed him around the corner in his own kick of speed, spotted him up ahead, and hung back, knowing he could never catch up.

But the Goober put on the brakes, came to a sudden stop, and looked back over his shoulder.

"Sorry," he called, waiting, running in place, legs churning.

As Jerry came abreast, the Goober pointed to an unoccupied bench at a nearby bus stop. "Let's rest," he suggested, noticing Jerry's labored breathing, his face grooved with the agony of exertion.

Jerry was grateful for the pause, realizing that he was very much out of shape. He knew that he had to convince the Goober that he was not to blame for what had happened to Brother Eugene, hoped he could find the proper words.

"I hope you're not feeling guilty," Jerry said as he sat down, waiting for his body to calm, his heart to resume its normal silent beat. "It can't be your fault, Goob."

"I keep telling myself that," the Goober said. "But I keep wondering what would have happened if we hadn't taken Room Nineteen apart. Would Brother Eugene still be alive?"

"You can't second-guess a thing like that, Goober," Jerry said, groping for the right words. But could any words mollify his friend? "Room Nineteen happened last fall. Brother Eugene wasn't young anymore. You've got to forget the past—"

"It's not that easy."

"I know," Jerry said, thinking of the chocolates.

"I can't wait to leave that rotten school," Goober said, voice bitter, pounding the earth with his foot.

"I'm not going back either," Jerry said. "I might go back

to Canada," he added, discovering that possibility only as he spoke the words.

"You liked Canada that much?"

Jerry shrugged. "It's peaceful there." He thought of the Talking Church, knew he couldn't possibly explain to the Goober how he felt about those weeks in Quebec. "This parish I lived in with my uncle and aunt is only a few miles north of Montreal. Maybe I can commute to an English-language school in Montreal." More possibilities that he had not realized existed until this moment.

"Monument High for me," Goober said flatly. "No more Brother Leon. No more Archie Costello. No more Vigils. No more crap—"

"Is Archie Costello still riding high?" Jerry asked tentatively, wondering if he really wanted to know.

"I try not to pay attention," Goober said. Then amended his reply: "Yeah, sure he is. You hear rumors all the time about assignments. Secret stuff. Some poor kid given a stupid stunt to perform." Like me, he thought, and Room Nineteen.

"Let's run some more," Jerry said, on edge suddenly. All this talk of Brother Eugene and Archie Costello brought back memories he had been avoiding. Room Nineteen was bad enough. But what about the chocolates? He didn't want to think about the chocolates.

They ran now in companionable silence, like last fall, finding a balm and benediction in the movement of their bodies, down hills and across streets, arriving finally at Monument Park and coming to a halt near a Civil War cannon. Sitting, stretching, Jerry was languid in the aftermath of exertion, felt as though his bones and muscles were deliciously melting.

"Why so quiet, Jerry?"

"Know what I keep thinking, Goober? How many Archie Costellos there are in the world. Out there. Everywhere. Waiting." A thought crept into his mind: It would be nice to avoid the world, to leave it and all its threats and unhappiness. Not to die or anything like that, but to find a place of solitude and solace. Nuns retreated to their convents. Priests lived in rectories, separate from other people, or in monasteries. Was it possible for him to do the same? Become a priest? Or a brother? A good and kind brother like Brother Eugene? And take his place in the world, someone to fight the Archie Costellos and even the Brother Leons? Hey, what's going on here? Me a priest? A brother? Ridiculous. Yet he remembered those exquisite moments of peace in Canada.

"What do you want to do with your life, Goob?" he asked.

"Who knows?" the Goober mused. "Sometimes I wake up at night in a panic. Wondering: What will my life be like? And sometimes I even wonder: Who am I? What am I doing here, on this planet, in this city, in this house? And it gives me the shivers, makes me panic." This is what he liked about Jerry Renault. He could talk to him like this, tell him his fears and hopes.

"That happens to me, too," Jerry said. "I remember a poem from somewhere, school, probably.

> *"I, a stranger and afraid*
> *In a world I never made.*

"That's me, Goob. That's us." That was also Trinity. A world he had not made. In which he had been afraid. He didn't want to be afraid anymore. He remembered the poster in his locker: *Do I dare disturb the universe?* He had disturbed the universe of Trinity. Look what had happened. He would do no more disturbing.

"Oh, Christ."

Jerry looked up as the Goober spoke, startled at his words, knowing that the Goob seldom if ever swore.

"What's the matter?" Jerry asked. And then followed the Goober's eyes. Goob was staring at something across the street. Jerry looked and saw that it was not something but someone. There was no mistaking who that someone was. Emile Janza. The blunt, compact body, head sunk into his shoulders, the small eyes visibly piglike even at this distance. Or maybe he couldn't see the eyes after all but remembered them vividly. He remembered vividly everything about Emile Janza. The fight in the boxing ring; the day Emile and his buddies had attacked him in a wooded area near the school. And now Emile Janza stood across the street, hands on hips, looking in Jerry's direction. The noise of passing cars and trucks, the movement of pedestrians on the sidewalk, the quick dart of a small kid faded into the background. And for a moment Jerry and Janza seemed to be locked in a confrontation by eyeball. But were they? Jerry couldn't be certain. Too far away to tell, really. Janza might be merely staring vacantly into space, eyes unfocused.

A bus lumbered into view from Jerry's right and slowed down, veering toward the curb, passing in front of Janza, obliterating him completely as if wiping him from the surface of the earth. Jerry waited, not looking at the Goober, not speaking, not even thinking. Remaining blank, a cipher, zero. The bus lurched into action again, belching purple exhaust, moving forward, revealing the sidewalk and the spot where Janza had stood. Janza was no longer there. Had evidently boarded the bus. Or walked away while the bus paused at the curb.

"Do you think he saw us?" the Goober asked.

"Maybe."

"What an animal."

"I know."

Jerry leaped to his feet.

"Come on, Goober," he urged. The hell with Emile Janza. "I'll race you to the library."

And as he started to run, he knew he was really racing toward another place altogether, to Canada. Hey, Canada, here I come.

"What time is it?" Janza asked.

Obie glanced at his watch. "Ten after."

"Ten after what?"

Obie tried to hide his exasperation. "What do you think? I told you to meet me here at seven o'clock. That was ten minutes ago. You think an hour's gone by?"

Obie wondered whether he had made a mistake by enlisting Janza's aid in his confrontation with Cornacchio. They were standing in a shadowed doorway across the street from Vivaldi's Supermarket, the small grocery store where Cornacchio worked part-time. The store closed at seven, but Cornacchio always stayed behind to bring inside the vegetables and other groceries the market displayed on the sidewalk. Obie had once worked in a store after school, but was fired for being late because of the demands of Archie and the Vigils.

"I'm getting hungry," Janza said.

Obie didn't bother to answer. He didn't want to engage in conversation with him. He hated the thought of using Janza, becoming involved with him at all, and yet Janza was the muscle he needed. Both Cornacchio and Janza were brutes: either one would cancel the threat of the other. Obie's instructions to Janza had been simple: "You don't have to say anything. Just play dumb." Which wouldn't require any acting at all on Janza's part. "Look menacing." As if he had to make an effort to look menacing.

The evening had turned cool, and the wind hustled assorted debris along the sidewalk: pages of a newspaper, dry leaves, candy wrappers. Obie's eyes were slits. Painful dry slits. As if someone had removed them for inspection and put them back in the wrong sockets.

Cornacchio finally emerged from the store, arching his back, stretching his muscles. Looked tough. Which made Obie glad now that he'd brought Janza along.

"There he is," Janza said. He had a faculty for stating the obvious.

Cornacchio walked with a swagger, the rhythmic bouncing gait of an athlete, as if his shoes contained hidden springs. Broad shoulders, legs like tree stumps.

As Cornacchio crossed the street at an angle, Obie moved forward to intercept him, Janza at his elbow. Obie checked the damaged loafer, the brass buckle winking in the dusk, and felt again the anger and horror of that terrible night.

"Hi, Cornacchio," he said, stepping in front of him.

Cornacchio looked at Janza, although Obie had greeted him. And he got the message immediately, knew what this was all about. Turned his attention to Obie, Obie's deadly calm, his attitude of determination joined with Janza's silent menace. Cornacchio was not a coward and not shy about using his muscle: he had emerged triumphant from countless schoolyard skirmishes since the third grade. But he knew when he was hopelessly outclassed, not only by

Janza, who was probably the only guy in school whose strength he respected, but by Obie, who was a key figure in the Vigils, powerful, next to Archie Costello. He knew that Bunting couldn't help him at this moment, no matter how clever Bunting was.

"What's happening?" Cornacchio asked, dancing a bit like a fighter warming up, instinctively putting up a front, not wanting to betray his nervousness.

"It's not what's happening, Corny," Obie said, deliberately using the nickname Cornacchio despised. "It's what's already happened."

"I don't know what you're talking about," Cornacchio said, making an effort to pass by.

Janza stepped into his path.

"You know what I'm talking about," Obie said. So calm, so certain of himself, so implacable. Voice flat, deadly, quiet. And something terrible in the quietness.

"Okay, okay," Cornacchio said, lifting his arms, his shoulders, like a spy discovered in enemy territory, knowing that he would be shot at dawn, alone and friendless, abandoned by his comrades.

"It's not what you think it was," Cornacchio said.

Obie felt himself sagging, relaxing, unfolding, the relief from his tension so sudden and strong that he was afraid he would collapse on the sidewalk like a puppet whose strings had been severed. "What was it, then?" he asked.

Cornacchio hesitated, glanced down at his feet, kicked at a piece of broken glass, looked up at Obie, then at Janza, then at Obie again. Held on to Obie's eyes. Obie sensed a hidden message there. Then got the message. Of course: Janza. Cornacchio didn't want to talk in front of Janza. And Obie realized how ridiculous it was to have brought Janza along. He had been duped by loss of sleep, the obsessive nature of his search for the attacker, had lost all perspective. He realized that he certainly didn't want Janza to know what had happened. The less Janza knew, the better it would be for everybody.

"Hey, Janza," Obie said.

Janza had not removed his eyes from Cornacchio for an instant. He had decided that he didn't like Cornacchio. He didn't like the way Cornacchio had ignored him, had barely glanced his way. Janza liked to be recognized, did not like to be ignored.

"What?" Janza said, his voice a brief bark.

"Check the other end of the street," Obie said. "I thought I saw someone there."

Janza didn't want to appear to be taking orders from Obie or anybody else. On the other hand, if somebody *was* lurking down the street, it was an opportunity for action, for the use of muscle.

"Okay," he said, spitting out the word, continuing to glare at Cornacchio to show that he was not simply an errand boy.

Obie and Cornacchio watched Janza lumbering away, shoulders swinging.

"I hate that scumbag," Cornacchio said.

Obie ignored the remark. He knew that he and Cornacchio were connected with each other by the Vigils and that Janza was an outsider. But the brotherhood of the Vigils did not make any difference to Obie as far as the attack was concerned. Cornacchio was the enemy; he was the scumbag, not Janza.

"Okay, Corny, explain. If it's not what I think it was, then what was it?"

Cornacchio flinched at the use of his nickname, knew

that Obie was deliberately taunting him. But he was in no position to protest.

"The Vigils," Cornacchio said.

Obie stepped back as if Cornacchio had spit in his face.

"An assignment," Cornacchio said, pleased at Obie's reaction, gaining confidence. "Bunting told Archie Costello about you and that girl. How we spotted you one night making out at the Chasm. He told Bunting to do something about it. Said the Vigils would provide an alibi."

More than spit in Obie's face: as if a bomb had detonated nearby, leaving his body intact but sending shock waves throughout his system.

"Archie Costello gave the orders?" Disbelief in his voice. Impossible. Yet nothing was impossible with Archie.

Cornacchio nodded, gulping nervously, surprised at the way Obie had gone pale, hands groping at the air. Cornacchio was still troubled about that night at the Chasm, had replayed it a thousand times in his mind. He'd never done anything like that before. Actually, he hadn't *done* anything, after all, had merely held Obie a prisoner under the car. He was aware of feeling horny as he and Bunting and Harley approached the car and saw Obie and the girl. His lust and desire died, however, as he held Obie on the ground, realizing the rotten thing they were doing. *But nothing had happened.* That's what Bunting claimed, and Cornacchio believed him, needed to believe him. Bunting said later that it was all Archie Costello's idea, an unofficial assignment. This knowledge had greatly relieved Cornacchio. The involvement of Archie and the Vigils made it seem less serious, not such a rotten thing, more like a kind of stunt.

And nobody, but nobody, had been hurt.

Obie had regained his composure.

"Okay, tell me. What did Archie say? Precisely?"

"I can't be precise," Cornacchio said. "I wasn't there. Bunting told us later that it was an assignment. Unofficial but still an assignment. Look, Obie, nothing happened. Okay, I held you down, but I was only following orders." Cornacchio knew he was stretching a point here, but he was a bit alarmed by what he saw in Obie's eyes. Wasn't sure what he saw but knew it was something to beware.

Obie's mind reeled and he ran his hand through his hair. His thoughts were a jumble of images—Archie and Laurie and Janza and Bunting and this kid in front of him, Cornacchio. Who seemed to be telling the truth. Was too smart to lie, knowing that his story could be checked. With Archie. With Bunting.

"The assignment," Obie said. "What was the assignment? To bushwhack? Or to do more than that?" Obie didn't want to use the word *rape*.

"Bunting said Archie told him: Do something. He didn't say what. Do something about Obie and the girl. So we did." Cornacchio was confused now, realizing that Bunting had not gone into detail about the assignment. And he was worried—had he told Obie too much? He was happy to see Janza approaching.

"Nobody there," Janza said to Obie.

His voice jolted Obie.

"Nothing but shadows."

"I've got to get home," Cornacchio said, doing his fighter's dance again, avoiding Obie's eyes, sensing the study Obie was making of him.

Obie nodded, eyes huge, face still pale. Looked lost. Cornacchio felt sorry for him, then remembered that Obie had called him Corny. He hated every bastard who'd ever called him Corny.

"Okay, get out of here," Obie said at last, turning away, his voice weary, shoulders drooping.

"What the hell was that all about?" Janza asked, keeping his eye on Cornacchio until he had disappeared around the corner.

"What you don't know can't hurt you," Obie said. Numb now, bones singing with the pain of exhaustion, all exhilaration gone. And thinking: What a guy knows *can* hurt him.

Rain. Pelting the streets and sidewalks and lashing at Obie as he walked toward Laurie's house. He had taken to keeping a vigil across the street from her house at various times of the day and evening, drawing comfort from being near the house she lived in, slept in, took showers in (the vision of her naked under the water's spray caused an ache in his groin), ate her meals in. The house was precious to him because she lived in it. Standing under a leafy tree for shelter, clothes soaked, hair matted—he had neglected to wear a hat or raincoat—stamping his feet now and then, he realized the futility of the solitary watch.

He saw her brother approaching from the far end of the street. Clutching a book bag to his chest, he kept his eyes down as he approached Obie, as if afraid he might be robbed. He always looked as if he expected the worst to happen. And only twelve years old. Wait until he gets to high school, Obie thought.

"When's Laurie coming home?" Obie asked, not wanting to ask this particular kid anything but the question emerging from his frustration, soaked and lonely here on this rotten street when he should be home trying to catch up on homework.

The kid didn't stop walking and called over his shoulder: "She's home. She's been home two days."

"Oh," Obie said stupidly, mouth hanging open, the taste of rain bitter on his tongue.

"I don't think she likes you anymore," her brother said, not viciously but with the uncluttered honesty of a twelve-year-old kid.

Obie did not reply, said nothing, stood miserable and abandoned, all the lights in the world dimmed and dying, knowing in the deep places of his being that he had lost Laurie Gundarson forever.

PART THREE

The heat wave came without warning. In May, for crying out loud. Out of season, too early, arriving before the body was prepared, blood too thick, skin too pale. The heat rose from the streets and sidewalks as the sun hammered at the earth without mercy, shimmering from budding trees and flowering shrubs.

The heat turned the Trinity student body into a sluggish army of sleepwalkers. The exhilaration of the seniors, aware that final days had arrived and that classes were meaningless now, was muted by the waves of heat and humidity that moved indolently across the campus. Posters plastered to corridor walls and classroom bulletin boards announcing the coming of Fair Day, the last event of the year, were met with indifferent stares or yawns.

Archie loved the heat. He loved it because other people were so uncomfortable, sweating and groaning, stalking through the heavy air as if their shoes were made of lead.

He had many ways of avoiding the blistering temperatures. Keeping cool thoughts. Controlling his emotions. Laying low. No Vigil meetings or activities. His leadership of the Vigils was a thing of delicate calibration, and he knew instinctively when to call meetings, to adjourn them, or to allow the Vigil members to go their way. Like now. Knowing everyone's discomfort, knowing they would resent any extra effort, any assignment.

The heat also took the pressure off current events. Although maintaining a reserved attitude, Archie had as usual been keen-eyed without seeming to be, watching, observing. Two targets of observation, Obie and Carter, seemed like twins. Both walking trancelike, preoccupied with their thoughts and worries. Which meant they would be unlikely to do anything foolish or threatening. At certain moments Archie was a bit apprehensive—what was going on inside Obie? Was he plotting revenge in a quiet way or merely accepting his fate? Carter was easier to read. The swaggering athlete had turned into a shoulders-hunched, narrow-eyed specimen these days, like a hunted creature, passing quickly by, not talking to anybody. Archie knew what was going on inside him and delighted in the knowledge. Let him stew awhile in his thoughts and fry in the heat. Time enough to take care of Carter, the traitor, in his own way. Meanwhile, Carter was torturing himself—a sweet Archie touch, letting the victim be his own torturer. All in all, Archie found a certain satisfaction in the heat wave.

The heat did not touch Caroni, either.

He had erected a screen around himself, invisible obviously, which the heat could not penetrate. Neither could anything else in this world.

His world was without seasons. And, thus, without weather. He operated beautifully in this atmosphere, his mind clear and sharp, a thing apart from his body. He marveled at the way he responded to the necessities of life, performing his silly but necessary duties as a student, son, brother. He could perform so well because he knew that he would not have to do so forever. He knew there was a moment when the command would be given, and events would be set in motion.

David was drawn incessantly to the parlor and the piano. The parlor was cool, windows closed, curtains drawn, isolated from the rest of the world. David raised the piano lid, sounding middle C. Waiting. For an echo? He didn't know.

He was a bit afraid of the piano, the keys grinning at him in the shadowed room. As he was staring at the keys one afternoon, a thought occurred to him. Transmitted somehow from the piano to himself. The thought was actually an image. A knife. The butcher knife his father used on occasion for big roasts and turkeys. He checked to see if the butcher knife was in the special drawer with the other kitchen utensils. He touched the knife, ran his finger across the blade, and announced: "Yes, I found it." He did not know whom he had said his words to. But knew that someone, something, had heard him. And that he was drawing closer to the time of the command.

Thus, in the heat, David Caroni waited. For the signal. Knew it must come soon. He didn't mind waiting, he didn't mind the heat. Every day he went into the cool parlor and stood near the piano, waiting.

The heat always made Emile Janza horny. Actually he was almost always horny, but the heat intensified his feelings. Girls dressed flimsily in the heat, of course, wearing sleeveless, see-through blouses, brief skirts, or short shorts that exposed their bodies beautifully.

Other things made him horny as well, something he noticed increasingly as time went on. He noticed it first in football during plays in which he tackled his opponents bruisingly and without mercy. A distinct wave of sexual pleasure swept him on these occasions. Sometimes when he engaged in a scuffle in the parking lot—Trinity was a very physical place—he would be instantly aroused. He had felt that kind of swift pleasure last fall when he had faced the Renault kid in the boxing ring, and even earlier when he had beat him up in the woods behind the school. Those were beautiful moments, really.

The beauty had returned the other day when he spotted Renault in the park. Sitting on the lawn with his creepy friend whose name Emile did not know. Spotting Renault, recognizing him even from that distance, he was surprised to find he had returned to Monument. Janza had heard the kid had run off to Canada, afraid he might get beat up again. And now he was back. Asking for more trouble. Janza was tempted to tell Archie Costello about Renault's return. Then decided against it. He wanted to keep Renault for himself.

Now, in the heat, in his house, nobody home, Janza picked up the telephone book. Looked up the *R*'s. Felt nice and sexy.

Flipping the pages, he found Rathburn . . . Raucher . . . Red Cross Hdqtrs . . . Reed, and, finally, Renault. Two Renaults in the book. Easy to check out.

Renault, that little jerk. He should not have come back to Monument. He should have stayed in Canada.

Sudden booming thunderstorms interrupted the hammering of the heat. The skies exploded with thunder, split radiantly with lightning. Rain sluiced down as if from giant faucets turned on full force. Steam hissed from the concrete pavement as rain drummed on heated surfaces. Gutters overflowed, debris bobbed along like tiny boats to the catch basins and sewers. Drippings from the edges of buildings and trees struck like a thousand small water tortures. Or so it seemed to Obie, who was undergoing a special kind of torture. The torture of losing Laurie.

It had taken a few days to track Laurie down after her brother had disclosed the news of her return to Monument. The telephone route still did not work: she was never at home when he called or, at least, did not come to the phone. Making his way wearily through the steaming streets, he stood watch in front of Monument High, checked out her friends, all those Debbies and Donnas who regarded him with blank faces as if they had never seen him before, giving him no information whatever. *Laurie? She was here a minute ago.* Or *Haven't seen her for, oh, two or three days.* He hounded bus stops and the stores in the vicinity of the school, moist with sweat, eyes stinging from the relentless sun, itchy and sniffling, realizing with dismay and disgust that he had somehow caught a cold. He sneezed three times in succession—maybe an allergy? Catching a cold in a heat wave would be the final indignity.

His vigil was finally rewarded when he saw her emerging from Baker's Drugstore (he had missed her going in) and walking to a mailbox, where she slid a letter into the slot. A farewell letter to him, saying good-bye forever? Not even that. A renewal of her subscription to *Seventeen*, she told him.

On a busy sidewalk with the smell of bus exhaust fouling the heavy air, one of her girl friends, a blonde with bangs that almost covered her eyes, waiting near a yellow fire hydrant, a screaming child being pushed in a baby carriage while a young mother licked a melting strawberry ice cream cone, that was where Laurie Gundarson said good-bye to Obie. No throbbing background music, no hushed intimacy. Her eyes told him the truth before she said a word, her expression distant, as if her mind was on more important matters than Obie's plight. He could have been a beggar asking for a handout, somebody passing out leaflets, a stranger asking directions. She answered his questions—he couldn't remember afterward what words he'd used, what questions he'd asked—in monosyllables, patiently, as if talking to someone slightly retarded. Until she said: "Obie, it's over." Addressing him at last directly, recognizing him as a person.

A kid on a skateboard zipped by, brushing Obie's sleeve, spinning away.

"Why?" he asked.

"A million things," she said. "God, it's hot." Touching a stray strand of hair. "But mostly because I don't feel anything anymore. Nothing."

"Was it because of what happened that night?"

She shook her head. "That was bad, Obie. And I always thought your creepy friends at Trinity did it. But don't blame them. Blame me." She looked around, as if the words she wanted were written in a store window or on the side of a passing bus. "I don't know. It was all too physical. We hardly knew each other—"

"We went out four weeks," Obie said. "More than that. Thirty-one days . . ."

Laurie lifted her shoulders, dropped them. Christ, she acted bored.

"I don't believe what you're doing, Laurie. People just don't fall out of love like that—"

"Who said it was love?" she asked.

"You did. More than once."

"Love . . . it's just a word," she said.

He wiped his nose, jammed the damp Kleenex into his pocket, and braced himself. Then asked the question he had been dreading to ask:

"Was it all that stuff about Archie Costello? And that secret society?"

She looked away. "I knew you were lying, Obie. I knew you were a part of it. One of the . . . bunch." Had she almost said *stooges*? "I heard all about the dirty tricks you guys played on people."

"Okay, okay. But after we met, after we started going together, things were different. I was breaking away—"

"But you didn't, did you? You still belonged, still served your lord and master, that monster Archie Costello. . . ." Her voice lacked conviction, as if she were only going through the motions of responding.

"Yes, but . . ."

And saw the futility of explanations. Because the spark was gone, the glow had disappeared, replaced by a terrible indifference. Something rare and precious that had flowed between them was no longer there. Nothing left. *That monster Archie Costello* . . .

Her girl friend, tossing her long hair impatiently, called: "Hey, Gundarson, you coming or what?"

Laurie turned toward her, answered: "I'm coming, I'm coming." Then, looking at him again: "Obie, it was nice while it lasted, but then it was over. It happens like that. Blame me—it's happened to me before. I mean, I like someone and then I don't feel the same way anymore. . . ." She ran her hand across her forehead, wiping away a small cluster of perspiration. "I'm sorry." Looking up at the sky, she said, "I hope it rains pretty soon." And walked away, out of his life, catching up to her girl friend, going down the street and around the corner without a backward glance. While he stood there, motionless. *I hope it rains pretty soon.* Her final words to him, banal, a comment on the weather, for crissakes, something you'd say to a stranger.

In the terrible vacancy left by her departure, he floundered, turned around, mouth agape, as if appealing to the world to witness what had happened to him. Hey, look, I loved this girl and she loved me and it all went wrong. What went wrong? The attack, yes. Bunting, that bastard. He had avoided Bunting since his encounter with Cornacchio. A showdown was meaningless without Laurie in his life. But he knew without any doubt whatever who the real villain was. Archie Costello. He doubted that Archie had given any direct orders to Bunting to attack Laurie, but he also knew how Archie worked, playing one kid against another, toying with Bunting, dangling the role of Assigner before him so that Bunting would be willing to do anything to impress Archie Costello. Including an attempted rape. So he hated Bunting and would someday, somehow, make him pay. But the attack had not broken up his relationship with Laurie. They could have weathered that together. The breakup had been caused by what he had become and what Laurie had discovered him to be—a stooge of Archie Costello, a member of the Vigils, one of the guys playing dirty tricks on others. How could she love him, knowing that?

The rain that Laurie Gundarson hoped for came with the thunderstorms—Obie would never again see rain fall without being haunted by all the possible heavens he might have missed. He walked aimlessly in the rain, aching with longing and, under the aching, a growing anger, an anger that was almost sweet as it surged within him. The ache and the anger warring inside him. The ache for Laurie, acknowledging his loss of her. And a seething anger focused on Archie. Archie, who had ruined his chances for Laurie, ruining his life as well. He thought sadly of graduation, how he was lucky to be escaping Trinity with a dull *B* average, no honors, no achievements. He had been a top student at Monument Elementary, with great promise for his high school years, both in scholastics and athletics. His parents had long ago stopped asking: What happened to you, Obie? The Vigils had happened. Archie Costello had happened. Because of Archie he had lost everything, his high school years and the only girl he had ever loved.

The relief brought by the rain was only temporary. Within an hour the heat returned with a vengeance, worse than before, penetrating, merciless. The sales of air conditioners boomed although summer was officially a month away. The Monument *Times* published a photo showing a reporter trying to fry an egg on Main Street. In this new blast of heat, sneezing and wheezing, swallowing capsules and chewing aspirins, Obie held on. Held on to what must happen, what he must make happen. Soon. Before school ended. When the heat subsided. Must make happen to Archie Costello. And through Archie to the rest of this terrible world he now inhabited.

The heat vanished.

With a final thunderstorm, more violent than earlier storms. Trees fell, power lines snapped, a small bridge over the Moosock River collapsed, sweeping a seventy-two-year-old man to his doom. Darkness enveloped Monument, broken only by occasional lightning splits.

Toward morning thunder echoed wearily in the distance and lightning scrawled faint flashes near the horizon. Bird cries greeted the dawn, and dawn itself brought the sun and fresh breezes. The breezes leaped from tree to tree, through the streets and avenues of the town. Early risers stretched magnificently, filling their lungs with the clean, bracing air of morning.

At seven thirty Obie left for school, his cold miraculously gone with the heat and the thunder and lightning. Maybe it had been an allergy, after all. He drove through the streets with purpose and determination, knuckles pale as he grasped the steering wheel, impatient with traffic lights. He drove with hope in his heart. Hope and hate. The hate, he knew, was his only means of surviving.

That, and Fair Day.

Some people called it Fool Day.

This year he would make it Fear Day for Archie Costello.

Afternoon: classes over for the day. Air sizzling with a thousand scents and colors, sun dazzling on car roofs, setting Trinity windows aflame, but the heat of the sun benevolent now, the sun of springtime.

The Trinity campus leaped with activity—baseball players jogging to the athletic field, volleyballers lunging in the air, students in the assembly hall rehearsing the sketches for Skit Night.

Obie searched for Archie in the halls and classrooms, on the steps, in the parking lot. He finally found him in the stands at the athletic field, languidly watching the action below.

The hardest thing of all: approaching him.

"Hi, Archie."

The long slow look from Archie, the slight lifting of eyebrows but quick to hide surprise, proud of his ability to remain always cool. Ah, Obie knew him like a book, like he knew himself.

"Obie." The name hung in the air, noncommittal. Not welcoming, not rejecting. Letting Obie make the move.

"How's things?" Obie asked, trying to keep his voice normal.

"In control."

Down on the field the baseball practice went on. Players throwing the ball, hitting the ball, scooping up the ball. All that activity centered on a small round object. Obie thought of that other small round object, the black marble.

"How's things with you?" Archie asked.

Obie felt as if he were poised on the edge of a chasm, a thousand feet above sea level. Tensing his stomach, he leaped.

"Not so good. But I'll recover." Not wanting to say too much, letting Archie draw the information from him.

"Recover from what?"

Another leap:

"That girl. Laurie Gundarson." Despite his determination, her name on his lips almost brought tears to his eyes. "We broke up."

And then, astonishingly—but Archie was always astonishing—Archie turned to him, eyes melting with compassion, face twisted in an attitude of commiseration, understanding. As if Obie's pain was his own pain, Obie's loss taken upon himself like a cross.

"Tough," Archie said. But the single solitary word was imbued with such emotion that Obie felt Archie Costello was truly his only friend in the world, the only person who could understand his misery and loss. He had to forcibly remind himself that Archie was the architect of his defeat with Laurie.

He was surprised to find Archie reaching out, touching his shoulder. Archie, who never touched another guy, who always held himself isolated.

"Welcome back," Archie said.

184

Obie did not move. The leap was over. He had plunged into the deep, not knowing if he would sink or swim. He had come to the surface. The scheme was launched.

Down on the field, a throaty voice called: *C'mon, Croteau!* Joined by other voices: *Get the lead out, Croteau. Hey, Croteau, you dumb or what?*

"Poor Croteau," Archie said. "Whoever he is."

Archie seemed to be having one of his compassionate days. Obie wondered: Should he press his luck? Why not?

"Fair Day," he said, as casually as possible.

"What did you say?"

"Fool Day."

"I thought you said Fair Day."

"I did."

They laughed, sharing the joke, the old play on words. Maybe he's actually glad I'm back in the fold, Obie thought. Which encouraged him to go on.

"It's coming up soon."

"Got to go easy on Fair Day," Archie said. "All those fathers and mothers and little kids." A touch of W.C. Fields in his voice.

"I know. But we have the Fool."

"True. Any candidates?"

"I'll check the notebook."

Archie looked down at the field. "Croteau," he said. "He'll make a great Fool. Sign him up, Obie."

Poor Croteau. So much for Archie's compassion. Then Obie tensed himself again. Big moment coming up. Walking the tightrope, with the drop far below.

"How about Skit Night?"

"What *about* Shit Night?" Archie parried.

"Remember that kid, Ray Bannister?"

"The new one?"

"Right. He's a magician, Archie. Does all those magic tricks."

Archie said nothing, eyes on the field, waiting.

"He does tricks with cards and balls. Stuff like that." Paused, hoped Archie didn't notice him taking a deep breath. "He also has a trick he does with the guillotine—"

"The guillotine?" A question in Archie's voice, and a flash in his eyes. *Guillotine* was a deadly word, an Archie Costello kind of word.

"Right. The guillotine. This kid, Ray Bannister, has built an honest-to-God guillotine. A trick, of course. But it seems too good to pass up. The guillotine and Skit Night. Some kid's head—like the Fool—on the block . . ." Get the picture, Archie? He waited for Archie to get the picture.

"Let me think about it," Archie said, moody suddenly, brooding, going deep within himself. Obie knew all the signs. He had gone as far as he dared at the moment.

"See you later," Archie said, dismissal in his voice. But something else, too.

He's hooked, Obie thought gleefully.

The Goober spotted Janza across the street from Jerry Renault's apartment building in the dusk of evening and stopped short, fading into the shadows. He swallowed hard, pressing his body flat against a stone wall. After a while he peeked around the corner to make sure it *was* Janza, and saw without a doubt the figure of Emile Janza pacing the sidewalk.

What was he doing here? And why was he out in the open like that, walking up and down like someone in a picket line? The Goober didn't know the answers to those questions, but he knew that there was something sinister about Janza's presence on the street. Every once in a while

Janza's eyes swept over the building, his head thrown back, as if he were issuing some kind of silent challenge to Jerry, a challenge only Jerry could hear, the way a dog hears the high-pitched whistle that human ears can't pick up.

What do I do? the Goober thought. Should he run by Janza, show himself? Or slink away in the direction he had come from? The Goober wanted to do the right thing. He didn't want to betray Jerry Renault again.

I've got to warn him, he said silently. Then stopped short. Janza was making no secret of his presence, strutting around like that in the open. Jerry must have already seen him. Okay, so what do I do? Do I face Janza now? Tell him to bug off? Get out of there? He shivered in the night air, as he always did when he paused in his running.

What would Jerry want him to do? Christ, I've got to do the right thing. This time. Can't let him down.

He peeked around the corner, carefully, squinting, one-eyed, didn't see Janza. Had he gone away or was he hiding in the shadows? Probably gone away. No reason for Janza to hide in the shadows. When Goober first spotted him, he was obviously making his presence known.

Goober looked up at Jerry's bedroom window. The window dark, curtain drawn. Other windows also dark, no signs of life. Jerry was not home, apparently, and neither was his father. Nobody home.

He glanced again toward the spot where Janza had paced the sidewalk. Still not there. No confrontation, then. He knew what he had to do. He had to warn Jerry. Put him on his guard, in the event he didn't know about Janza. And, for God's sake, offer his assistance. Jerry was in no condition to face Janza, the animal. Not alone, anyway.

Best thing was to suspend the rest of his run and go home. Start calling Jerry. Keep calling until he returned to the apartment. Keep calling all night if necessary.

Checking the front of Jerry's apartment again, satisfied that Janza was no longer there or in the vicinity, the Goober struck out for home. As he ran he told himself: I won't betray Jerry again. I won't let him down this time.

The balls, colored marbles really, danced in the air, playing games with the lights, and Obie learned that you didn't look at all of them but only at the ball that concerned you.

The ball. Playing hide-and-seek, peekaboo, here today and gone tomorrow or, rather, here this minute and gone the next. Ah, the ball, sleek and eloquent in its tiny perfection, the ball that would provide him with the means of revenge.

"Beautiful," Ray Bannister said. "You really catch on fast, Obie."

Pleased, Obie decided to try the ultimate test. Holding the ball out, on the tips of his fingers, he made a pass with his other hand, felt his fingers fighting their own impulses and following his commands. Lo, the ball appeared against Ray's cheek, held between the thumb and middle finger of Obie's right hand.

Ray shook his head in undisguised admiration.

"Now show me how the guillotine works," Obie said.

Ray hesitated, drawing back, frowning. "Hey, Obie, what's going on, anyway?"

Obie squirmed, wondered: Is it too soon to tell him? Stall a bit. "What do you mean?"

"This magic stuff. You and the Cups and Balls. You and the guillotine. You figure on going into business for yourself? Like, magician business?"

No more stalling, Obie.

"In a way, you're right, Ray."

Ray walked over to the guillotine, his hands caressing the polished wood.

Obie said: "I thought we'd go into business together. You, the magician." He waved his hand slowly in the air, his finger like a plane skywriting. "Bafflement by Bannister," he announced dramatically. "Assisted by Obie the Obedient . . ."

"I don't know what the hell you're talking about," Ray said, sorry he had shown Obie his tricks, feeling as though Obie had invaded the most private part of his life.

"The annual Fair Day is coming up. And Skit Night. Skits, songs, and dances, making fun of the faculty."

Ray nodded. "I've seen the posters."

"Right," Obie said. "Anyway, I thought your magic act would be perfect. As the big climax, in fact. You know, the Scarves, and Cups and Balls." Careful now, Obie. "And the guillotine. Every magician needs an assistant—I figure I'd be yours."

Ray stepped behind the guillotine, as if for protection.

"I don't know, Obie. I've never performed in public before."

"Look, it's just the school. The guys and the teachers. And it's a loose kind of night. Everybody hams it up. Even if you goof a bit—and I don't think you will—nobody will care. . . ."

Ray Bannister was tugged by the fingers of temptation. He had often longed for an audience, besides Obie, particularly when he worked one of the effects to perfection, yearning for admiring glances, whispers of awe and delight. The guillotine, he knew, would knock their eyes out. And it was a thing of particular pride to him because he had constructed it himself, had not merely spent money on an effect. He also considered how sweet it would be to announce himself to the world of Trinity, to let them know he existed after months of being ignored and neglected.

"We'll see," Ray said, still behind the guillotine.

Obie was elated. *We'll see:* the words his mother and father used when they meant *yes* but wanted to postpone the decision for a while.

"Okay," Obie said. "Take your time. Let me know later."

As he left he glanced back at Ray, who was still standing behind the guillotine. But his face held a soft, dreamy expression, his eyes far away, and Obie knew that Ray Bannister was at that moment already performing on the stage of the assembly hall.

He answered the telephone, finally. Had listened to the rings, too many to count, and then picked up the receiver, knowing that whatever had to be done must begin with answering the phone.

Glancing outside once more—Janza not in sight at the moment—he said: "Hello."

Goober's voice took him by surprise.

"Jerry, I've been trying to reach you since last night. Where've you been?"

Do I lie or not? Jerry wondered. And knew he had to tell the truth.

"I've been right here."

"Are you sick? Anything wrong? I called last night, then this noon during lunch. Something wrong with the phone?"

"My father's away," Jerry said. "On a swing around

New England. On a business trip. But I've been here. And I heard the phone ringing . . ."

"You know about Janza, then?" Goober asked. Because why else wouldn't Jerry answer the phone?

"I know." Weary, accepting.

"He's been pacing up and down across the street from your apartment. I saw him last night. I spotted him again today, after school. I made a detour to check up on him."

"Thanks, Goob."

"I wanted to warn you," Goober said. "Wait. More than that, I wanted you to know, *want* you to know that we're in this together. Janza's always looking for trouble. Okay, he'll get it. From both of us."

"Wait a minute, Goob. You're going too fast."

"What do you mean, too fast?"

"Slow down. Just because Janza's been down on the street a couple of times doesn't mean it's an emergency—"

"What is it, then?" Goober asked, slowing down, curious, as if waiting for Jerry to come up with some marvelous, stunning truth.

"I don't know. But it's time to sit and wait awhile. . . ."

Silence from Goober. Which Jerry expected.

"Look, Goober, I'm glad you called. I appreciate what you're doing. But I don't know yet what I'm going to do. That's why I didn't answer the phone. I thought it might be Janza and I wasn't ready to talk to him—I'm still not ready."

"You don't have to do anything, Jerry. He can't keep this up forever. He'll get tired of it. Just sit tight for a while, Jerry. When's your father coming home?"

He heard the nervousness in Goober's voice.

"Tomorrow night. But that doesn't matter, Goober. Whether my father comes home or not doesn't matter."

"You shouldn't be alone, Jerry. Janza's such an animal, you never know what he's going to do. He's one of Archie Costello's stooges. He might be doing this on an assignment from the Vigils."

"You're going too fast again, Goob. Way too fast. All we know is that Janza's been walking up and down out there. He's not there right now. So the best thing to do is wait and see."

"Want me to come over? I can spend the night—"

"Hey, Goob, I don't need a bodyguard. Janza's not going to launch an invasion."

Another pause, more silence.

"Why didn't you answer the phone, Jerry? Last night I must have called three, four times. Again today. Why didn't you answer?"

"I already told you, Goob. Because I'm not sure what I want to do. I don't know yet—"

"Well, don't do anything crazy. Don't try to fight him. That's probably what he's looking for."

"I'm not going to fight him," Jerry said. "But I have to do something. I can't sit in this apartment forever."

"Wait him out. Let me come over."

"Course not, Goob. I'm safe here. Janza's not going to murder me. Look, it's getting late, and Janza hasn't shown his face for an hour. Wait a minute. Let me look. . . ."

He glanced out the window, saw the empty street, all grays and shadows like a scene in a black-and-white movie. A car passed, headlights probing the shadows. Nobody in those shadows. No Janza.

"He's not there. We'll probably never see him again. Get some sleep, Goob. I'll be okay. Let's wait and see what happens tomorrow." Felt the need to say more. "I appreciate your call. You're a good friend, Goob. . . ."

"What are friends for, right, Jerry?"

"Right . . ."

After he had hung up, Jerry glanced out the window again.

And saw Janza again. Rain had started to fall, the sidewalks glistened with wetness, but Janza stood there, hands on hips, looking up, black hair plastered to his skull, ignoring the rain.

Jerry thought of the fight last fall and he thought of Trinity and he thought of the chocolates and he thought of his father, and his thoughts were like a tired caravan of images.

Most of all, he thought of Canada. Wistfully. Those beautiful moments on that frozen landscape, the wind whispering in the Talking Church. He suddenly felt homesick for a place that was not really home. Or maybe it was. Or could be.

"I'm going back to Canada," he said, speaking the words aloud to give them life and impact like a pledge that had to be spoken in order to verify its truth.

Back to Canada.

But first—Janza.

While Janza continued to stare up at the building, his short blunt figure dripping with rain, cold and dark and implacable, as if he had emerged from a block of ice.

Carter was reluctant to help.

But then Carter was reluctant about everything these days, walking around school like a zombie.

Obie needed him, however.

"I don't know," Carter said, rubbing his chin. Dark sharp bristles on his chin, cheeks. Carter hadn't shaved yet today. And probably not yesterday.

They were sitting in Obie's car in front of Carter's house. Twilight muffled the neighborhood sounds of evening.

"I thought you were all hot to start a mutiny against Archie," Obie said. "Remember when you called me about the Bishop's visit?"

"What's the Bishop's visit got to do with this?" Carter asked suspiciously.

"Nothing," Obie said, studying the athlete, his bloodshot eyes, damp, pale face. Like he was suffering a hangover or the aftermath of drugs. But Obie knew that Carter didn't do drugs, didn't want to ruin that precious physique. It was evident, however, that Carter was in turmoil. Obie felt, crazily, as if he was looking into a mirror. He didn't know what kind of demons had invaded Carter's life, but he recognized a suffering, kindred soul. "This has got nothing to do with the Bishop's visit. It's got to do with Fair Day. And Skit Night . . ."

Carter raked his hand along his unshaved cheek. "What do you want me to do?" he asked, still reluctant.

"It's simple," Obie said. "I need you to create a diversion. For a minute or two." He couldn't spell out the entire scheme. Hell, Carter would head for the hills if he knew the plan.

Now it was Carter's turn to study Obie. Obie had changed in the past few weeks. Not physically, of course: he was the same scrawny kid. But something was different about him. His eyes, for instance. Carter remembered Brother Andrew in Religion describing missionaries who challenged jungles and cannibals as "God's holy men." That was Obie now, the gleam in his eyes, his intensity, his missionary zeal. Carter knew, of course, that Obie had broken up with his girl. Had heard rumors of a gang rape.

He also knew that Bunting had split Archie and Obie apart. Otherwise he wouldn't trust Obie at all.

"Tell me about the diversion," Carter said.

Obie told him. He required two pieces of action by Carter. The first at the Vigil meeting when the Fool would be chosen. The second during Skit Night.

"Is that all?" Carter asked.

"That's all."

"Then tell me why. Why you need these diversions."

"It's better if you don't know the details, Carter. Then you can't be blamed for anything later."

"Archie's the target, right?"

"Right."

Carter wondered if he should confide in Obie, if he could tell him about the letter to Brother Leon and the telephone call, about these terrible days and nights while he waited for Archie to take his revenge.

But Obie, he realized, was too preoccupied with his own concerns. And suddenly Carter felt a wave of optimism. Obie was taking action against Archie. And this action, whatever it was, could draw Archie's attention away from himself.

"Okay," Carter said.

Obie punched his shoulder. "Terrific," he said.

"Details," Carter ordered.

"Later. But I'll tell you this much. Archie Costello will never be the same again."

"Good," Carter said, slapping his hand against the dashboard, the sound like a gunshot in the car.

"Unfinished business," Obie said, flipping through his notebook, using it as a prop in order to avoid looking Archie in the eye.

"The Fool, right?" Archie asked, running his hand over the hood of his car, flicking a speck of dust off the gleaming metal.

"Right," Obie said.

"And the guillotine," Archie added, studying his car with a critical eye. He disliked dust and dirt, kept the car properly polished and shining all the time. "Frankly, Obie, it doesn't excite me. . . ."

But then nothing ever excited Archie.

Obie was prepared for that reaction but could not show too much eagerness.

"I've got a few ideas," Obie said.

"What ideas?" Having concluded his inspection of the car, Archie leaned against it now as he fumbled in his pocket for a Hershey.

Obie told him, spelled it all out in detail, as much detail as he dared to risk, knowing Archie would want to provide the final finishing touches. Which he did, of course.

"You surprise me, Obie," Archie said as he opened the car and slid easily behind the wheel. "You're developing a devious mind."

"I learned it all from you, Archie."

But Archie had already roared away, leaving Obie in a cloud of blue exhaust.

As Carter turned into the main corridor, a book slid from the bunch he was carrying and dropped to the floor. The others also spilled out of his hands. Sheepishly, he bent to pick them up. Disgusted with himself, he pondered the possibility that he was losing his coordination along with everything else.

A commotion farther along the corridor caught his attention. A group of guys had gathered at the trophy case across from Brother Leon's office. Marty Heller, pimple-faced, greasy-haired, called down the corridor. "Hey, Carter, take a gander at this. . . ."

Carter hurried toward the cluster of students, curious about what he would encounter at the trophy case. *His* case, because most of the trophies in it had been won through his efforts.

Marty Heller stepped back and swept the other kids aside. "Look," he said.

Carter looked. Aware that the other guys were not looking at the trophy case but at him as *he* looked.

It was a trophy case no longer. A trophy case has trophies and this case no longer had any. It was empty. But not really empty. On the middle shelf stood a small porcelain ashtray, the kind purchased in a joke shop or trick store. The ashtray was in the shape of a toilet.

"Who the hell would steal the trophies?" Marty Heller asked in his squeaky off-key voice. His voice had been changing for three years now, was still totally unpredictable.

"They're not stolen," somebody said, a voice Carter did not recognize, probably a Vigil plant, courtesy of Archie Costello.

Stunned silence then, but a silence filled with the knowledge of what the voice meant. There was only one alternative to the theft of the trophies. The Vigils. And everybody knew that.

"Jeez," Marty Heller said, "Brother Leon'll go ape when he finds out. . . ."

But Brother Leon did not go ape. Because he never found out. He was away for the day at a conference of headmasters and school principals in Worcester. By the time he returned the next day, the trophies were mysteriously back in place, the small toilet gone.

Marty Heller confronted Carter before the bell rang the next morning. "What the hell's going on?" he asked.

"I don't know," Carter told him, hurrying on his way.

But he did know, of course. The knowledge had kept him awake most of the night. And had given him nightmares when he slept.

The cafeteria. First lunch period. A group of guys huddled around the table nearest the entrance to the kitchen. They were staring so intently at a hidden object on the table that everyone else felt it must be a pornographic magazine, something dirty.

Richard Rondell stumbled away from the table in utter disgust. He had in fact expected to see a beautiful dirty picture when he made his way into the group—Rondell was the raunchiest guy in the senior class, with only one thing on his mind—and he was angered to learn what all the excitement was about. Newspaper headlines, for crying out loud.

STUDENT BEHEADED IN MAGIC ACT

And below, in smaller type:

AMATEUR MAGICIAN
GETS PROBATION

The clipping was frayed and wrinkled, edges tattered, obviously ripped from a newspaper. Obie handled it delicately as he held it up for display. He had chosen this moment carefully, making certain that Bannister had been assigned to the second lunch period. The clipping needed only a minimum amount of exposure. Only a few students had to see it. But Obie knew the outcome. The word would be carried to all reaches of the school, exaggerated and embellished probably, racing from student to student, class to class.

By the time the last bell had sounded and everyone headed home or to afternoon jobs, the effect of the newspaper story was firmly established. Now everyone thought that Ray Bannister was a killer.

With a guillotine.

Nobody knew yet that Ray Bannister and the guillotine would become the highlight of Skit Night.

Nobody but Archie Costello and Obie, who'd had the fake newspaper made to order at the magic store in Worcester.

The command came to David Caroni from the piano in the parlor as he went down the stairs on his way to take a walk. He had taken a lot of walks in recent days. Had to get out of the house. Away from prying eyes.

The command was earsplitting, a chord played off-key, followed by another, as if a maniac were in the parlor playing madly away at a song no one could recognize.

Except David Caroni.

He walked to the kitchen, through the dining room, drawn by the sound of the broken music. The French doors had been thrown open. His mother, her hair hidden in the white cap she wore when she charged into her spring housecleaning, an event that shook up the entire routine of the Caroni household for at least a month, was dusting the keyboard with a white cloth. David stood transfixed, surprised but somewhat pleased that his mother was the medium through which he would receive the message. He had been waiting for so long. For the sign, the signal, the command, the order. Knowing that it must come and trying to be patient. And now it was here.

He listened, silent, still. His mother, unaware of his presence, continued to produce the discordant music that was telling David what he must do.

David listened, smiling. Listened to what he must do and how he must do it and when it must be done.

At last.

Bunting caught up to Archie at his locker, timing it beautifully, waiting until most everyone else had left the vicinity.

"Hi, Archie," Bunting said, a bit breathless and not sure why.

"What do you say, Bunting?" Archie was arranging his textbooks on the shelf of the locker. Bunting realized that he had never seen Archie Costello carrying books out of the building. Didn't Archie ever do homework?

In Archie's presence, he abandoned all his preconceived notions and the conversation he had been rehearsing in his mind.

"Know what gets me, Archie?" he asked instead, going in a direction he hadn't intended.

"What gets you, Bunting?"

"If I didn't come to find you, you'd never come to find me."

"That's right, Bunting." Archie continued to shuffle his books around on the shelf.

"Suppose I stopped coming around?"

"Then you'd just stop coming around."

Bunting wanted to say: Look at me, will you? Instead: "Wouldn't you want to find out why?"

"Not particularly. It's a free country, Bunting. You can come and go as you please." Archie had opened a book, looked through the pages, speaking absently as if his mind were on more important matters.

Dismayed, Bunting said: "But I thought—" And paused, wondering how he could say what he wanted to say delicately, diplomatically.

"Thought what?"

"I thought, you know, next year . . ." And let the sentence dribble away. Archie sometimes made him feel like he was still in the fourth grade, for crissakes.

"Next year?"

Bunting knew that Archie was making him spell it out. He knew he should just walk away, tell Archie *Screw you* and split. But knew he couldn't. There was too much at stake.

"Yes, next year. Making me, like, the Assigner. You know. After you graduate."

Archie replaced the first book on the locker shelf and took down another. A math book, spanking new, it looked as if it had never been opened.

"You *are* going to be the Assigner, Bunting."

"What did you say?" Bunting asked, blinking.

"I said, Bunting, that you *are* going to be the Assigner next year."

"Oh." He had a desire to leap and shout, go bounding down the corridor, but maintained his cool. Let the "oh" echo. Had to play it smart. The way Archie always played it. "Don't the Vigils have to vote on it or something?" Bunting said, knowing he had blundered as soon as the words were out of his mouth. Asking that question was definitely not playing it cool.

Archie looked at him for the first time, a pained expression on his face.

"Don't you take my word for it, Bunting?"

"Sure, sure," Bunting said hurriedly. "I just thought—"

"There you go, thinking again, Bunting," Archie said, turning back to the locker, taking down another textbook, looking at it as if he'd never seen it before. "There's one condition, however."

"Name it," Bunting said.

"You'll need an assistant. A strong right arm, right?"

"Right," Bunting snapped.

"I know you've got your stooges. Cornacchio and Harley. Keep them around, if you want. But your right arm will be Janza. Emile Janza . . ."

"Janza?" Trying not to betray his dismay. Dismay? Hell, disgust. Complete disgust.

"Emile will serve you well. He's an animal, but animals come in handy if they're trained right."

"Right," Bunting said, but thinking: When you're gone, Archie, I'll be boss and I'll choose my own right arms.

"Bunting," Archie said, looking up again, looking at him with those cool blue appraising eyes. "I'll be telling Emile about it. Emile Janza will be looking forward to his job as your assistant. And Emile doesn't like to be disappointed. He's very unpredictable and gets very physical when he's disappointed. Never disappoint Emile Janza, Bunting."

"I won't," Bunting said, trying to swallow and finding it difficult, his throat dry and parched.

"Good," Archie said, studying the book in his hand, turned away from Bunting now.

Bunting stood there, not knowing what else to say. Wanting to ask a million questions about the duties of the Assigner, but not quite sure how to proceed. And afraid to ask another dumb question.

Archie looked up, surprised. "You still here, Bunting?"

"Oh, no," he said, which was stupid. "I'm leaving. I'm just leaving. . . ."

Archie smiled, a smile as cold as frost on a winter window. "We'll go into details later, Bunting. Okay?"

"Sure," Bunting said, "sure, Archie."

And got out of there as fast as he could, not wanting to risk screwing up the biggest thing—despite Emile Janza—that had ever happened in his life.

Later, leaving school, without any books in his arms, of course, Archie paused to drink in the spring air. He spotted Obie walking across the campus in his usual hurried stride, as if hounded by pursuers. Poor Obie, always worried.

Obie saw him and waved, waited for Archie to catch up to him at the entrance to the parking lot.

"What's up, Archie?" Obie said, the mechanical greeting that really asked nothing.

But Archie chose to answer. "I've just spent a few minutes guaranteeing the ruin of Trinity next year," he said.

And said no more.

"Are you going to explain what you said or just let it hang there?" Obie asked, trying to mask his impatience and not doing a very god job.

"I just told Bunting that he will be the Assigner next year," Archie said, "and that Emile Janza will be his right-hand man."

"Boy, Archie, you really hate this school, don't you? And everybody in it."

Archie registered surprise. "I don't hate anything or anybody, Obie."

Obie sensed the sincerity of Archie's reply. The moment

seemed suspended, breathless, as they walked toward their cars. Obie wanted to ask: Do you love anything, then, or anybody? Or is it that you just don't have any feelings at all?

He knew he would never find out.

Carter saw his chance: Archie parking his car in the driveway at his house, stepping out of the car, pausing as if testing the atmosphere, his thin body knifelike and lethal silhouetted against the rays of a spotlight above the garage door.

The pause propelled Carter into action. Otherwise he might have hesitated, and then Archie—and the moment—would be gone.

"Archie," he called, walking toward him.

Archie turned, saw him, waited, his head haloed by the spotlight.

Carter stopped within a few feet of Archie, was tempted to turn away and get out of there but instead heard himself saying:

"I did it, Archie."

"Did what, Carter?"

"Wrote that letter."

"What letter?"

"To Brother Leon."

"I know that, Carter."

What do I do now? Carter wondered. He had never faced Archie as an adversary before.

"I want to explain about the letter."

"There's nothing to explain," Archie said, cool, unforgiving.

"Yes, there is!" Carter cried, a tremor in his voice. He had to get this over with, couldn't endure the waiting anymore, waiting for Archie to strike. He knew the trophy case was only the beginning and dreaded what would come later. "Archie, I wrote that letter to protect the school. I didn't do it for myself. I was afraid the assignment would screw us all up. I didn't do it to double-cross the Vigils. . . ."

"The Vigils are more important than the school," Archie snapped. "You should have come to me, Carter. Told me your doubts. I'm not the enemy. Instead, you went to the enemy—"

"I thought it was the right thing to do."

"The right thing to do," Archie mocked. "You guys make me want to vomit. With your precious honor and pride. Football hero. Boxing champ. Strutting the campus with your chest out and your head high. Carter, the ace of aces . . ."

Carter had never heard such rancor, such venom in Archie's voice, Archie who was always so cool, so detached, as he had been a moment before.

"I'm sorry, Archie. I made a mistake. And I'm sorry."

Archie studied him for a moment and then turned away, his movement indicating finality, meeting over, so long, Carter.

Panicky, Carter stepped forward, hand shooting out, almost touching Archie's shoulder but stopping short at the last moment.

"Archie, wait."

Over his shoulder, Archie asked: "Something else, Carter?"

"No ... yes ... I mean ..." Flustered. Groping for words and not finding any. But having to detain Archie somehow. "What happens now?"

Archie turned full face toward him again.

"What do you want to happen?"

Is this the moment? Carter wondered. Is this when he should make his move? He had approached Archie with a bargain on his mind. First, to make his confession about the letter. Then, as amends, to tip Archie off to Obie's plan for revenge, on Fair Day and Skit Night. He paused now, deciding to stall awhile longer.

"I guess I want things to be like they were before. Hell, we're almost ready to graduate."

"Tell you what, Carter," Archie said. "Let things stay the same as before, like you just said. Let the last days come and go. Graduation. But that's not the end of it, Carter. You were a traitor and you're going to pay for that. Some way, someday. Not tomorrow, not next month. Or even next year, maybe. But someday. And who knows? Maybe next month, after all. That's a promise, Carter. When you least expect it. When everything is rosy and beautiful. Then comes the payoff. Because you can't be allowed to get away clean, without paying for it, Carter."

God, Carter thought, all those years ahead. He had never heard Archie's voice so deadly, so somber, almost sad, and this sadness gave his words a devastating impact and power. Carter had thought graduation would be the end. Of Archie Costello and the Vigils and everything rotten in this world. He knew, too, that the bargain he had been about to propose would serve no purpose now, that his best course was to help Obie, although he shied away from what that meant, what Obie had in mind.

"Remember that, Carter. Nobody double-crosses Archie Costello and gets away with it. When you least expect it, the revenge will come."

Without a further word, Archie stepped across the driveway, in front of the car, under the spotlight, and up to his front door. Then was gone into the house.

He left Carter there, shaken, not only by the prospect of Archie's revenge sometime in the future but by what he had almost done. He'd almost turned traitor against Obie. Which meant being a traitor a second time. Not once but twice. Christ, he thought, what have I become? Archie's words rang in his mind as he stood there shivering in the evening air. *You guys make me want to vomit.*

Carter left the driveway, empty, hollow, without honor or pride, like something haunted, and he was both the ghost and the thing that was haunted.

Archie, Obie, and Carter always examined the black box just before Vigil meetings began. From that moment on, the box was not touched by anyone and rested on the small shelf in the crate Carter used as an improvised desk.

Carter held the box aloft now, opened, the six marbles rolling and clicking together as he tilted the box this way and that, the black marble ugly and forbidding in sharp contrast to the five white marbles. Carter avoided Archie's eyes. After the encounter in Archie's driveway last night he wanted to avoid Archie altogether, but knew he had to play his part in Obie's drama. Archie barely glanced into the box, indifferent as always. He nodded his satisfaction and turned away.

That was Obie's chance, a chance calling for swift movements in a matter of seconds. He passed his hand over the box as Carter began to lower the lid. Carter delayed the closing, paused, turning his head as if interrupted by someone calling his name. In that brief interval Obie deftly picked up three white marbles. Carter looked panicky, couldn't help glancing at Archie, who was walking toward the center of the storage room. With his other hand Obie dropped three black marbles into the jewelry box, the sound of their dropping muffled by the velvet interior. So now the score stood: two white marbles remaining in the box and four black. Obie glanced at Archie, who was watching the members of the Vigils entering the storage room and taking their places. As Obie and Carter moved toward the desk, Obie's hand shot out again, like a darting bird, and plucked up the other two white marbles, pocketing them.

Carter then closed the box with a clap of finality, looked at Obie doubtfully, unconvinced the trick would work. Because now there were only four marbles in the box. All black, of course. But two missing. Wouldn't Archie notice that two were missing when he put his hand into the box to pick a marble? No, Obie had explained, because of the illusion. All magic is illusion, that's what Ray Bannister had said. A magician guided the audience to see what the magician wanted them to see, made them *think* they were seeing one thing while another surprise awaited them. Archie thought there were six marbles in the box; thus, he would believe they were there. We can't go wrong, Obie had said. But now he was feeling nervous and tried to cover up with a weak smile. He regained his composure looking at Archie, letting the full force of his anger and hate overcome him. Archie, you bastard, you are about to get the black marble.

But first the meeting and Tubs Casper standing there, the bathroom scale at his feet. Poor Tubs, bloated and miserable, perspiring as usual.

"Step up, Ernest," Archie advised.

Tubs stepped on the scale that Bunting, always the brownnose, had brought from home. He felt immense, ponderous, and slightly nauseated as well. Ashamed, too. Ashamed? Yes, for following Archie's orders, eating like a madman, having, for once, an excuse to eat, making a pig of himself. Ashamed and guilty and, more terrible than anything: enjoying himself.

"Read the numbers, Bunting," Archie commanded.

"One hundred ninety-nine," Bunting sang out, bending over the scale. "Four pounds over."

"Terrific," Archie said, smiling his approval. "You look great, Ernest. What you have to admit is that you are fat. Don't fight it. Follow Archie's advice: Eat and be happy. Right, Ernest?"

"Right," Tubs echoed, wanting to end the ordeal and get out of there. And thinking: I'm not going to be fat all my life. I'll go on a diet. Curb my appetite. Get nice and trim. Maybe even ring Rita's doorbell again.

"That's all, Ernest," Archie said, voice flat, indicating his sudden uninterest in Ernest Casper and his weight problem. "Send in Croteau on your way out. . . ."

Tubs stepped down from the scale, slowly, deliberately. He'd show Archie Costello and everybody else what he could do: lose weight, slim down. He marched to the doorway, turned, and paused, knowing he looked ridiculous now but later a different Tubs Casper would be seen. First things first, though: get out of here and upstairs to his locker. Where a box of Ring Dings waited. They would satisfy his craving, relieve his tension, and then he would map his plans for dieting. Beginning tomorrow. He managed a smile for the benefit of the Vigils, a smile that said: Someday you'll see a new Tubs Casper.

Obie watched him as he departed. Poor Tubs. Obscene

in all that fat. Another score to settle with Archie Costello: what he had done to Tubs Casper.

Croteau entered, wearing his baseball uniform, for crying out loud. Sweat stains at his armpits. A thin kid, a shortstop, with long arms hanging apelike at his sides. Poor Croteau. Worried looking, of course. Everybody summoned before the Vigils wore worried looks.

Archie proceeded to outline the rules as usual, in his friendliest fashion. Nothing personal, Croteau. A Trinity tradition, Croteau.

"You are scheduled to play the Fool," Archie ordained.

Croteau swallowed hard, his chin almost meeting his chest.

"Don't look so worried, Croteau," Archie said pleasantly. "You won't get hurt. You'll have the Water Game. And the Sign, of course . . . a little fun . . . and a bit of magic . . ."

Suddenly Archie seemed to grow bored with the entire proceedings, looking at Croteau impersonally, as if he had strayed in here by mistake. He stifled a yawn, sniffed the stale air of the storage room.

Turning to Carter, he said: "The gavel."

Carter banged the gavel automatically, his eyes seeking Obie. But Obie was looking elsewhere, looking at nothing.

"Any other business?" Archie asked diffidently.

Obie snapped his notebook shut. "That's it," he said briskly.

Archie gestured toward Carter. "The box," he commanded.

Were Carter's hands trembling as he drew the box from the shelf and held it aloft? Obie couldn't tell. He blinked as Archie walked slowly toward Carter. Tension gathered in the room, all eyes fastened on Archie. Croteau regarded the box with a mute appeal in his eyes, knowing that the proper marble drawn by Archie could deliver him from the humiliations of Fair Day.

Archie reached into the box, pulled out a marble, tossed it carelessly into the air. The black marble caught the light. The marble like a streak of black lightning sizzling through the air.

Startled, Archie failed to catch the marble as it fell. It bounced off the tips of his fingers and clattered to the floor, rolling crazily across the concrete surface, lost somewhere in the shadows.

"Jesus," someone murmured.

Not a prayer or a curse but an expression of awe and wonder. As if a world had just been destroyed. And that's exactly what had happened. Archie's world, shattered, annihilated by a rolling black marble.

The Vigil members looked at each other in bewilderment. Archie was not supposed to choose the black marble, just as the sun was not supposed to rise in the west. Logical, a fact of life. But logic had been demolished. And all eyes turned to Archie as if he could do something, anything, to show them that what they had seen had not really happened.

Archie smiled at the gathering. But Obie had never seen such a smile. Without mirth or joy or warmth, an arrangement of lips, as if an undertaker had fashioned flesh into a grotesque parody of a smile. But Archie's eyes did not smile. The eyes pinned Obie as if Obie were an insect struggling to be free. Held and caught, Obie stared helplessly at Archie. Then the spell broke. The smile on Archie's lips was suddenly the smile of someone who had just lost a bet or a fortune, gracious enough to accept defeat without whimpering.

"See you at the fair," Archie said, looking directly at Obie.

He turned back to the assembly of Vigils.

"Dismissed," Archie called.

For a split second, nobody moved, nobody *dared* move, and then there was the thunder of sound and action as everybody tried to get out of there at the same time.

See you at the fair.

As Obie joined the throng rushing toward the single doorway, he wondered whether those words were a statement of fact, a promise, or a threat.

They picked up Janza's trail at the Sweet Shoppe where he was operating, business as usual. Which meant that he was going from booth to booth and table to table, intimidating, threatening, and extorting, not always in that order. Intimidating by merely standing at the edge of a booth and glaring at the occupants, inspecting them up and down.

Janza's presence was always a threat. Violent vibrations emanated from him. He seemed liable to explode into violence without warning or any reason at all, and that's why animated conversations stopped when he came into view, why kids turned half away from him or refused to meet his little pig eyes.

Now as he strolled around the Sweet Shoppe, pausing here and there, "borrowing" a dollar from a nervous sophomore whose name he had forgotten, a dollar the sophomore would never see again, Janza was in his element. Swaggering, strutting, knowing the effect his presence had on other people, and enjoying it all.

Jerry and the Goober watched from outside the store, standing in the shadows. The Goober stood on one foot, then the other, whistling softly, impatient, uneasy. Jerry merely stood there, watching Janza's every move, craning his neck now and then to keep Janza in sight.

After a while Jerry said: "Here he comes."

"I hope you know what you're doing," Goober said.

"Don't worry," Jerry replied.

Actually, Jerry did not know what course he would pursue with Janza, what steps he would take. It was all too hazy in his mind to explain to the Goober. All he knew was that he must confront the animal, had known this from the moment he had spotted Janza across the street from his apartment.

When Janza left the Sweet Shoppe, slamming the door and rattling the window, a typical Emile Janza exit, he began walking south toward the downtown district. Jerry and the Goober fell in behind him, keeping a distance of about thirty yards between them.

"If he turns around, he'll see us," the Goober whispered.

"Good," Jerry said.

They followed Janza down West Street across Park to Elm and into the area of the Apples, a new development, so called because all the streets were named for apples. McIntosh Street, Baldwin, Delicious. Imagine telling people you live at 20 Delicious Street, Jerry thought, half giggling, knowing the giggle came from nervousness.

"I wonder where he's going," the Goober said. "He doesn't live around here."

Another neighborhood now: decayed buildings, sagging apartment houses, littered streets, ashcans at the curb. Sudden yawning alleys, like dark forbidding caves.

Janza turned a corner and they quickened their steps, anxious not to lose him. Old-fashioned streetlights threw feeble light on the street, emphasizing the many shadowed areas. Janza was not in sight.

Jerry and the Goober stood there, puzzled. The Goober was anxious to get away. He felt somehow responsible for Jerry's safety. Jerry kicked at a telephone pole.

"Hi, fellas."

Janza's voice came out of the shadows of a nearby alley.

"You think I didn't know you were following me?" he asked, leaning against a wall, enjoying himself as usual. "Jesus, Renault, you're a glutton for punishment, know that?"

"You're the glutton, Janza," Jerry said, pleasantly surprised at how calm he was, heartbeat normal, everything normal.

Emile stepped out of the shadows. Anger glinted in his eyes. Mouth turned down. Nobody talked to Emile Janza that way, least of all this scrawny freshman.

"You always were a wise guy, Renault. That's why I had to beat you up last year. That's why I've got to beat you up again." He scratched his crotch. "Welcome to my parlor, said the spider to the fly," he added, half bowing, indicating the alley behind him. "See? I know poetry, too."

Poetry? "The Spider and the Fly"? If the situation hadn't been so dangerous, the Goober might have laughed. Instead, he urged: "Let's go, Jerry. . . ."

Jerry shook his head. "I'm not going anywhere."

"Hit the road, kid," Janza said to the Goober. "I got no gripe with you. Your buddy here. He's the one—"

"I'm not leaving," the Goober said, hoping the quaver in his voice wasn't discernible.

Janza stepped forward threateningly. "Yes you are."

"Go ahead, Goob," Jerry said. "Wait around the corner."

The Goober stood his ground, stubbornly, shaking his head.

Emile Janza's foot shot out, caught Goober in the groin, the pain excruciating as it spread through his lower body, nausea developing in his stomach. He felt himself capsizing, legs buckling.

As Jerry turned to help his friend in distress, Janza struck him from his blind side, a blow to the cheek that touched off an explosion of lights in Jerry's eyes. He raised his hands to his face and knew immediately that he had made a mistake. Two mistakes. The first mistake was not expecting Janza to strike without warning. The second mistake was to leave his stomach unguarded. The blow to the stomach was soft. Janza's fist sank into Jerry's flesh almost tenderly, but an extra thrust made Jerry cave almost in two. He heard the Goober retching beside him where he was kneeling on the ground.

Janza stepped back, smiling, fists up and ready. "Come on, Renault," he said, retreating, beckoning Jerry into the alley. "Your friend's not interested anymore, is he?"

And Jerry saw now what he must do. Cheek still dancing with pain, his intestines twisted sickeningly inside him, he stalked toward Janza, determined now, not unsure or uncertain anymore. Arms at his sides, looking defenseless but knowing where his strength *was*, where it had to be, he advanced toward Janza.

Two or three lights flashed on in windows facing the alley, spraying the narrow passage with light. A window went up. Jerry had a sense now of spectators, people watching the scene, elbows on sills. Nobody said anything. Nobody cheered or booed.

"Put 'em up, Renault," Janza said, his own fists ready at chest level.

Jerry shook his head.

"I don't put them up." Voice steady.

"You afraid to fight?"

"You're the one who fights, Janza." Taking a breath. "Not me."

"Okay," Janza said. "It's your funeral, buddy."

Jerry braced himself, remembering last fall, when Janza had struck him in the boxing ring, but both of them then at the mercy of Archie Costello, puppets playing roles Archie had created. This time, however, Jerry was on his own two feet, by choice.

Janza hit him twice in succession, both blows to the face, first his jaw, then his right cheek. Jerry's head swiveled instinctively with the blows, which took some of the sting out of Janza's fists.

Janza paused, setting his feet again, squinting, taking aim. He faked a blow to Jerry's face, hit him instead in the stomach, but his fist did not land with full force. Grunting in disgust at his lack of efficiency, he lashed out at Jerry's face and body, a series of one-two blows. Jerry stood his ground. Tasted blood in his mouth, knew one eye had closed, absorbed the pain but found it bearable. And surprised by the fact that he was not only on his feet but steady, having taken a pace or two backward but solidly planted there.

Janza's breathing tore at the silence of the alley. He looked up, taking a deep breath, saw the scattered faces at the windows, bellowed: "What are you looking at?" And lashed out again, but not looking at Jerry as his fists flew. A glancing blow, Jerry's right cheek absorbing it. Jerry was surprised to find how strong, impregnable really, cheeks were. Hard bones, not much flesh. But one of his teeth had been jarred loose, and the taste of blood was stronger in his mouth now.

"What's the matter with you, Renault?" Janza asked, arm cocked, fist ready. But pausing, his breath ragged. "Why don't you fight?"

Jerry shook his head, beckoned with his hands, the gesture saying, *Come on, hit me again.*

Janza hit him again. A furious telling blow that sent Jerry back three paces, his knees turning liquid, sending a sheet of flame up the right side of his head, snapping his neck. He fell against the brick building but pulled himself away from it. Another blow followed before Jerry could recover and establish himself solidly on his feet again. This one to the chest. Then another that almost missed his jaw but scraped his ear, tearing his earlobe a bit.

Wobbly, weaving, Jerry remained on his feet, his body arranging itself somehow to meet the blows and absorb them.

"Hit back, will ya?" Janza said, pausing again, breath still ragged. Was the great Emile Janza out of shape? Running out of steam? Had he used up his best blows?

"I am hitting back," Jerry said.

"You crazy?" Janza yelled, outrage in his voice. Or frustration, maybe. "This is for the birds—"

"Come on, Janza," Jerry said, lips swollen, that loose tooth beginning to throb, voice bubbling with either saliva or blood. He swallowed both, not wanting to spit, not wanting Janza to see his blood.

"You're nuts, know that?" Janza cried, arms at his sides. "You're crazy. . . ."

Jerry smiled at him. He knew it must be a grotesque and pathetic smile. But a smile all the same.

"Tell you what I'm going to do, Renault," Janza said, calmer now, having caught his breath, rubbing his fists together, massaging his knuckles. "I'm letting you go. For now. You've had enough. I've had enough. But every time I see you—I don't care where it is—I'm gonna beat you up. So keep your ass away from me...."

A solitary person clapped his hands at one of the windows, a hollow pathetic sound in the alley.

Janza walked toward the building to his right, leaning against it, sucking his knuckles, studying Jerry. He felt drained, something missing, not feeling horny, nothing sexual in his combat with Renault. Like he had lost something. But what? And he hated that smile on Renault's face. Hated what that smile said. What did it say? He didn't want to think about it. Christ, his knuckles hurt. He wanted to get out of here.

"Remember what I said, Renault," Janza threatened, pushing past Jerry, and then over his shoulder: "Keep out of my way...."

Renault watched him go. He looked around for the Goober. He had forgotten about Goob. He stumbled to the corner, saw Goober leaning against the mailbox. Still clutching his groin.

"Jesus, Jerry," he said. "I'm sorry. I should have—"

"Forget it," Jerry said.

"You look terrible. I let you down again. The thing I'm best at."

"No," Jerry said, placing his hand on the Goober's mouth. "It's something I had to do. And I had to do it without you."

They turned and watched Janza's retreating figure, still swaggering as he walked, arms swinging, shoulders moving as if to some unheard bully's music.

* * *

"Know what, Goober?"

"What?"

"I'm not going back to Canada next fall."

"You're not?" Feeling miserable, never felt so lousy in his life, worse than last year during the chocolate sale.

"I'm not going to Monument High, either."

"Where are you going, then?" Goober asked, automatically responding. Am I doomed to let Jerry Renault down forever?

"I'm going back to Trinity."

Jerry's words struck Goober like blows.

"That's crazy, Jerry. Why do you want to do something like that?"

"I don't know. It's hard to explain." He limped painfully as they walked, had somehow wrenched his knee during the fight without realizing it. His knee felt swollen, twice its size, but he refused to look down. He needed to concentrate on what he must tell Goober. "Just now, Janza was beating me up. But he wasn't winning. I mean, you can get beat up and still not lose. You can look like a loser but don't have to be one." Saw Goober's puzzled expression and felt frustrated because he couldn't make him see what he knew was the truth. "Janza's the loser, Goober. He'll be a loser all his life. He beat me up but he couldn't beat me. . . ."

"It's not only Emile Janza," the Goober said. "It's the school itself. Brother Leon, who lets the Vigils and guys like Archie Costello get away with murder. Okay, Archie Costello's graduating, but somebody else will take his place. And what about the chocolates, Jerry? There'll be another chocolate sale. And what will you do?"

"Sell them," Jerry said. "I'll sell their chocolates. Every

stupid box." The pain of Janza's blows still resounded in his body, and he knew somehow that the answer to everything was in the echo of that pain. And in the fact that Janza had walked away. "They want you to fight, Goober. And you can really lose only if you fight them. That's what the goons want. And guys like Archie Costello. You have to outlast them, that's all."

"Even if they kill you?"

"Even if they kill you."

The Goober kept shaking his head as he walked along beside Jerry. He didn't understand what Jerry was talking about, just as he hadn't understood why Jerry hadn't sold the chocolates last fall. All he knew was that he didn't want to return to Trinity. And if Jerry did, then he'd have to return, as well. And he sure as hell didn't want to do that. Couldn't. From the moment that Jerry's father had called him a few weeks go, everything had gone wrong. Tracking down Emile Janza. The fight in the alley and Janza's kick that had immobilized him, leaving Jerry to face Janza alone. Now this: Jerry returning to Trinity. All Goober wanted was to run. Get on the team at Monument High. Find a girl, maybe. No complications, no fights or talks about fighting. Or winning. Or losing.

"I'm not going back to Trinity," he said stubbornly.

Jerry glanced at his friend, saw the utter misery on his face, as if he were being tortured, and realized suddenly how his decision to return to Trinity was affecting him. He felt stricken with guilt, inflicting guilt on his friend, Goober. And knew instantly what he must do.

"Look, Goober, okay, I'm not going back. Forget what I said. I guess that was just crazy talk."

Goober looked at him guardedly. "You sure?"

Jerry nodded. "I'm sure."

The Goober relaxed visibly, slowed his pace.

"Good, Jerry. For a minute there—"

"I know. It was crazy." *But it isn't crazy. I'm going back. To Trinity.*

"Nothing to be gained by going back . . ."

"Right." *Wrong. A lot to be gained but not sure what.* His tooth was hurting now, killing him, and he felt blood gathering on his gums, the taste warm and sweet on his tongue. And his knee still hurt. He hurt all over, but a clean hurt.

"Summer's coming. We'll have a great summer. Running, swimming . . ." The Goober's voice vibrated with excitement as he thought of good times coming.

Jerry knew what he had to do. Break off with the Goober, end their relationship. Gradually, over the course of the summer, so that when next September came and he returned to Trinity, the Goober wouldn't know about it. Or care. Because by then Jerry would be a stranger. Jerry felt rotten about that, his only friend becoming a stranger.

For a moment Jerry wavered, poised between decisions, overcome by a sadness, drenching him with—what?— loneliness, maybe. Longing for the peace of the Canadian countryside and his uncle and aunt and the Talking Church. Or maybe Monument High with Goober as his friend. Trying out for football, the snap of the ball, calling signals, the pass . . . good-bye to that. For a while. He knew somehow he would make his way back to Canada. And especially to the Talking Church. And beyond that to something else. Something he could not even consider now. But first he had to return to Trinity.

"We'll have a great summer," Jerry said, hoping the words did not sound as false to Goober as they sounded to himself.

• • •

He ran. Through darkened streets, taking occasional walkers or strollers by surprise, his feet on the pavement keeping time to his beating heart.

He heard the sound when he was a half mile from his home. At first he thought the sound was behind him. Or ahead. And then realized it came from inside him. A sound like something wounded. Or crying. Or maybe sobbing. Him? Yes, him.

This little piggy went to market . . .

When he was just a little kid, his mother used to recite the nursery rhyme to him, every night at bedtime. And later when he began running, he would run to the rhythm of songs he knew. And sometimes that old nursery rhyme.

And this little piggy stayed home.

Not wanting to think about Jerry Renault and the way he had betrayed him again tonight, groveling on the sidewalk, clutching his stomach in pain. Not wanting to think that he had done it again. And knowing, too, that Jerry *was* going back to Trinity. Pretending for Goober's sake that he wasn't, but going. And the Goober not wanting to go. He'd had enough of Trinity. Of being put to the test. Of betrayal. He'd break off from Jerry, a bit at a time this summer, little by little. Because, damn it, he did not want to go back to Trinity. Wouldn't. Couldn't. He didn't want to betray him again.

And he sang silently as he ran:

This little piggy cried wee, wee, wee, all the way home. Wee, wee, wee . . .

For Obie, at this moment, it was not Fair Day or Fear Day but Fool Day.

And Archie Costello was the Fool, being led now across the campus to the parking lot where the Water Game had been installed, Obie surveying the scene with a kind of satisfaction he had never known before. If only he still had Laurie and could share with her this beautiful moment and all the other beautiful moments to come: Archie as the Fool. Archie walked with his head held high, despite the Sign on the back of his white jersey, block letters spelling out KICK ME. The Fool was required to wear the Sign throughout the day and students understood that it was proper to kick the wearer. One of the traditions of Fair Day, a mild enough diversion allowed by the brothers. No one had yet kicked Archie. Ah, but the day was young, barely an hour old.

Obie watched at a discreet distance as Archie arrived at the Water Game. His arrival didn't cause a big stir; too much other activity was going on. The campus was thronged with parents and students and smaller children. Music blared over a loudspeaker, clashing with the tinny sound of a calliope. Squeals of laughter and delight came from the merry-go-round. Clerks dispensed amazing amounts of pizza and submarine sandwiches and soda pop. Booths with all kinds of merchandise, from handmade crafts to home-baked goods, did a thriving business. All profits for the Trinity School Fund. Thus, Archie Costello's drama was only a small part of the entire scene. But an important drama for most of the students at Trinity. Nothing their mothers or fathers or younger brothers or sisters knew about as they participated in the day's activities, but important to the Trinity student body.

Archie did not protest as he was directed to the Water Game chair. The arrangement was simple. The chair was situated above a pool of water. The price was one dollar for three balls. The balls were thrown at a bull's-eye target to the left of the chair. If the center of the target was hit by a ball, an unseen mechanism dropped the chair into the water, submerging the occupant. The occupant at this moment was Archie Costello. Neat and spotless in his chino pants and white jersey, the KICK ME sign hidden from view, Archie sat quietly, feet dangling, his Nikes almost touching the water. He waited patiently, looking at the crowd with cool, appraising eyes.

"Okay, okay, a dollar for three balls," the hawker called, juggling the balls as he talked. His face was sunburned, his scalp beneath his thinning gray hair also fiery red. His voice was hoarse, challenging.

Obie detached himself from his vantage point at the front steps and made his way closer to the game. He wanted full measure, wanted to hear the splash of water when Archie dropped, wanted to see him soaked and struggling in the pool.

"Let's go, let's go," the hawker urged.

Nobody went forward to buy the balls. The crowd hung back. While Archie sat, silent and unmoving, patient, waiting.

"What d'ya say, kids," the hawker yelled. "Not only do you dunk the victim, but you win a teddy bear for the girl friend. C'mon, kids, step right up. . . ."

Nobody stepped right up. Obie studied the gathering, puzzled, disappointed. He nudged John Consalvo, who stood beside him. Consalvo was a silent member of the Vigils, someone who never questioned a decision, always carried out orders.

"Here's a buck, Consalvo," Obie said, handing him a dollar bill. "Get in there and throw the balls. . . ."

"Not me," Consalvo said, backing away.

"Why not? It's fun time on Trinity campus. . . ."

Consalvo shook his head, his black-olive eyes shining with apprehension. "I'm not throwing any balls at Archie Costello."

"You don't throw the balls at him. You throw them at the target and Archie Costello gets dunked—"

Consalvo had backed away several feet now. Having achieved what he considered a safe distance, he said: "I'm not dunking any Archie Costello."

A chorus of shouts drew Obie's attention back to the scene. A sophomore by the name of Bracken had stepped up, paid his money, and taken the three balls. He turned to the crowd, flexing his muscles comically. The crowd responded, a chorus of cheers and catcalls. Obie added his voice to the vocal fray.

Bracken was one of the wise guys. Loved dirty jokes, sly pokes in the ribs of other kids, tripping people in the corridor. Always sneaky, though, then putting on an innocent act.

He faced Archie, holding one of the balls in the palm of his right hand. As if weighing it. He looked over his shoulder at the shouting crowd, and as he turned to Archie again, the volume of shouts and calls died down. The immediate area had suddenly become a pocket of stillness. Bracken studied Archie for what seemed a long time while Archie sat there imperviously, untouched by it all, looking merely curious, apparently wondering what Bracken was about to do. As if it had nothing to do with him, really.

Bracken cocked his arm, stuck his tongue in his cheek, leaned back, pumped his arm, and let the ball fly. The ball was a bit wide of the mark. Hoots and jeers from the crowd, which Bracken accepted with an exaggerated bow.

He turned to the target again, pumped his arm, paused, waited. Studying his target. The crowd was quiet, the calliope music faint in the air. Bracken threw the ball. But softly. No pep, no steam in the throw, Obie realized. He also realized that now Bracken was only going through the motions, not intending to hit the target. Sure enough, Bracken threw the last ball without hesitation, without a windup, and again it went wide of the mark. He turned, shrugged, smiling weakly.

Obie couldn't help glancing at Archie, although he did so against his will. Archie was still perched in the chair and now there was a half smile on his face—what was the other half? Obie didn't know. Didn't want to know.

The small crowd began to disperse as the hawker tossed his balls in the air again, imploring someone to "hit the target, dunk the kid." The guys ignored his plea as they drifted away, avoiding one another's eyes. Sensing a lost cause, the hawker shook his head in dismay and looked at Archie curiously, a question in his eyes. Obie knew what the question was: Why won't anybody dunk you? Good question, Obie thought, and he knew the answer. The answer angered him. More than angered, frustrated him. Even as a victim, Archie retained his goddam hold over them.

"Okay, guy," the hawker said, motioning to Archie. "Out. I'd go broke with you there all day long. . . ."

Archie leaped from the chair in a graceful motion, landing lightly on his feet. Obie saw the flash of KICK ME on Archie's jersey as he joined the crowd. No one kicked Archie, of course. Several guys glanced at the Sign and then looked quickly away. Obie tried to stifle his disappointment. He knew that if nobody was willing to dunk him, nobody would be willing to kick him.

But wait for the guillotine, Obie said silently. That's what counts, the guillotine. Just wait for the guillotine to fall. And Archie Costello will smile no more.

"What are you doing here, Caroni?" Brother Leon asked, looking up from his desk. He squinted toward the doorway. "It *is* Caroni, isn't it?"

"Yes, it is," David answered, closing the door soundlessly, hiding the object in his hand behind his back.

The windows were closed, but he could hear the sounds of Fair Day faintly: the carnival calliope, the muffled shouts of hawkers, typical crowd noises.

Brother Leon regarded him sternly. "I didn't hear the doorbell. Were you announced, Caroni?"

David Caroni shook his head. He was glad to see the surprise on Brother Leon's face. Surprise had been a key element in the command. *Catch Brother Leon on Fair Day when he least expects it.* David was pleased at the clarity of that inner voice. Pleased, too, at how much he was in control of the situation, everything sharp and beautiful in its clarity. Clarity, that was the word of the day.

"Repeat," Brother Leon snapped. "Repeat: What are you doing here?"

"Detention," David said.

"Detention?"

232

"Yes," David said, enjoying Leon's bewilderment, puzzlement.

"I don't understand."

"Detention, Brother Leon, is from the word *detained*. Students are detained after class when they break a rule or do something wrong—"

"I need no lectures, Caroni," Brother Leon said, beginning to rise to his feet, pushing himself away from the desk.

"I'm not going to lecture you," Caroni said. "I am merely saying that you are having a detention. For breaking the rules, for doing something wrong. . . ."

Ah, he loved the look on Brother Leon's face, the look that said: Have you gone mad, Caroni? An unbelieving look, a look of surprise and a bit of curiosity, too. Nothing more, yet. No fear yet. Caroni was eager for that moment of fear. But not yet, not yet.

"Have you gone crazy, Caroni?"

"I am not crazy, Brother Leon. Not now. I may have been crazy before. Before the Letter . . ."

"What letter?"

For a moment he had forgotten about the code and had called it the Letter. To disguise the disgusting thing to himself. But now he could use the real letter again. Especially to Brother Leon.

"*F*," David said, exulting. It was going beautifully, exactly as planned, his mind clear, the words glib and perfect as he pronounced them. "The sixth letter of the alphabet. But a terrible letter . . ."

Leon had gained his feet and leaned a bit against the desk.

"Tell me what this is all about," he demanded, his voice crackling with sudden authority. But a false authority, Caroni knew.

"It's about the *F* you gave me," Caroni said, exactly as he had planned to say the words for so long. "And about this," he added, drawing his arm from behind his back and brandishing the butcher knife.

"Put that down," Leon snapped, immediately becoming the teacher, as if this office were a classroom and Caroni his only student.

Caroni did not answer, merely smiled, allowing the smile to permeate his features.

Leon stepped to his right, but David anticipated his move. As Leon came around the corner of the desk, David intercepted him, slashing the air with the knife, causing Leon to fall back against the wall. Which was a mistake on Leon's part. As the Headmaster instinctively lifted his hands to protect his face, David thrust the knife into Leon's neck, just above the Adam's apple, the knife point penetrating a bit into Leon's flesh. Caroni smiled, enjoying the spectacle of Leon pinned to the wall, at bay, eyes wide with fright, skin gushing perspiration.

"Be careful, Caroni," Leon managed to say without moving his lips, as if any movement would bring death. Which, David considered, was exactly correct.

"I am being very careful, Brother Leon," he said. "I don't want to harm you, don't want to injure you, don't wish to kill you." Perfect, exactly as rehearsed. "Not yet . . ."

The effect of David's last words—"not yet"—and the knife at Leon's throat was marvelous to behold. More than David had hoped for. Brother Leon immobilized, paralyzed by fear. David felt strong and resolute, felt as though he could stay like this for hours, both he and Leon in this wonderful tableau, as if frozen on a movie screen, the projector halted or broken or both.

234

"Caroni, for God's sake," Leon said through gritted teeth. "Why are you doing this?"

"Let me tell you why," David said. And this was the best part, this is what he had been waiting for all this time, all these months. This moment, this opportunity, this chance. "The *F*, Brother Leon. You haven't forgotten that *F*, have you?"

"Take the knife away, David, and we'll talk," Leon said, squeezing the words out slowly as if each utterance were painful.

"It's too late for talk," David said, holding the knife steady. "Besides, we already talked, remember?"

Ah, how they had talked. About that *F*. Brother Leon and his evil pass-fail tests. The kinds of tests that kept students on edge. Questions with ambiguous answers, answers that called for educated guesses. As a result, Leon in complete command of the results. Could pass or fail students at will. No other teacher did this. Worst of all, Leon used the tests for his own purposes. Brought students into his classroom for discussions of the probable results. Meanwhile, probing, questioning. Using the students. Sounding them out about their classmates, seeking secrets, confidences, by dangling a possible *F* in front of them. Leon had used David, too. David Caroni of the straight *A*'s, top-ranking student, a certainty for valedictorian at graduation. Until the *F*. David Caroni had told Leon what he wanted to know during that sly questioning, fed him information about Jerry Renault during the chocolate sale last fall, told him why Renault refused to sell the chocolates. Thus assuring his passing mark, but sickeningly, nauseatingly, realizing for the first time how terrible a teacher could be, how rotten the world really was, a world in which even teachers were corrupt. Until that moment, his ambition had been to be a teacher someday. He had stumbled home after that terrible session with Brother Leon, feeling soiled, unclean.

When the test results were published, he was shocked to find an *F* on his paper. The first *F* of his life. He had appealed to Brother Leon, hating himself for doing so. And Leon had dismissed his appeal, ho-humming David's concern away. I have more important matters at hand, Leon had said. The *F* had stood. A mark of shame as well as corruption.

"Please," Brother Leon said. And now it was his turn to plead, his turn to speak with a quivering voice.

"It's too late for pleas," David said, delighted with his pun. *Please* and *pleas.* You see, Brother Leon, I am not stupid, despite the *F*. I commit a pun with a knife at your throat and commit murder with the same knife. "It's even too late for an *A*."

"*A*'s ... *F*'s ..." Brother Leon said, voice gurgling. "What's all this about *A*'s and *F*'s?"

At last. Now he could tell Brother Leon, get it all off his chest.

"*C*'s, too," David said. "Don't forget the *C*'s. I never got a *C* in my life before the *F*. But then I got another *F*. Because I didn't care. And then a *C* from Brother Armand in Math. Which I never got before."

Leon stared at him in disbelief. "You mean all this is about marks? *F*'s and *C*'s?" He giggled, an idiot giggle. As if, lo, the problem was solved: This is only a misunderstanding about marks. Which angered David, causing him to thrust the knife point just a bit deeper, wondering if it was deep enough to draw blood. And then speaking his anger, not with the knife but with his mouth:

"Yes, all this is about marks. And about my life. And my

future. And my mother and father. Who wonder now what happened to their nice smart son David. Who doesn't always get *A*'s anymore. They don't say anything, they are too nice to say anything, but their hearts are broken. I can tell their hearts are broken. They look at me with hurt in their eyes because they know that I am the bearer of *F*'s. I, who do not deserve *F*'s. I am an *A* student." Screaming the words, having to make Leon see his sin, having to let the world know what had happened. "I deserve *A*'s. My mother cries at night in her room." He had refused to acknowledge the truth of her tears until this moment. "Over what I have become. . . ."

"Yes, yes, I remember now," Brother Leon said, voice scrambling, rushing. "That *F* . . . an oversight. I had meant to correct it, to give you the mark you deserved. But we've had terrible months here at Trinity. The illness of the Headmaster, the violence of the chocolate sale . . . I did not realize you were so sensitive to the mark. All that can be changed."

"Not just the mark, Brother Leon," David said, unimpressed by Leon's arguments. "You can change the mark, but it's too late. There are other things you can't change. . . ."

"What? Tell me. Nothing is irrevocable. . . ." Suddenly David was weary, felt energy draining from the arm that held the knife, from his entire body. He did not want to argue anymore, knew he could never express to Brother Leon or anyone the sickness of his soul, the despair of his life, the meaninglessness of his existence. He clung to one thing only, the voice inside him, the voice that had emerged from the broken music of the piano, the voice that was a command. A command he could not ignore or dismiss although it filled him with sadness. Sadness for all that might have been and could be no more. Brother Leon had said: *Nothing is irrevocable.* But some things were. The act he was committing even now with the knife at Leon's throat. The act he must commit if only to find peace.

"Listen," Brother Leon said, lips still stiff in order not to disturb the knife. "Listen to what is going on out there."

David listened, granting Leon this much at least, a man's last wish. The sounds of Fair Day, still faint, still far removed. Distant voices breaking into laughter. All of which made David sadder still.

"That is Trinity too, David," Brother Leon said, his voice a whisper. "Not only marks. Not only *F*'s and *A*'s and *C*'s. Education . . . families . . . listen to the voices out there . . . students and parents . . . enjoying themselves . . ."

"What has all this got to do with—" David began.

And saw that Brother Leon had tricked him, diverted his attention, gotten him to let down his guard, loosening his grasp on the knife, losing his concentration as he inclined his head to listen to the sounds from outside. Astonishingly, without warning, he was seized from behind and a hand struck his wrist, pain shooting up his arm, stinging and burning, causing him to drop the knife. Cries filled the room, and scuffling, and David closed his eyes, flailing his arms, striking out blindly at whoever had sneaked in while he was talking to Brother Leon. Anger or madness or something beyond both gripped him. He whirled, tore at his attackers, kicked out, heard clothes ripping, tasted something warm in his mouth as he spun away.

"Watch out . . ."

"Get him . . ."

He opened his eyes and found himself at bay facing Brother Leon and Brother Armand.

They were crouched, hands on their knees, stalking him as if he were an animal on the loose.

"Give up, Caroni," Brother Leon urged. "You cannot escape. . . ."

Brother Armand's voice was softer, more compelling. "You need help, David. We will help you . . ."

But the voice within him was stronger:

Get away. Leave this place. It's too late to carry out the command now. You have botched it up.

Ah, he answered, there's one other thing I can do. That I won't botch up.

The knife lay on the floor, useless to him now.

He knew he had one advantage:

The door was at his back.

He backed toward it cautiously, one step at a time, hoping no one else was in the residence. Please, dear God, he prayed silently, let me get away and then end this agony.

He was in the doorway at last.

Saw Brother Leon's hand reaching for the telephone on the desk. A call to the police would doom him.

Knew this was the moment when he must act, get away. Yet had to wait for the command. He stood there breathless. At last the command came.

He turned and ran.

The Trinity grounds lay battered and bruised in the fading sunlight. The lawn and parking lot were free now of the debris left by hundreds of people playing, eating, drinking, cavorting, and making merry in the carnival atmosphere of Fair Day. Ground crews had moved in to scoop up the accumulation of paper cups, popcorn boxes, hot dog containers, and all the other rubbish left over from the event. The lawn was trampled and tired, the abandoned booths and tables looming like the skeletons of awkward animals in the dying light.

It had been a typical Fair Day, thronged with young and old, blessed with sunshine and high spirits. The only sobering incident had been the arrival of a police cruiser at mid-afternoon, howling its way to the front door of the residence, where Brother Leon greeted the officers as they leaped from the vehicle. A small crowd flowed toward the cruiser and rumors immediately ran rampant. A bomb scare, someone said, which was not at all unusual. A robbery foiled by Brother Leon, someone else reported, with the robber running off toward Main Street. In fact, Brother

240

Leon pointed in that direction as he talked to the police officers. When a second cruiser arrived a moment later, the first cruiser sped off in the direction of Main Street. Meanwhile, a massive policeman, with beefy jowls and a huge stomach that rippled as he walked, waved off the onlookers, dispersing the crowd. "It's all over," he kept saying, and refused to answer any questions.

A few minutes later Brother Leon's voice crackled over the loudspeakers, interrupting a medley of disco tunes.

"We have had a minor disturbance in the residence, but all has returned to normal," he said. "Please continue to enjoy yourselves. There is no cause for alarm or a disruption of this pleasant occasion."

The music resumed, and so did the festivities. By the time the fair drew to its conclusion in early evening, the visit of the police cruisers had either been completely forgotten or had become an object of idle curiosity and speculation, apparently not serious at all.

Ray Bannister wished the afternoon incident had been serious . . . serious enough to call a halt to the proceedings of Fair Day and, in particular, the evening program. He walked reluctantly toward the main school building, head down, as if searching for dropped money. He was not searching for money. He was searching for a valid reason to call off tonight's program. He honestly did not want any part of it. Earlier, of course, he had been excited about the performance, his stage debut before the student body: anticipating the attention and applause of the audience. But Obie's behavior of the past few days had made him uneasy. More than uneasy, suspicious. Obie had conducted himself like a madman, in a frenzy, rushing into Ray's house at all hours to rehearse the small part he would play as Ray's assistant, eyes too bright, talking too much, pacing the floor, then falling into sudden brooding silences.

"What's wrong, Obie?" Ray had finally asked.

"Nothing's wrong," Obie snapped. "Why do you ask?"

"Because you're acting . . . strange. Like this is a life-and-death proposition. It's only a magic show. Hell, *I* should be nervous."

"I want everything to go right," Obie said. "This is the big senior night at Trinity."

"It'll go fine," Ray assured him, although himself unconvinced.

"Let's rehearse again," Obie said. "Show me again how the guillotine works. . . ."

Ray paused now, before entering the building, wishing he were home or back at Cape Cod. A few stragglers preceded him, one of the kids holding the door open, an unexpected politeness. Ray's name had appeared on posters announcing the "Magic Night" program—Bafflement by Bannister. He had felt like a minor celebrity, aware of students glancing at him. Tom Chiumento, one of the good guys, nodded in friendly fashion as they met in the corridor. All this pleased Ray, at first. Then made him uneasy. Not quite sure why, but then everything about Trinity made him uneasy. And especially Obie. More than once Ray had thought about canceling his appearance, but he hated the idea of disappointing Obie, the only student at Trinity to extend friendship. Or what seemed to be friendship.

Stepping into the building, Ray heard a rustling sound, like a distant gathering of insects. He followed it along the corridor, the buzzing now louder, now softer, inconsistent, strange to his ears. Not the usual rowdy sounds of typical Trinity assemblies or gatherings for basketball or baseball games. In the assembly hall Ray's eyes were drawn immediately to the stage, where he saw the reason for the curious attitude of the students. Center stage, in a spotlight, standing alone in what seemed like an immensity of space, was the guillotine. Ugly, dangerous, blade gleaming in the harshness of the spotlight's glare, a nightmare object suddenly thrust into reality. Or maybe, Ray Bannister thought, it's me, dramatizing, exaggerating. But as he looked around the auditorium at the other students leaning forward or tilting toward each other, puzzled, whispering, he realized the full impact of the guillotine on their sensibilities. He thought of Obie. He also thought: My God, what's happening here?

What was happening there was exactly what Obie had planned. Pressing himself against the wall backstage, listening to the murmuring of the students, imagining the effect of the guillotine, Obie smiled with satisfaction. In a moment the show would begin. Songs, sketches, the usual parade of antics that marked every Skit Night. All the while, the guillotine would be visible, at the side of the stage during the various acts but never out of sight of the audience, a grim reminder of things to come. Archie was out there, in the audience, waiting, surrounded by the members of the Vigils, knowing that when the last skit was over, he would face the guillotine.

Obie leaped a bit as a hand touched his arm. "Are you okay?" Ray Bannister asked.

"Of course I'm okay," Obie said, a giggle escaping his lips. "What makes you think I'm not okay?"

"I don't know," Ray said unhappily. And he didn't

know, really. All he knew was that Obie still looked hyper, too excited, eyes fever bright.

"Look, the show's about to begin but it's got nothing to do with us," Obie said. "Maybe we can rehearse the guillotine act somewhere out back—"

"Without the guillotine?" Ray asked.

"I mean, the positions, where we'll be standing. The patter . . . . didn't you say the patter was important?"

"We already rehearsed a million times," Ray said. "And the patter is nothing. Cripes, Obie, you're getting spooky, know that?"

"I just want everything to go right," Obie said.

Ray sighed. "Look, I'm going to watch the show from out front. I'll come back when the skits are over, okay?"

"Okay, okay," Obie said impatiently. He wanted to be alone, anyway, didn't want company at this moment.

Ray drew back and started for the small hallway that led to the assembly hall. At the last moment he turned and looked doubtfully at Obie.

"Are you sure you know what you're doing, Obie?" he said. Allowing himself for one moment to contemplate a possibility he had avoided for a long time. He wondered whether this was a life-and-death matter, after all.

"Get going," Obie said. "The show's about to begin. . . ."

Ray lifted his shoulders and let them fall. He knew that Obie planned to give Archie Costello the scare of his life. He also suspected that Obie planned to go further, to carry out some kind of weird plot against Archie. But he refused to contemplate more than that. One last look at Obie, still pressed against the wall, and he hurried down the stairway as the first burst of music from a stereo filled the air. An old Beatles song, "Yellow Submarine."

* * *

He looks at me as if I'm crazy, but I'm not crazy, am I? Crazy people aren't eighteen-year-old seniors in high school. And anyway, I'm not going to do anything. I'm just going to scare the hell out of Archie Costello. Humiliate him in front of the entire student body. Get him on his knees. Okay, so nobody wanted to dunk him in the water and nobody wanted to kick him in the ass. But they'll have to sit there and see him on his knees, his neck on the block. That's all.

Ah, but that isn't all, Obie, is it? You know what you're planning to do. And that's where the crazy part comes in, the insane part. Insane, Obie baby. You are out of your mind. You can't do what you're planning to do. Not in a high school in Monument, Massachusetts, in the last quarter of the twentieth century.

Obie recoiled from the voice in his mind, paced the floor restlessly, let the Beatles song carry him, heard the scattering of applause as the first skit began, the whoops and cries of the actors. As usual, when he stopped thinking about Archie and the guillotine, he encountered Laurie Gundarson, a ghost lurking in his heart. He was doing all this for her sake, of course. Couldn't simply let her go out of his life without this gesture.

Christ, Laurie.

One more chance, he thought, one more chance.

He fumbled in his pocket for change, isolated a dime from the other coins, paused, tossed it in the air—it came up heads—and then made his way out to the corridor. He stopped at the pay phone, stared at it a moment, said out loud: "Okay, Laurie, I'll let you decide. . . ."

He inserted the coin, dialed her number, listened to the blurt of ringing.

"Hello." Her father, rough-tough voice, a heavyweight-boxer voice although he sold automobiles.

"Is Laurie there?" Obie's own voice thin and sparse by contrast.

"Is this you again?" A brutal, give-no-quarter voice.

He ignored the question, had become accustomed to ignoring her father's voice.

"Could I talk to Laurie, please?"

"Look, kid, she doesn't want to talk to you."

"Is she there?" he asked patiently. This was the last try. If she came to the telephone, if he heard her voice again, he would take it as a good omen. It would give him hope. And he could call it all off, wouldn't have to go through with the plan.

He heard an exasperated sigh at the other end of the line and then her father's voice, threatening now: "Do you know what harassment is, kid? You call here again and you'll be in big trouble."

The receiver slammed in Obie's ear and he sagged against the wall. Last chance gone. He had his answer now. Knew there was no turning back. Knew what he had to do.

Brother Leon arrived late for the performance. His late entrance was not a surprise. Everybody knew that Leon hated the student skits and sketches. Too often there had been hilarious takeoffs on the faculty and, a few years ago, a devastating burlesque of Brother Leon by a student named Henry Boudreau. Boudreau had minced across the stage, speaking in a prissy voice, wielding an oversized baseball bat the way Leon used his teacher's pointer, as a weapon. The performance had become a legend at Trinity.

But funny thing about Boudreau: He had flunked out at the end of the year.

Brian Cochran, watching Brother Leon settle into the seat, looked at him with undisguised dislike. Leon had forced Brian into the role of treasurer at last fall's chocolate sale, meaning that Brian had had to consult with him on a daily basis. Since then Brian had avoided contact with Leon, which was about par, of course, for most students at Trinity. Looking at Leon now, Brian noticed that he was rumpled, hair a bit mussed, seemed distraught, as if his thoughts were elsewhere. Beautiful: Leon worried and apprehensive about something—the skits tonight? Or probably the incident this afternoon. Brian had heard rumors that an unidentified student had fled the residence after robbing the place. Another rumor, also unfounded: a student had attacked Brother Leon, threatened to kill him.

Brian Cochran was not a saint by any means, although he went to communion every Sunday, had served as an altar boy until his sixteenth birthday, knelt and said his prayers every night. He considered himself a good Catholic but admitted that he would have enjoyed seeing Brother Leon under attack by someone with a knife or a gun. He wouldn't wish for Leon to be killed or wounded, but a good scare would be terrific.

Turning his attention to the stage, Brian pondered the presence of the guillotine, acknowledged its ugliness and the threat it represented. He was aware of the wild stories about Ray Bannister accidentally cutting a student's head off down on the Cape. Another rumor, of course. Just like the rumor that Obie and the Vigils had engineered Archie Costello into picking the black marble the other day. After all these years. Which meant Archie would be placing his neck on the block.

Brian searched for Archie, saw him in the seat near the front, surrounded by the Vigil members as usual. He wondered whom he disliked more—hated, really—Brother Leon or Archie Costello. He conjured mental pictures: Leon wounded and gasping for help, the blade descending on Archie's neck.

Shuddering a bit, he tried to escape the images—and wondered whether these were sins he would have to tell the priest the next time he went to confession.

Carter sat next to Archie Costello.

He did not look at Archie at all during the entire program.

And Archie did not look at Carter.

Archie, in fact, did not seem to be looking anywhere. He stared at the stage, but he neither laughed nor groaned nor shook his head like other students as the antics unfolded before him. Some of the skits were downright funny, Carter thought, although Carter did not laugh either. He could recognize the funny part of a skit without having to laugh. Which was funny—strange, that is—in itself, wasn't it?

At first Carter had been uncomfortable sitting silently beside Archie. Carter did not like silences. But when Archie seemed content to sit there, immobile, like a figure in a trance, Carter shrugged and permitted himself silence as well. The other Vigil members took their cues from Archie and Carter, did not make conversation but responded to the crazy stuff on stage. Laughed at the good jokes, and groaned and hissed at the jokes that fell flat, the skits that failed. A lot of the skits failed, probably because this year nobody dared poke fun at the faculty. The skits mostly had to do with student life. And what was funny about homework, lockers with broken locks, the furnace that gave no heat, and all the other inconveniences of life at Trinity? That was not stage stuff. That was real life.

Carter moved only once. He glanced at his watch. Impatient for the show to end, for the entire evening to end. He refused to think of the guillotine, blotted it from his mind as if erasing a piece of music from a tape.

And all the while, Archie sat there, impassive, expressionless, looking as if he could sit there forever, through eternity, although Carter knew that Archie recognized no eternity, neither heaven nor hell.

The moment.

The stage cleared away, the lights subdued except for one spot on the guillotine.

And the hush.

Along with bodies leaning forward in the chairs, knees pressed together, faces thrust upward, eyes bulging slightly, an entire audience caught in one reaction, one pose, as if the students were multiplications of themselves in a hall of mirrors.

Even the faculty seemed to sense that this was a special moment, although Carter realized that they could not know what was going on.

Obie walked to center stage, dressed in a neat dark suit, plaid shirt, plain dark tie, followed by Ray Bannister, also in suit and tie, walking haltingly behind Obie as if maimed in a way, leg wounds. They stood on either side of the guillotine. Obie looked down, squinted, found Carter with his eyes, and nodded.

Carter touched Archie's shoulder but did not look at him.

"It's time," Carter said. Like a warden in a prison movie.

Archie rose to his feet, twisted away from Carter's hand. Like the condemned prisoner in the same movie.

This time the head of cabbage did not explode into a thousand pieces of raw vegetable as it had in Ray's cellar. Instead, the blade cut through the folds of cabbage precisely, and so swiftly the eye could not catch the movement as the cabbage split into two pieces, one piece remaining on the block and the other bouncing to the floor of the stage, then rolling awkwardly, crazily, drunkenly, to the stage's lip, where it hovered for a moment and then dropped out of sight.

The silence in the assembly hall was awesome as the audience regarded the figures on the stage—Ray standing beside the guillotine, his hand a fraction of an inch away from the button; Obie beside him, slightly hidden from the audience; Archie calm on the other side of the guillotine, looking at the apparatus as if it were the most fascinating piece of merchandise he had ever encountered; plus Carter, bulky and massive, like a bodyguard who didn't quite know whom he was guarding. After that immense silence, the audience drew one big collective breath that seemed to Carter strong enough to suck them all offstage.

Ray bowed, came up again, managed to say *"Voilà"* in his best imitation French, realized that his voice had been too soft and reedy, cleared his throat, and called out, stronger now, *"Voilà!"*

For some reason the audience began to applaud and whistle, as if someone had scored a touchdown or hit a home run. Ray flushed with pleasure—cripes, he hadn't *done* anything yet, wait until they saw the real tricks—and bowed again.

Obie prodded him gently, reminding him of the next step, and Ray, frowning, stepped aside, reluctant to share the spotlight.

"And now," Obie called, "the *pièce de résistance.*" Pronouncing the words as Ray had taught him: the *pea*-ess duh ray-ziss-*tahnce.*

The audience hushed again.

Obie glanced at Carter. And Carter nudged Archie.

Archie ended his contemplation of the guillotine and looked up, beyond the audience somewhere, smiling remotely, as if he found this all very, very amusing but nothing to do with him, really: he was merely lending his body to the affair, as if it were out on loan like a library book.

Obie's hands were itchy, tingling. He realized it was nerves, like the nerves of an Olympic star waiting for the starting gun to go off, the nerves that sing a sweet song, not jangled or out of tune. He was eager for Archie to reach the guillotine, to stoop, kneel, and place his head upon the block. As Obie watched, Archie did those very things, easily and smoothly as if it had all been rehearsed, his body loose and relaxed as usual, all his movements casual and almost in rhythm. He'd always hated Archie's coolness and hated him more at this moment for displaying that cool, that aloofness, at a time when he should be shaking in his shoes or at least showing signs of embarrassment.

Archie was lodged now in the guillotine, neck resting on the block, facedown. Obie smiled, ignored his itching fingers, and looked at Ray Bannister.

"Begin . . ." he said, letting his words carry over the audience.

And Ray began. His bag of tricks. Making the deck of cards appear as if at will and playing them along his sleeve, tumbling them this way and that. Ray felt in command. Went down the brief steps to the audience, asked a student to select a card and then cajoled the kid—he made sure ahead of time that he was young, a freshman from the looks of him—onto the stage.

While Obie watched. Watched Ray and his magic show, but also watched Archie in his perch on the guillotine. This was part of the plan. To let him squirm. To make him wait. To prolong the drama. To build up the anticipation.

Ray Bannister was performing beautifully. He wished his mother and father were here to see the way he had mastered the tricks. He had chosen surefire effects, blowing his savings on tricks at the magic store in Worcester. The deck of cards he now worked with would be effective in the hands of a ten-year-old, but the audience didn't know that. They also didn't know the secret of the unending scarves, the rainbow cascading from his mouth. So deceptively simple. The old Chinese ring trick was equally effective, although it required at one particular point a touch of sleight of hand, the kind of deception that Ray had been a bit apprehensive about. But didn't need to be, he learned. The audience was in the palm of his hand, and he was able to misdirect them without problems. He forgot about Archie Costello and Obie and everything else, even his rotten first semester at Trinity, as he clicked the rings in triumph, bowed, and felt carried away on the waves of applause.

He turned, breathless, exhilarated, the way people must feel when they take a whiff of oxygen from a tank, feeling light as air, and looked at Obie. Then at Archie. Archie still on his knees, waiting.

Ray had performed in silence, except for occasional thrusts of applause or approving murmurings from the audience. Now, as his final applause ended, a burst of music jarred the air, martial military music deafeningly loud, played on Obie's cue. The music stopped as Ray moved toward the guillotine.

Now the hush again.

Ray Bannister and Obie stepped up to the guillotine as they had rehearsed, with Obie nearest the button on the right side of the apparatus.

Obie glanced at the button, small, mother-of-pearl, no larger than a dime. His eyes traveled downward, saw the small disk in place. Which meant that everything was in readiness, that Ray Bannister had touched the almost-invisible disk that had placed the mechanism in the slice position, causing the blade to slice through the cabbage. The rehearsal had called for Ray to advance now to the guillotine, run his hand over the top bar casually but actually touch a lever, likewise almost invisible, that switched the mechanism to the second position, so that the lethalness of the guillotine was removed and the blade would fall harmlessly, without touching Archie's neck at all.

Obie observed Ray's casual movement and admired the offhand way he now ran his hand along the guillotine, touching the lever. Then bowing to Obie.

Obie turned to the audience:

"And now the climax of the evening, by the illustrious master of illusion. May we present Bafflement by Bannister!"

Good-natured cheers and jeers filled the air, the crowd enjoying itself, all of them vicarious magicians for the moment.

Now it was Obie's turn for deception, the sleight of hand, for putting to use again the lessons Ray Bannister had taught him. This was where Carter came in. And Carter acted perfectly on cue, following the instructions Obie had given him earlier.

As Obie stepped to the guillotine, Carter left his position at the side of the stage and approached Ray Bannister, catching his attention.

That was all the time Obie needed to imitate Ray's manner precisely. He ran his hand across the top bar of the guillotine. He had instructed Carter to distract Ray, using whatever gimmick he could come up with, it didn't matter. "Tell him he's got a speck of dirt on his cheek." By the time Ray had returned his attention to Obie and the guillotine, the deed was done.

I actually did it, Obie told himself, looking at the audience and then unable to resist glancing at Archie, still patiently waiting.

The hush continued. Obie felt as though a thousand suns burned down on him but it was only the spotlight. He glanced toward Carter and Ray Bannister, saw something on Ray's face—what? He couldn't place it, couldn't name it—and then looked down at Archie again, his neck white and naked and vulnerable.

Obie stepped forward.

I am going to press the button.

No you're not.

Of course I am.

But that's—

Don't say what it is. Whatever it is, it must happen. For Laurie, for me, for Trinity, for every rotten thing that Archie did and made others do.

254

His arm traveled a million miles as it went through the air, his finger like the barrel of a pistol. He touched the button, pressed, heart stopped, breath held, time halted, clocks frozen.

He heard the click of the mechanism as it changed gears inside the guillotine.

He waited for the blade to fall.

Thinking for the first time of blood.

All that blood.

At that moment he heard the swish of the blade.

The railroad tracks so far below looked like the tines of a fork, like his mother's best silver, gleaming in the twilight.

Leaning over the iron railing, he felt dizzy but a good dizziness, lightheaded really, and he drew back, started a prayer: *Hail, Mary, full of grace*... sighed, why pray now? Prayer couldn't help. Too late for prayer.

He had botched everything, spoiled everything, but must not spoil this final act.

Lifting his head, he listened. For footsteps, for cars that might be following.

Heard no one, nothing.

Oh, he'd been clever enough, as if to compensate for failing so completely at the residence, allowing Brother Leon to trick him like that. Fleeing, he had known that he must hide. Like an animal. Ah, but with animal cunning.

He had slipped through the streets of Monument, running behind cars, through parking lots, heard sirens in the distance, felt hunted and at bay. Like in the movies. The movies, of course.

Purchasing a ticket to a matinee at Cinema 3, he had padded into the darkened theater, slouched in a seat, knees drawn up, only a few people scattered around, did not know the name of the movie, distantly recognized the actors on the screen, Dustin Hoffman maybe, whom he always mixed up with Al Pacino. Clung to himself. Waiting. Clever. Then out again, running the streets again, wanting to go home but not able to.

Listening, on the bridge, a car approaching, sweep of headlights interrupting dusk, making him feel like an insect pinned against a wall. But the light moved across and away, the car passing, motor purring catlike.

He looked down. A long way down.

It's now or never, David.

The last thing you can do to reclaim yourself, save yourself, obliterate the humiliation.

He grabbed the railing, testing it for firmness, and then climbed onto it, perched himself there, legs dangling over the edge, looking down into the blackness, pondering the height of the drop. Two hundred feet, maybe. To the tracks below.

This was the best way, the clean way, a flight through air, like a dive from the high board at the Y pool and then beautiful blessed oblivion. All of it over. And no one hurt except himself. And he himself did not matter.

Carefully, slowly, he slipped off the railing, stood on the narrow ledge where the bridge jutted out about a foot or so. Mustn't lose his footing and go hurtling below unprepared, undignified.

A sob escaped him.

Such a sad sound.

But it was too late now to cry.

This was the moment he had awaited for so long. The command he had been awaiting for so many days and weeks and months.

He took a deep breath, leaned his body into the night, but still held on, with his arms thrust behind him, his hands still grasping the rail.

Good-bye, Mama.

Good-bye, Papa.

Using the names he had called them as a baby.

Good-bye, Anthony. Little Tone-Tone, he had called him.

Paused. Sad now. Thinking how nice everything could have been.

All he had to do was loosen his grip on the railing, bring his arms forward, pretend he was diving—a swan dive, maybe—and then a nice flight through the air.

He did exactly that.

Relaxed his grip, let his fingers come loose. At the same time, he drew himself up, chest out, neck arched, face raised to the darkness, aware of a sweep of headlights approaching, the cough of a faulty engine. He thrust himself forward, felt the pull of gravity, the yawning emptiness of *nothing* in front of him or below him, he was falling, not diving, falling . . .

And *Mama, I don't want to . . . I didn't mean to . . .* this terrible flash of clarity like lightning striking . . . *What am I doing here? . . . Mama . . . Papa . . .*

Trying frantically to hold on, grab something, not fall but, yes, he was falling, loosened from the bridge, wrong, a mistake, *I didn't mean to do this. . . .*

Heard his scream in the night as he fell.

But did not hear the hollow thudding sound his body made as it struck the railroad tracks below.

"**Y**ou wanted to kill me, Obie."

Archie's voice was softened with a kind of awe and his eyes were wide with disbelief as he spoke.

"Right, Archie."

"But you couldn't do it, Obie, could you?" The old Archie voice restored, casual, edged with contempt.

"What do you mean—I couldn't do it?"

"Just what I said. You turned chicken at the last moment."

They were standing near Archie's car in the parking lot, watching the kids scattering after the program, heading home with hurried footsteps. The evening had turned cool, a chill in the air. The deserted booths gave the campus a surreal look, like an abandoned movie set.

"I wasn't chicken, Archie. I rigged the guillotine so the blade would fall, the real blade. . . ."

"And cut my head off?" Archie mocked. "But what happened, Obie?"

"Ray Bannister happened. There was a foolproof safety catch he had never bothered to tell me about. Not until tonight after the show."

Obie pulled away, still stung by the swift turn of events on the stage.

He had waited, eyes shut, knowing that in a split second the blade would fall and the screaming would start, plus the blood and Archie's head on the floor or dangling from the block . . . murder, for crissake, he was committing murder . . . and trying to deny the thought while knowing the terrible truth of it. Then, the absence of sound, a pause, only a split second but like an eternity, and then an explosion of sound, not screams of horror but applause, a thousand hands clapping and hoots and cheers, and Obie opened his eyes to look down and see the blade *below* Archie's neck and Archie safe and untouched, body intact. He had looked toward Ray Bannister for an answer. But Ray was taking his bows, responding to the wild applause and the drumming of feet on the floor, always reserved for special accolades. He gestured toward Archie, who leaped to his feet in a quick, graceful movement and stood motionless, erect as a knife blade as the air sizzled with applause and shouts of approbation.

Later, as the students filed from the hall, Ray Bannister confronted Obie: "I don't know what the hell you had in mind, Obie, and I don't want to know. But I'm glad the safety lock was working. Are you crazy or something?"

He turned away with such a withering look of disdain and disbelief that Obie began to shake and sweat, thinking how close he had come to murder, and didn't know whether to curse or thank Ray Bannister for the safety lock.

Archie, leaning against his car, shook his head, admitting for once that someone had been capable of surprising him, amazing him with actions he had been unable to predict.

"Congratulations, Obie. You've got more guts than I ever gave you credit for."

"Christ, Archie . . " Obie said, dismayed. For the first time in their relationship, Obie had heard admiration in Archie's voice, and words that could be construed as praise. For a sweet tempting moment, Obie almost succumbed to that praise and admiration. Then realized what had happened to him. What Archie had done to him. He had driven him to the point of murder. In order to earn Archie's praise, you had to be willing to murder someone, even if the murdered person had to be Archie himself.

He peered at Archie through slitted eyes, marveling at his confidence and ease despite the ordeal he had just endured, then saw something else, too, in Archie's eyes— what?—and made a leap of thought that almost took his breath away.

"Wait a minute, Archie," he said. "The black marble . . ."

"What about the black marble?" Archie asked, amused. That was the light in Archie's eyes: amusement.

"You knew about the switch, didn't you? Saw Carter and me with the black box."

Archie nodded. "Never turn to a life of crime, Obie. You're too obvious. You always look suspicious. And you're clumsy."

"Then why did you go through with it? Why did you take the black marble?"

"I had to know, Obie."

"Know what?"

"What would happen. How far you would go."

"You took that chance?" Obie said, his turn to be awed now.

"Not much of a chance, Obie. I knew that I would win, that nobody at Trinity—you, Carter, even Brother Leon—could make me a loser."

"Why didn't you ever get the black marble all these years?" But Obie knew, of course. He realized he had known ever since Ray Bannister had demonstrated the tricks with marbles at his home, the day they met.

Archie waved his hand and produced a white marble from nowhere, rolling it on his fingers, tossing it from one hand to another, the marble like a small, pale moon leaping in space. "I knew about that Worcester store a long, long time ago," he said, laughing lightly. Then inclined his head and spoke almost dreamily. "But I didn't always play the trick, Obie. A lot of times I just took a chance. Had to do it that way. Testing. And I never lost. . . ."

Obie shook his head. Seemed he was always shaking his head when Archie was around. Shaking his head in dismay or admiration or disgust. And didn't quite know which at this moment.

"Can I ask you something, Obie?"

"Sure." But get it over with, Archie. He wanted suddenly to get away from him, away from Trinity, as if the crime had actually been committed. Like any murderer wanting to leave the scene of the crime.

"Why, Obie?"

"What do you mean—why?"

"Why did you want to kill me?"

"Why?" Obie asked, his turn to be surprised now. "Are you blind, Archie? Don't you see what's been going on at Trinity all this time? What you've done to me? To everybody?"

"What have I done, Obie? You tell me what I've done."

Obie flung his hand in the air, the gesture encompassing all the rotten things that had occurred under Archie's command, at Archie's direction. The ruined kids, the capsized hopes. Renault last fall and poor Tubs Casper and all the others, including even the faculty. Like Brother Eugene.

"You know what you've done, Archie. I don't need to draw up a list—"

"You blame me for everything, right, Obie? You and Carter and all the others. Archie Costello, the bad guy. The villain. Archie, the bastard. Trinity would be such a beautiful place without Archie Costello. Right, Obie? But it's not me, Obie, it's not me. . . ."

"Not you?" Obie cried, fury gathering in his throat, his chest, his guts. "What the hell do you mean, not you? This could have been a beautiful place to be, Archie. A beautiful time for all of us. Christ, who else, if not you?"

"You really want to know who?"

"Okay, who, then?" Impatient with his crap, the old Archie crap.

"It's you, Obie. You and Carter and Bunting and Leon and everybody. But especially you, Obie. Nobody forced you to do anything, buddy. Nobody made you join the Vigils. Nobody twisted your arm to make you secretary of the Vigils. Nobody paid you to keep a notebook with all that crap about the students, all their weaknesses, soft points. The notebook made your job easier, didn't it, Obie? And what was your job? Finding the victims. You found them, Obie. You found Renault and Tubs Casper and Gendreau—the first one, remember, when we were sophomores?—how you loved it all, didn't you, Obie?" Archie flicked a finger against the metal of the car, and the *ping* was like a verbal exclamation mark. "Know what, Obie? You could have said *no* anytime, anytime at all. But you didn't. . . ." Archie's voice was filled with contempt, and he pronounced Obie's name as if it were something to be flushed down a toilet.

"Oh, I'm an easy scapegoat, Obie. For you and everybody else at Trinity. Always have been. But you had free choice, buddy. Just like Brother Andrew always says in Religion. Free choice, Obie, and you did the choosing. . . ."

A sound escaped from Obie's lips, the sound a child might make hearing that his mother and father had been killed in an auto accident on their way home. The sound had death in it. And truth. The terrible truth that Archie was right, of course. He had blamed Archie all along. Had been willing to cut off his head, for crissake.

"Don't feel bad, Obie," Archie said, the tenderness in his voice again. "You've just joined the human race. . . ."

Obie shook his head. "Not your kind of human race, Archie. Okay, maybe I'm not the good guy anymore. I admit that, I accept it. Maybe I'll confess it at church. But what about you? You just go on and on. What the hell are you?"

"I am Archie Costello," he said. "And I'll always be there, Obie. You'll always have me wherever you go and whatever you do. Tomorrow, ten years from now. Know why, Obie? Because I'm you. I'm all the things you hide inside you. That's me—"

"Cut it out," Obie said. He hated it when Archie began to get fancy, spinning his wheels. "What you're saying is a lot of crap. I know who you are. And I know who I am." But do I, he wondered, do I?

He wrenched himself away from Archie although Archie had not been touching him or holding him back.

Archie shrugged, opened his car door, movements casual and cool as usual, as he slipped into the seat. Obie could feel Archie's eyes on him as he walked away, those cold intelligent eyes.

"Good-bye, Obie," he called.

He had never said good-bye before.

PART FOUR

"I have a confession to make. A confession of guilt," Brother Leon said, addressing the final assembly of the year at Trinity High School.

"My guilt is my involvement in the recent tragic death of a Trinity student, David Caroni.

"You have heard the rumors, I trust.

"And have read accounts in the newspaper.

"I have called this extraordinary assembly in the last days of the school year to set the record straight because of what Trinity is—a school of both academic and athletic splendor, a place of honor.

"We have many traditions here at Trinity.

"And a search for truth is one of them. We search for truth in our classrooms, in our informal discussions, in our daily lives.

"Thus, we must admit and face the truth about David Caroni."

Henry Malloran had brought his lunch today because he was tired of cafeteria food. Not tired as in sleepy, exhausted, but tired as in fed up, disgusted. Everything tasted the same in the cafeteria and the taste was rotten. His lunchbag sat on his lap now because Brother Leon had called this meeting before classes began and he hadn't had time to put it in his locker. Henry let Leon's words roll over him. He had been shocked at David Caroni's death even though he had barely known the kid. But death at an early age was shocking, suicide even worse. He wished Brother Leon would shut up about it. What the hell did he know about how a kid felt, anyway?

"The truth is that David Caroni performed that most tragic of acts—the taking of his own life. An act such as this always touches off rumors, conjectures. Even our local newspaper, so supportive of educational endeavors, could not resist bold headlines.

"We must face those headlines as we must face the truth at all times.

" 'Student Kills Self After Attack on Headmaster.'

"Yes, David Caroni took his own life and, yes, he did attack the Headmaster of Trinity.

"Another headline:

" 'Suicide Note Puzzling.'

"We may never know the reason for David Caroni's tragic act. The reason lies somewhere in the note he left behind, a note that was a reflection of his troubled mind. I know that some of you have been asked about the note, his strange mention of a letter or letters. No one seems to know what this poor tortured boy meant.

"His visit to the residence on his final day of life has been a shock, I know, to all of you here at Trinity. And a mystery as well. It is known that troubled persons often turn their anger against those who try to help. Investigators have been thorough in their search for the truth. They have weighed all the evidence. They have interviewed faculty and staff members here at Trinity and the students who knew him best, although it is true that this sensitive boy did not have many close friends."

Henry Malloran's mother was a great cook, very inventive, and although some of her new concoctions failed—like cucumber soup, for instance—she was never discouraged. Her sandwiches, too, were fancy. Like the two tuna fish salad sandwiches she'd made this morning: tuna fish and Miracle Whip and bits of celery, a dousing of garlic salt, and some herbal kind of stuff, dill or something. Plus an apple for fruit and a tomato, which she said was also a fruit, which Henry hadn't known. And chocolate chip cookies for dessert. He was getting hungry just thinking about it and wondered if he could sneak a cookie as Leon rattled on about the note and everything that had happened, although Leon was probably one of the people who had made David Caroni's life miserable, like he made everything at Trinity miserable. Henry probed around in the bag for the cookies, found them, carefully slid one out of its plastic wrapper, and prepared to slip it into his mouth.

"The verdict of the investigation was: No one at Trinity is implicated in David Caroni's death. His attack upon your Headmaster was declared unprovoked and clearly without motive.

"And yet I am guilty.

"Of ignorance. Ignorance concerning a student in my school who went through his classes troubled and unhappy, in need of attention and care.

"But you, also, are guilty.

"All of you.

"If I am guilty of ignorance, you are guilty of neglect. Of blindness. David Caroni was one of you, a student like you,

271

an adolescent like you. He sat beside you in classes. He walked the corridors with you. He ate beside you in the cafeteria. He talked to you.

"And you did not listen.

"You did not see.

"You did not respond.

"The troubled person always sends out signals.

"But you did not acknowledge those signals.

"And for this you should be ashamed. You should hang your heads in shame."

Henry Malloran wondered what the hell Brother Leon meant when he said everybody was guilty. And should be ashamed. I'm not guilty, he thought, I didn't even know the kid. Never even said hello to him in my life. He was tired of Brother Leon, as tired of him as he was tired of cafeteria food. Why should Leon try to make everybody feel rotten all the time? *You should hang your heads in shame.* Henry Malloran let the anger course through his body and reached into his bag for another cookie, couldn't find it, his fingers touching the apple, the tomato. . . . Where the hell was the other cookie?

"But let us pause. Let kindness rule the day. Let us not dwell upon the terrible events of these past days. Let us pledge to go forward toward the future. Let us not forget the past but learn from it instead. Those who ignore history are doomed to repeat it.

"I have searched my heart and have sought forgiveness for my ignorance and found it.

"And I have looked into your eyes, as I am doing now, and I forgive you for your part in David Caroni's tragedy.

"We must go forward and make Trinity such a splendid educational facility that the honors we attain in the future will diminish this tragic act.

"Thus, remembering the past, let us go to our future.

"Not even the present counts, since our school term will end in a few days.

"The future counts. And it can be glorious for all of us here at Trinity.

"Let us now bow our heads and pray silently for the soul of David Caroni.

"And for ourselves.

"And the future."

The tomato hit Brother Leon on his left cheek, a ripe tomato that exploded in juicy fury, splattering his shirt and his hair and smearing his face with what looked like blood. Nobody said anything. Nobody moved. Nobody cheered or booed. Everybody sat there in a profound silence as Brother Leon, mouth agape, wiped the tomato from his face, still silent as he stalked from the stage, leaving an assembly hall full of students who sat stunned, silent for a few minutes, and then quietly filed out of the hall. Brother Leon never learned the culprit's name. He, in fact, never made an effort to do so. Nobody else ever mentioned the incident. But Henry Malloran was elected president of the senior class at the next day's election and nobody ran against him.

Bunting sat on the front steps of the school, basking in a late-spring breeze, conscious that he was sitting exactly where Archie Costello always held court. But Archie was gone now, with the rest of the seniors. And all the other students were waiting for the term to finally end.

Bunting sat there, waiting for something to happen.

Ten minutes later nothing had happened. The final school bells had rung and students had abandoned the place, without looking behind, without giving Bunting a glance. Ah, but wait till September, when they realized who Bunting was.

He hated to admit it, but he wished Cornacchio or Harley or someone would come along. He knew, however, that Cornacchio was definitely out of the picture. Ever since that night at the Chasm, Cornacchio had been avoiding him. Which was fine with Bunting. He himself felt guilty about that night, was grateful that there had been no repercussions. He had acted stupidly and Cornacchio was a reminder of that stupid act. So good-bye, Cornacchio. Harley was off brooding somewhere—Bunting had explained to him about Emile Janza. How Emile had to be second in command. Harley's lips had curled up, as if tasting something distasteful. "But I still need you, Harley. Someone smart, someone I can trust." Harley always responded to flattery, and Bunting was an expert at providing that flattery. Harley would sulk awhile but would come around.

The breeze turned a bit chilly. Only a few students lingered on the lawn, watching the last school bus lurching away. Bunting had decided to give it up, to abandon his lonesome vigil, when he saw Emile Janza approaching. He kept his face expressionless, his eyes vacant as Janza drew near. Emile was like a pebble in his shoe, a sliver in his flesh, a piece of dirt in his eye. And there was nothing he could do about it.

Janza stood below him, his squat figure almost at attention. This pleased Bunting and he nodded his hello, not speaking, playing it cool.

"We ought to have a meeting this summer," Emile said. "Me and you. To go over plans."

"Plans?"

"Right. I figure we should get organized. Like an army. I mean, Archie was too soft with his psychological crap. I think we have to use muscle. None of that subtle shit." He smacked his right fist into his left palm.

Bunting winced as if Janza's fist had sunk into his stomach. Yet he saw the logic of Janza's suggestion. It would be good to have muscle and brawn on his side.

"Then I think we ought to have some weapons," Janza said.

"Weapons?" Bunting asked, horrified but trying to stay cool.

"Oh, not guns. But, like, brass knuckles. And rubber

clubs. You strap the club to your leg under your pants. They hardly leave a mark. And Mace. Mace is beautiful. Like chemical warfare . . ."

Bunting shuddered inside. "I don't know, Janza. . . ." Had to treat Janza gingerly.

"Look, let me take care of all that. Training the guys, getting the weapons. You be the general. I'll carry out the orders. . . ."

General Bunting—it sounded faintly ridiculous. And yet Janza had a point. Bunting saw himself surrounded by loyal people, troops, all of them ready to follow orders.

"Another thing," Janza said. "I think we need a treasury."

"A treasury?" Janza was full of surprises. Maybe he wasn't as dumb as he looked, after all. But that also made him dangerous.

"Right. Have the guys pay, like, dues."

"Have the Vigils pay dues?"

"No. The Vigils *collect* the dues. The rest of the school pays them. All the students. They pay and we see that everything runs smooth and easy. Nobody gets hurt. And we build up a treasury. For ourselves . . ."

Bunting was always scratching for money. Was always practically broke, his stupid allowance not enough to cover expenses, and he hated the thought of working part-time.

"And how about grass?" Janza said, really on a roll now. "I think we ought to do a little business in grass. Or pills. Archie Costello never allowed drugs, which was stupid. As long as we control the supply, we can have this place in our pockets."

Emile Janza studied Bunting as he talked, looking for the clues and seeing them. The way Bunting had at first looked horrified and then just reluctant and now his eyes bright, sizzling almost, with the plans Janza had been unfolding. Hell, you had to admire Archie. He had predicted exactly how Bunting would react to the suggestions Janza was grateful to Archie for all these suggestions, although Archie said that Janza's thanks were unnecessary. They were a gift to Emile for service loyally rendered. Let's see, what else did Archie suggest?

"And Bunting. We ought to do something about the faculty."

"The faculty?" Bunting's voice was getting higher and higher every time he spoke, and Janza grinned.

"Yeah. To keep them distracted." Wonderful word: *distracted.* Archie's word but sounding natural on Janza's tongue. "Classroom disruption." More Archie words. "Show the faculty who's in charge . . ."

Bunting drew up his knees, curled his arms around them, rested his chin in the space between his knees, needing time to think, to absorb Janza's suggestions. Wild suggestions, but they made sense. They opened all sorts of possibilities. The great part was that Janza seemed perfectly happy to be the good right arm. With Bunting in charge. King of the place. Yet he sensed that Janza would always represent a danger. He'd have to keep alert, on his toes. But then, Janza could always be eliminated. A loose stair rail, say, on the third floor.

"What do you think, Bunting? What do you think, O leader of us all?"

Bunting pretended to be deep in thought, letting Janza dangle a bit, not wanting to appear too eager, too ready to accept Janza's plans.

"We'll see," he said finally. "I've got some plans of my own, you know. But I think it will work out okay. . . ."

Janza grinned, amazed at the accuracy of Archie's predictions. You'll have a great year, Archie had said. Which Janza echoed now: "We're going to have a great year, Bunting."

Bunting nodded. Continued to stare into space. Not wanting to look at Janza now or anybody or anything. Staring into the future, next year, beyond. Him, Bunting, in command of the entire school. Stooges at his beck and call. An army at his disposal. No rules except those he made up. The boss. More than that. Like a dictator, for crissake.

Beautiful.